COYOTE SONG

COYOTE SONG

D.J. MOLLES
THE REMAINING
UNIVERSE

D.J. MOLLES

Copyright © 2024 by D.J. Molles Books LLC

All rights reserved.

No part of this publication may be reproduced, distributed, or transmitted in any form or by any means, including photocopying, recording, or other electronic or mechanical methods, without the prior written permission of the publisher, except as permitted by U.S. copyright law.

For permission requests, contact info@djmolles.com.

The story, all names, characters, and incidents portrayed in this production are fictitious. No identification with actual persons (living or deceased), places, buildings, and products is intended or should be inferred.

Book Cover by Tara Molles

ISBN Print Paperback: 9798343200973

ASIN: B0DJMY8MZN

First edition

THE REMAINING UNIVERSE

It began with a bacteria called Febrile Urocanic Reactive Yersinia. When exposed to a host's blood or mucous membrane, the bacteria would burrow holes through the frontal lobe, destroying the host's ability to reason and speak.

The FURY bacteria spread so rapidly that it burned itself out in a matter of months. But by then, the damage had been done. Nine out of ten people had been infected by it. Many of those infected experienced a massive spike in their metabolic rates, causing them to feel insatiably hungry. Due to their damaged frontal lobes, these infected turned hyper-aggressive, and preyed on anything they could get their hands on—including other humans.

After a year, most of the infected died out due to starvation and exposure. But of those billions, a few were gifted–or cursed–with genetics that favored extreme adaptability. These individuals not only survived, but began to thrive. Their bodies underwent a period of macroevolution, resulting in morphological changes that made them better suited to be an apex predator: elongated forelimbs, hardening of the fingernails, widening of the mandible, and lengthening of the canine teeth. These came to be known as primals.

Three years after the plague first swept the globe, it was discovered that the primals were not only breeding, but doing so at an alarming rate. A female primal's gestation was estimated to be 3-4 months, and their offspring were able to move independently within a day. After a single year, they were large enough to be dangerous and mature enough to reproduce on their own.

The primals began to form large colonies capable of overrunning human settlements that were previously considered secure. Reports began to surface, claiming that the primals were being led by females whose physical mutations were not as extreme. As human settlements began to fall to these massive primal colonies, another trend was discovered: All the men were killed and eaten. But the women were taken alive.

The pieces began to fall into place: the primals were taking human women and forcing them to breed, creating half-human and half-primal hybrids. These were the matriarchs whose physical mutations were not as extreme. It was a survival strategy, designed to establish a leader over the colony with all the strengths of a primal, but with increased cognitive abilities.

Over the following years, more hybridization between the primals and humans occurred–most often forced, but in some cases, willingly. This continued hybridization has resulted in individuals who look mostly human, except for their larger-than-normal teeth and jaws, claw-like fingernails, and propensity for extreme violence. With one-quarter or less of primal genetics in them, this new breed of hybrids are able to reason, and even speak.

This new off-shoot of homo sapiens is viewed by most to be a threat to human existence.

But when Lee Harden and his team are forced to accept a mission deep into territory controlled by primals, they will have to put their prejudices aside. Because hybrids—one in particular, whom they've had previous run-ins with—might be their only way to stay alive.

Chapter 1

It was only because Abe was on the very peak of the roof that he happened to see them coming.

He crouched, one knee on either side of the peak, inspecting the shingles with a clinical eye. There was a patch of freshly-carved cedarwood shingles in amongst the old, gray ones. Abe's cabin had sprung a leak during a hard rain the week prior, and he'd gone up the morning after and fixed it.

Or at least he *thought* he'd fixed it. Then came last night's rain, which revealed his poor craftsmanship with fat drops that spattered right on his face when he was trying to sleep.

With no clear idea of what he'd done wrong the first time around, Abe had just finished ripping out his old work and replacing it. He now gave the shingles a hard, distrustful stare as he pulled the one-liter water bottle from where it protruded out of his cargo pocket.

"I swear to fuck," he growled at the shingles. "You pieces of shit better work or I'm gonna burn the whole goddamn cabin down."

Because a sternly-worded reprimand would surely make up for his lack of carpentry skills.

He poured the water over his patch job, then hollered down below, "Marie, how's it looking?"

He heard her voice come from inside the cabin. "Did you put the water on it?"

"Yeah. Any drips?"

"Not yet. Give it a minute."

His lovely partner clearly didn't believe he'd actually fixed the leak.

Huffing irritably, Abe looked out over the vista of Oregon's Gearhart Mountain Wilderness, from which the settlement of Gearhart got its name. Twenty, inexpertly-built log cabins surrounded the original six that had been a part of a developed campground.

Abe's was one of the inexpertly-built cabins that had been constructed *after* the plague had wiped out society six years ago. All in all, Gearhart had done well for themselves. They were tucked back way in the middle of nowhere, and due to the mountainous terrain, didn't even have to worry about primals much.

Most other settlements that had survived this long had either high-voltage fencing or a shit-ton of guards with guns to keep the primals out. But the mountain was its own fortification because primals did not seem to care for elevation change, and stuck mostly to the flatlands.

Mostly. But not always.

So, since he was sitting around waiting to see how bad he'd fucked his roof up this time, Abe peered through the distant landscape of winter-bare trees and evergreens, instinctively looking for movement.

That's when he saw them. He knew in an instant that they weren't primals. They were still a ways off, but he could see they were clothed, with rucks on their backs, and...

Yes—rifles in their hands.

"Motherfuckers." Abe immediately started clambering over to the ladder propped on the side of the roof. "Marie!"

"Yeah, I think I see a little water coming through."

"Seriously?" Abe mounted the ladder, casting one last glare at his patch job before he started to descend. "Fuck—nevermind. Twelve bogeys incoming."

Marie burst out of the house as Abe reached the ground. Her eyes scoured the terrain, but Abe doubted she could see the approaching men from the ground.

"Bogeys?" she commented. "What're you, a fighter pilot?"

He frowned at her as he brushed past, moving for the front door of the cabin they shared. "Really, Marie? You gotta bust my balls *right now*?"

"I've just never heard you call them bogeys before," she said, following him through the front door to where their armor and rifles were hung up, right in the entryway.

"Yes, you have. I've said it before." Abe threw his armor over his head and began strapping into it, giving Marie a sour look. "You just never remember anything I say."

Marie slipped her plate carrier over her giant frizz of dark curls, then paused. "This is about the gunpowder, isn't it?"

Abe grabbed his rifle and slung into it. "It's about attention to detail, Marie," he said, a bit loud in his defensiveness. "I need a very specific type for my reloads, or they won't be as accurate. And it's called 'propellant,' not 'gunpowder.'"

Marie took her rifle from its pegs, checking the mag and chamber. "Well, next time *you* can call in the resupply, since you have to have everything just-so."

"Maybe I will! And when you ask for fucking heavy-flow tampons or some shit, *I'll* remember, because I listen and I pay attention to details and I love you."

Marie got both of her hands in Abe's bushy beard and gripped it in a way that wasn't painful, but clearly could be if he pissed her off anymore. "I love you too, you salty fuck."

Then she gave him a quick peck, because they'd agreed not to take their old-couple-arguments into potentially dangerous situations. It would be a shame if one of them died when they were mad at each other.

They headed out the door.

"You think it's Badger and his fucktards?" Marie asked, casting a glance towards the other denizens of Gearhart, out and about doing their business for the day. They spotted Marie and Abe in their armor and immediately perked up like a pack of meerkats.

"Who else?" Abe grunted.

"The hell is wrong with this guy?" Marie murmured, then raised a hand to the small crowd of people that had halted in their daily duties to stare worriedly. "Everything's fine! Got some visitors coming—we'll handle it. Someone holler at Jeff, though."

Several people took off to jointly holler at Jeff, the settlement's head of security.

"I'll get Sam and Jones," Abe said. "You get Lee."

Marie nodded and peeled off to the right. Abe went to the left.

The cabins were not arranged in any logical way. They all sat on whatever patch of ground had been clear cut to provide the timbers for building, with no discernible pattern. But after being here for the last three months, Abe had memorized where everyone's cabins were.

Sam and Jones shared a larger cabin with a family. Now, Abe would never know whether the family had invited Sam and

Jones, or if they'd invited themselves. Sam and Jones would deny it until the day they died, but Abe was pretty sure they'd ingratiated themselves, on account of the two, twenty-year-old women that lived with that family—one a daughter, and the other a friend of that daughter.

Abe's suspicion was bolstered by the fact that Sam and Jones had both begged off of helping him with roof repair, claiming the family needed help harvesting the pumpkin patch that day. And yet, when Abe rounded the corner of the family's cabin and looked out at the pumpkin patch, he didn't see much harvesting going on.

Sam—dark skinned and dark haired, of middle-eastern ethnicity, like Abe.

Jones—white as white could be, with sandy hair that he'd been letting grow into a mop.

And two, pretty young women, smiling, wide-eyed, as Jones animatedly regaled them with some tale of heroism that was probably only half true and the rest greatly exaggerated.

It was Abe's eternal pleasure to cock-block Jones any time he could.

"Yo! Dumbasses!" Abe hollered.

Sam and Jones immediately spun, both looking like they'd been caught.

Abe waved a hand at the pumpkin patch. "Nice pumpkin harvesting. Grab your shit. Badger's on the way with a dozen of his goons."

Sam and Jones were mirror-images of each other: As one, their shoulders slumped and their faces looked skyward, as though seeking heavenly intercession.

"Again?" Jones moaned.

"The fuck is wrong with this guy?" Sam grouched.

They recovered quickly, then gave a few parting words to the ladies, and came running.

"How far out?" Sam asked, as Abe followed the two young men at a jog, around the front of the cabin, and into the entryway, where their armor and rifles were stowed, much like Abe and Marie's had been.

"Couple miles," Abe answered.

Sam and Jones grabbed their gear and toted it outside, strapping up as they followed Abe towards where their pickup was parked.

"I'm on record," Jones pronounced. "We should've killed this idiot two years ago."

Abe spotted their pickup, close to Lee's tiny, one-man cabin. He started patting his pockets, and realized he hadn't grabbed the keys. He cast a guilty glance towards Jones. "Y'all wait at the truck. I'll be right back."

He started jogging back towards his own cabin.

"What'd you forget?" Jones asked, in a way that told Abe he knew exactly what had been forgotten.

"Don't worry about it!" he barked over his shoulder.

"Did you forget *the keys*?" Jones sang with high glee. Then, shouting after him: "Attention to detail, Abe!"

As Abe passed Lee's cabin, Marie came running from behind it, then looked at Abe, confused. "Where are you going?"

"Gotta grab something."

"Keys?"

Abe didn't answer.

"Attention to detail!" she sniped at him.

"Where's Lee?" he deflected.

"Not in his cabin."

Abe turned to jog backwards for a few strides, quirking an eyebrow at Marie. "You know where he is."

"Oh, Jesus," Lee groaned, his face mushed into the ground, muffling his words as Bethany raked her elbow slowly over the knotted muscles of his back.

She laughed evilly.

Lee cracked an eyelid, giving her a sidelong frown. "Why do you love hurting me?"

Bethany was seated on his back, which was nice—he could feel the warmth of her there. She was a pretty thing, with bright blue eyes and a big smile that, at first glance, seemed girlishly innocent, but upon closer inspection, concealed what was apparently a predilection for sadism.

She'd been a physical therapist in her old life. Which was one of the reasons Lee had chosen to come back to Gearhart to convalesce after his team's last mission had left him with some broken ribs and a shit ton of soft-tissue damage.

That was the *main* reason he'd come back here.

Bethany leaned over him, her hair tickling his face as she hovered over his ear and whispered, "Because the hurt's the healing, baby."

Yeah. That was the *other* reason.

In addition to needing some time to heal up, Lee and his team had been coming off a run of tough losses. The last settlement they helped, down in Northern California, had ultimately been successful, but the team needed a break. They needed to spend some time doing normal-people-shit, in a friendly settlement where everyone knew them and treated them like family.

Gearhart was as close to a home base as Lee and his team had. They'd helped the settlement out two years ago, and it had become a frequent stopover point for them as they continued to journey up and down the west coast.

Here, they were all able to take a breath, and pause the unforgiving tempo of their near-constant combat operations.

There were practical reasons why this was necessary. Experience was the best teacher for sure, but every once in a while, it helped to take a break and let your mind consolidate all the little things you'd learned along the way. So they hadn't just spent their time lounging about and carousing with the people of Gearhart.

Abe and Lee were diligent, not only in keeping their own skills sharp, but in continuing to mentor Sam and Jones. Marie was not exempt from daily drills, but as their team's medic, her focus remained more on healing than death-dealing. At this point, she probably had more experience in combat medicine than any corpsman or medic Lee had ever worked with, but she still spent evenings pouring over a battered copy of a Tactical Combat Casualty Care workbook, like a monk might pour over scripture. And at least once a week she would make house calls around Gearhart, practicing more generalized medicine.

Lee hadn't planned on staying in Gearhart as long as they had. But his body, now closing on forty years old, disagreed with his plans to be healed up and gone within a month. Busted bones and torn ligaments didn't heal as quick as they used to. Lee's severe limp—courtesy of a gunshot wound to his right hip several years back—combined with the broken ribs, conspired to set his body out of whack in a variety of unseen ways.

Bethany had done a stellar job rehabbing him, and he was almost back to a hundred percent—or at least what passed for it these days. But now winter was coming on, and there was a lot of work to be done in Gearhart. And though the others were antsy to get moving, Lee didn't feel...

He didn't feel...

Honestly, he just didn't feel like going back out there.

This created no small amount of confusion in Lee's head. Because it wasn't like he wanted to settle down. As nice as Gearhart was, and as much as he enjoyed Bethany's company, the prospect of hanging it up and living a life of peace still felt like a prison to him.

But every time he turned his mind to going back out there, and finding another settlement to help, his stomach would drop and he would think, *What's the fucking point?*

He was supposed to be paving the way for the Interim American Government to expand out from the interior states. But their borders hadn't moved a single damn mile in the last three years. Lee's task had turned from a fresh start into a pointless slog.

Was he actually doing any good?

Did his life actually have any meaning anymore?

Bethany's therapeutic massage stopped. "What now?" she demanded. "You just got all tense again."

Lee sighed. "Oh, just pondering meaning and purpose again."

"Well, don't do *that*."

When Lee didn't respond, she made a disgruntled noise and laid on top of him. "I'm kidding," she murmured into his neck. "You can talk about it."

"Nah, it's alright."

"No, you should talk about it."

"What? Are you a shrink now too?"

She flicked his ear sharply. "Don't be surly or I'll use my elbows again."

"Oh, no," he said in mock terror. "Not that."

She waited him out.

He took a big breath, causing both their bodies to rise an inch. "It just all feels a bit...Sisyphus-ian. I know I'm supposed to go out there and help people, but half the people we help end up dead, and the other half are left wondering when the fucking IAG is gonna get off their asses and re-settle the coastal states. It's Whack-a-Mole. It's fingers in the dike. And...various other metaphors for pointless, never-ending tasks."

"You could always stay with us," Bethany said, in a way that made it clear she knew that would never be the case.

Lee grimaced. "No offense, but that sounds even worse. I'm *supposed* to be out there doing shit. It's what I'm made for. It's just..." he let out an ornery grumble. "I've been fighting wars my entire adult life. And I'm fine with that—I really am. I'm good at it. It's my calling. And just the thought of *not* doing it leaves me feeling...itchy. But it's starting to feel like there's no purpose to it. Like I'll just keep going out there and putting me and my team's lives in danger—for what? What's the point here? What are we actually accomplishing?"

Bethany righted herself and began to knead his muscles again, but it seemed to lack focus. "Yeah, I dunno, Lee. Life without meaning is no life at all."

"But how do you fix that?"

He felt her shrug. "Guess you're gonna have to find a new meaning."

Lee frowned, dissatisfied with the lack of clear direction he felt his life had taken.

The frown didn't last long, though. Bethany's half-hearted massage began to drift into other explorations.

Yeah, Lee could get on board with a few more months of this. Sure, he was starting to feel that itch—the frustrated malaise of a working dog kept in a kennel for too long—but it wasn't like the shitty world out beyond Gearhart would be any less shitty come spring. The warlords and the cartels and the primals weren't going anywhere.

Lee was just rolling onto his back to begin some exploration of his own, when someone slammed their fist into the door of Bethany's cabin.

"Jax! You in there?"

It was Marie, and Lee was instantly irritated.

Bethany's eyes twinkled with mischief as she continued to undo his belt, whispering, "Does she know that I know your real name?"

Lee shook his head, then called out, "Yeah?" to Marie, praying this was something that could be handled in, say, thirty minutes or so.

"Badger's inbound with a dozen guys."

All explorations ceased.

Lee wilted back onto the floor. "Sonofabitch. Are you serious?"

"Yeah, I'm serious," Marie called through the door. "He's about two miles out. Everyone else is waiting at the pickup."

"Goddammit," Lee grumbled, as Bethany unlimbered herself from his lap. "Alright. I'm coming."

"Not anymore," Bethany remarked with a shit-eating grin.

"I'm gonna kill this motherfucker," Lee swore as he sat up, cinching his belt back and reaching for his boots. "Swear to God, I'm just gonna shoot him in the face."

"No, you're not," Bethany observed.

Lee scowled at her, pulling his boots on. "I might."

Bethany sat on the ground, splay-legged, looking utterly inviting. "No, you're gonna talk him down like all the other times, because you're better than that."

Lee got to his feet, clawing his way back into his shirt. "My patience has limits."

Bethany raised and lowered her hands in an inhale-exhale gesture. "Deep breaths. Stay centered."

"Yeah," Lee grunted as he turned for the door. "I'm zen as a motherfucker."

Chapter 2

The pickup truck rumbled down the pitted mountain road, heading to where Badger and his group were hiking up. Whenever it rained, it all came rushing down this road, leaving big ruts where the water flowed, some of them about six-inches deep.

Lee was geared up, his rifle hanging between his legs as he restrained the jostling steering wheel with both hands. Marie was in the front passenger seat, and Sam, Jones, and Abe were in the back.

"Here," Abe said—needlessly, as Lee was already pulling to a stop.

Right off the side of the road, there was a narrow but well-worn path squirrelling off into the woods. At the end of that path was a little lookout that provided a perfect view of the road, all the way down to the bottom of the mountain.

The second the truck rocked to a halt, Abe hopped out, toting his big Remington MSR.

Lee began rolling forward again, glancing towards Marie. "I'm sensing some tension between you two."

Marie just rolled her eyes. "It's nothing. He's still pissed about the gunpowder."

"Ah." Lee dismissed it with a wave. "It only opened his groups by point-seventeen inches. It'll be fine."

"I'm with Abe on this one," Jones piped up.

"Of course you are," Marie said.

"It's not like that, Ma," Jones said, petting her shoulder in a placating fashion. "But seriously, those bullets are going right by our heads, you know. Point-seventeen inches—*at a hundred yards*. Kick it out to a thousand and that's…" he hesitated.

"One-point-seven inches," Sam provided.

"*Almost two inches*, Ma!" Jones proclaimed. "So, yeah, I'm with Abe. You better get his powder orders right next time."

Marie made a disgruntled noise and turned in her seat. "How'd the pumpkin harvesting go?" she asked, with clear accusation.

Sam and Jones both blinked innocently.

"Good," Sam said.

"Yeah, super," Jones concurred.

"Melons is more like it," Marie groused as she turned back around.

"Aw, don't be like that, Ma," Jones whined.

"I don't even understand the reference," Sam lied.

"I'm not just a tactical god," Jones went on. "I'm also a man. With needs. Lee knows what I'm talking about. Uh? Don't you, Lee?"

"No clue," Lee quipped, then redirected the conversation. "I'm gonna pull the truck diagonal in the road, about twenty yards from Badger. Y'all stay behind it. I'll walk out there and talk to him. You know the drill."

Mirth was banished as lungs filled up, eyes got focused, and minds got right. Sam and Jones both shifted to the rear passenger's side door.

The fact that Badger and his group were coming right up the road and not sneaking through the woods was a good sign. It seemed he wanted a conversation, not a shootout. But you never knew how shit was going to go down.

Especially since Lee was in no mood to handle the fucker with kid gloves, as had been Gearhart's long-running policy with Badger.

Lee touched off his comms. "Abe. You set?"

The truck rounded a bend, and there ahead of them was Badger and his group, right in the middle of the road. They saw the pickup and stopped, the guys spreading out a bit, while Badger remained front and center.

Lee slowed the pickup to a crawl, closing the last few hundred yards. Marie shouldered her rifle, preparing to pump a magazine into the first twat to get froggy.

Abe came back: "Yeah. All set. Got visual on you and the visitors."

"Copy," Lee said, letting the truck coast down the hill. "We're on approach."

Lee pulled the truck across the road so Marie, Sam, and Jones could take cover on the passenger's side, then rolled to a stop. Looking out his window, Lee made eye contact with Badger, and knew he should've forced a smile to put things on a cordial footing, but...

No. Not today.

He thrust the shifter into park and popped his door. Marie, Sam, and Jones slid out their side and posted up, not pointing their weapons, but holding them ready and positioning themselves behind the engine block and rear axle.

Lee took a moment longer to hoist his bum leg out of the cab and get his boots on the ground. He let his rifle hang, as nonthreatening as he could be when kitted out for combat. He shut the driver's door and started crossing the twenty yards to Badger.

Lee didn't know whether Badger had been named for his general resemblance to the animal, or if the man had curated his appearance to match the nickname. He was squat and wide, though not fat, with wild eyes and a two-tone beard of black and gray.

At this point, six years after the collapse of society, Lee was getting pretty tired of animal names in general. There was just something so juvenile about them. They never failed to irritate him. In his years, he'd dealt with a whole menagerie of Spiders, Scorpions, Wolfs, Bears, etcetera. So far, naming themselves after scary animals hadn't stopped the bullets from going through them, or kept them from bleeding out afterward.

Still, Lee approached the situation with caution. For all his disdain for this man, Badger was armed, and so were his guys—ten of them, actually, now that Lee was counting.

Badger was the leader of a smaller settlement that also occupied the Gearhart Mountain Wilderness. They called their settlement—Lee almost had to cringe—The Badger's Den.

Badger had never been directly hostile towards the Gearhart settlement, which was to say, they'd never fired shots. But the relationship between the two settlements had always been strained.

Gearhart was high on a mountain plateau, protected by the terrain, with well-insulated log cabin homes, and fertile soil for successful crops, as well as plenty of hunting.

The Badger's Den was at the foot of the mountain, regularly endured raids by both primals and humans, was comprised mostly of trash-constructed shanties, and relied almost solely on foraging to feed the thirty-or-so people that called it home.

So, basically, their life sucked, and they occasionally liked to take it out on Gearhart by issuing stupid demands and thinly-veiled threats.

A policy of appeasement had been enacted by the generous humanitarians of Gearhart. After all, they had enough, so why not help another settlement out?

But, as Lee had warned them, *If you give a mouse a cookie, they're gonna want a glass of milk.*

"Afternoon, Badger," Lee greeted the man, keeping his hands visible as he stopped about five yards shy of the man.

Badger somehow managed to be wide-eyed and glaring at the same time. He had a basic AR-platform rifle slung on his chest, but seemed to be keeping his hands clear of it.

Badger wagged a finger at Lee. "It's...Jax, isn't it?"

Lee nodded, cataloguing the other members of Badger's group. There was a mix of deer guns, shotguns, and assault rifles. Most of these were slung on shoulders. One guy had his shotgun in hand, but pointed down. Another guy was holding his bolt action, but carrying it like a civil-war soldier might march with their musket.

"Yeah, I remember you too, Badger," Lee said, keeping his tone even—not too hostile, not too nice. Right in that Goldilocks-zone of *I'll be civil, but let's get this over with.* He squinted his one eye at the man. "Something I can help you boys with today?"

Badger looked skyward, then all around. "Gonna be a bad winter this year."

"Oh?"

"Yeah."

"Okay."

Badger lowered his chin. "Foraging's been rough."

"Sorry to hear that."

An insinuating glare. "Gonna have a lot of hungry mouths to feed, once the snow starts falling."

Lee took a big breath, like Bethany had told him to, eyeing the group before him. The thought occurred to him: If he sprinted into the woods, Marie, Sam, and Jones would start spraying on automatic, while Abe started perforating heads from afar, and Lee could work the angles and clean up the rest.

It'd probably only take about ten seconds to murder all these people.

He decided not to.

He was better than that. According to Bethany.

"I mean," Badger went on. "I'm the leader, sure. But once folk get hungry? Once their kids start crying because their bellies are empty? Well, they might be a little hard to control. And we both know where they're gonna go to get food." He glanced significantly up the mountain road. "Me, personally? I'd like to handle things peacefully today, so they don't get violent tomorrow."

Lee had been holding the breath he'd taken, waiting for his urge to murder to subside. It didn't quite work. He sighed the breath out through his nose. "We really gonna do this again, Badger?"

Badger glanced from side to side, almost guiltily, but not quite.

"What happened to the hundred pounds of barley we gave you?"

Badger blinked. "We ate it."

"Huh. See, that was for *planting*."

"We needed the food."

"If you'd've planted it, you'd *have* food right now."

Badger shifted his feet. "We needed the food *then*."

Lee nodded. "And what about the two hundred pounds of seed potatoes? Did you eat them too?"

Badger huffed. "They were bad seeds. Didn't grow. So we dug 'em up and ate 'em."

"They didn't grow, because they need full sun."

Badger thrust a hand out to encompass the terrain. "We're in the fucking woods! There's no full sun!"

"You ever thought about clear cutting an area for crops, Badger?"

Badger's face screwed up. "Clear cutting? We're not fucking lumberjacks, you gimpy fucking cyclops."

Lee rubbed a finger across an eyebrow. "Very nice." He rested his hands on the butt of his rifle. "Lemme ask you a question, Badger. Why in the fuck do I have to keep giving you shit, when you're either too dumb or too lazy to provide for yourself?"

Badger bristled, eyes going wide again. "Who in the fuck do you think you are?"

"I'm the guy saying 'no' to you."

"No?" Badger seemed agog, as though he'd never heard the word before.

"No," Lee confirmed. "No more handouts. No more freebies. You shoulda planted the fucking barley and cleared an area for the potatoes, and then all your people would be fat and happy. But you didn't, and I'm not going to keep protecting you from inevitable natural selection."

Badger had gone very still, eyes narrowed at Lee.

Everyone behind him was tense. Waiting.

Lee slowly shook his head. "Gearhart is no longer interested in subsidizing your existence. Also, I should point out to you, that me and my team are planning to stay for the winter. So if you get it in your head to come up that mountain again, don't plan on coming back down."

Badger regarded him from under heavy brows for a long moment. "You'd rather see us all starve to death?"

"No, Badger," Lee snapped. "I'd rather you have planted the fucking barley and potatoes we gave you, but I guess that ship has sailed, huh?" He leaned towards the squat man. "Your settlement is starving because of *poor leadership*."

Badger began nodding, very slow, as though he were realizing something. "Jax. Let's cut the shit, shall we? I know you. I know your team. I know there's five of you, and the fifth one—the guy with the beard, yeah?—he's probably pointing a big rifle at my nose right now, isn't he?"

Lee neither confirmed nor denied it.

Badger took a small step forward, his voice lowering. "But let's be honest—you're not who you claim to be. I know you got the Gearhart folks believing you're some special forces guy..." he made a significant glance towards Marie, Sam, and Jones, then quirked a dubious eyebrow at Lee. "But you and I both know that's bullshit."

Lee's ears pricked at a distant noise, and his attention shifted skyward.

Badger didn't seem to notice, and kept going. "You can play tactical dress-up all you want, with your armor and your fancy fucking guns. But you're not fooling me. You're just another pack of drifters, out conning folk to give you food and a place to sleep. You're a con man, Jax. You don't actually have the backing of the interim government, and..."

The noise became loud enough that Badger finally noticed it. He was a bit late to the party, as the rest of his guys were already looking skyward.

It was the sound of rotors.

This was immediately alarming to Lee—far more than Badger's threats had been.

People didn't just fly aircraft around anymore. The only aircraft in service—the only ones that should be flying over this airspace—belonged to the Interim American Government. And with the exception of exactly two people, no one else in the IAG should know where Lee and his team were.

Badger looked at Lee, and for just a flash, there was real fear in his eyes. "What the fuck is that?"

"Aircraft," Lee said, his throat a little tight as he searched the sky and tried to categorize the heavy, punchy sound of these particular rotors. Not a fixed-wing aircraft, he didn't think. But it didn't sound like a Blackhawk, nor an Apache...

The noise reached a sudden crescendo, and Lee watched a V-22 Osprey come hurtling around the side of the mountain, flying low.

Shit—that was a troop transport craft. And there really was no other explanation for it being in this lonely section of Oregon wilderness unless it had something to do with Lee.

Badger and his men ducked as though they were under fire as the twin-rotor aircraft roared over their heads. Lee tracked it, wondering if some black ops faction of the IAG had come to put him down.

He didn't know why that would be, but the why was immaterial—it was there, and it was heading straight toward Gearhart.

Lee swung back to Badger, doing his best to hide the worry in his expression. That aircraft might not be friendly, but Badger didn't know that.

Lee forced a confident smirk, even as his mind ran amok. "What were you saying about me not having any backing from the IAG?"

Badger's eyes were wide, snapping back and forth between the aircraft and Lee.

Then he took a step back. Raised his hands, as though Lee had won—this time.

He smiled back at Lee, and it was an ugly, threatening thing.

Neither said a word to the other.

Badger twirled a finger in the air, and all of his men seemed awfully happy to turn their asses around and head back down the mountain.

"Who the fuck is that?" Abe demanded over the radio.

Lee spun and began running back to the truck. "I have no idea," Lee transmitted back to Abe. "But we need to get back to Gearhart *now*."

Marie, Sam, and Jones were already piling into the truck by the time Lee reached it.

Ahead of them, the Osprey transitioned its rotors for vertical landing, and began to descend, seemingly right on top of Gearhart.

"Shit-shit-shit," Lee spat as he threw himself behind the wheel, tore through a three-point turn, and then began roaring up the mountain road.

"Please tell me that's a supply drop," Sam begged, though he didn't sound hopeful.

"I didn't call for a supply drop!" Marie shouted over the sound of the engine and the equally-loud rattle and rumble of the tires slamming over the bad road.

"We never drop inside settlements anyway," Lee said, watching as the Osprey disappeared below the trees. "Who knows we're here?"

"Just Angela and Ron!"

Angela was their single point of contact with the IAG base in Aspen, Colorado, and she reported to Major Ronald Paige. No one else should know shit about Lee and where he was holed up, and there was no reason why Angela or Ron would send a troop transport aircraft their way without warning.

Lee skidded to a stop at the trailhead, and Abe burst out of the brush, clambering into the backseat with Sam and Jones.

"Haven't heard any shooting yet," Abe said, breathlessly.

Lee peeled out again, slaloming his way up the mountain. He rolled his window down as he went, ears straining for the sound of gunfire. The Osprey had armaments, yes, but it could also carry three or four squads.

With no evidence to the contrary, and with life's habit of ruining anything good that Lee found, he began to imagine nightmare scenarios: Cabins burning, and tracer rounds flying, and people—*Bethany*—getting shot to mincemeat.

His heart was slamming much faster than it had when dealing with Badger.

Was that a gunshot? Or was he just imagining it?

Marie laid a hand on his arm, gripping him as she cringed. "Easy-easy-easy!"

Lee almost lost control of the truck as they spun through a hard turn with a nasty drop to one side. He had the presence of mind to take his foot off the gas for a beat. The tires got purchase, and he pushed the accelerator again.

They sped into Gearhart and...

No burning cabins. No tracers. No dead people.

There were plenty of people, but they were all streaming for the far end of the settlement, where the fields had recently been harvested. Lee slowed down enough that he wouldn't accidentally run someone over, then drove towards the field, honking his horn to get people out of the way.

Right smack dab in the middle of one of the fields, sat the big, gray bulk of the Osprey, its rotors still spinning, but slowing. The back ramp was lowered, and a single man stood there, dressed in fatigues. He wore no armor, and had only a pistol holstered on his hip.

Lee drove the pickup past the crowd of people and right up to the back of the Osprey.

The second he put it in park, he was out the door, confused, uncertain, and fuming.

"The fuck are you doing here?" Lee shouted over the whine of the slowing engines.

Major Ronald Paige took a pair of aviator sunglasses from his eyes, folded them, and put them in his pocket. He gave Lee a brittle smile, which seemed right on par with how the man felt about Lee.

Then he cupped one hand to the side of his mouth, and used the other to make a sweeping, inviting gesture towards the interior of the Osprey as he shouted back, "How 'bout you step into my office?"

Chapter 3

Lee stared at Ron Paige. Ron stared back.

The major folded his arms across his chest, waiting, albeit impatiently.

Lee's brain was still pulling at a dozen different threads, trying to figure out what the fuck was happening here, and whether or not he and his team were in danger.

And what about Gearhart? Surely, Ron wouldn't do some black-hearted shit like wiping one of the settlements out. Especially after spending the last three years supporting Lee's mission to help them until the IAG could get its ass in gear.

Lee ducked his head a bit to get a good look at the interior of the aircraft.

It appeared that Ron was alone.

So...no kill squad. That was encouraging.

Lee turned and looked at the people of Gearhart, scanning faces until he alighted upon Bethany, who happened to be standing next to Jeff, the guy that ran the settlement's security. Both of them looked worried and plenty confused.

Lee gave them a nod and a thumbs up, assuaging their worries, even as his own continued to mount.

Then he checked out his team. Marie, Sam, and Jones were all wearing pursed expressions of uncertainty. Abe looked pissed as hell. He knew Ron better than Lee, and their animosity had some weighty history to it.

Lee waved a hand, garnering his team's attention, then jerked his head toward the back of the Osprey. It looked like they were going to do this.

Lee and his team approached, squinting against rotor wash that had turned into more of a stiff breeze. As they reached the lowered ramp, Ron turned his back on them, strode to the top of the ramp, then put his hand on the controls, as though waiting for them to get inside.

They stepped in, cautiously.

Ron didn't even wait for them to clear the ramp. Sam was the last one on, and the second he had both feet on the ramp, Ron hit the controls and it started to trundle closed, causing Sam to swear and scamper forward until he was clear of the moving machinery.

He shot Ron an acidic look.

Then they all just stood there until the ramp sealed itself, and the noise from without became slightly duller. The engines were still spooling down, and Ron seemed willing enough to hold his silence until they could speak without shouting. He motioned for them to take some of the jump seats against the right wall of the Osprey's cargo hold.

Lee noted that he and his entire team were still strapped up. That was also encouraging. If Ron had some dirty shit planned, Lee doubted he'd be willing to stand around with five heavily-armed operators, when he only had a pistol.

Lee took the lead in claiming a jump seat, and the rest followed.

Ron chose a jump seat directly across from Lee and settled in, crossing one knee over the other, looking pretty relaxed.

After another minute, the engines had quieted enough that conversation was possible.

"Again," Lee said. "What are you doing here, Ron? This is not how we do things."

Ron frowned, then made a show of looking around his person. "Oh? Is there a rulebook? I can't seem to find it. Nope. No rulebook."

Lee tilted his head to one side. "That's real odd, because a couple months ago, back in California, we almost got our shit pushed in because you were afraid of breaking the rules."

Ron harrumphed. "Hey, I showed up, didn't I? You're welcome."

"Point being," Lee pressed. "There *are* rules. You and I don't talk. We call in supplies through Angela, she gives you the requests, and you drop them *where we tell you to drop them*. We do not meet in person, and we definitely don't show up on each other's doorsteps unannounced."

Ron nodded slowly along with this. "All of that's true. But, just like I made an exception for you when you requested an AC-130 for fire support—which is not a part of the original agreement—I'm now calling in the repayment."

"Oh, we're swapping favors now?" Lee scoffed. "See, I thought we just had jobs to do. You do your job so I can do my job. Didn't realize it was a favor-system."

Ron groaned. "Fuckssake, Lee, get a grip. I know you're really enjoying your new role as the mysterious white knight for random groups of survivors, but let's not just gloss over the fact that you're a terrorist and a war criminal, whose irradiated particles *should* be drifting about the ionosphere."

"Poetic."

Ron leaned forward, elbows on knees. "Just saying, Lee, I think you've spent so much time pretending to be a hero instead of a monster, you might've forgotten that there's a whole big world out beyond the confines of your personal messiah complex."

Abe recoiled his head. "The fuck does that even mean?"

Ron gave him a sharp look. "It means there are bigger issues at play, and I don't give a good goddamn if your feathers are ruffled because I dared to treat you like what you are—assets. Not fucking national heroes. Not someone who gets to tell me how shit's done. Assets." He leaned back again. "God. Get over yourselves."

Lee sighed and patted a hand in the air. "Alright. Obligatory dick-comparing aside, what is it you need from us?"

Ron smiled. "Hey, remember that time I saved your asses with an AC-130?"

No one responded.

Ron didn't seem to mind. "I read over the reports—such as they were. Is it true you were able to infiltrate a nest of primals? Walk right into their colony?"

"We had help," Lee said, carefully.

"Right, right. The hybrid girl. Like, part primal, part human? Able to think and talk, but also able to control the primals?"

"To a certain extent."

Ron pursed his lips. "Elaborate on that."

Lee chewed his lip for a moment, wondering how much to tell Ron. The reports Lee issued were bare-bones, and heavily obfuscated. He gave them verbally to Angela, who then wrote them down and issued them to Ron. Lee had intentionally left out all but the most basic details about the hybrids, because he had a well-founded concern about getting sucked into some sort of government-run experiments.

"Hybrids seem to have some status in the primal hierarchy," Lee trudged on. "The one that worked with us was able to get us through the door. However, when shit popped off and the primals got nasty, her influence over them was...minimal."

There was a flare of interest in Ron's eyes. "But you *were* able to work with a hybrid, and she *was* able to get you in amongst the primals without being attacked?"

"Initially."

Ron considered this for a few beats. "Did she make it out alive? It's not mentioned in your report."

Lee didn't like the direction this was going. He needed to tread very carefully. "She was alive the last time I saw her."

Ron's eyes twinkled with dark amusement. He knew Lee was omitting details. "Do you know where to find her?"

"No," Lee said.

That was a complete lie. Only the week prior, while doing a long-range patrol from Gearhart, Lee and his team had come across a group of drifters. They'd been friendly enough, and Lee had given them food and water and then pumped them for information. Turned out, they'd just come through a few settlements on the western side of Oregon, and they had stories to tell about some guy who'd made friends with a girl that was part primal.

It was either one hell of a coincidence, or it was their old "friends" from California: Bran and Kat.

Those settlements—one was called Winchuck, and the other O'Brien—were in relatively close proximity to the valley in Northern California where Lee had met Bran and Kat. Initially, their relationship had been combative. But after Jones had tagged Bran twice in the back during a shoot-out, Kat had come, offering to help them infiltrate the primal colony if they saved Bran's life.

After everything had gone down, Bran and Kat had lit out north, searching for a place where they were not hated and feared. Apparently, they'd wound up somewhere around Winchuck and O'Brien, which was about 150 miles west of Gearhart.

Again, Ron seemed to know that Lee was hiding something, but he didn't press—not directly anyway. "Alright, lemme back up a few steps," he said. "Give you a fuller picture of what we're dealing with here."

His gaze panned over Lee and the others. "This information is classified—and when I say classified, I mean full-blown, I find out you breathed a word about this and I'll carpet bomb you and everyone who might've heard, and I am not fucking around. *That* type of classified. We clear on that point?"

Lee made a writing motion in the air. "Should we sign NDAs? Or just cut our palms and make a blood oath?"

Emboldened by Lee's sarcasm, Jones raised a hand. "Is there any way we can *not* hear the classified information?"

Ron gave Jones a laconic side-eye. "No."

Jones's hand fell. "Oh. Alright. Fine."

Ron pointed to his own nodding head. "Everyone nod like this, so I know you understand the consequences."

Begrudgingly, they all nodded.

"Great." He dusted his hands together. "My conscience is clear then. Okay, here's the situation that has brought me to your door." He addressed himself to Lee again. "Weird shit's going down in Virginia. IAG has been trying to push a bit into the northeastern states and reclaim some of that territory that was lost to all the hordes that came out of the cities—you remember that, don't you, Lee?"

"Intimately."

Ron nodded. "Well, most of it's a fucking wasteland now. But they did locate one pocket of survivors. Little settlement that somehow made it through all that shit. Seems they survived by developing some sort of fucked up relationship with a colony of primals—don't ask me how that works, I'm not privy to the details. Suffice it to say, they've managed to survive by working *with* the primals, not against them."

This was already giving Lee all kinds of bad vibes, but he stayed silent and let Ron continue.

"This is where the details get even fuzzier. All I know for sure is that a team of researchers was sent to this settlement, and everything was hunky dory, until last week when the researchers went dark."

Lee scratched a fingernail gingerly around the scar tissue of his ruined eye socket. "What were they researching?"

Ron shrugged. "We'll get to that later. What I can tell you right now is that the upper echelons of the IAG are freaking the fuck out. They want to handle things without bloodshed, but the settlement has closed themselves off, and refuses to speak with any government officials. Two separate teams have been sent in to try and recover the researchers. They went dark as well. At which point, our mutual friend, ICAO Griffin, offered a possible solution that doesn't require aggressive military action."

Ron gestured to Lee with both hands.

"Us," Lee said, flatly.

"Yes, you guys. Overt military action is still on the table, but Griffin would like to see if things can be handled quietly, without any blowback onto the government. Who better to accomplish this task than a black ops team that doesn't even exist on paper?"

Lee squeezed his eye shut, pinching the bridge of his nose. "Alright. So, basically, Griffin wants to curry some political favor with the IAG's higher ups, and he's going to use us to get it." He opened his eye. "That about right?"

Ron bobbled his head. "Well. You guys…and the hybrid girl."

"Because you think she can get us in without getting ripped to shreds by primals. Which is what happened to the other two teams, isn't it?"

"I don't know how they got taken out, but I think that's a reasonable conclusion, yes."

Lee leaned forward. "See, when I made this agreement—which, by the way, I made with ICAO Griffin, not you—I was promised that we wouldn't be used as a kill team to do dirty shit for the government."

Ron frowned. "Were you not listening? That's the whole reason why Griffin wants *you guys* to do it. They've got an entire military detachment within striking range of the settlement—if they wanted to wipe them out, they'd just cut those guys loose. Which, again, is still on the table. What they want *you guys* to do is what you've been doing for the past three years: Stroll in, smooth talk them, get them on our side if possible, and retrieve the research."

Lee cocked an eyebrow. "You mean retrieve the *researchers*."

Ron waved it off. "Yeah, them too—assuming they're still alive."

"With the hybrid girl," Lee added. "Because otherwise we won't make it past the primals."

Ron nodded.

"I already told you I don't know where she is."

"Yeah, you did say that," Ron sighed. "And I don't buy it."

Lee pressed himself back in his seat. "I'd like some time to talk this over with my team."

Ron gave him a pained expression. "Alright. I'm gonna level with you, Lee. You and I have never cared for each other. I didn't come here, hat in hand, trying to ingratiate myself with you, for two reasons: First, because you'd know it was bullshit; and second, because...you don't have a choice."

Ah, there it was.

Abe let out an ornery, growling noise.

"Well, I mean, you *do* have a choice," Ron amended. "You could tell me to go fuck myself. I'd smile and wave and take off in this nice shiny Osprey, and you'd never hear from me again. Then you and your friends can spend the rest of their lives here doing...you know...farming or whatever."

It was funny—for all that the two men disliked each other, they did understand each other perfectly. Ron knew what type of creature Lee was. He knew that, while Lee might enjoy—or even need—some downtime every once in a while, the prospect of settling down and living in peace was anathema to him.

So, while that sounded like a dandy offer to a normal person, to Lee and his team it sounded more like a life sentence.

Surprisingly, Ron did not seem to take pleasure in this, as he had with the rest of his goading bullshit. His eyes went to each of the team, speaking to all of them now, not just to Lee. "If you want to keep doing what you do, then this is the price of that. And it's not a big price—it's doing what you usually do. Helping people."

"Helping Griffin, you mean," Abe retorted.

"Yeah," Ron acknowledged. "And keeping a settlement of people from getting wiped out." His head suddenly drooped with a sigh. He looked exhausted. "Look, this shit wasn't my idea, okay? I work for Griffin, just like you do. He tells me what he wants. I get it done. This is what he wants. And you gotta do it or your deal with him is off."

Well, at that point, Lee had pretty much been boxed into a corner.

Finding a way out of it was not an option, so Lee forced his mind into finding a way through it.

"Alright," Lee dredged out of himself. "Well, you got us by the short and curlies. Let's bury the hatchet, at least for the next ten minutes, and figure out how we're going to move forward."

Ron waited, expectantly.

"Assuming I can find the hybrid girl, what's our timeline on this?"

"Immediate."

Lee shook his head. "Can't be immediate. At the very least, I'm gonna need a day, maybe two, to track the hybrid girl down."

Ron slid his palms across his thighs. Drummed on his knees a few times. "Reason I said immediate, is because you're gonna be on the clock. Like I said, higher ups are ready to pull the trigger on that settlement. Griffin convinced them to wait, because he's confident you can get it done without a fucking massacre, but the higher ups only gave him a week. As of last night. Which means you got—"

"Yeah, I can do math," Lee interrupted, leaning forward onto his elbows and rubbing the short beard on his jaw.

If it really was Bran and Kat down by Winchuck and O'Brien, Lee could get there by that evening. Maybe get in touch with

Kat sometime tomorrow, if they were lucky. That'd only leave them five days to get the job done—one of which would probably be spent in transit from Oregon to Virginia.

That was not a lot of time. Could they run this op safely with only four days?

It was a stretch.

But what other options did he have?

He looked at Ron again. "Any way Griffin can push for more time?"

Ron shook his head. "He's already out on a limb here."

Lee considered. "If I find the hybrid girl, it'll be faster if I could call for a pickup wherever I find her, instead of having to transport her back here. Can you do that?"

"Depends on where you find her. Our fixed wings are currently on other operations, and you'd need an airfield anyway. As long as it's within the thousand-mile range of an Osprey, though...then, yeah. I can do that."

"Alright. One other problem."

Ron made a *go-ahead* gesture.

"There's a smaller settlement at the bottom of this mountain," Lee said. "They're getting a bit uppity with this settlement we've been staying in. I don't want to leave these folks vulnerable while I'm gone."

Ron looked confused. "Do they not have weapons? Have you not been training them?"

"They have weapons. We've been training them."

Ron's eyes narrowed. "Am I missing something?"

Lee clenched his teeth. No, Ron wasn't missing anything. Fact was, Lee was just thinking about Bethany. Not wanting to leave her and her people in the lurch. But, if he looked at the situation clinically—and took his affection for Bethany out of it—he knew that A) Badger likely wouldn't try anything so soon after Lee had warned him away, and B) if he did, Gearhart still had the advantage of high-ground, numbers, and the training they'd received.

He just wished he could've left them with some heavier weapons. A handful of machine-gun nests around the perimeter would do nicely.

Maybe Lee could work on that when they came back. This op would only take a week.

"Alright," Lee finally sighed. "I guess we better get going."

CHAPTER 4

THEY WERE DRIVING DOWN the mountain, and Jones had concerns: "Alright, so clearly we're doing this thing with Kat. And since we're definitely doing it, I'll skip all the parts about how it's a wildly fucked up idea, and move on to how in the hell we're gonna make this work."

"Aw," Sam said, reaching across Abe to pinch Jones's cheek. "Look at that. You're maturing."

Jones batted his hand away. "Stop. Be serious."

That actually made Lee look in the rearview at Jones, whose face was indeed serious. "Jones, calling for the rest of us to be serious? It truly is the end times."

Jones gave him a flat look. "Someone's gotta bring the mood up between all you sourpusses—*would you stop that?*" Jones recoiled from where Sam had snaked his arm over Abe's shoulders and was twiddling Jones's earlobe.

"Geez," Sam said, retracting his hand, mock affronted. "Who's the sourpuss now?"

Jones glared. "So, all I gotta do is be serious, and then you fucks will lighten up?"

"Yeah," Sam sniffed. "Gotta bring balance to the Force."

Not happy being stuck between the two younger members of the squad, but handling it admirably, Abe raised both hands like a referee. "Jones has very reasonable concerns."

"Thank you," Jones said. "So, we worked with Kat back in the Valley. But she did that shit to save her friend's life. That kept her motivated and obedient." His eyebrows climbed in question. "What makes you think she'll even agree to work with us, let alone follow orders?"

Silence for a long moment.

"You're asking me?" Lee said. "I don't fucking know, Jones. I have all the same information that you have."

Jones wilted a bit. "Well, I was hoping you had some master plan."

Lee shook his head. "Nope. Just gonna roll in there and hope for the best."

"Alright, next question—what if Kat doesn't come with us? Is Griffin still going to kick us to the curb?"

"I don't know."

"So, you literally have no plan."

Lee stretched his back. "Let's try this, Jones—what's *your* plan?"

Jones entered into a period of quiet contemplation.

After a few moments of silence, he said, "Well, we gotta talk to her to figure out what might motivate her."

"Ding-ding-ding," Lee said. "You figured it out."

"Okay. Very clever. I walked into that one. But we're still left with the problem of Kat being half primal."

"I thought she was only a quarter primal," Sam said.

"She is," Lee confirmed.

"Whatever," Jones rejoined. "She's got primal in her. So, like, what? Do we put her on a leash or some shit? How do we keep her from running off, chewing on people we don't want her to chew on, or even worse, just running off period, and leaving us to face the primals on our own?"

Sam leaned forward in his seat. "All joking aside, Jones does have a point. I saw her get pissed when I was with her on that ranch. She completely lost her shit. That's a bit concerning if she's gonna be embedded with us on an op."

"Yeah," Lee said, remembering how she'd tackled her own biological father—a human—and bit his throat out. "I saw."

Marie spoke up. "So far, I'm hearing a lot of problems, and no solutions." She twisted in her seat to look back at Jones. "And don't say the leash idea was your solution. It's a non-starter."

"Guys," Abe said. "We're just gonna have to trust her."

Jones looked at him like he was crazy. "Trust a hybrid?"

Abe nodded, sagely. "Yeah, Jonesy. Sometimes you get stuck on a team with some wingnut and you just gotta roll with it and hope for the best."

Jones scowled. "I feel like that was a shot at me."

"It wasn't," Abe said, though the smile hidden in his beard said that it was. "Look: You, me, and Lee were all in the military before. Remember the idiots you had to go into combat with sometimes? You didn't just get to say, 'no, I don't trust this idiot,' you had to just suck it up and go. And you know what? Most of the time it turned out fine."

"You're talking about idiot *humans*, though," Jones pointed out. "I feel like Kat could be a lot more harmful."

Abe made an uncertain noise. "Retarded eighteen-year-old on a ma deuce can be pretty harmful."

"You know," Lee put in. "Jonesy and Sam, you both rode with me right into that city with Kat. Right into the primals' nest."

"And it turned into an utter fuckfest," Jones observed.

"That wasn't Kat's fault. You were both nervous as shit having her ride along with us, but she didn't do anything crazy. She did exactly what we asked of her."

"Again—because she wanted to save her friend."

"I dunno," Lee said. "I don't think you're giving her enough credit. If she's capable of controlling her instincts to save her friend, then, at the end of the day, she's capable of controlling her instincts. Will she? I can't say. What motivates *you* to control *your* instincts?"

Jones seemed confused. "My instincts for what? Eating people?"

"Come on, Jones," Lee chided. "How many times have you stared at someone and just thought about killing them? Even when they weren't doing anything wrong. Maybe just being slightly annoying. And you have that idea pop into your head, 'I could just choke slam this person and then keep bashing their head against the ground until they stop twitching.'" He glanced in the rearview again. "You know?"

Silence.

Abe raised his hand. "I know what you're talking about."

Lee frowned. "Oh, come on, Jonesy."

Jones looked out the window. "Y'all're fucked up."

Sam boo'd him, while Abe elbowed him.

"Don't lie," Lee challenged. "This is a safe space."

"Alright, okay," Jones said, fending Abe off. "Maybe. Occasionally."

"Okay, well, see?" Lee said. "We're all fighters, and we're all killers, and all of us know that we can take a life pretty fucking easy. But we restrain our base instincts."

"Yeah, but we're humans," Jones argued. "She's not."

"Then what is she?"

"She's a hybrid."

"And what does that mean?"

"Means she's a quarter primal and three-quarters human."

"Okay, so she's got a seventy-five percent chance of being able to control her instincts just as well as you do, Jones." Lee shook his head. "Hate to break it to you, but I don't think this hybrid issue is going anywhere. I think it's something we're going to have to learn how to deal with. And I don't feel real great about just saying that someone like Kat, who's still mostly human, is nothing but an animal."

Jones thrust himself into the space between the two front seats. "She's gonna be sleeping next to us, Lee. Did you think about that?"

"Yeah, I did," Lee admitted. "And I'll cite my previous point on the matter."

"Psssh." Jones wilted back into his seat, defeated and shaking his head. "Just another fucking level in the game."

Sam rolled his eyes. "Here we fuckin' go."

Curious, Marie glanced between Sam and Jones. "What?"

"It's a simulation," Jones said with conviction. "All of this. Life. The universe. It's a fucking simulation."

Marie's eyes crinkled with amusement. "Like the Matrix?"

"No, not like the Matrix," Jones replied, defensive. "I don't think we're actually in tubes, plugged into a virtual reality." He began to make expansive gestures. "More like we're disembodied consciousnesses, floating in some cosmic medium, all experiencing the same ridiculous simulation that we call reality."

Sam patted Marie's arm and spoke sotto voce: "Please, don't get him going."

Marie ignored Sam. "So, who's running the simulation? Aliens?"

Jones shrugged. "Aliens. AIs. What difference does it make? Whoever it is, they're basically God. And God's basically a DM."

"A DM?" Marie asked.

It was Abe that answered: "Dungeon Master."

Jones looked gobsmacked. "Bro, did you play D&D?"

"Fuck yeah, I played D&D."

Jones went for an excited high-five.

"But only on deployment, because I have self-respect," Abe finished.

Jones pulled his hand away, chagrinned. "That's cold."

Marie gave Abe a hooded look. "You were a D&D nerd?"

"No, I wasn't a D&D *nerd*," Abe corrected. "I said I played it on deployment. Why? Does that make me more or less attractive?"

Marie pulled her head back, evaluating him through slitted eyes. "I'm not sure."

Lee decided to back his friend up. "Everybody played D&D on deployment. Good way to pass the time."

Jones flagged the air with his palms. "Wait-wait-wait. You mean to tell me this whole time we could've been having epic D&D nights?"

"No," Abe and Lee said in unison.

They arrived in the settlement of O'Brien just as the sun dipped below the horizon. It was a trading settlement, and so they didn't balk at newcomers as much as some other settlement might have. They actually had signs posted telling folks how to approach without getting shot.

Lee thought that was a nice touch.

The checkpoint seemed a little alarmed at the contents of Lee's truck—namely, five people with armor and weapons. But Marie smiled real nice, and everyone kept their hands visible while Lee explained why they were there.

He opted not to mention Kat, and instead asked after Bran Potter, and gave a description.

The guard at Lee's window gave him a cautious look, and instructed Lee to park off to the side. Lee complied, noticing that two of the guards seemed to be hovering—not threatening, but definitely keeping them covered.

"Well," Lee remarked as he pushed the shifter into park, but left the truck running. "Seems they know who Bran is, at least."

"He definitely knew who you were talking about," Marie confirmed.

Whether or not to be honest had been another topic of debate in the truck. When strangers showed up asking after a particular person, it had the tendency to make folks think they had a bone to pick with the person they were looking for.

In the end, honesty had won out for pure expediency: Lee didn't have time to waste, acting like they were there for trade, and slowly beating around the bush.

One of the guards that was not-so-subtly keeping an eye on them approached, seeming suspicious.

Lee smiled as cordially as he was able.

The guy made a show of sniffing the air. "Truck smells like gas," he said.

Lee nodded. "Yup."

Narrowed eyes. "Where'd you get gas?"

There really was nothing Lee could say that would sound innocent. So he went with, "Dinosaurs."

The man glowered, then moved to cover their truck from the rear quarter panel.

Lee kept an eye on him in the sideview, but the guard didn't make any overtly-hostile moves.

After about fifteen minutes of sitting there, quietly speculating amongst themselves on how they could extract themselves from the situation if shit went down, a small convoy of vehicles appeared on the road behind them.

The vehicles approached quickly, led by a two-tone Ford F-150 with an armed guard standing in the back bed.

Lee's first instinct was that the checkpoint guards had called in backup. But the occupants of the convoy acted pretty casual. None of them even looking towards the strange white pickup parked just outside their gates.

The lead guard approached the guy in the bed of the two-tone Ford as he hopped down. They conversed briefly, the guard shooting glances at Lee and his team. The guy from the two-tone Ford gave them a look, nodded to the guard, and walked over.

Lee took in the pertinent details of the guy at a glance.

Average height. Average build. An earnest face. Not a hard-case. Armed with a lever action and a holstered pistol.

He stopped just behind the cab, meeting Lee's one-eyed gaze in the sideview mirror. "You in the driver's seat," the guy said. "You the leader?"

"Yeah, something like that."

"You mind stepping out and talking to me back here?"

Having had a lot of experience making contact with various settlements, Lee knew to keep everything as above-board and non-threatening as possible. So he stuck both his hands out of his open window, showing they were empty, then opened his door from the outside, and stepped out. He didn't raise his hands, but he kept them palms-out at his sides as he stepped over to the man.

"What's your name, stranger?" the guy asked, taking in Lee's armor, hanging rifle, and holstered sidearm.

"Name's Jax," Lee said. "You?"

The guy hesitated, but only for a second. "Patrick." He jerked his head towards the lead guard. "My friend tells me you're looking for someone."

Lee kept his tone even and friendly—but not too friendly, as that made people feel like you were trying to manipulate them. "Yeah. Looking for a man named Bran Potter. You know him?"

Patrick didn't directly answer. "Why are you looking for this Bran Potter guy?"

It was clear to Lee that Patrick knew him and was covering for him. But he thought that was a good sign. Because if Patrick was covering for Bran, that meant they were more or less on friendly terms. Which meant Bran probably hadn't gone back to being an asshole.

"Me and my team have a job that we need his help with."

"Oh? What kind of job?"

Lee smiled, but shook his head. "Alright, Patrick. I appreciate what you're trying to do, but I can't tell you what the job is."

Patrick raised his brows. "And what is it you think I'm trying to do?"

"You're trying to protect Bran. But it's unnecessary. We're not here looking for trouble, and I'm certainly not going to hurt anyone—not you, your people, or Bran. But I am on a bit of a time-crunch, and I need to find Bran ASAP. So, let's lay our cards on the table. You know Bran, and you know where to find him. I need to speak to him, but I know you have no reason to trust me. So, what can I do to get a meeting with Bran by, say, tomorrow morning at the latest?"

Patrick scoffed lightly and shifted his feet. Looked at the rest of Lee's team, still sitting in the truck. He looked at Lee again. Then stared off at nothing, contemplating.

"Alright," Patrick said. "I might—*might*—be able to help you. But we're not going anywhere tonight."

Lee allowed it with a nod. "I didn't figure."

"Y'all are welcome to stay inside the gates tonight, but we don't have extra room, so you'll be sleeping in your truck. And, don't take offense to this, but you'll be under guard."

Lee sighed, not relishing the idea of being cramped in the truck all night, but it was a common discomfort. "I understand."

"Y'all stay on your best behavior, and tomorrow morning you can hop in with our caravan—just you. Your team stays here."

That wasn't Lee's favorite idea, but he didn't get any bad vibes from Patrick, and the settlement seemed normal. None of the weird shit that Lee occasionally saw from people left too long without oversight—corpses on walls, necklaces of ears, shit like that.

"I can get on board with that," Lee said.

Patrick gave him a look that wasn't exactly threatening, but was nonetheless deadly serious. "I wouldn't call Bran a close personal friend, but if I start to feel like your intentions towards him aren't what you said, I will have you and your team killed."

Lee shrugged. "Since I have no ill intentions, that's no skin off my back."

Without further ado, Patrick instructed Lee where to park his truck inside the gates, then assigned two guards to watch them. Lee complied with everything they told him to do.

The one amenity they were provided was access to an outhouse, which was greatly appreciated.

They stretched their legs and hung around the tailgate as they ate a meager dinner of bread, jerky, and pumpkin seeds from Gearhart. As Lee was finishing the last of the bread—which was dense, but pretty damn tasty—he spotted five guys he recognized from Patrick's earlier convoy.

At first, he thought that perhaps O'Brien had decided to renege on their agreement to let Lee and his team stay there overnight. But then he noticed that, save for two of the guys that had pistols on their hips, none of them appeared to be armed.

Curious, Lee watched them as they approached the front gates of O'Brien—not towards Lee, but to the line of vehicles they had parked nearby. They went to one of the pickups and stationed themselves at the tailgate. When they dropped it, Lee spotted what looked like a stack of papers, bound tightly with twine.

In the old world, this would have been nothing to comment on. Back then, paper was everywhere, and more of a trash-nuisance than anything. Nowadays, it was a commodity, and seeing a whole stack of it got Lee wondering where these people had got it, and what they were doing with it.

He brushed bread crumbs off on his pants as he watched one of the guys cut the twine with a pocket knife and begin separating the papers into five equal stacks.

"I'll be right back," Lee commented to his team as he walked over, keeping his pace casual and his hands visible.

The two guards that had been stationed to watch them followed Lee with their eyes, but didn't move to intervene. Lee cut wide of the tailgate, not wanting to walk right up behind the guys and alarm them. He managed to catch one guy's attention as he approached the pickup bed. The guy startled a bit, glancing worriedly to his friends, then over to Lee's guards.

Lee held up his hands and stopped advancing. "What's up, gentlemen?" He nodded towards the five stacks of paper. Now that he was closer, he noticed that they were crammed with tiny, printed lettering. "Just curious what you got going on here. Haven't seen that much paper in a while."

He got a few blank stares, but the guy that was distributing the papers into stacks gave him a cautious smile and held one of the sheets out to him. "Go ahead. Take one."

Lee accepted the paper with a nod of thanks and looked it over. As he did, his eyebrows climbed. The words were typed in a small font, designed to save space. Three columns of lettering, with no margin on the edges. The back was printed in much the same way.

Lee glanced up at the guy that'd given him the paper. "Is this...a newspaper?"

The man's cautious smile turned into a big grin. "Yeah, man. IAG just started rollin' these out. We get 'em once a month."

Lee blinked rapidly. "Where do you get them from?"

The guy jerked his head. "Winchuck. They're the ones got the printer. See, IAG made these special printers with a satellite connection. As long as you can hook 'em to some sort of power source, they download and print off a newspaper once a month. This is only the second time we've got them." He shrugged. "It's pretty bare-bones—not exactly 'all the news that's fit to print,' but it gives us the gist of what's going on inside the interior states."

One of the other guys chuckled darkly. "At least we know they're doing *something*. For a while there, I thought the IAG was just a myth."

Lee scanned the lines of cramped lettering again, then glanced up. "You mind if I show this to my team? I'll bring it back."

The guy waved him off. "Keep it. We got enough."

Lee gave him something of a salute with the sheet of paper, thanked him, and walked slowly back to his team, reading as he went.

"Watcha got there?" Jones queried while chewing noisily. "That a manual or somethin'?"

"No," Lee said, sidling up to their pickup bed and resting his arms on the side. "This is a newspaper, direct from the IAG." He lowered the paper out of his eyeline to see frozen, shocked faces. "Did you know we have a new president?"

"Get the fuck out," Jones marveled.

Abe snatched the paper. "Lemme see that." He read for a moment, his gaze becoming almost irate. "You gotta be shitting me. New fucking president. James Morton. Old air force colonel. Says he won in a landslide." Abe raised his eyes, glowering. "I didn't get a fucking vote."

Marie, Sam, and Jones came hustling around from the other side of the truck bed to jostle in tight with Lee and Abe, everyone reading random snippets aloud.

"The MCR," Marie pointed. "Multinational Coalition for Reconstruction. What the fuck? And apparently they're having a summit, and we're in it—or at least the IAG is."

"Who the hell is James Morton?" Jones griped. "I've never heard of the guy. How'd he win a landslide and I've never even heard of him?"

"Chicago?" Sam cried. "What the fuck are they trying retake Chicago for? There's a bajillian settlements out here that need the IAG's support, and they're focused on *Chicago*?"

Lee had to laugh, which caused Sam to glare at him.

"What's funny?" Sam demanded.

Lee shook his head. "You were probably too young to remember American politics, but that's just how it goes. Ignoring the majority, and coddling the fucking city-dwellers. Par for the course."

Abe got a troubled look on his face. "American politics," he breathed, glancing at Lee. "Of all the things to bring back, that's possibly the last thing I wanted them to resurrect."

The smile fell from Lee's face. "Yeah. If it hadn't already happened six years ago, I'd say this was the beginning of the apocalypse."

Chapter 5

"Okay," Kat said.

Standing on the side of a stretch of road between the settlements of O'Brien and Winchuck, Lee blinked in surprise. He'd just made his initial sales pitch, entirely prepared for bargaining and arguments to follow.

Instead, Kat was smiling with all of her considerable teeth, clearly not needing to be convinced.

The morning had proceeded just as Patrick had outlined. Lee had left his team under the watchful eyes of a few guards they probably could've killed without much of a fight. The sole occupant of his truck, Lee had then followed the trading caravan out of O'Brien about an hour after sunrise.

Roaring down a long, straight section of road with brush encroaching on either side, Lee had spotted Bran, standing on the side of the road like a hitchhiker. Patrick had been in the lead vehicle again, and pulled their convoy to a stop, then had a brief conversation with Bran.

Even from all the way in the back of the convoy, Lee could see the disconcerted expression on Bran's face. That expression turned into full oh-shit-mode when Lee emerged from his truck and approached.

Lee couldn't really blame the guy. The last time he'd seen Lee, he'd been on the cusp of dying from two bullet holes Jones had put in him.

Lee didn't give them a lot of details—just the broad strokes: He needed Kat's help with a mission. Bran was welcome, but Kat was a necessity for his team's success—and survival.

Bran was clearly not interested.

Kat, on the other hand, seemed rarin' to go.

"Okay?" Lee asked, still recovering from his surprise at how easy that had been. "Like...you're in?"

"Yes," Kat said, immediately. "I'm in."

Lee was once again impressed by how improved her speech had become. When he'd first met Kat, she'd barely been able to string a full sentence together. Her voice was still low and raspy, the words still a bit unwieldy due to the mutation of her jaws and teeth, but she spoke much more fluidly than she had before.

Bran spun on her, eyes wide. "What the fuck, Kat?"

She looked at him like a minor annoyance on a path to ultimate glory. "I want to go."

"I thought you liked it at the monastery!" Bran cried. "What about Elijah? You're not going to miss Elijah?" Bran made an unconscious gesture into the woods, then seemed to catch himself, but Lee had already seen it and looked into the brush.

He tensed at the sight of a large, dark-skinned face peering through the foliage at them.

A face with an inhumanly-wide mouth under a snout-like nose.

Lee's hands instinctively twitched towards his rifle, but he restrained himself from actually taking it up. Standing to the side, Patrick also seemed surprised that another hybrid was present, which struck Lee as odd.

Bran immediately realized his error and raised both hands, one towards Patrick, and one towards Lee. "No-no, it's okay, he's not a threat. He's just like Kat—he's one of the good ones."

Lee goggled at Bran. "He? As in…"

Bran nodded. "Yeah, he's a male hybrid."

Lee shook his head. "I thought there were only female hybrids."

"Well, you thought wrong," Bran said, a bit testily. "Primal packs only want female hybrids, so any time a male is born, they kill it. That's why you never see male hybrids."

Lee's mind raced to keep up. "So where'd this one come from?"

Bran heaved a sigh. "Look, it's a long story that I don't want to get into right now."

The male hybrid—Elijah, apparently—started to come out from behind the stand of vegetation he'd been hiding in, but Bran shot up a hand to stop him. "Stay put, Elijah. We're good."

Lee was surprised to see the hybrid immediately obey.

Bran looked sternly at Kat. "You don't wanna leave Elijah, do you?"

Kat looked a little torn, and Lee had the urge to tell Bran to shut his fucking mouth before he ruined everything. But then Kat seemed to brighten and looked at Lee. "He could come with us," she said, hopefully. "You need hybrid help. Two is better than one."

Lee's first thought was *fuck no*, but then his second thought was, *well…*

He didn't get much further, because Bran chopped a hand through the air as though to behead the idea. "No. Absolutely-fucking-not. Are you kidding me, Kat? Shay would murder me."

Kat gave Bran a thoroughly-displeased look, which Lee imagined was something like having a partially-tamed lioness snarl at you—extremely disconcerting.

Bran however, did not seem intimidated at all.

"Well, I'm going," Kat announced, resolute.

Bran opened his mouth to object. Then stopped himself. Then slumped a bit. "Why? I thought...I thought you liked what we had going on."

Kat's expression softened. "I do." She placed a hand on his shoulder. It looked like any other hand at first glance. But at second glance, you would notice how those fingers were oddly long, and that the nails were thick and hardened, and came to a claw-like point. "Love you. Love Shay and the boys." She shook her head, looking almost sad. "But...I am not you. You like peace. No fighting. All farming." Her pretty, copper-colored eyes went down to her feet. "I am...I feel..."

A strange silence fell on them, as Lee, Bran, and Patrick all waited intently. It could not be easy for someone like Kat to articulate her emotions. Hell, it was hard for most people, and Kat had a speech barrier to maneuver around, and probably an extreme lack of practice with introspection.

"Trapped," Kat finally said.

Lee kept his face level, but inwardly, he smiled.

"Kat," he said, getting her to look at him again. "I think you're gonna fit in great with my team."

Things moved quickly.

A half-hour after finding Kat, Lee was back at O'Brien introducing her to the crew.

Surprisingly, Abe seemed to be the most comfortable with her, while Marie remained cordial, but aloof, and Sam and Jones were both obviously nervous.

"Welcome to the team, Kat. I'm Abe." He thrust a hand out to her.

She stared at it.

Abe kept it out there, a breath of sympathy coming to his eyes as he realized this might be the first time someone had offered to shake her hand. When she glanced up at him, he covered it quickly with a smile.

"It's alright," he said, casually. "This is what we weird fucking humans do to show trust. We clasp hands together."

Kat looked at his outstretched hand again. Then raised her own and slowly seated it into Abe's. Judging by her bloodless knuckles, and Abe's slight wince, Lee figured she was really cranking down on him.

"Why?" Kat rasped, not letting go.

"I dunno. Some old-timey shit about showing you don't have weapons."

Kat looked at the rifle on Abe's chest. "But you have weapons."

"Yeah," he said, casting a glance at Lee. "It's just...a tradition, I guess."

Kat stared at him for a few beats. "How long do we hold hands?"

"We're probably good now."

She released him, but kept her hand out and turned it on Marie, expectantly.

"Alright," Marie said, tightly. "No time like the present for a lesson in etiquette." She took Kat's hand and managed to hide her discomfort as Kat squeezed. "Okay, loosen your grip a bit,"

Marie instructed. "Good. Now we do this..." Marie gave Kat's hand a single pump. "...and then we let go." They released. "I'm Marie, by the way."

Etiquette lesson complete, Kat pivoted the hand to Jones.

"Yup, we're doin' this," Jones murmured, then dove in, his eyes a little wide as he took Kat's hand and, instead of pumping it, rotated it to look at her claw-like fingernails. "You, uh...sharpen those things? Or do they just stay that way?"

"They stay sharp," she answered, a slight frown crossing her brow as she stared at Jones. "You're supposed to go up and down."

"Oh. Right." Jones shook her hand. "I'm Jonesy."

Lee noticed that Jones surreptitiously wiped his hand on his pant leg when he got it back. Lee gave him a castigating look. He responded with a defensive shrug and a mouthed, *What?*

Kat shook hands with Sam last, who peered at her distrustfully.

"Sam," he said. "You remember me and Jones?"

Kat nodded. "I remember."

Lee glanced around their environment. They were outside the gates of O'Brien. When he'd arrived at the checkpoint, the lead guard—the same one from last night—had taken one look at Kat and backed off, clearly terrified of her.

He'd pointed to the side and growled, "You're not taking that inside O'Brien."

Lee had glanced worriedly at Kat to judge her reaction to this.

She seemed to take it in stride, but those predatory eyes of hers remained fixed on the guard as he backed away from them. Then she let out a small, nasal huff and appeared to let it go.

Now, standing around the pickup right outside the gates, they were the center of much unfriendly attention. The guards held their rifles a little more ready, none of them daring to turn their back on Kat. Beyond the gates, people were gawking as they passed, and several had formed a tight knot from which Lee could hear derisive whispers.

He wondered if Kat could hear what they were saying—primals, and by extension, hybrids, had incredible senses.

Lee cleared his throat. "Kat, you ready to get out of here?"

Her face brightened, eyes looking eager. "Yes. Ready."

"Yeah," Lee remarked, frowning at the faces staring back at them. "Me too."

They piled into the truck. The center console folded up into a small seat, and that's where Lee put Kat, squashed between him and Marie. Lee noted that Marie seemed to be avoiding elbow-rubbing with Kat by keeping herself pressed against the passenger's side door.

They drove ten minutes north until Lee found a clearing big enough for an Osprey to set down in. He pulled the truck through the field and stationed it in the brush where he hoped to God it wouldn't be molested while they were gone. Then he placed a call on his satphone.

Chapter 6

Ron Paige walked to the lip of the Osprey's ramp as it lowered.

Lee and his team hustled through the field, rotor wash buffeting them as they lugged their packs and gear aboard. Kat and Lee took up the rear, hauling a large Pelican case between them.

Ron stepped off the ramp, making room for the others to scamper up into the Osprey's hold. He was giving Kat the stink-eye pretty hard.

Coming abreast of him, Kat paused and thrust her hand out.

Ron gave it the slimmest glance, then ignored it.

Lee tugged on the Pelican case to get Kat moving again, then hollered over the rotors, "Don't worry about it. He's an asshole to everyone."

They deposited the case with a few others. Lee's team had taken jump seats across from each other towards the front. Kat looked at the available seating like the new kid on the school bus. She chose a seat next to Jones, who was clearly displeased with the development.

Maybe it was just the fact that Lee had spent a half hour alone with her when he'd driven back to O'Brien, but his nervousness about her—and what she was—had lessened, and he found himself a bit irritated with his team.

During that drive to O'Brien, Lee had asked a lot of questions about what the last few months had been like for Kat and Bran, and she'd opened up. By the time he'd arrived at O'Brien, he'd almost forgotten what she was. Felt more like he was just talking to a normal person with a slight speech impediment.

Lee felt a nudge to his back, and turned to find Ron looming.

"The fuck is this?" Ron bellowed over the engines. "Why didn't you restrain her?"

Lee scowled at the man, then looked pointedly at Kat, who was currently puzzling out the harness on the jump seat. "Yeah. She's *real* fuckin' wild. What was I thinking?"

Ron leaned in closer, which really wasn't necessary, since Lee could smell the coffee on his breath already. "She's a fucking animal."

"You know she can probably hear you, right?"

Ron shook his head, not even deigning to glance at her. "I don't care." He thumped a forefinger in Lee's chest. "You better keep a fucking close eye on her—she does some crazy shit, it's on your head."

Lee raised a thumbs up and, since Ron was being a dick, repaid him in kind by pushing the thumbs-up nearly to Ron's nose. "Wilco, Major Paige."

Two and a half hours later they landed in Aspen, Colorado.

A great deal of taxying was done while Lee and his team, freshly awoken from fitful naps, were getting out of their harnesses and into their packs.

Kat seemed so out of place. She and the rest of the team wore civilian clothes, but the team had their armor, rifles, and helmets on, and were all clustered around their Pelican cases, while Kat stood awkwardly to the side, oh-so-clearly not a part of their group.

The Osprey came to a stop somewhere on the Aspen airfield, and the engines began to spool down. Ron still did not open the ramp. They waited until the engine noise in the hold got low enough, at which point Ron called out, "Leave the cases. There's a black Suburban outside. When I lower this ramp, you are all going to keep your heads down and get your asses into the back of that SUV *immediately*. Do not stop. Do not look around. Do not speak. I'll have some guys get your gear."

They nodded their understanding. Ron turned and lowered the ramp.

They scuttled out onto a shadowed airfield, the sun having already dipped below the nearby mountain peaks. As promised, a black Suburban waited, parked sidelong to the rear of the aircraft, close enough that the tail almost touched the roof rack.

They piled into the Suburban, sitting with their packs on their laps. The driver was some kid in fatigues that didn't look old enough for the captain's bars on his collar. Or maybe Lee was just getting old. Ron took the front passenger seat, as Lee and Kat were getting in. Lee was about to sit directly behind him, but then decided to let Kat have that honor. Lee was rewarded with an acidic glare once Ron noticed it.

As soon as the last door slammed, the Suburban took off at an aggressive pace.

They drove the entire length of the airfield, then hung a sharp right and skidded to a stop inside an empty hangar. The second they were inside, a couple soldiers began closing the hangar's massive doors.

"Don't get out yet," Ron said, twisting around to watch the doors as they closed. But Lee noticed that his eyes kept flicking over to Kat.

There was an audible *clunk* as the doors closed.

"Alright, come with me." Ron exited, and the team followed.

Conspicuous in the vast, empty space, was a single table. No chairs, Lee noted, but that was okay. He'd been sitting too long anyway, and his hip was aching. Ron took them over to the table and waited for everyone to assemble around it.

There was nothing on the table, but Ron now had a manila folder in his hand, which Lee supposed had been waiting in the Suburban. Standing at the center of the table, Ron flipped the folder open and withdrew five packets of papers, stapled at the corners. These he distributed to Lee and the others, excluding Kat.

"This is your mission briefing," Ron said, looking at a sixth packet which he kept to himself in the folder. "Objective is to locate three missing scientists and their research. If you find them alive, you will extract them. If you find them dead, you will attempt to recover proof of their deaths. In either case, it is paramount that you recover their research and bring it with you when you extract. By the time you get on the ground, you will have roughly ninety-six hours to complete these objectives and get to the extract point. At hour ninety-seven, if you have not completed the mission, a special detachment will move in and eliminate all hostiles in and around your AO. Because you are not technically military, and no one knows you exist, that will include you, if you haven't gotten out of there, so don't dilly-dally when your time's up."

Still reading the first page, Ron continued: "Enemy is unknown at this time. You will almost certainly take contact from primals." He gave Kat a pointed look. "Which is why...*she* is here."

"Kat," Lee said, helpfully. "That's her name."

Ron just grunted, then went on. "It is also possible that the settlement the researchers were embedded with will be hostile. They were somewhat neutral towards us for the last few months, but since the researchers went dark, they have refused all contact, so we're not really sure how they'll react to you. Proceed with caution. And, again, though you are to take no action against the military element we already have on the ground, they will be hostile towards you if you haven't unassed the AO by the appointed time.

"Terrain will be relatively flat, with a lot of forest and heavy brush until you get to the settlement. Weather should be clear and cold for the next two days, but expect some precipitation towards the tail end of your time window.

"You are, as you know, going in unsupported. The only call you should be making to me is for extract, which will have a one-hour window from the time of your request to it arriving at your extract point."

Having given the overview, Ron turned the page, and the others followed suit.

On the second page, Lee found a satellite image. Four points were denoted on the image—A, B, C, and D. A was clearly their insertion point, with a dotted line to point B, which was in the center of a highlighted area—their AO. Another dotted line swooped down away from point B to point C, which was their extract.

Which left the mysterious point D, maybe twenty miles northwest of their insertion point.

"In about one hour," Ron said. "You'll get on a C-130, which will hop you over to the recently-reclaimed Fort Campbell Army Airfield. From there, a Blackhawk will take you to an outpost in Kentucky for refuel, and then to your insertion point in Virginia—Alpha on your map. You will then move overland about fifteen miles east to Bravo, which is the settlement of Appomattox. Flip over to the next page."

Papers shuffled.

Lee glanced at Kat and found her staring blankly at the center of the table. She stood to his right, so he scooted over and inclined his packet so she could see it. She seemed to appreciate the gesture.

On the next page, Lee found another satellite image, this one a detailed rendering of the town of Appomattox, Virginia.

"You will note the line that bisects the town," Ron said. There was indeed a red line that appeared to follow some streets, carving off the northwestern third of the town. "You will also notice the three, large structures that have been highlighted on the northwestern side of that line. According to reports from the researchers before they went dark, those are three separate colonies of primals."

"Whoa-whoa-whoa," Jones said, pumping a hand in the air as though to apply brakes to the conversation. "*Three separate colonies?*"

"That's correct," Ron nodded at their astonished faces. "You can see why the IAG sent in researchers. Because, in addition to the fact that we've never seen colonies exist in such close proximity to each other, we've also never seen a settlement of humans surviving right across the fucking road from them. By all accounts, the area is crawling with primals, and yet the humans stay on their side of the town, and the primals stay on theirs."

"Do they have defenses?" Abe asked. "Barricades? High voltage wires?"

Ron shook his head. "Nothing."

Abe's brow furrowed. "That's not possible."

"That's why they sent researchers," Ron said with a shrug. "Trying to find out how in the fuck this settlement is coexisting with these primals. Back to those three colonies, you'll notice the biggest structure there in the middle. That is, predictably, also the biggest colony. The structure was some sort of metal fabrication plant. The next biggest colony is just north of that, and have made their home in an old Wal-Mart. Then, down below the fabrication plant, the smallest colony is in the former Appomattox Primary School." Ron eyed them over his papers. "Suffice it to say, you'll want to come in from the south, even with..." He squinted at Kat. "What'd you say her name was again?"

Lee opened his mouth, a bit peeved, but Kat cut him off.

"My name is Kat," she growled, her words just slightly piquant. "And I can talk for myself."

Ron did a good job of hiding his shock, but Lee saw the way the cords of his neck briefly stood out. "Alright then." A little off his game, Ron blinked at his papers a few times before flipping the page and continuing. "Moving on. On the next page you'll find the three researchers you're looking for and their biographical data. It's pretty self-explanatory."

Lee eyed the faces on the page and their accompanying information.

They looked like ID photos—heads and shoulders squared to the camera, with that certain blankness in the eyes that non-photogenic people get when someone says "look into the camera."

At the top was one Bruce Ballmer, who looked to be the oldest of the three—forty-six, according to his data. Long, narrow face. Large, bifocals over mud-brown eyes, with a rime of graying hair that looked like he'd woken up right before they snapped the photo. Five-foot-nine, a hundred and sixty pounds.

Next was a guy named Michael Schwartz, whose slim smile looked like he was supremely annoyed with the photographer. Almost-skeletal features. Dark eyes, and dark hair that looked like it was either slicked back, or pulled into a ponytail. Thirty-nine years old. Six-foot-one, a hundred and eighty pounds. Lanky fucker.

Last was a much younger-looking character by the name of Jeremy Tuttle, who seemed to be Michael Schwartz's opposite—his smile looked youthful and genuinely excited in a wide face with a blond beard and short-cropped hair. At only twenty-nine, he was the pup of the trio. Five-foot-ten, and also a hundred and eighty pounds.

"What exactly were they scientists in?" Marie asked, glancing up at Ron. "I don't see that specified anywhere."

"I wasn't given that information, and it's not germane to your mission. Flip to the last page."

Marie sucked irritably on her teeth, but did as instructed, along with everyone else.

The last page was a bit odd.

It featured two images that looked like they'd been copied and pasted from a product manual. One was a ruggedized laptop. The other was a ruggedized...box.

Sam held the paper up, as though to get a better focus on it. "What am I looking at here?"

"Computers and a hard drive," Ron answered. "There should be three laptops identical to the one pictured here, and one hard drive. Ideally, you will recover all four items. We'll take what we can get, but prioritize the hard drive. And before you ask, no, I don't know what's on it. All I know is what I was told by ICAO Griffin: Someone at the top of the IAG is prepared to mount a small invasion on the settlement to get those things back."

Lee made a dissatisfied noise in the back of his throat. "Yeah. This really sounds like some shit I don't wanna be anywhere near."

"I don't blame you for that," Ron admitted. "I wouldn't either, and neither does Griffin. Which is why you'll turn everything over to an intelligence analyst as soon as you get back. And then no one will ever talk about this shit again."

Abe shook his head. "All this secrecy stinks to high heaven, Ron."

"Such is life," was Ron's reply. "Questions?"

"Yeah," Sam said, flipping back a few pages. "You never mentioned what Point Delta was on the main satellite image."

Lee had been wondering the same thing.

Ron looked at each of them, his expression stern. "That is the location of the strike force that is currently on the ground, waiting for you to fail so they can blow the fuck out of Appomattox. Actually, check that, they're not waiting on you to do shit, because they don't even know you're going to be there. All they know is that they were told to stand down for a week. Their location is on the map so you know where *not* to go. You get anywhere near them, they *will* dust you, no questions asked."

Jones began wafting his papers in front of his face, wrinkling his nose. "You know what, Abe? I smell it now too."

Lee heard a snuffling noise from his side, and looked to find Kat scenting the air with a somewhat confused look. The others took notice as well.

"There's not actually a smell, Kat," Lee murmured.

She turned a frown on him. "What?"

"They were speaking figuratively."

She glowered. "I don't understand."

Lee gave Ron a pointed look. "It's kind of a joke, Kat. You see, sometimes when you get the sense that you're being lied to or manipulated, you say it stinks. But there's not really a smell. Just a feeling."

Ron ignored them, placing a blank sheet of paper and a pen on the table. "Write down your wishlist. If we have it, I'll get it on the C-130 for you." He straightened and placed his hands on his hips, his expression suddenly grave. "I haven't lied to you guys. I gave you every single bit of information that was given to me. But you guys are right. This shit stinks." He sighed. "Lee. Abe. I know we've butted heads..."

"And by 'butted heads,'" Abe interrupted. "You mean 'spent years trying to kill each other'?"

Ron's expression remained unchanged. "Among other things, yes. But as hard as this might be for y'all to believe, I don't want to see anything bad happen to you. Doesn't mean we're friends, or that I wanna have a drink with any of you. But..." He lowered his chin, his eyes becoming intense. "Seriously. Watch your backs out there. Don't fucking trust anyone but each other. Just get the shit done, and get out."

Chapter 7

At roughly 0400 the following morning, a single Blackhawk thundered low over the Virginia foothills.

Inside, Lee sat on the deck, leaning back on his ruck and looking out the window at nothing but darkness. He faced the front of the helicopter, and saw the crew chief, sitting in a jump seat right behind the cockpit. He seemed to be speaking with the pilots. Lee had one of the intercom headsets on, but didn't hear anything.

After a moment, the crew chief turned to Lee, made an adjustment on his own headset, and Lee heard the man's voice come over the intercom.

"Insertion point is clear. Five minutes."

Lee nodded, then doffed the headset.

Flying out of the outpost in Kentucky, an Apache gunship had gone ahead of them to circle their insertion point. Using their thermal imaging systems, they'd scoped the ground and made sure Lee and his team weren't being dumped in the middle of a pack of primals.

Lee motioned to the others to get ready, then popped his helmet on.

Due to the people of Appomattox not being too keen on military forces at the moment, Lee's team had remained in civilian clothes, though they had changed into pants and tops in more earthen tones.

Seated beside him, Kat wore the same clothes they'd picked her up in, though Marie had given her a tan, softshell jacket to hide the white-and-red-plaid shirt she wore. They'd also equipped her with a ruck, containing mostly food and water.

Lee had wrestled with whether to offer a firearm to an untrained individual, but it turned out to be a non-issue. She didn't *want* a firearm. Said she preferred to work with her claws and teeth.

Jones had tittered nervously at this.

However, she'd flat-out refused to wear the armor or a radio. She said the armor was too constricting—though she'd never even tried it on—and that the radio earpiece blocked her natural hearing—which she *had* tried on, only to recoil when it touched her ear canal like someone had given her a wet willy.

This being something of a trial run of how well they could work as a team, Lee decided to let it go, though he still had some reservations about having a teammate unarmored and off-comms. He did, however, order her to keep the items in her ruck, just in case.

This was going to be…interesting.

Everyone roused themselves and got into position. They'd managed to get something like sleep while on the C-130, but they were all still a bit groggy from the day.

The crew chief slid the Blackhawk's doors open. A blast of cold air knocked any residual sleepiness out of Lee. His eye watered and he blinked rapidly to clear it as he scooted himself into position.

He felt the helicopter decelerate and drop altitude.

Lee lowered the single-tube NOD over his eye. The blackness of the world beyond turned into crisp, monochromatic white phosphor, overlaid with thermal. This was the first time Lee had used these "enhanced" night vision devices. He'd put them on his wishlist, and Ron had accommodated.

Lee was impressed. This was some tricky shit. He couldn't help a small smile.

You get so used to doing high-speed shit that it becomes rote and boring. But every once in a while, you get to experience something that reminds you why you thought it'd be cool to get involved with all this nonsense in the first place.

For just that one moment, as the Blackhawk came to a hover and began to descend, Lee felt like that nineteen-year-old grunt again, experiencing his first insertion by helicopter.

It dissipated rapidly as his mind turned to matters of the present.

The Blackhawk touched down, and the team spilled out both sides, rifles up and scanning. The sound of the rotors became punchier, and the downdraft pressed harder as the Blackhawk dusted off. The hurricane wind lessened as the helicopter gained altitude, then swooped off and away.

As the noise faded, Lee called out to check in with everyone. They were good—no one had busted an ankle hopping off the helicopter.

"Bro, these NODs are *hot*," Jones observed with a boyish sort of glee. "I feel like the Predator."

Lee turned to look at Kat, her facial features even stranger through the enhanced night vision. "You got anything?"

She stretched her neck out, peering around them and sniffing. She did not have NODs. She didn't need them. After a moment, she shook her head. "We're alone."

They were in a large field of low-lying brush. Lee panned his gaze around, spotting a nearby section of woods. "Everyone on me." He stood up and motioned for Kat to take the lead. "Take us into those woods right there."

The team jogged out of the open, moving single file. Once in the woods, Lee stopped them with a gesture and pulled out his DAGR. Ron had actually offered him a fancy, upgraded navigation system, with a color screen and all, but Lee had neither the time nor the inclination to learn a new device. He was comfortable with the older Defense Advanced GPS Receiver, and it would do just fine for their fifteen-mile ruck.

He oriented himself to a preset waypoint, about two miles south of Appomattox.

Kat had not alerted them to anyone in the area, so Lee gave his instructions in a low voice rather than hand-signals. "Single-file. Kat's on point. I'll stay with her. Abe you're behind me. Sam, you're right. Jones, you're left. Marie, pull rear security."

They took their positions. Lee, Abe, and Marie were armed with their usual suppressed carbines as a primary weapon, while Sam and Jones had been given some heavier hitting equipment. They'd grumbled about the weight, but accepted that, as the young hard-chargers of the group, their backs and knees were regularly sacrificed on the altar of superior firepower.

Jones was kitted out with a Milkor M32 grenade launcher, while Sam took charge of the M249 Para light machine gun. They'd Rochambeau'd over it, the prize being the M249 Para, since it was two pounds lighter.

With Kat's superior senses in the lead, they headed out into the predawn gloom.

So far, Kat was a little disappointed.

Life at the monastery had been pleasant, but boring. When she and Bran first arrived, it had been much more exciting. But after all the initial fighting that got Kat's blood pumping so beautifully, things had settled into a slog, each day identical to the last.

Bran had seemed to really love that. And Kat had even enjoyed it herself...for a few weeks. Then she'd started to get itchy. She wasn't sure what that feeling was called, but it was like something in the center of her chest felt constricted. Confined. Fidgety and dissatisfied.

That feeling had worsened over the subsequent months. She'd wrestled with herself about it. This is what it meant to control her primal instincts, right? This was supposed to be a good thing. So why didn't she feel good? Why did she find herself constantly thinking back to all those times she and Bran had killed whole settlements of people? And why did she remember those incidents with a sense of longing?

Did that mean she was bad?

She had a hard time reconciling herself to the idea of morality. She'd never really shared in Bran's guilt for the people they'd killed. Those times when Bran would say the words "Dark Mode" to her? They'd been the bright spots in an otherwise miserable life of trying to pretend to be something she was not.

Oh, but when he said Dark Mode, she was free. Free to stop thinking. Free to stop hiding. Free to let loose all that pent-up aggression she held inside of her.

No, morality didn't make a lot of sense to her. But then again, when she'd been able to unleash that violence on other primals to protect the monastery, well...that'd felt *really* good. Better than just slaughtering random people. And she thought there was something to that—being able to fight for a good reason.

But there'd been no good reasons to fight for months on end.

So, when Jax—who apparently also went by Lee, which was kind of confusing—had shown up out of the blue and offered her a chance to fight for a good reason, she'd been overcome with joy and excitement for the opportunity.

She hadn't realized there'd be so much sitting around, and waiting, and driving, and being in planes and helicopters—which was initially interesting, because she'd never flown before, but quickly lost its verve. Then she'd had to stand around and listen to the man named Ron talk, and talk, and talk, and she had to pretend to be interested in the papers when Jax/Lee had shown them to her, but really, it all seemed like a bunch of nonsense.

While her language skills had improved greatly, Kat still found herself getting overwhelmed when too much information came at her at once. But she'd understood the gist of what they were doing here.

They were going to try and rescue three guys. That was also a little disappointing. It didn't sound like she was going to do much fighting. Sounded like she was just going to sneak around in the woods.

Plus she had to carry this damned rucksack. The weight didn't bother her. But it was awkward, and she couldn't move as fluidly as she was used to.

Frankly, this was all starting to look like a whole lot of bullshit.

And then she smelled something.

She did what Lee had told her to do—she stopped and raised a fist, then went down to one knee, scenting the air. She pivoted a bit, facing into the wind, and sensed Lee moving up close behind her.

"Whatcha got?" he whispered.

What *did* she have?

Kat did not know the word "synesthesia," but that is what occurred in her brain when scenting. She couldn't really describe it, but she perceived smells as visual tendrils, almost like threads of luminescent fog. The world was alive with these smells—leaf mold, animals, fungi, various forms of scat. Gunmetal. Lubricants. Sweat. Body odors.

Once she perceived a scent, it was as easy to recognize as a face. So she knew the scents of Lee and his team—those had become distinct and familiar in her mind, since she'd been cooped up in various vehicles with them for the last day.

But there were two new scents wafting to her on the breeze—misty little trails, one coming to her as a light blue, the other as kind of gray.

"Primals?" Lee prompted.

"No," Kat said, very confident. She knew the scent of primals, which was distinct from both human-scent, and her own hybrid scent. These new scents were people.

She explained as much to Lee.

"How many?" he asked. "And can you tell where they are?"

Initially, she'd only perceived two threads of scent, but as she continued snuffling at the air, trying to determine their direction and distance—which was not easy to do under any circumstances—she began to realize there were more.

The gray thread was actually two different scents—one kind of whitish, and the other kind of golden. Then there was a fourth, greenish scent. All of them individual people.

"Four," she decided after a moment. She pointed into the wind, which wasn't really much of a wind, but just a current of slow-moving air. "That way."

Lee clicked something on his gear and spoke in a whisper: "Kat's scenting four people, north, northwest of our location." Then, to her, he asked, "Can you tell how far?"

That was really hard to do. She could tell that the strangers weren't right on top of them, or their scents would've been stronger. But really, they could be anywhere from a hundred paces away, to nearly a mile.

"Not *very* close," she said. "Maybe—"

zzzZZIP!

"Shit!" Lee belted out, grabbing Kat and slamming her to the ground.

Her immediate instinct was to explode to her feet again, but then she recognized what that noise had been, as it was immediately followed by a lot more of the same.

Bullets, Kat realized, even as Lee shouted, "Contact! Left!"

The air was suddenly filled with the whine of hurtling projectiles and the chatter of the team's suppressed weapons spitting back, chopping through branches and brush, spraying with no clear sense of a target.

Kat's perception of the scents was obliterated as the smell of gunsmoke blotted out everything else. But as that sense deflated, overwhelmed, another sense barged to the forefront of her mind: She could hear their attackers calling to each other. She couldn't understand what they were saying, but that didn't matter.

Her brain triangulated those noises, and she knew instantly where they were, and how far.

She grabbed Lee's shoulder as he was in the midst of a reload, then pointed right where she'd heard the voices. "There! Two hundred paces!"

"Got it," Lee snapped, finishing his reload and shouting to the others, "Marking the targets!"

There was a lull in their return fire as the others in the team looked to where Lee was shooting. Kat had no idea how they could see where he was aiming in the dark, but they seemed to figure it out, and then all of them were concentrating their fire on that spot.

The incoming bullets didn't let up. Kat felt her rucksack jerk on her shoulders as it was peppered by passing rounds.

Someone yelped, "Fuck! Hit!"

It sounded like the woman, Marie.

Kat had to do something. She could feel the conscious thought ebbing away from her, while something else rose up. Her blood roared in her head, her natural night vision flaring crisper and brighter than before, and she was hot all over, all through her muscles.

She began shucking the rucksack from her shoulders. "Jax—Lee! Keep firing for one minute! Then stop!"

"What?" Lee shouted back, clearly incredulous.

But Kat knew he had to have heard her—she'd barked it practically right in his ear.

The second she had the rucksack off her back, she rolled, then sprang to her feet and took off on all fours. Her human side became a distant voice, and she was unleashed to be what she truly was: An apex predator.

"Kat! What're you—aw, fuck!" Lee gave up as her thermal signature disappeared into the brush. There was no calling her back now.

Information filled his head, filtering instantly through his years of combat experience. Four hostiles, and by the amount of rounds he was hearing splash the brush around him, they all had automatic weapons and were letting them eat. Marie was hit—how bad, he didn't know, and no one had time to check.

They needed cover.

First instinct—break contact.

Except Kat had just run out there. It wasn't exactly a conscious thought process, but breaking contact immediately became a non-starter.

Which left assaulting through the ambush.

He'd splashed the area that Kat had indicated with his infrared aiming laser, so the others could mark his aim through their NODs, but immediately switched it off, not wanting to give his location away if the enemy also had night vision capabilities.

All of this careening through his brain in a single second.

He fired off five rounds, shucked off his pack, fired five more, then hit his PTT. "Sam—keep that base of fire! Jones, hit 'em with HE! Moving forward!"

Off to Lee's left he heard Abe shout, "Moving!" and Sam responded, "Move-move-move!"

Lee scrambled to his feet, his stiff hip forgotten in the surge of adrenaline. He sprinted for the nearest, thickest tree he could find and dove for cover behind it. Bullets chased him and smacked the trunk.

No way they could've tracked him like that unless they had some sort of night vision.

Another realization: he hadn't heard a single damn report, which meant they had suppressors.

Who the fuck were these guys? Lee had *just* checked their heading, and they were nowhere even close to the strike force, so it couldn't be them.

He rolled up onto a knee and began firing into the darkness at a steady pace.

WHUMP! WHUMP! WHUMP!

The sound of Jones's grenade launcher going off, followed about two seconds later by the crash of high explosive rounds. A section of the woods a couple hundred yards ahead flared brilliantly in Lee's NOD.

"Moving!" Sam screamed.

"Move!" Lee and Abe shouted back in unison.

Lee took a bare glimpse over his left shoulder to check Abe's location, and spotted him on his side behind a fallen tree, about ten yards over.

WHUMP! WHUMP! WHUMP!

Jones sent his last three HE rounds, and Lee clocked him moving laterally towards where Marie was prone on the ground, alternately firing and crawling for the cover of tree. Jones snagged her drag strap as he reached her and began hauling her for cover.

As the last three 40mm rounds detonated, Sam shot to his feet and sprinted forward of Abe and Lee. He slid into cover behind a trunk and immediately blasted out controlled bursts of suppressive fire.

How long since Kat had told him *one minute*?

Maybe thirty seconds.

Lee leaned out from the tree and aimed as best he could without his infrared laser, targeting the dissipating heat signature from the last three explosions. He fired until he went empty, slapped in a reload from his chest rig, and called his movement.

Sam laid hate, and Lee and Abe sprinted forward again.

They gained another twenty yards, and as Lee went prone behind an upturned root system, he spotted them.

Four heat signatures, glimmering through the trees.

He rolled back into cover and keyed up. "Visual. Eleven o'clock. Hundred and fifty yards."

Ten seconds.

He popped up, thumbing his infrared laser on. The beam speared out, jiggling over one of the heat signatures, and Lee immediately sent three rounds. He turned off his laser as he dropped back into cover. Rolled to the opposite end of the root system. Came out the side of it. Thumbed the laser and fired again.

Then he rammed himself back into cover as a multitude of projectiles chewed up the root system, spraying him with bark and dirt. "Cease fire! Cease fire!"

His team wouldn't know why he'd called a cease fire in the middle of assaulting through an ambush, but their response to the command was reflexive. Abruptly, their weapons went silent, and Lee could hear the muted chatter of the enemy guns.

Seizing some control over his breathing, Lee panned his NOD rapidly over his team.

Sam and Abe were in cover. They seemed to be looking at him as though somewhat confused. Further back, Jones and Marie were both huddled behind a tree, and it looked like Jones was working on her. He could see the way Marie's leg was kicking. She was hurting. Fuck, he hoped it wasn't bad.

"What're we doin' here, Lee?" Abe demanded over the comms.

"Just hold fire! Kat's out there! Jones, talk to me!"

Bullets zipped and whined and clacked through the branches. One of them smacked *very* close to Lee's left foot, and he squinched in tighter, dirt and wood fragments dribbling down his collar.

Jones came back: "She took a skimmer to the face—took her ear off, but I think she'll be okay!"

Right on the tail of Jones's transmission, Sam reported in: "I took one." His voice was tight, and a bit frazzled. "My leg. Uh…"

Lee shot his gaze to Sam's position, and saw him squirming around behind his tree.

"Not squirting," he said. "I think I'm good."

He saw Sam getting his tourniquet out and looping it around his leg.

And then, like falling into the eye of a storm, all the incoming fire suddenly ceased.

That lasted for a single beat of Lee's heart, and was immediately followed by the sound of men screaming.

CHAPTER 8

THEY DIDN'T EVEN SEE her coming.

She'd sprinted hard, fast, and low, moving on all fours. She'd moved wide around the firefight and come in on their blindside. She'd held back, as rounds from Lee and the others were still incoming. She stood behind a tree, breathing steadily through flared nostrils.

She smelled blood. It called to her. Spurred her on. But she held back, knowing she had to wait just a little longer.

There were three of them still firing from behind cover. One was on the ground, flopping around. He was the one giving off that blood-scent, rich and strong, making Kat's jaws clench and unclench.

They were spread out, the closest one about fifty paces from Kat.

Then Lee and his team stopped shooting.

The three men across from Kat continued on for a handful of seconds. Then one of them barked something to the others, and they stopped shooting as well. In the silence, they all heard the rush of something coming at them through the trees, but by then, Kat had closed the gap.

She slammed into the first one, tackling him high, claws finding the tender flesh of his neck as they slammed to the ground and rolled. He was on top of her for an instant, and then she was on top of him, wrenching his trachea out in a spray of blood. She exploded off of him as the others began to shout and scream.

The already-wounded one tried to scramble for his rifle. Kat stomped her foot into his right arm. His wrist bones popped like muted gunshots and he gasped. Then she kicked him in the face so hard his neck snapped and what would have been his scream of pain melted into a death rattle.

One of them sighted for her, and she heard bullets cracking through the air and pocking against trees. She sprinted diagonally to him, his rounds chasing her, nipping at her heels, and it was pure joy. Then she leapt, bounded off a tree, and landed on the man, pummeling the rifle out of his hands. It caught on a sling as they went to the ground, and she seized the strap of it and pulled it across his neck, choking him.

She slammed her fingers into his gut, but her claws hit hard armor plating.

They were wearing armor?

The man was croaking, reaching for a sidearm on his hip. She rammed her head into his, jaws open wide, teeth clamping down on his face. She ripped back and forth, savaging him. He thrashed against her, his blood spurting into her mouth as he cried his hot breath down her throat. He got his pistol unholstered, but Kat simply kicked a foot out and sent it flying from his grip. Then she snaked her hand under his armor, sank her claws into his belly, and ripped.

More bullets whizzing by her. Something snapped across her hunched back, hot and stinging. Still attached to the man she was tearing apart, she rolled so his body covered hers. Felt the incoming rounds smack against his back plate. Then one went through his throat and punched a hole in Kat's left breast.

The pain did nothing but infuriate her more.

The last man shooting realized he was putting holes in his comrade and stopped firing for an instant, screaming words that meant nothing to Kat. She immediately detached herself from the dead prey in her jaws and sprang for a nearby tree.

She could see the last man aggressing on her as she got behind the thick trunk. She leapt, claws finding purchase in the rough bark. Clambering up the trunk, she kept it between her and the man as he came around the base of the tree, his rifle pointing as though he expected to find her on the ground.

She dropped on him and promptly bit his throat out.

He was still alive, struggling against her, trying to bring his weapon to bear, but she mounted his chest, her muscular thighs clamping down hard on his arms, pinning him. Then she slashed his face to tatters as his writhing weakened. Then he gurgled, and was still.

Panting now, blood and drool dribbling down her chin, she cast her wild eyes about for more prey. The first one she'd hit—the one she'd torn the throat out of—was still squirming around, legs kicking.

She growled, stalking towards him on all fours. It seemed she'd ripped his trachea out so cleanly, she hadn't severed the arteries in his neck, and he was somehow still getting air through the end of that throat tube.

His eyes hit hers as she reached him. No, not eyes. He was wearing goggles like the ones Lee and his team were wearing. Something about that tickled her interest, but she was still in the throes of bloodlust, and didn't think too much about it.

She squatted on her haunches beside him while he rasped and coughed, still struggling to breathe. She thought about savaging him just for the entertainment value of it, but was starting to come down from the rush, like a cat might get bored with a mouse that is no longer trying to get away.

Still. He needed to die.

She reached out, taking the ribbed tube of his trachea in her fist. She waited for him to exhale, then squeezed it shut. He began jerking, but was already half gone. With her other hand, she wrenched the goggles away from his eyes, bending the mount that attached it to his helmet.

He stared up at her, eyes terrified of what he saw, lips moving with soundless words.

She actually didn't care for how he was looking at her. She covered his eyes with her hand.

"Ssh," she hissed, softly. "This is death."

Jones knelt in front of Marie, holding the bandage to her shredded ear as he stared out into the night and listened to the sounds of absolute carnage.

If he were being honest, it was creeping him way the fuck out.

He couldn't see much but flashes of thermal signatures. One was much hotter than the others, and moving much faster. One by one, the other thermal signatures were taken down. Then there were no more screams.

"It's okay," Jones said, not liking how high his voice came out. "You're okay."

He felt Marie's hand touch his and he looked down at her—two sets of NODs staring at each other. "You saying that to me or yourself?" Marie ground out, taking the bandage from him.

"Me? What? No. I'm fine," he protested. "I was talking to you. You're gonna be okay."

Lee's voice broke the eerie quiet. "Kat! You alright over there?"

For a moment, there was no response.

Then, like a kid that's unsure if they're in trouble or not: "Yes?"

Another pause.

"Talk to me, Kat," Lee barked. "How many hostiles left?"

"No hostiles left," her voice growled back.

"Jesus," Jones whispered. "Did you hear that shit?"

"Yeah," Marie said, straining to sit up more. "I heard it."

Lee's voice came over the comms now: "How we looking, Sam?"

Jones leaned out a little further from around the tree. He could see Sam up ahead maybe twenty yards, sitting against a tree, much like Marie was. Abe squatted next to him, fiddling with Sam's leg.

"I'm good," Sam said, sounding calmer now than he'd been right after getting shot. "Just meat. Through and through on my left calf."

"Roger that. Stay put. Marie, what about you?"

Marie seethed a disconsolate noise through her teeth, then keyed up. "Just a missing fucking ear. Think it clipped my jaw muscle—talking hurts."

"Can you move up and hang out with Sam for a minute?"

Marie got to her feet. "Yeah, gimme a sec." When she released her PTT, she looked at Jones. "See if you can tape that bandage down or something. I need both hands."

"Right." Jones rummaged through her open IFAK and came up with the medical tape. The wound was in an awkward spot, right next to her hair, so he had to apply an exorbitant amount to get the bandage to stay.

That done, they both hustled over to where Sam and Abe were.

"Marie, stay with Sam," Lee transmitted. "Abe and Jones, on me."

They moved up to Lee's position. He was kneeling now, looking over the top of the root system he'd been covering behind.

"Kat," he called out. "We're coming to you."

After a moment, she acknowledged with a curt, "Okay."

Jones could see the hybrid, standing now, a bright, hot signature in the midst of four others on the ground that were already cooling. As they approached, Jones found himself morbidly curious. He kinda wanted to see the damage she'd done. And he also kinda *didn't*.

Drawing closer, Kat's features came into focus. She was just standing there, watching them, and her eyes were weirding Jones out. In the white phosphor light amplification, they looked like the eyeshine you get when you spotlight an animal.

Jones stopped well clear of her and worked his NODs over the bodies strewn across the ground. The night vision sanitized the scene somewhat, but one of the men had clearly been disemboweled.

That wasn't what caught Jones's attention though.

"Yo. These dudes were military," he said, observing obvious tactical fatigues, armor, helmets, and night vision of their own.

"Yeah," Lee murmured, kneeling over the closest one. Then he paused and looked at Kat for a beat. "Good job, by the way." He held out a fist.

Kat seemed to grasp the concept of a fist bump better than she'd understood the handshake. Hesitantly, she touched her knuckles to his.

Lee jerked his head out to the woods. "Can you sense anyone else nearby, or was this it?"

Kat turned in a slow circle, alternately peering and scenting. "No one else."

"Alright," Lee said, flipping his NOD up. "Use white light and search these bodies. Kat, pull security."

"Pull security?" she echoed, confused.

"It means keep an eye out for bad guys," Jones provided as he pushed his NODs up and saw nothing but darkness. He felt a brief touch of panic that he couldn't see Kat, and imagined her lunging for him. He hurriedly swiped up his pocket light and clicked it on.

"Oh, Jesus." He jerked back a bit as Kat was illuminated. She hadn't gotten any closer to him, but—holy fuckoly—she was covered in blood. It was all over her face, dripping down her neck, slaking her chest, and coating her hands.

She looked like a lioness that's just had her face in a zebra. This was some straight up National Geographic shit.

Then he realized that not all of the blood was from the men she'd shredded. She was wearing a coyote brown, soft-shell jacket that Marie had given her. There was a hole in the left breast, dark with blood that was still flowing, beading down the moisture-resistant fabric.

Jones's instinct to help a wounded teammate kicked in, and he stepped quickly forward.

She swung her eyes on him, and he froze.

Cautiously, he pointed at her chest. "You're shot."

She looked down at the wound. Then back at him. "I know."

Jones felt his eyebrows rise. "Well. Do you wanna do anything about that?"

She shook her head. "I'll be fine."

"Are you sure? It didn't go into your chest cavity? Sometimes you can't tell how bad you're hurt when your blood's up, you know?"

"It's just my boob."

Jones couldn't help a sudden snort of laughter. He took a step back from her. "Roger that. Well. If you need help with it. You know. Holler."

Christ, did that make it sound like he was trying to get his hands on some hybrid titties?

This was all super fucking weird.

He turned and approached one of the dead men. It happened to be the disemboweled one. Viscera was leaking out from under his armor. His fatigues were OCP. The rifle strapped to him was some sort of M4 variant, with a suppressor, and an NGAL—the same type of IR aiming laser they had on their rifles.

"Shit." Jones knelt over the body. "Did we just kill our own fucking guys?"

"They're not *our* fucking guys," Abe replied. "And I have no fucking clue what's going on here."

Jones squinted at the corpse, playing the beam of his light over all the little details of it. Half the guy's face was gone beneath a set of NODs. But it was neither that, nor the disemboweling that'd killed him. It looked like he'd caught a round through the neck, which had severed his spine. Something in Cyrillic letters was tattooed on the side of his neck, speckled with gore. Other than that, the guy had no way to identify him. No nametape. No rank or unit insignia. No flag.

Jones frowned as he stuck his hand down the guy's collar, feeling for the beaded chain of his dog tags, but there were none. He checked every pocket in the guy's uniform and found jack shit.

He stood up and looked towards Abe and Lee. "You guys find any identifiers? Patches? Dog tags? Anything?"

"Negative," Lee grunted.

Abe finished roughly searching one of the bodies. "Fuckin' nothin'."

"We need to roll out of here," Lee said, turning off his white light. "I don't know if they called for backup, but I don't wanna stand around and find out."

Jones was very intentional in how he waited for Kat to follow Lee and Abe back towards the others, before falling in behind. Was he being paranoid about this? Yeah, maybe. But he had good damn reasons for that paranoia.

He'd been fighting primals for fucking years now. He'd run from them, killed them, infiltrated their nests, seen the women they'd taken and raped, seen the bodies they stored up as food for later. He'd witnessed them savage people to death—much like Kat had just done to those boys back there—and seen whole settlements overrun by them. Hell, he'd been there when they'd overrun Fort Bragg.

She might only be a quarter primal, but she could still move and kill like them.

Trust her? Ehhh—no. Because one look in her eyes as she'd stood there with other people's blood all over her face, and Jones had seen the truth: the quarter primal in her had taken control.

Lee faded back to Kat's side, noticing how Jones was keeping his distance from her. He couldn't really blame the guy. They'd all seen that look in her eyes. The girl he'd talked to on their drive over to O'Brien was gone, and in her place was something entirely different, though still very familiar to Lee.

The feral aggression of a primal.

He lifted his NOD again and used his handheld light to splash her, muting the beam by curling his fingers around the lens so just a shaft of it played over her.

The wildness in her eyes was still there, but seemed to be fading.

He felt a tiny chill skitter up his spine.

"Lemme see that wound," Lee said as they kept moving.

She didn't object, because it hadn't been a question. She unzipped her jacket, unbuttoned the plaid shirt she wore beneath it, and, without an ounce of shame, exposed her breast.

Lee eyeballed it clinically, craning his neck to see both the entrance and exit. The bullet had gone in just above her nipple, and exited close to her armpit, but looked like it had only carved through breast fat, and hadn't clipped the pectoral muscle beneath. Still, he could imagine it hurt like a motherfucker. And yet Kat didn't seem to even notice.

He also noted that the wound had already begun to clot, the blood coming out at a slow ooze now. Primals and hybrids had extremely tough constitutions. The wound probably wouldn't even get infected.

Wouldn't hurt to slap a bandage on it, though.

"Alright," Lee said. "Have Marie put a bandage on it. You get hit anywhere else?"

Kat closed her shirt, but didn't bother buttoning or zipping up. "Across my back."

Lee leaned as they walked, spotting a line of shredded fabric across the back of the jacket. "Not much blood, but it won't hurt to patch that up, too."

"I'll be fine," she asserted.

"Yeah, but you're still gonna patch it up," Lee said, making it clear he wasn't asking. With her welfare addressed, he moved on to the real issue. "You did good, Kat. But in the future, you can't just go running off like that. You're a part of a team, and you need to make sure you're coordinating with them. No one else knew what you were doing but me. If I'd been taken out, no one would have known you were out there and you woulda been fucked. Communication is key. You understand?"

Kat made a huffy noise, but nodded. "Understand."

"Also, I know you said you didn't want to wear armor or a radio, but you're putting them on."

"Earpiece makes it hard to hear."

"You'll manage."

They reached Sam and Marie, who were both on their feet now, facing opposite directions as they scanned for threats.

Lee went to Marie first, because she was closest. He put a hand on her shoulder and made "eye contact"—such as it was with their NODs on. "You good?"

What he could see of her facial expression looked more irritated than wounded. "Yeah, I'm good," she said. "Bit pissed that they fucked up my pretty face, but that's all."

Lee offered a smile at that.

Neither Marie nor Sam had had military experience prior to getting mixed up with Lee, but the days of having to prompt them for an ACE report after an engagement were long gone. Marie immediately gave him the rundown on Ammo, Casualties, and Equipment—the casualty part being that her ear had been shot off.

"One and a half mags left," Marie told him. "All equipment's up."

"Good deal," Lee said, patting her shoulder. They all had extra mags in their rucks. They could refresh their empty pouches when they got back to where they'd all dumped their packs.

He moved to Sam, doing much the same with him—make physical contact with your troop, and look them in the face. Sam's eyes were invisible, but his mouth was pressed into a grim line.

"How you doing?" Lee queried, glancing down at Sam's leg. He'd initially applied the tourniquet to his thigh, as they typically trained to put it on as high on the injured limb as possible. But after determining it wasn't an arterial bleed, Sam had chosen to move the tourniquet down just below his knee. Lee approved of the decision, because they needed to be mobile, and it's real fucking hard to hump a ruck with a tourniquet cranked down around your thigh.

Sam had rolled up his pant leg rather than cut through it with his medical shears. He'd stuffed the holes in his calf with combat gauze and wrapped them up with an Israeli bandage.

"I'm fine," Sam grunted, sounding a bit sullen. "I'll be stiff, but I'll keep up. Two mags left. Equipment's up."

"Roger 'at," Lee said, then turned to the group. "Kat, I want you on rear guard now. Everyone, police up your mags if you can find 'em but don't waste time. We're getting back to our rucks and moving way off this line."

No one argued with that.

They were able to retrieve a few mags as they went, but most were lost in the leaves and deadfall of the forest. They found their rucks, took a quick moment to refresh their mag pouches and make sure their rifles were topped off, then they slung into their packs and hoofed it straight south.

After about a mile, Lee called a halt and the team circled up, taking knees.

"Alright, here's the situation," Lee said in a low voice. "We got off fucking easy. Every one of those four dudes were kitted out like pros, and they all had NGALs on their rifles. The only reason they didn't tag all of us right at the outset is that they never used their NGALs."

The team understood—if the hostiles had activated their IR aiming lasers, they would've given away their position. The infrared laser was invisible to the naked eye, but anyone with NODs would see the beam and be able to spot its source.

"Which means," Abe put in. "They knew *we* had NODs."

"They might've just seen that we had them equipped," Lee said. "Just because they didn't use their NGALs doesn't mean this was a pre-planned ambush."

Jones blew a dissatisfied raspberry noise. "But they knew right where we'd be."

"And the only other person who knew our route," Sam observed. "Was fucking Ron."

Lee grimaced. "I'm not saying y'all are wrong. I just don't wanna get carried away with supposition. And when it comes to Ron, as much as he nitpicks us, I believed him when he said he didn't want anything bad to happen to us. Anything's possible, but I don't think Ron would sell us out like that."

"Sure seems like someone did," Marie said, bitterly.

"Maybe," Lee allowed. "Regardless, I think it'd be smart to change our infiltration strategy."

Marie's mouth opened in shock. "Whoa—hang on. You wanna move forward with this shit?"

Lee nodded. "Yeah, I do. If we call in for an extract, one of two things is gonna happen—we get extracted, and then Griffin blacklists us. Or, if someone in the IAG *did* dime us out, then they'll know about our extract and either hit us at the extract point, or just blow the fucking Blackhawk out of the sky with us in it. We're already here, and if someone really is gunning for us, then I wanna figure out who it is. But the original plan is obviously a no-go."

"Lee's right," Abe asserted. "If we got an enemy somewhere in the IAG, I wanna know who they are, and what's motivating them. Best chance at getting that info is finding out what shady shit's going down around here."

"Yeah, you know what?" Jones hissed. "I'm feelin' kinda hot about this shit. They zipped up Ma's face, and shot my boy, Sam. If someone fucked us, I feel like we need to fuck them back, just on principle."

Lee fished out the DAGR and checked their location, then stood up, the others following. "We're gonna keep cutting south for a bit, then go wide around Appomattox and come in from the east side. Set up an overwatch and see what there is to see by daylight. Y'all know we have limited time, so let's hump it. We can rest while we recon. Kat, you're on point. Same positions. Sam—don't kill yourself. If you need to slow up, just tell me."

Sam scoffed and spoke in an affected drawl. "Pff. I ain't no bee-itch. Let's go."

Chapter 9

Dawn came, cold and clear.

The sun was just peeking over the trees in a brilliant pink ball when they reached a road. According to the DAGR, they were about four miles south of Appomattox. The road was one of the main highways that ran south out of the settlement.

Kat stopped, several yards shy of the roadway. They were heading east, right into the rising sun. The road didn't look like it had been traveled in years. Sapling pines crowded the shoulders, fallen pine needles and leaves having long moldered into a dark loam that covered most of the blacktop, with no evidence of tire marks.

Either the people of Appomattox did not have vehicles, or they did not use this road. Considering how isolated the settlement had been up until being located by the IAG's expansion, he figured it was likely they didn't have access to fuel.

Lee moved up to squat at Kat's shoulder. "You got anything?"

She was scenting like something had caught her attention. She took a few more sniffs, then did an odd thing that Lee had only seen dogs do: She appeared to hold the scent in her mouth and pulse her jaw a bit to circulate it through her nose. Almost like a sommelier with a fine glass of wine.

"Ash," she stated. "Char. Stale—like it was rained on. And..." She appeared to think for a moment. "Burned flesh. But it's old."

"How old?"

She gave a minimal shrug. "Few days? Maybe more?"

"Maybe even a week or so?"

"Maybe."

Lee puzzled over that. Burned flesh could be many things. But if it was an animal that had been burned, then why? Why not eat it? It could be primals that'd been burned—that was a common technique to dispose of their bodies after you'd had a run-in with them. But Appomattox was supposed to be coexisting with the primals.

Which left burned humans.

Who had been burned, and why?

Lee had his suspicions. "Can you take me to this burn site?"

Kat nodded confidently. "Need to cross the road."

Lee keyed his comms, noticing how Kat twitched and grimaced just slightly as the channel popped in her newly-fitted earpiece. She'd grumbled about it, but accepted Lee's command. That was a good sign. At least she was compliant when her blood wasn't up.

"Kat's catching the scent of possible burned human remains," Lee transmitted. "She's gonna track to it so we can investigate, but we gotta cross this road."

The rest of the team packed in tight to where Lee and Kat were already positioned. Sam and Jones took the wings, addressing their weapons up and down the road. Kat scuttled across the road on all fours, keeping her body low to the ground. It was a disturbing thing to witness, but also had a creepy sort of grace to it.

On the other side, she scented, looked all around, and listened. Then looked back across to Lee and nodded.

Lee and Abe went next, mirroring Sam and Jones on the opposite side of the road. Then Marie, and lastly Sam and Jones. Standard road-crossing. All was quiet.

They took their positions in their usual column and followed Kat as she moved through the woods. Her progress zig-zagged a bit as she followed her nose, but the track curved steadily north, towards Appomattox. Lee didn't want to get too close to the settlement at this point, but he figured they could afford to keep going for a bit longer.

About five hundred yards up from where they'd crossed the road, she stopped.

Lee moved up to her, noting that their course had returned them closer to the road—he could see it about thirty yards off to his left. But, directly in front of them, there was a shallow, blackened depression in the earth.

Lee could smell it himself now. Like the scent of an old, dirty grill, with the charred remnants of a previous barbecue still clinging to it. Except there was a rancid greasiness to it as well, along with a faint whiff of woodsmoke, and something else that Lee associated with burnt hair.

Also, there were clearly bones in there. Blackened, and partially crumbled, but identifiable nonetheless.

Lee squatted stiffly at the lip of the depression, still inspecting its contents. He straightened a bit and circled a finger in the air. "Gimme three-sixty. I'm gonna poke around a bit."

The others spread themselves out into a rough circle, about fifteen yards in diameter.

Lee slung his rifle off to the side, unsheathed his fixed blade knife, and stepped down into the burn pit. The carbonized remains crunched a bit under his boots, but it was also moist. Almost like wet concrete, but more...viscous.

Rendered body fat, Lee surmised as he squatted again, poking his knife through the charred remains. The bones were clearly humanoid, but they'd been burned enough that it was impossible to tell if they'd come from humans or primals.

Bodies didn't burn all by themselves. You couldn't simply light meat on fire. The fact that the bones in this burn pit were so broken down, meant that whoever set this fire had added a shit-ton of wood to get it hot enough to effectively cremate the bodies.

Which was odd, in and of itself.

Winter was coming, and Lee knew from hard experience that having a sufficient supply of dry firewood was labor intensive. Why waste so much of it just to burn these bodies? Burning bodies was practical to avoid health issues from exposed, rotting corpses. But if that's all you were looking to accomplish, you didn't need to make the fire so hot that it burned the bones to cinders.

A funeral pyre, perhaps? That was possible. But it implied some emotional connection to the deceased. And if that was the case, then why do it out here in the middle of nowhere, so far removed from your settlement? This seemed a lonesome place to cremate a loved one.

Which left another possibility: Destruction of evidence.

Someone either wanted to make these bodies unidentifiable, or had hoped to incinerate them completely, and just fallen a bit short.

And yes, at this point, as Lee continued to poke through the ashes, he was certain that more than one body had been burned. He'd found two pieces of lower jawbone that could not have come from the same person. One of those pieces had a few blackened teeth still in it. Lee couldn't be absolutely positive, but he didn't think they looked like the elongated teeth of a primal.

His fingers coated in gritty, greasy blackness, Lee continued to sift around with his knife, his nose slightly curled against the stench, which seemed to get worse the more he disturbed the burn pit.

Then his knife clinked against something metallic.

He flicked the point of his knife, unearthing the object from its shallow grave. Liquefied fats, dirt, and ashes had congealed to form a lump around the object, but he could see a dull glimmer of metal sticking out. He spiked his knife into the dirt and took the object in his fingers, cringing a bit as he worked the piece of metal out from the clod of organic debris.

Well, now. This was interesting.

It seemed to be a ring of some sort, except it was made up of three, interlocked bands. Two seemed to be gold, and one was silver. An odd ring, but clearly a piece of jewelry. Definitely not anything mechanical.

He buffed the ring on his pants and held it up for closer inspection. It was still dirty, but he thought he saw the hint of some inscription on the inside. He'd need to wash it off to be able to read it.

He stood up. "Yo, Abe," he called in a low voice. "Check this out."

Abe trotted over as Lee stepped out of the burn pit. He eyed the thing in Lee's fingers.

"That a ring?" he asked.

"Yeah." Lee gingerly took the tube of his hydration pack—careful not to get his grimy fingers anywhere near the mouthpiece. He sucked on it, then spat the water over the ring, working it around with his fingers to clean most of the muck off.

Abe leaned in close as Lee held it up again to read the inscription.

"That ain't English," Lee observed, frowning.

"No," Abe agreed. "Pretty sure that's Cyrillic."

"Yeah. I mean...I don't speak Russian, but that *looks* like Russian writing."

Abe looked out over the rest of the team. "Hey, any of you happen to be able to read Russian?"

Nobody said they could, but Jones twisted around and gave them a weird look.

"Why?" Jones asked.

Lee held out the ring. "Got a ring here with some Cyrillic writing on it. We think it might be Russian."

Jones's eyes widened bit. "Dude. One of those fuckers that ambushed us?" Jones gestured to the side of his neck. "He had a neck tattoo in Cyrillic."

Abe gave him a suspicious look. "Jonesy, don't take offense to this, but are you sure you can tell the difference between Cyrillic and, like, Greek? Or wingdings?"

Jones looked put upon. "How'm I supposed to *not* take offense to that? Yeah, I fucking know what Cyrillic looks like. I had a girlfriend from the Ukraine one time."

Abe shook his head. "You never cease to amaze me, Jonesy."

Jones stood up and started over. "Well, that tracks, because I'm an amazing guy. Lemme take a look at it."

He gave it the barest of glances before nodding with the utmost confidence. "No, yeah, that's a Russian wedding ring. They do the three-band thing."

Lee gave him a quizzical look. "How in the fuck do you know that?"

Jones peddled a hand slowly through the air, like a kindergarten teacher trying to get their class to remember what they'd just been taught. "Because of my Ukrainian girlfriend. Who..." he looked just a touch guilty. "...was technically still married."

"Ah," Lee and Abe said at the same time.

Lee smiled. "Now it makes more sense."

"So, she wore a ring like this one?" Abe asked.

"No," Jones said, defensively. "She was *separated*, you dicks. I'm not a homewrecker. I just saw—you know what? I don't have to defend my life choices to either of you." He pointed to the ring still in Lee's fingers. "That's a Russian wedding ring. There. That's all you need to know."

Lee grew suddenly very serious, rolling the ring thoughtfully between thumb and forefinger. He looked up at Abe and saw his own misgivings reflected in the man's dark gaze.

"Alright," Lee said, puzzling aloud. "At least two bodies were burned here. One of 'em had a Russian wedding ring. Kat says this burn pit smells stale, like it's been here a few days—maybe even a week or so. And we're looking for three scientists that went dark about that same time."

Abe grunted. "How much do you believe in coincidences?"

"Not much."

"None of those scientists had names that sounded Russian or eastern European."

"No, they didn't," Lee admitted.

"And what about the guy with the tattoo?" Jones asked.

Lee shrugged. "People get all kinds of shit tattooed on themselves."

Jones peered at him. "Thought you didn't believe in coincidences."

"I said I didn't believe in them *much*," Lee corrected. "I can buy that maybe one of the scientists had a Russian wife or something, and that's why he's got a Russian wedding ring with a Russian inscription. But if you're implying that those guys that ambushed us were Russian troops?" Lee shook his head. "That makes no sense to me. Besides, they were kitted out like us. If they were Russian troops, they'd be rocking AK variants. They all had M4 variants."

Jones began stubbornly ticking off fingers. "And no dog tags, and no unit patches, and no nametapes. Clearly someone's doing some shady shit, and doesn't want to be identified."

"Yeah," Lee nodded. "I'll agree with you on that, at least."

Abe slung his pack off and knelt, going into a side compartment. "At what point do we make contact with Ron about this shit?"

Jones started shaking his head vehemently. "I'm still not sure he wasn't the one that fucked us."

Abe gave him a caustic look. "I was asking Lee."

"No, I'm with Jones here," Lee said—which caused Jones to give Abe a triumphant look. "I'd like a little more intel before I take that leap. I don't *think* Ron would do something like that. But I don't *know* it."

Abe stood up with a small, digital camera. "Do you think Griffin would?"

"No. But right now, anyone not on our team is a suspect."

Abe took a photo of the ring, then took several photos of the burn pit, and some close ups of the jawbone fragments Lee had found. The camera had been given to them for just this purpose—to collect proof that the scientists were dead. Lee still didn't know if the bodies in the burn pit were those of the scientists they were looking for, but things were certainly pointing in that direction.

So, someone in Appomattox maybe killed the scientists and burned their bodies to get rid of the evidence. But why? And what had they been researching? And why was that research so fucking sensitive that a strike force had been assembled to wipe out a whole settlement of civilians to get it back?

And if the higher ups in the IAG wanted that research so bad, why would they try to kill Lee and his team, whose whole mission was to get the stuff they wanted?

None of this made any sense.

"Maybe we're reading into things too much," Lee said, as Abe finished his evidence gathering and stowed the camera. "Maybe those boys that hit us were just a long-range patrol from the strike force. They saw some heavily-armed folks they didn't recognize and decided to engage."

Abe hiked his ruck onto his shoulders. He didn't look convinced. "Feels like a stretch."

"More of a stretch than some convoluted conspiracy theory about someone in the IAG trying to kill us while we're on a mission to retrieve research they want so bad they're willing to wipe out a settlement to get it back?"

Abe got a contemplative look on his face as he shouldered his rifle again. "You know, I'd really hoped the new government would be better."

Lee gave his friend a grim smirk. "Meet the new boss. Same as the old boss."

Abe chuffed, bitterly. "Guess we *did* get fooled again."

Chapter 10

As soon as Kat was out of sight, she stopped and stripped down to her bare skin.

It was approaching midday now. Lee and his team had worked their way around to the east side of Appomattox and set up in an abandoned farmhouse. Due to the terrain, there was no good way to recon the settlement without getting close.

Best way to get close? Send in Kat.

Lee had been very specific about how he wanted her to remain on the radio. But as Kat had slipped off through the woods in the direction of Appomattox, she decided that was dumb. Part of the reason they were sending her was because she was stealthier than they were. But the other part was that if someone happened to catch sight of her, they might just think she was a primal.

Except primals didn't wear clothes. And they certainly didn't carry radios with earpieces.

She piled her clothes at the base of a tree, knowing she'd have no problem finding them again. She looked at the radio for a moment, feeling like she might be doing something wrong. But no. This was a good idea. Lee wanted her to get eyes on the settlement. Appomattox was supposed to be friendly with the primals, so it just made sense that she should look as much like a primal as possible. That would allow her to get in very close.

If anyone took notice of her, she would simply scamper away. They'd just see a naked form moving on all fours and assume it was a primal.

Lee might be irritated with her that she'd left the radio, but Kat figured he'd get over it if she was able to get good information.

She looked down at her bare skin. The bandages Marie had applied to her breast and back were a giveaway, though. And they were pointless—her body could heal from those minor flesh wounds without all this shit they'd slapped on her.

She peeled the bandages off the two holes in her breast, hissing as she did. Admittedly, now that she wasn't pumped full of rage and adrenaline, the pain was significant. The wounds beneath were swollen and red, now oozing pinkish fluid.

The bandage on her back was harder to get to. She bent and contorted herself, but just couldn't reach it. Grunting irritably, she put her back to a tree, steeled herself, then scraped the bandage off on the bark. The pain was sharp and insistent and made her breath lock up for a moment. But then it was over.

That done, Kat squatted down and took handfuls of black, forest loam in her hands, then rubbed it over every inch of her skin. Ground it into her hair. Made sure to really scrub her armpits and her crotch. The dirt was less about making her look like a primal—actually, primals tended to keep their bodies fairly clean. But it was a way to keep her scent down.

Then she set off through the woods again.

She felt good. The best she'd felt in a long while. The shade of the forest was chilly and invigorating, while the patches of sunlight she passed through glowed warmly on her skin. There was no one else around. No one to look at her, or to talk at her, or to judge her, or tell her what to do. Just her and the forest.

Her past became inconsequential. Her future, immaterial. All that existed was the present. The scents of the woods. The feel of the air, and the leaves under her feet and hands, and the healthy exertion of her steady, loping stride.

She lost track of herself. Wasn't really thinking about anything. Not about Bran, or the mission, or the team, or the men she'd killed, or the way Jones had looked at her after she'd done it.

She was so lost in the sheer *presentness* of the moment, that she'd gone almost five minutes off course before she realized she was following a scent.

The freedom of the moment evaporated. She came to a stop, breathing steadily, just a tiny bit of sweat along her hairline, despite the chilly air.

What was wrong with her? Why'd she just gone off like that? She hadn't even been thinking. Was that what it was like to be a full-blooded primal? To just be lost in the flow of instinct, with no active, conscious thought?

It'd been invigorating, yes. But now that she'd come back to herself, she realized that it scared her. Like the human side of her—the side that thought deeply about things, and communicated those thoughts in words, and had feelings and opinions on matters—was something that she could lose, if she didn't hold onto it tight enough.

Was that possible? If she stayed in that primal frame of mind for long enough, would she forget how to be human?

Only moments ago, being human had seemed like a farce—something she had to pretend at, and the act was a prison from which she might escape and be her true self. But now, what she'd thought of as freedom just seemed like mindlessness. And she liked her mind. She liked thinking, and having opinions about things, and talking to other people. She didn't want to lose that.

Without those things, she wouldn't be Kat. She'd just be...one of them.

Alarm shocked her back into the realm of conscious thought, and she refocused herself. She was supposed to be spying on the settlement, and she'd gotten distracted by a scent. But now that she was actively thinking about it, that scent *was* very intriguing.

It was actually several, distinct smells, all mixed together.

Several individuals. Humans.

But that wasn't what had her interested.

What had her interested was the fact that their scents were mixed with the scents of several *other* individuals, and those others were...hybrids?

"Here's something else I don't like," Jones announced, standing to the side of a mildewed pane of glass and peering out.

Abe was on the opposite side of the old farmhouse's living room, looking out his own window. They were on watch while the others slept in a separate room. The farmhouse was in surprisingly good condition. The front door had been kicked in. Clearly someone had looted it. But it still had glass in the windows, no one had lit it on fire, and it didn't appear to have been a home for squatters or critters.

Jones was clearly waiting for Abe to acknowledge him, because he hadn't gone on.

Abe gave the exterior of the farmhouse another once-over and then glanced over his shoulder. "I'm listening."

Jones paced to another window and stared out for a moment. "I didn't mention it before because I was all like, 'don't be weird about shit, Jonesy.' And I know you're just going to make fun of me and say that I'm being a conspiracy theorist—"

"Christ, Jones. Just spit it out."

"Alright," Jones sighed, then seemed to gird himself as he turned to meet Abe's gaze. He raised his hands like a presenter introducing a topic. "Appomattox."

Abe stared. Jones seemed frozen, eyes somewhat feverish as he waited for Abe to connect some crazy dots that no normal person would connect.

Abe blinked a few times. "Yes. That is the settlement we're investigating."

Jones's face screwed up, his presenter-hands dropping to his side, dejected. "Really? You don't know about military history and shit?"

Abe shifted his weight. "Well, I know *some* military history. What era are we talking about here?"

"The Civil War."

Abe shook his head. "Never learned much about that."

Jones seemed excited to educate him. "Bro. Appomattox is the town where Confederate General Lee surrendered to Union General Grant."

Abe blinked again.

Jones huffed. "Appomattox is where...*Lee...surrendered*."

Ah, okay. Abe had now successfully connected the dots.

Which made him roll his eyes. "Alright. So, what you're trying to say is that you think this is all just a big setup to do Lee in or whatever, and someone intentionally chose the town of Appomattox as the location, because they wanted...what? Historical symmetry?"

Jones looked pained. "Don't...don't fuckin' look at me with those judgy eyes. It's just weird, alright? That's all I'm saying. It's very *coincidental*. Makes me hinky."

"I think you're seeing patterns that don't exist, brother."

"Maybe," Jones said, noncommittally. He turned back to looking out the window. "I guess we'll find out, huh?"

Abe couldn't help but smile as he looked back through his own window. Despite how much they all enjoyed giving Jones a hard time, Abe really did like the guy. The team wouldn't be the same without him. Abe probably wouldn't tolerate his humor as much if Jones was a tactical idiot. But, once you got past the verbal diarrhea, Jones was as good an operator as any Abe had worked with.

"I'll tell you what, Jonesy," Abe said, still smirking. "If your theory turns out to be true, and someone masterminded Lee's downfall to happen in Appomattox because some general two hundred years ago with the same name surrendered there, then I'll never make fun of you again."

"Pssh. I've heard that before."

Abe turned to frown at him. "I've never promised that before. I love picking on you too much to offer that up."

"No," Jones said, whirling on him. "You remember that guy in Nevada with the shaky hands?"

"The fuck are you talking about?"

"The guy with the shaky hands in Nevada!" Jones was getting indignant. "Remember, I said his hands were shaky because he was a fuckin' cannibal and the prions fucked with his nervous system, and you said I was full of shit, and I said I'd seen that in a movie before, and you said that if he actually turned out to be a cannibal, you'd never make fun of me again, and then he turned out to be a cannibal, and I was totally right, and I'm still taking your shit."

Abe squinted skyward for a moment. "Nope. Not ringing any bells."

Jones's face became deadpan. "You seriously don't remember Shaky-Hand Cannibal Guy?"

"From Nevada?"

"Yes, Nevada."

Abe shook his head. "Nope. Pretty sure you dreamed that up."

"Oh!" Jones smiled ruefully and pointed a finger at him. "Oh, we're gonna see about this. I'm gonna tell Ma, and she's gonna remember. Put you in your fuckin' place, you geriatric, Alzheimer's, memory-losing sonofabitch."

Abe chuckled quietly to himself. He remembered Shaky-Hand Cannibal Guy perfectly fine. But it was just so easy to get Jones riled up.

He reached for his PTT, but stopped just before pressing it, as Jones grumbled, "Go change your Depends."

He waited. Started to key up again—and again was interrupted.

"Mix you up some nice Jell-O, you old fuck."

"Jones."

"Fuckin' lace that shit with Centrum Silver for your old-ass brain."

"Jones."

"What?"

"Shut up. I'm tryna transmit."

"Your arthritic fingers can't push the button or something? You need me to do it for you?"

"Ssh-ssh-ssh," Abe said, putting a finger to his lips as he waited for Jones to be done. After a moment, Jones let out a final scoff and was quiet.

Abe keyed up and spoke very slowly and deliberately. "Abe to Kat. Abe to Kat. Can you give me a sitrep?"

Five seconds passed. No response.

Maybe she wasn't sure what a sitrep was.

"Abe to Kat. Can you tell me what's going on? I'd like to know where you're at, and what you're seeing."

She should've made it pretty close to Appomattox by now.

Again, he got no response.

Perhaps she'd gotten so close that she was unable to speak without giving herself away. "Kat, if you can hear me, just click your transmit button twice."

The living room of the old farmhouse was absolutely still as both Abe and Jones waited in tense silence.

"Kat. I need you to respond in some way. Either speak to me, or click your transmit button."

Initially, Abe felt a flush of irritation, thinking that Kat was either ignoring him, or was simply too dumb to figure out how to transmit back. As the seconds ticked by, that began to cool into worry.

"Maybe she took her earpiece out," Jones suggested.

"Better fucking not have," Abe growled.

"Coulda fallen out too."

Abe transmitted once more, raising his voice to a shout: "Kat! Answer your fucking radio! Answer! Your fucking! Radio!" The hope being that, if her earpiece had fallen out, she might hear the buzz of his yelling voice and put it back in.

After another twenty seconds, the only response they got was Lee, storming out of the back bedroom with his one eye squinting, his face sleep-puffed and irritated.

"The fuck are you yelling about?" Lee demanded.

Abe gestured to the radio on his plate carrier. "Kat's not answering up."

It seemed to take a second or two for that to fully compute for Lee.

Then he swore and turned to yell over his shoulder, "Sam! Marie! Grab your shit!"

Kat crept closer to the strange group.

She was on all fours, so low to the ground that fallen leaves would sometimes tickle her chest and stomach. Moving across dry leaves was never soundless, but she was still very quiet, and the slight crunching she did make would not be audible to the people she was sneaking up on—they were still too far away.

She'd caught a glimpse of a red shirt or jacket through the trees ahead, maybe another hundred strides or so. This area of the forest was a little thicker, so visibility had shrunk.

She paused to scent and listen.

The smells remained the same. She was pretty sure it was four humans. The other smells that she thought might be hybrids were...a little harder to pin down. She was guessing there were a few more hybrids than there were humans.

She could hear voices speaking in low tones.

It seemed they were heading in her direction.

She considered retreating, but decided to stay put. She wanted to get a better look at these people. The wind was coming crosswise to her, and it was muddling their scents so she couldn't tell how many of them there were, or even if the hybrids were a part of the human group.

The thought that they might be excited her for some reason.

She moved forward, but only to get behind a cluster of fallen pine trees, their branches cluttered with pine cones so that it created a nice screen for her to conceal herself behind. She kept that between herself and the slowly-approaching humans as she crawled up to it.

Then she leaned this way and that, and found a keyhole through the jumble of pine cones and twigs.

That flash of red again. Definitely a guy in a bright red jacket. With him were three others, spaced out in a line, each of them about ten yards from the other. They were moving slow, and were fairly quiet for humans, though to Kat's hyper-attuned ears, they still made a racket.

Also of note: They all had weapons.

Two of them had weapons she did not recognize. She'd never seen a compound bow or a crossbow before, and wasn't sure what she was looking at, only that it was clear they were weapons of some sort.

The guy in the red jacket had a pump shotgun. A woman beside him was holding a black pistol.

She saw no others with them, hybrids or otherwise.

Interesting. Perhaps the hybrids she'd smelled were *not* a part of this group.

The party of four was closing within fifty strides of her, and she realized she might need to make a run for it. They seemed to be coming straight at her. There was a chance she could get real low and squirm in amongst the pine twigs to hide herself. But that seemed like a bad choice—its only chance of success was if they didn't check their surroundings very hard, and these four humans seemed to be keeping their heads on a swivel.

She decided she'd move straight back, keeping the fallen pine between her and the group. There was a slight swale about twenty-five yards back. If she could make it there without being seen, she could cut wide around them—

She heard something to her right.

Immediately, her head snapped in that direction. It'd been a small noise—maybe just a bird rustling through the leaves. Except that something about it seemed...heavy.

She stared in the direction of the noise, unbreathing and unmoving.

Then she realized that the humans weren't making their racket anymore.

Everything was completely still.

"Hey," a human voice called out—not aggressively, but almost soothing. "It's okay. We know you're there."

Shit.

Kat still hadn't pulled her eyes away from where she'd heard that noise to her right. Almost at the same time, five shapes melted out from behind tree trunks and low-lying brush. They moved fluidly on all fours in a way that no normal human could. And yet they were clothed.

Hybrids.

And they'd circled around downwind of her.

Also, all five of them were looking right at her.

"It's okay," the voice came again—a man's voice.

Kat's eyes jagged through the keyhole. It was the man in the red jacket that was speaking.

"You don't need to run. We're not here to hurt you. Can you understand what I'm saying?"

Run. She needed to run now.

Her thighs tensed, preparing to bolt, when a fresh wave of scent hit her, coming from the left.

Her head snapped in that direction, and saw three more shapes scuttling through the trees, maybe fifty yards to her left.

They had her pinned in. Almost surrounded.

If it'd just been the humans, Kat would've run.

But there were eight hybrids, and they were working as a pack.

Kat versus some humans? She was the apex predator.

Kat versus more hybrids? She had no advantage.

The hybrids to either side of her seemed to be holding their positions. As were the humans.

"If you can understand me," the man went on. "Then stand up. If you're friendly with us, we'll be friendly with you. There's no need to run or fight. Let's just talk. Can you talk?"

Kat did not stand up. She remained ready to bolt, but let out a low, warning growl and then rasped, loud enough to be heard, "Talking is not my favorite."

Chapter 11

Abe had continued to hail Kat on the radio every minute or so, just in case.

But at this point, Lee didn't think she was going to answer up.

He sat on the musty remnants of a living room couch, lacing up his boots, with his gear next to him. "We don't know," he suddenly barked, silencing the rampant speculation between Sam and Jones. "We don't know if she took the earpiece out, or it fell out, or she turned the fucking radio off, or she's dead. There's no way to know, and it doesn't matter anyway. She's out of contact."

Sitting on the arm of the couch, Marie was already geared up. "So, what? We're just gonna go out there and mount a fucking search and rescue?"

"I'm still deciding."

"Well, you're gonna need to decide quick."

He paused, mid-lace-up, to give Marie a sour look. "I'll have a fucking decision by the time I finish gearing up."

"Strong chance we might be compromised," Abe said.

"Yeah," Lee agreed, finishing with his boots and standing up. "Also a strong chance she might've just disobeyed me and turned the radio off. Again, we don't know."

"I fuckin' told you," Jones sang from over by the window where he was still alternately arguing, claiming he'd known this would be a disaster all along, and keeping watch. "Hybrid on a tactical team? That's just asking for trouble. She don't know how to follow orders. Of course she disobeyed you. You see the way she up and ran off the second we were in a firefight?"

"It worked out for us," Sam snapped.

"Oh, so now you're Team Kat?" Jones cried.

Sam glowered at his friend. "There is no 'Team Kat.' There's *this* team—*our* team—and she's a fucking part of it whether you like it or not."

"You're about to hit me with some 'never leave a man behind' bullshit?"

Sam spread his hands as though to say, *Yeah? What of it?*

"She's not a man!"

"Don't get fucking pedantic with me—Marie's not a man either, and you wouldn't leave her if she went dark."

"That's because I know Marie wouldn't do something stupid," Jones countered. "So if she went dark, we can assume she's in trouble."

Lee dropped his armor over his head and took his time cinching the straps. Why did everything have to be a fucking dilemma? Why couldn't things ever just be clear-cut cases of right and wrong?

He let everyone air their opinions. Ultimately, it would be his call to make, as he was the nominal leader, but he didn't mind hearing his team's arguments. It'd become a part of his decision-making process. He was a good leader, but that didn't mean he always thought of everything, and he relied on his teammates to articulate perspectives he might've missed. Those fresh perspectives had led him to solutions on more than one occasion.

Sam stabbed a finger at Jones. "There's a chance she did get snatched up, Jones. And that feels way shitty to me to just abandon her. We were the ones that sent her out there solo."

Jones gaped at the ceiling. "Oh. My. God. We sent her out there solo because she swore up and down she was the stealthiest fucking thing in the world and we'd only—" he started putting up air quotes. "*Slow her down*, and *move too noisy*. Shit, man, she all but strong-armed us into letting her go by herself. She *wanted* to go by herself. Probably so she could run off and be one with nature."

"Abe to Kat. Abe to Kat. Please respond."

Lee glanced at Abe and made a cutting motion across his neck. "Abe, don't transmit anymore. If someone managed to take her down, they might have her radio. If they don't already know we're out here, I don't wanna advertise."

"Won't get an argument from me," Abe murmured and let his hand fall from the PTT.

"Look," Marie said. "I'm with Jones here. This op's been fucked six ways from Sunday since we got off that helicopter. I think we need to cut our losses and get out of here before it gets worse."

"Yes!" Jones proclaimed, thrusting his hands at Marie. "Thank you! Ma's the only reasonable one here!"

Lee shook his head. "Yeah, well, that's not gonna fly. We already talked about baling, and we made the decision to stick around and find out what's going on here and who's gunning for us."

"The circumstances may have changed a bit," Marie noted, coolly.

"No, the circumstances haven't changed," Lee countered, slowly and deliberately checking each piece of equipment—maybe stalling just a tad. "Someone in the IAG's doing some shady shit, and they looped us into it. Now we're here, and our options are to move forward and learn who our enemies are, or go on the run with no clear idea of who's gunning for us. That how you wanna live the rest of your lives until a laser-guided missile incinerates you while you sleep?"

"Great." Marie threw up her hands. "Here comes Lee Harden on his white horse, taking on the government. By himself. Again."

Lee actually smiled at her as he slung into his rifle. "Well, Marie. We did it before, didn't we? Operative word there being 'we.'" Lee drew a circle to encompass his team. "I didn't do it by myself. I did it with y'all. We're alive because we stuck together. We *won*—and continue to win—because we have each other's backs. Does that not extend to Kat?"

"No, it does not," Marie said. "Because she's not a part of the team."

"She is while she's on this op," Lee stated. "At the end of the day, we don't know what happened to Kat, only that we sent her in to recon the settlement, and now she's not responding." He shrugged. "I can't, in good conscience, just do nothing."

Marie rubbed her face. "Here we go with the conscience thing again."

Lee checked the mag in his rifle, then the chamber, then thumbed the forward-assist a few times. He looked at Marie and spoke calmly. "Would you really wanna be a part of my team if I didn't have one?"

Marie sighed heavily, refusing to look at him. "No," she admitted, sullenly.

"I don't want you to be a sociopath or nothin'," Jones put in. "I'm just saying, your conscience tends to put us in danger."

"Yeah," Lee allowed it with a nod. "That's fair. But what do I always say about doing the right thing, Jonesy?"

Jones stuck his chin out, petulant. "I'm not gonna say it."

"Doing the right thing is never easy," Lee provided his own answer. "Look at it like this: If Kat wasn't with us, what would we be doing right now?"

"Sleeping," Sam commented, picking some leftover crust out of his eyes.

Lee ignored him. "We'd be sneaking up to Appomattox and conducting recon. And that's all we're gonna do right now. We gave Kat that task. She's not answering up. So we're going to do it ourselves. Just so happens that finding out what happened to Kat coincides nicely with what we'd already be doing."

"So you made your decision?" Marie asked.

"Yeah, pretty much." Lee looked around. "Unless one of you has some alternate idea that doesn't entail going on the run or sitting around and being useless, then, as I see it, the only way forward is through."

"Ugh," Jones shook his head. "You're like a soundboard for tactical motivational quotes."

Lee gave him a laconic side-eye. "Do you have an alternate idea?"

"Nooo-uh," Jones sulked.

Lee glanced to the others. "Anyone else?"

Marie and Jones were clearly in the camp of *No, we don't have any ideas, but we don't like yours*. Sam and Abe seemed to be on board though.

"I agree," Abe said, putting the final nail in the coffin of the detractors. "Not like we gotta roll in there, guns blazing, and do a rescue mission. But it sure as shit behooves us to put some eyes on these folks and figure out what their game is and how they fit into this giant clusterfuck."

Abe was still standing to the side of the window he'd posted up on, and if Lee hadn't been looking at him as he spoke, he wouldn't have seen it.

Abe immediately saw the way Lee's eye fixed on something, and he whirled towards the window, snatching up his rifle.

"Movement," Lee said in the same instant, sidestepping to the left while Abe took the right side of the window. "No ID—Jones, heads up."

Lee didn't take his eye off of where he'd seen something, but he heard the others scuttling into various positions. The farmhouse sat in the middle of a field, long-since turned to high brush. Being on a slightly elevated foundation, Lee was able to see across the tops of the brush and into the surrounding woods. What he'd seen was just a flash of something through a spot of sunlight coming through the trees.

"In the woods," Lee said to Abe. "Maybe fifty yards out."

It could've been wildlife. Maybe a deer. But until Lee confirmed that, they were going on high-alert.

Out of his peripheral, Lee saw Marie moving quickly towards the front door, which was visible from the living room, and gave them an additional angle on their perimeter.

He hadn't seen any more movement. Which was not a comfort at all. If it'd been a deer, Lee should've been able to spot it again. The fact that he only saw that one flash of movement made him feel like whatever was out there was trying to be sneaky.

Three separate colonies of primals patrolled this area. It was feeling more and more likely to Lee that something had sniffed them out and was creeping in to investigate.

He didn't particularly want to be pinned down in a farmhouse. But being out in the open would be worse for them. They had to work with what they had, and what they had was a structure that could provide at least *some* fortification.

There was an upstairs. One stairwell, off the living room, going up to an attic space that'd been converted into a bedroom. Going up limited their escape routes to taking a two-story jump out the attic window—not ideal. But the stairwell would provide a bottleneck. And with the five of them fully loaded up, they could hold that bottleneck against a lot of bodies.

"Movement," Marie said in a low voice from the front of the house.

"Over here, too," Sam snapped.

Lee cinched the buttstock of his rifle tight into his shoulder pocket. "Hold fire until I—"

"Primals," Sam interrupted. "Two primals—positive ID. Wait. Check that. They're wearing clothes. Lee, I think I got two hybrids on this side, looking right in these windows."

"Hold fire," Lee repeated. "Until they make a go at us, we don't shoot."

"Heard," Sam said tightly.

"Contact," Marie called out. "Got someone approaching from the front. Walking on two legs—I think...yeah, they're human. Shit. Lee, come check this out!"

Lee darted towards the front of the house.

"Contact," Abe called as Lee moved past him. "Two on my side. All I got is faces—primals or hybrids, I can't tell."

Marie was looking through a sidelight on the front door, but she was backed off of it a couple paces so she wouldn't be as visible through the glass. As Lee reached her, he called over his shoulder, "They attack, we're moving upstairs to hold them at the stairwell, copy?"

"Copy," Sam, Abe, and Jones called back in unison.

Leering over Marie's shoulder, Lee spotted the approaching human. As well as what appeared to be two other humans—both of them armed—and two more hybrids lurking in the woods.

Lee's mind was fixated on the tactical aspects of what he was facing—how to make them dead, and not get any of his team dead in the process—but a small part of him marveled at what he was seeing. Multiple humans, working in concert with multiple hybrids?

So far, Virginia was blowing his mind.

The person that Marie had initially spotted now stopped, just a handful of strides into the brushy field, standing fully visible in an area of lower growth. It was a woman in a green, canvas jacket. She was lugging a bundle of stuff that looked like it had some heft to it. Then she unceremoniously dumped it on the ground.

It looked like mostly clothing.

Lee spotted a tan soft-shell jacket, and a plate carrier in the mix.

"Shit," he murmured. "That's Kat's stuff."

He raised his rifle, bringing the optic up to his eye. The red dot traced little circular patterns around the woman's chest.

Lee noted that the two humans behind her—both men—were armed with AR variants. They had their rifles shouldered and addressed towards the house. He decided to pivot his aim to one of them, since the woman had only a sidearm, which was still holstered.

Then the woman cupped her hands over her mouth and yelled, "We know you're in there! We have you completely surrounded. You start some shit, we're gonna rip you to shreds. You wanna get out of this alive, you come out and talk to us—unarmed, with your hands over your head!"

Well. This was looking shittier by the second.

"Think we can take 'em?" Marie asked.

"Maybe," Lee answered, keying his radio. "Everyone stay quiet, but I need a headcount on hostiles."

Abe: "Got two hybrids, one human with a shotgun."

Sam: "Three hybrids, one guy with a pistol, one guy with a bolt action."

Plus the two hybrids, and the two guys with rifles right in front of Lee.

"We can take twelve if we bottleneck 'em," Marie said.

"Twelve—that we can see," Lee pointed out.

The woman started yelling again, seeming to work herself up: "We told you motherfuckers not to come back here! We told you what would happen if you did! The only way you're getting out of this alive is by turning yourselves over to us!"

"She seems awfully confident," Marie remarked.

"She also thinks we're someone else."

Right. Okay. So the options were A) bloodbath, or B) talk it out.

Lee's brain shot through the pros and cons of each in a few seconds flat.

Option A appealed to Lee, simply because that was what he was good at. But, to play it safe and account for the fact that they might not be seeing all the hostiles that had them surrounded, he decided to double their number in his mind. Could they hold out in the attic against twenty-four attackers?

Possibly. But these weren't mindless infected. They wouldn't just throw themselves into the meatgrinder of a bottleneck. They'd take a few losses, then back off, and then...what? Back to talking it out, while Lee and his team huddled in the attic?

Another possibility was that the people with guns just started pumping rounds through the house. Depending on how much ammunition they had, that could be a bad day for Lee and the others.

Even considering all that, Option B was still not attractive to Lee, simply because there were too many unknowns. Who did these people think Lee and his team were? The military? It'd be hard to convince them that they *weren't* tied to the military once they saw all their gear.

On the other hand, ever since the ambush last night, Lee had been considering making direct contact with the people of Appomattox. That hadn't been in the original gameplan, but now he had a lot of questions and wanted some answers. Did they kill the researchers? If so, why? Did they know what the scientists had been researching?

Because if they could tell Lee that, he might have a better understanding of why he seemed to be caught in the middle of some high-level fuckery. And if he could understand that, he might figure out who had betrayed them.

Which really had supplanted the original mission in his mind.

If his team was ever going to get out of this debacle and not spend the rest of their lives looking over their shoulders for some black-ops kill team, then Lee needed information. He needed a clearer picture of what was happening in Appomattox. Which made Option A a pointless endeavor, and Option B the only possibility with a positive outcome—as slim as it might be.

Lee sighed irritably as he came to this conclusion. "Goddammit. Alright, Marie, go swap out with Sam." He keyed his comms. "Sam, bring that SAW up to the front door and cover me. I'm gonna go out and talk to them—don't give me any lip about it, this is what we're doing. Y'all copy? Maintain three-sixty and if shit goes bad, take the attic and hold 'em off. Abe, you're in charge."

Marie gave Lee a look that spoke volumes—again, the general sentiment communicated through her glare was *I don't like your idea, but I don't have a better one.*

Or maybe she was just not giving him lip about it like he'd asked.

She hustled off, and Sam appeared with the M249 Para.

"If I drop to the ground," Lee said as he unslung his rifle and set it to the side of the foyer. "You hose the fuck out of 'em."

Sam gave him a similar look to Marie, but nodded and said, "Roger that."

Lee unholstered his sidearm. Looked at the Glock 17 for one moment of indecision, then swore under his breath and deposited it with his rifle.

The woman was starting to yell at them again, her voice gaining a shrill quality to it that promised no quarter if her demands were not met in short order.

Lee opened the front door a crack and shouted through it. "Alright! That's enough! Everyone calm down! I'm coming out, unarmed, with my hands up! Don't fuckin' shoot!"

Chapter 12

His one eye peering around the door frame, Lee saw the two men with rifles tense up, heads sinking lower into their sights. The woman's gaze darted around the front door until it met his eye and locked on. She immediately put a hand on her sidearm, but didn't draw it.

Lee held his position for a beat, his heart in his throat as he waited to see if the shooting was going to start. But everyone held their fire. So far.

Lee pushed the door open a little further, careful not to expose Sam, who was standing in the shadows, pointing his SAW at the woman and her gunmen. He put his hands out first, waving them a bit to make sure everyone saw he had no weapon. Again, no shooting, so he stepped out.

He stopped on the front porch. With a wide field of view now, Lee glanced quickly around the entirety of the field and the surrounding forest, spotting a few more shapes that hadn't been accounted for just yet.

Yeah, they definitely had more than twelve. Which meant they'd come out here expecting some shit to go down.

"Keep your hands up!" the woman bawled at him. "Walk towards me!"

Lee kept his hands raised and stepped slowly down off the porch. "Alright, I'm coming to you. I'm compliant, and I am *not* who you think I am." Lee didn't exactly exaggerate his limp as he walked toward the woman, but he certainly took no pains to hide it.

When people thought of special forces teams sent to fuck their shit up, they typically did not picture forty-year-old guys with one eye and a severe limp. That worked in his favor—he wanted to look as far from *hostile government operative* as he could get.

The woman's incensed expression turned to something more in line with bitterness and heavy suspicion. She didn't say anything, holding her ground over the pile of Kat's clothing and armor she'd dumped.

Lee stopped with about five yards between them. Glanced at the two gunmen with their rifles trained at his face, then made eye contact with the woman. "I'm not who you think I am," Lee said. "I'm not a threat to your people."

"I'll decide if you're a threat or not," the woman snapped. "How many guys do you have in that house with you?"

Lee briefly considered lying, but obfuscating their numbers seemed like such a paltry advantage that it wasn't worth the risk of burning trust this early on. "Four others," he said. "We are not with the military."

She looked him over, obviously taking in his armor, stuffed with magazines, and his empty holster. Lee was glad they'd stuck to civilian clothing. She was clearly not convinced, but being in his OCP fatigues would've only made it worse.

"Bullshit," she spat. "Some of our patrols heard explosions last night, and we were searching the area today, and what do we find?" she kicked the items on the ground. "Armor and a fucking radio. So tell me again how you're not with the military."

"We're not with the military," Lee repeated. "If we were, then why the fuck would we leave armor and radios and clothing laying around in the woods?"

The woman gave him an acidic smile. "Don't fuck with me, stranger." She leaned towards him, raising an arm and pointing all around at the woods. "You see all those figures that look like primals? They're not. They're hybrids. And they scented out this pile of shit and tracked the scent back here."

Lee frowned, surprised to hear her call them primals and hybrids. Lee'd been all over the country since the plague hit, and it seemed every isolated group of people had their own names for the infected. What were the chances that these folks he'd never met before used the same terminology?

He recovered quickly. "I didn't say those *weren't* ours," he pointed out. "I said that if we were a military unit, we wouldn't have left them in the woods." He nodded to the pile on the ground between them. "Your hybrids get a good scent off that shit? Did they tell you it was a hybrid that was wearing it?"

The woman's face screwed up, like this made no sense to her.

Lee jerked his chin out to the two hybrids standing in the woods several yards back. "Go ahead. Ask 'em. They talk, don't they?"

The woman's eyes turned to slits. "The fact that you know hybrids can talk means you're with the military."

Lee was a bit confused by that assertion, but rolled with it. "No, it means I have a hybrid on my team, and *that's* how I know they talk. Her name's Kat. That gear you just tossed on the ground belongs to her. And frankly, we're a bit concerned about what happened to her. We lost radio contact with her a half hour or so ago. Do you know anything about that?"

The woman shook her head violently as though tasting something foul, then pumped her hands in the air. "Wait. Stop."

Lee remained silent.

She peered at him dubiously, then, still holding eye contact, she called over her shoulder, "Baba, up here."

One of the hybrids loped quickly forward—a dark-skinned female with curly black hair cut short around her distended jawline. Hard to tell ethnicity due to the mutations, but Lee thought she looked Indian or Pakistani.

The hybrid named Baba stopped at the woman's side, glancing curiously at her, but mostly keeping her eyes on Lee, with apparent caution and plenty of held-back aggression.

"This shit we found," the woman said. "The scent on it—is it from a hybrid?"

Baba lowered her gaze to the items on the ground. Her nostrils flared, but she didn't move in for a closer sniff. The single-word answer came out guttural and harsh, but nonetheless pretty articulate: "Yes."

Lee gave the woman a *See? I told you so* look.

The woman's jaw worked for a moment. It didn't escape Lee that a lot of the tension came out of her shoulders. She still did not look friendly, but perhaps a bit less murderous.

"Alright," the woman said sharply. "What kinda shit is this? What're y'all trying to pull? This another fucking hairbrained scheme to infiltrate our settlement? Because we warned you! If you ever came back we'd—"

Lee shook his head. "No, you never warned *us* of anything. You might've warned the *military*, but I already told you, that's not us."

"Don't interrupt me," the woman seethed.

"Just didn't want you to waste your breath with spurious accusations when you don't have the whole picture. Unfortunately, we don't have the whole picture either." Lee let that dangle there like bait, and saw the curiosity flash through the woman's eyes. "By the way, my name's Jax. You got something I can call you by?"

"Yeah. You can call me Pissed-Off Bitch That's Going to Kill You If You Don't Start Making Sense."

"That's a mouthful. How about Stacey?"

"You think you're fucking funny right now?"

Lee sighed. "No, not really."

"Ma'am. How about that? You call me ma'am."

"Fair enough, ma'am. Can I lower my arms?"

"No. You explain to me who you are and why you're here, and then maybe, if I don't kill you, you can put your arms down."

"Alright." Lee considered his options for truth versus lies. He tended to heavily favor the truth, but he also wasn't an idiot. At the very least, he'd need to omit some things. "Like I said, my name is Jax. I'm a *former* operative for the US Army, but I no longer work for them, and I don't work for the IAG either. Me and my team are more like..." How to put this? "Freelancers."

The woman was getting impatient. "None of that explains what you're doing in my backyard."

"I'm getting there."

"Get there faster."

"An anonymous entity hired us to find some folks that went missing in this area."

The woman's face betrayed an instant of shock and worry. She covered it quickly. "The only people in this area are us, and the fucking military that's been harassing us. None of our people are missing. So you're here to find someone attached to the military. Which means this 'anonymous entity' that hired you is the military. Which means you're working for the military."

"Yeah, we've started to suspect as much," Lee said, carefully. "We've also started to suspect that someone in the military wants us dead."

"That doesn't make any sense. They hired you."

"No, it doesn't make sense, does it? We're a bit confused on the matter ourselves. You mentioned you had some patrols out last night that heard some explosions, yeah?"

She nodded.

"Well, that was a small squad from the military that tried to ambush us not long after we got here. So, frankly, I'm about as flummoxed as you as to what the fuck's going on around here. I'd like to try and figure out who sold my team down the river, but at this point, I'm a lot more concerned with what happened to Kat."

"Who's Kat again?"

"The hybrid on our team. The one whose gear that is. Her name's Kat."

The woman stewed, seeming at a loss for words.

Lee decided to press his advantage. "Look, ma'am. I'm gonna level with you. Me and my team got into this, thinking we were gonna help save some missing people. It has become obvious that we've been dragged into a serious fuckfest. I know you're suspicious as hell, and I don't blame you. I would be too. In fact, I am. Two of my team were injured in last night's gunfight. Frankly, I'm pissed. So if there's any information you can give me on what the hell's going down in Appomattox, and why the military would hire us to come out here, just to turn around and try to kill us, that'd be mighty helpful."

The woman pulled her head back. "And why the hell would we help you? We don't know you."

"You're right. You don't know us. The only thing we have in common is that we're both getting fucked by someone in the IAG. As for why you would help us? Well, we might be able to help you."

She scoffed. "How would *you* help *us*?"

"Because we have information you want, just like you have information we want. We can help each other, instead of fighting with each other." Lee girded himself up a bit. It was time to play a little hardball. "And, ma'am, I'll just be honest with you: You don't want to fight us."

Her eyes flared and she started to open her mouth to respond—doubtless with more threats—but Lee cut in, patting the air with his hands.

"I'm not saying you wouldn't eventually kill us. You got a lot more people than we do, and I know firsthand the damage all those hybrid friends of yours can do. No, you got us pinned into this house, and I highly doubt we'd walk away from that. But I also got a shit ton of ordnance in there, so if we can't play nice, this is gonna get real nasty for both of us, and I guaran-fuck-ing-tee you that before you wipe my team out, they'll take at least twenty of your people with them. I don't want that. I'm assuming you don't want that. We have a mutual enemy. Logic tells me we'd both benefit from working together. The only hurdle left is whether we can be intelligent human beings and put aside our instinctive stranger-danger responses and trust each other. You don't know me, but I've worked with a lot of different settlements, and I'm used to being the first to go out on a limb and show some trust." Lee motioned generally to his person. "Here I am, taking that first leap of faith, by coming out to talk to you, unarmed. Now, you can meet me in the middle and we can both benefit, or we can be assholes and start trying to kill each other. I'm comfortable with dying, but it wasn't exactly high on my list of things to do today. You?"

The woman did a lot of face-stuff as she mulled that over. Blinking. Sucking her teeth. Flaring her nostrils. Pursing her lips. "How do we know this isn't some ruse to get inside our settlement again?"

"Would we have a hybrid on our team if we were with the military?"

"I wouldn't put it past them."

Lee had to smirk darkly at that. "Yeah, me neither. Look, I got nothing. No way to prove to you that I'm not with the military—though, admittedly, I might've been hired by them. All I can offer is that we sit down and talk this out. We answer your questions, you answer ours. Maybe some trust develops, and we can move forward."

"Why can't you just fucking leave?"

"Would you let us go?"

She seemed conflicted for a moment. "I'd have to check on that."

"Be honest with you, ma'am—we coulda lit out after that gunfight last night when we realized we got sold out by someone. We chose to stick around because we hoped to get some answers. If we've somehow become enemies of the state, we kinda need to know why in order to figure out who's gunning for us. So I'd rather try to find a way to move forward." He nodded at her. "You said you'd have to check—is there someone in charge that should be here?"

She squinted and raised her eyebrows. "You asking for my supervisor?"

Lee thought he detected a glimmer of humor in that question. That was a very good sign. He offered a smile. "No, ma'am. But having been in this situation many times before, I know you're not going to walk us into the settlement without the say-so of whoever is in charge. I'm happy to talk to you, but if you're not the one running the show, then ultimately, I'll have to convince that person too, won't I?"

A thought occurred to him. Any information he had was a bargaining chip at this point in time, so he didn't want to give any away for free. But he also knew that high-pressure sales tactics were effective for a reason. The old "limited time only" thing really made people want to buy.

And he needed this woman to buy.

"And we're on a bit of a time-crunch, ma'am," Lee pressed. "As is everyone in your settlement. So it behooves us to come to an agreement quickly."

This clearly worried the woman. His words had struck home.

"How much time we talking?" she asked.

Lee shook his head. "Not trying to be a dick, but you got me in a situation where I need to preserve some bargaining power. We can help each other, but it can't be one-sided. Quid pro quo, you know?"

She considered this for a long moment. Then turned and looked at Baba. "Can you run back home and send for Judy?"

Baba gave a single nod, then immediately spun and took off at a four-legged sprint.

"Alright," the woman said. "She'll be on her way. Start talking."

"Tell you what," Lee said, daring to lower his hands by a degree. "There's a table and some chairs in the house. Let's have a sit down like civilized folks—you know, with less guns pointing at each other."

Her eyes darted to the house, alarm creeping back into them. "You got guns pointing at us?"

Lee chuckled. "Yeah, of course. Would you be standing here talking to me if you didn't have a bunch of guns pointed at my people? Like I said, quid pro quo. This can be as pleasant or as nasty as you want it to be."

"And you want me to just waltz inside the house with you and be surrounded by your goons?"

"First of all, they're not 'goons'...okay, maybe one of them is a bit of a goon, but even so, they're all good people. They know how to handle themselves, but they don't want bloodshed any more than I do. And no, you don't have to be surrounded. I got four others besides myself. You bring four of your own people. Make it fair."

"No," she said, resolutely. "I bring ten. Five guns, and five hybrids."

"Boy, you're really tryna bend me over backwards, huh?"

"No, I just don't trust you."

Lee took a moment to stare into the woman's eyes. She seemed to find the heavy silence this brought uncomfortable, but Lee was trying to figure her out. She had a plain face, and honest eyes. He tried to look past that, because faces were masks. Tried to see what peeked out from those two windows into her soul.

For the life of him, he couldn't detect a single shred of deception or cunning. Not that she was completely without guile, just that he got a very strong sense that this woman wasn't the type to try to pull one over on someone else. She wasn't trying to get a squad in his house to take them out. She was just trying to feel safe.

"Alright," Lee nodded. "I'll agree to that on the condition that my people can remain armed. I'll remain unarmed, if it makes you feel better. And they won't point guns at anyone. But they're gonna have 'em in hand. That seem fair to you?"

"No."

Lee sighed. "Well, I think it's *more* than fair. You're gonna have one more gun in there than I have, plus five hybrids? Come on. You know how much damage a hybrid can do in close quarters like that. I'm hanging my ass out here, ma'am. Don't take advantage of me."

Now she seemed to be taking *his* measure—staring him long and hard in his one eye.

She tilted her head to one side. "How'd you lose that eye?"

"Spall from a bullet hitting a wall next to my face."

"Yeah, but *how*? What were you doing?"

He thought about whether to tell the truth. Then went with his natural inclination. "I was fighting for the United Eastern States at the time."

Her guarded hostility melted in a flash and her eyes went wide. "The UES?" She actually took a step towards him—not aggressively, but almost excitedly. "You fought with the United Eastern States?"

Lee was a bit taken aback. He didn't think that would mean much to anyone north of the Carolinas. But clearly it did to this woman.

"Yes, ma'am."

Just the breath of a bewildered smile came to her face. "You fought with Captain Lee Harden?"

Well, that one damn near took his breath away.

He tried to recover as quickly as possible. "Well, I suppose we were on the same side, but I never met the man."

"Were you with him when he took over Greeley, Colorado?"

Holy shit. Apparently word had spread, even to these folks who Lee had figured had been living under a rock for the past six years.

Lee cleared his throat, suddenly uncomfortable. Part of the deal he'd made with Griffin after the fall of Greeley and its subsequent incineration by nuclear fireball, had been to maintain the lie that Lee Harden had been killed in the blast. Because the IAG, while still an improvement over the dictatorial regime Acting President Erwin Briggs had set up, still saw Lee Harden as an enemy of the state, a war criminal, and a domestic terrorist. But so long as everyone thought he was dead, then they wouldn't come looking for him.

All of this confirmed for Lee what he'd always known: One man's terrorist is another man's freedom fighter.

Cautiously, Lee said, "Well. I was in Greeley, yeah. Actually, my whole team was. But I wouldn't say we were there *with Lee Harden*. Like I said, we never met the guy."

The woman gave him another long, measuring gaze. Then, finally, she nodded. "Alright. I agree to your terms. Your people can hold onto their weapons, so long as they don't point them at me or my people."

Lee nodded. "So…can I have a name now?"

Still a little cautious, the woman extended her hand to him. "I'm Gale."

Slowly, Lee lowered his hands, then took Gale's. They shook, once. "Good to meet you, Gale."

CHAPTER 13

THE FARMHOUSE HAD A surprisingly open floor plan for such an old structure, and Lee wondered if it'd been remodeled before society fell.

In any case, Lee and Gale were seated at the kitchen table, and the kitchen sat between the living room and the front entryway, so Lee could see each member of his team.

Sam remained at the front door with his M249. Jones at one living room window with his M32, Abe at the other window with his rifle. Marie stood behind Lee, her carbine slung and pointing at the ground, her hands resting lightly on the grip.

Across from Lee, Gale sat with her back to the front door. Directly behind her stood quite the mixed bag of people. Four guys and one younger woman, all with assault rifles bearing high-capacity magazines—three AR variants, an AK variant, and one bullpup design of a make Lee was unfamiliar with.

And, of course, the five hybrids.

This was somewhat fascinating to Lee. Prior to coming to Virginia, he'd met only three hybrids, and two of those only briefly. One being Kat's sister, Freya, who had remained behind in Northern California after Kat and Bran had fled. The other being the big one named Elijah that had been with Kat when he'd found her in Oregon.

Looking up at the five hybrids standing behind Gale, Lee saw that there was a clear difference in the dose of primal genetics that each of them had. Some of them displayed more mutations than Kat—longer arms, and more severe changes to the normal human facial structure. Others were less mutated than Kat, and were barely even distinguishable from a regular human.

These less-mutated ones simply looked like very fit, very muscular people with unusually-strong jaws and wide mouths. They reminded Lee of people that took too much Human Growth Hormone as a performance-enhancing drug. He'd known a few guys like that in the military.

"I gotta ask," Lee said, after a moment of pregnant silence. "How many hybrids are there in your settlement?"

She gave him an odd look then, as though his question was mildly offensive.

That was weird, but he figured some clarity wouldn't hurt. "Reason I'm curious is that Kat is literally the first hybrid I ever met, and I've only had contact with two others besides her. So, to me..." he made a circular gesture, as though to include all the hybrids she still had lurking outside. "This is pretty wild."

Gale got a quizzical look on her face. "You mean to tell me you didn't have hybrids in the UES?"

Lee barely restrained a cough of surprise. "You mean, like, *in* the UES? As citizens?"

She nodded, seeming confused at his confusion.

"No," he said flatly. "Not at all. And Kat's from California."

"Well. That's interesting."

Lee leaned forward, settling his elbows on the table. "It's my understanding that Appomattox is coexisting with three colonies of primals. Is that correct?"

Another nod.

Lee considered his words carefully. "This might be hard for you to understand, then—I don't know the circumstances that led to your settlement coexisting with primals. But most everywhere else in the country? Primals are...a massive problem."

This did not seem surprising to Gale. "We gathered as much. It's not hard to understand. We've been very removed from everyone else here in Virginia. When we finally made contact with the outside world it was a bit of a shock to learn that what we had going on here had never been seen before." A wistful smile came to her lips. "As humans do, we figured we were pretty normal, and others' experiences would be similar."

Lee shook his head. "No, unfortunately not. This is the most hybrids I've seen in one place." He glanced at them, their faces running the gamut from impassive to glowering. "But you folks seem to be making it work."

"We do alright for ourselves."

Lee was extremely curious about the level of interbreeding that was occurring in Appomattox. And on a grosser, more personal level, he wanted to know how such a thing could be. But broaching those topics would likely not go over well, so he kept it to himself.

Instead, he asked, "How did your people get to the point where they were coexisting with the primals?"

Gale got a guarded look. "That's...something you should talk to Judy about. It's her story to tell, not mine. I'd like to move on to matters of more immediate importance."

"Such as?"

Gale put a hand on the table and picked at something. "You mentioned you were here looking for some missing people."

Lee nodded, but gave nothing else.

"Who are you looking for?"

Lee felt a bit of tension in his chest. He needed to be very careful with how he broached this subject. Currently, he suspected that Appomattox had killed the scientists he'd been sent to rescue, and burned their bodies to get rid of the evidence. If he came in too hot and made Gale feel like she was being interrogated, this might end up going quite poorly for him.

"A few scientists," Lee said casually. "As you pointed out earlier, it seems like my team was hired by the military. They didn't give me any details about why they wanted me to find these people. Just told me to come to Virginia and try to locate them. So I really don't know what they were doing, whether they were friendly with you folks, or if the relationship was more...combative." He shrugged. "If I'm being honest, after the firefight last night, I'm less concerned about the scientists, and more concerned with getting an idea of the big picture so I know where the pitfalls are and can avoid stepping in them. I'm sure you understand. We're all just trying to survive."

Gale nodded, slowly. "Have you found anything so far?"

God, Lee hated these fucking games. Hated dancing around things. Caution was called for, sure, but if Lee had taken Gale's measure correctly—and he considered himself decent at reading folks—then she liked things to be direct just as much as Lee did.

The trick was in being direct without sounding like you wanted a fight.

"Look, Gale." He fixed her with as earnest an expression as he could muster. "I'm not here to accuse anyone of anything. Frankly, I don't even care. That said, we found a burn pit with what appeared to be human remains in them, and I suspect those remains belong to the scientists that were in Appomattox." He held up a hand to forestall objections and excuses. "Again, I don't care. Or, at least, not in the way that you might think. I wanna know what those scientists were up to, but only so I can get an idea of why the IAG is so horny to get them and their research back."

Gale's expression was closed off. "You think we killed them?"

Lee forced a smile. "Well, that is the most logical conclusion." He shrugged. "But it's immaterial. Whoever killed them must've had a reason. If I can figure out what that reason was, it'll go a long way towards figuring out why my team was hired, only to be attacked by the people that hired us."

Gale looked thoughtfully up at the ceiling. "So. You were sent here to rescue some scientists." Her gaze dropped and skewered Lee. "Were you planning to hurt any of my people in the process?"

"Were we planning to? No. Would we have if it came to that? Yes, of course." Lee bobbed his head in the general direction of the other members of his team. "Hence all the hardware we're packing."

Gale seemed a bit indignant about that.

"You asked," Lee said. "I'm giving you an honest answer. Our original mission was to find the scientists and get them out. Obviously, if we'd encountered resistance, we would've done what was necessary to complete our mission. But the circumstances have changed. Which is why we're having a nice, peaceful sit down right now, and not trying to blow each other's brains out."

"You mentioned a timeline earlier. Care to expound on that?"

Lee arched an eyebrow. "Care to tell me what the scientists were researching in Appomattox?"

Gale pursed her lips and pressed herself back in her chair, causing the wood to creak. Her hand remained on the table, fingernails tapping a slow, thoughtful rhythm. Then she smiled, though it didn't reach her eyes.

"Us," she said. "Our relationship with both the primals and the hybrids."

Lee made a dubious face. "Well, that doesn't sound like a very good reason to kill some scientists."

"Who said we killed them?"

"No one. Maybe they burned themselves."

Gale did not appear to appreciate his sarcasm.

Lee decided to switch tacks. "Maybe we leave that for later. Here's something I'm curious about that shouldn't be too sensitive: I noticed you call them 'primals.'"

She frowned. "Yeah."

"Well, I been all over this country since the plague hit, and everyone's got their own colloquialism for them. You are the first folks I've come across that call them primals. The reason this is interesting to me, is because that's what *we* called them, back in the UES."

Gale gave a facial shrug. "UES started in North Carolina. We're in Virginia. Not that far apart."

"No," Lee admitted. "But Virginia was cut off from the rest of the southeastern states, so I don't know how the term could've traveled."

Gale took a big breath and regarded Lee for a long moment. "As I understand it, there's a few folks that came to Appomattox from another settlement. This was…oh, I dunno. Four or five years ago? Not long after everything went down. Their original settlement was centered around an underground CDC laboratory where some microbiologist was doing research on the bacteria and its effects on humans—particularly the physical changes that were happening to people. The term 'primals' came from them. Some theory the CDC guy had about certain people being genetically predisposed for adaptation to a primal lifestyle. I guess that made sense to us, so the term stuck."

Lee was positively floored.

Gale noticed his surprised look. "What? Why are you staring at me like that?"

"The people from that CDC laboratory—they had to abandon that settlement because it got overrun, didn't they?"

Gale nodded, still confused.

"His name was Jacob," Lee said, a small smile coming to his face as he remembered the man. Then it faded as he remembered how Jacob had died as their own settlement, a place called Camp Ryder, had been overrun.

"Who?" Gale asked.

"The microbiologist," Lee answered. "He came down to the UES—hell, this was before it was even the UES. He came to warn us about the hordes of infected that were migrating south out of the northeastern city centers."

"I figured he died," Gale said, a little flummoxed. "Did you know him?"

"No," Lee lied. "Just knew *of* him."

Gale nodded slowly. "Well. Seems like we have a lot in common, Jax. So, let me ask you…"

She cut herself off as the sound of shouts from outside reached them.

Lee immediately twisted in his seat to look at Abe, and in the same instant, heard a sort of vibratory hum in the air.

Abe was hunched, looking through the window, but with his eyes clearly on the sky.

Lee stood up. "That sounds like a—"

"Fuck!" Abe spun, his eyes wide. "Get down!"

The next thing Lee knew, the living room became a whirlwind of wood, glass, and drywall dust, everything exploding inwards to the sound of an ungodly amount of heavy projectiles keening through the air, pulverizing the couch into bits of fabric and fluff, and chewing up the floorboards.

Marie launched herself across the table, tackling Gale to the ground, using her body armor to protect the stranger.

Lee dropped as the flurry of incoming rounds tore through the house like a massive buzzsaw. He felt the air pop over his head as big projectiles created small sonic booms, still moving well over the speed of sound, even after slamming through the side of the house.

Debris peppered Lee's face and neck as he gasped, jerking his head to the left and seeing Gale's gunmen and hybrids come apart, bodies hurled back by the force of the impacts, limbs flying every which way, sending streamers of blood arcing through air that'd turned to red mist.

Lee's first conscious thought was *Minigun!*

Nothing else could throw a wall of lead like that.

The instant after he thought that, he heard the roar of a helicopter going over head—not the deep, throaty rumble of a Blackhawk, but the cicada-like chatter of an AH-6M Little Bird.

The second the strafing fire ceased, Lee was on his feet, staggering towards Marie and Gale. He cast a glance over his shoulder and saw Abe scrambling up from where he'd hit the floor near the window, glass and wood falling off of him as he stood. On the other side of the living room Jones was coming up to his knees.

Jones's eyes locked on Lee's and he shouted, "Get 'em out of here!"

Then he hurled himself through the shattered window he'd been guarding.

Lee stumbled into Marie as she wrestled herself off of Gale. The woman on the ground was coughing like the wind had been knocked out of her. Her eyes were wild and terrified.

Lee grabbed one of Gale's arms, and Marie grabbed the other, yanking her to her feet and immediately pushing her for the front door. She squirmed in their grip, not exactly fighting them, but trying to see the destruction that had been wrought on her friends.

Lee saw movement in the tangle of bodies, and knew *some* of them must still be alive. He thrust Gale and Marie towards the front door, catching a glimpse of Sam struggling to his feet on his wounded leg.

"Get into the woods!" Lee bellowed at anyone that could hear him, then spun around.

Abe practically knocked him over coming down the hall. "It's coming around again!" he shouted, as the sound of the Little Bird's rotors started to rise again. Abe shoved at Lee, trying to move him for the door, but Lee batted his hands away.

"Grab a survivor first!" Lee belted out, then dove for the writhing mass of blood and limbs.

BWAAAHHH came the sound of the minigun again, but the rounds weren't punching into the house. They were strafing the people outside in one long, protracted burst.

The first limb Lee grabbed was an arm that was not attached to anyone. He threw it to the side, then grabbed a fist-full of bloody shirt and jerked the wearer up—but there was nothing left of the man's face. He almost dropped the body back, but saw a woman pinned beneath him, and her eyes were open and she was gasping for breath.

Lee heaved the dead man to the side. The woman immediately thrust a hand out to Lee. He grabbed it and pulled her up. Then he noticed her other arm was gone at the elbow. She didn't appear to notice at first, but as Lee looped her good arm over his shoulders to support her, she looked groggily down at her shredded appendage and began wheezing.

"Where'd it go?" she whimpered as Lee started moving for the front door. She resisted, twisting around, trying to go back to the pile of carnage. "I needa find my arm!"

Lee ignored this and kept going, her dazed resistance not enough to keep him from hauling her out of there.

Abe was right behind him, hustling a hybrid male along with him who was clutching a bleeding stomach with both hands.

They got halfway to the front door before Lee heard the screech of multiple rockets being fired, one after the other. He felt everything in him clench at the sphincter-puckering noise and the destruction he knew would follow.

The blasts rocked him like sledgehammer blows to his back, taking the air out of his lungs and thrusting him forward. He felt things hitting the back of his armor, and he lost his feet. A wall of smoke overtook him as he pitched forward, and something clocked him in the back of his head.

He must've lost consciousness, because the next thing he knew he was much closer to the front door, crawling for it on all fours. He could see his rifle and pistol to the side of the door where he'd left them. Still stunned, he just wanted a fucking weapon in his hands, not even registering the fact that it would be useless against a Little Bird.

The woman.

Shit! The woman!

Lee stopped, still on hands and knees, and turned.

The woman was back a handful of yards, lying face down, unmoving. Beyond her, the entire living room area of the farmhouse was gone, shrouded in a fog of acrid smoke.

The hybrid male with the belly wound shambled past, growling, his eyes senseless.

Where the fuck was Abe?

Lee heaved himself to his feet and tottered back to the woman, though his eyes searched the wreckage for the body of his friend, his heart pounding in his throat with a dread he didn't even realize could still grip him.

He dropped stiffly to one knee, ramming his fingers into the woman's neck, feeling for the pulse of her carotids.

A collapsed section of wall shifted, and Lee heard a groan of effort. Abe emerged from the wreckage, blood staining his bared teeth, a trail of whitish snot clinging to his beard. He was coated in a fine layer of drywall dust, making the blood leaking from a scalp wound all the more livid.

"You good?" Lee croaked.

Abe glanced at him as he shuffled for the door, and for an instant, it was like Abe didn't even recognize him. He just grunted and kept going. Lee knew he must've been barely conscious or he would've stopped to help Lee with the woman.

Except Lee was not feeling a pulse.

Rotors screamed overhead, along with another burst of revving-chainsaw-noise as the minigun blazed.

Lee swore, then woozily stood up, abandoning the woman's body. His feet churned awkwardly into motion, but his faculties were coming back in a steadily-increasing flow as his jangled brain rebooted itself.

He lunged for his weapons, grabbing both and then tumbling out the door.

Daylight speared his eyes, making most of the world too bright to see. All he registered was the shadows of the woods ahead. He just needed to get there. The defoliated trees would only offer minimal concealment, and almost nothing in the way of cover against the helicopter's minigun, but it was better than being pinned down in a house.

Right?

Maybe his brain *wasn't* working quite right at that moment. But rather than stutter with indecision, Lee trusted his initial instincts and broke into a sprint for the woods.

He could see people running ahead of him. None of them were his team.

His head whipped around, searching for the tell-tale visual of their armored torsos, but all he saw were Gale's people, fleeing headlong away from the farmhouse.

Lee jerked his head up, in the direction of the rotor noise.

There that little bitch was—the machine known as a "Killer Egg" was in sideward hover, moving in a clockwise circle as it pummeled the forest with 7.62mm rounds, brass and links falling in a cloud from its minigun.

It went right over Lee's head as he ran. Scalding shell casings clattered over him, a few managing to slip into his collar and burn the skin of his back.

Lee didn't want to get the damn thing's attention, but he couldn't let the fucker just keep strafing. As he ran for the woods, he jammed his pistol into its holster, then shouldered his rifle, flicked the select fire to full auto, and dumped his entire mag at the Little Bird's underbelly.

He didn't know how many times he'd struck the helicopter, or if he'd actually done any damage, but it certainly distracted the pilot for a moment. The minigun stopped and the Little Bird juked, corrected itself, then began to rotate towards Lee.

Yeah, he was just full of great ideas at the moment.

Hopefully he'd saved a few lives with that stunt, but now he had the pilot's full attention, and it was never a good thing when someone with a minigun finds your existence offensive.

Lee hit the woods before the Little Bird completed its rotation, and he didn't stop, plunging headlong through the trees and brush, breath scraping in and out of raw lungs. He reloaded as he ran, hoping against hope that he'd manage to get some concealment before the pilot targeted him. The forest was filled with running figures, and Lee's only defense at that moment was the protection of a herd animal—scatter, and pray the lion chooses a different gazelle.

The minigun belched and Lee instinctively ducked his head, fully expecting to be dismembered by a flurry of bullets. He heard them shredding the woods to his left. Glanced over and saw a cluster of four people go down like they'd been tackled from behind. He couldn't tell whether they were humans or hybrids, but none of them moved after they hit the dirt, so Lee just kept running.

The minigun's bursts became more sporadic. Lee noticed that they were fading back. He was gaining distance, and the Little Bird seemed to be holding its position over the mutilated farmhouse.

Lee hazarded a glance over his shoulder and spotted the shape of the small, black helicopter from between the tangle of tree limbs. Then he saw another helicopter in the distance, but it was too far to see what kind it was.

What the hell was happening here? Ron had told them they had four days before any military action was to take place. Had the strike force jumped the gun? Or was this something else? Like the ambush last night?

Were they just trying to kill *him*?

He kept his pace through the woods for another few hundred yards. By then his mangled hip was screaming with cramps and he had a full dose of lactic acid coursing through his legs. He slowed to a jog, gasping.

"Lee—Jax!"

He spun, and saw Marie off to his right a few dozen yards. Gale was with her, as was a few of Gale's people—humans and hybrids alike. Abe was loping up from behind, looking about as gassed as Lee.

Lee hoofed it over to them, glancing warily at Gale, and wondering if she'd caught Marie's slip-up. But if she'd noticed Marie call him by his real name, she didn't show it. Her eyes were stricken with tears and terror. She was bleeding from a series of small cuts on her face—probably from the windows getting blown in.

"You alright?" Lee asked Marie as he reached them, giving the woman a once over and seeing no obvious injuries—new ones, anyway.

Her face screwed up. "I'm fine. You're bleeding all over the fucking place."

Lee looked down at himself, but didn't see any blood. Marie grabbed him by the shoulders, having to reach up because he was so much taller than her, and pulled his head down.

"It's your scalp," she said, her alarm turning to relief. Lee remembered getting hit in the back of the head by something after the Little Bird had unloaded a salvo of rockets on the farmhouse. "I'll look at it later," Marie hurried on. "We need to get the fuck out of here. Gale—you need to get us to Appomattox!"

Lee straightened after Marie's inspection of his head and looked at Abe as he met up with them. He was also bleeding from a head wound, but it must not have been too bad, since his eyes were sharp and hard as they hit Lee's.

"Where's Sam and Jones?" Abe demanded.

"You didn't see them?" Lee said by way of an answer.

"Shit," Abe spat, craning his neck to look back in the direction of the farmhouse. Lee followed his gaze, but there was nothing to see. Anyone that had taken off running was already past them. Lee couldn't even see the helicopters anymore—could only hear their rotors.

"Gale!" Marie said in a sharp tone, as though she was snapping the woman out of something. "We need you to take us back to your settlement!"

Lee interjected himself with an arm across Marie's chest. "Hang on. If those birds were gunning for us, we might not want to—"

Gale was already shaking her head. "They weren't gunning for you," she snapped, her voice rife with bitterness. "Fucker's have us cordoned off—anyone caught going in or out of this area has been getting shot up. This isn't the first time." Grief clenched her features, and she bent at the waist as though feeling some terrible pain in her guts. "Fuck! I didn't realize we'd gone out of the cordon! I thought we were still in our own goddamn territory!"

"Alright," Lee said, trying to affect some calm. "Marie, go on with Gale and head for the settlement. I'm gonna go back and check for Sam and Jones."

Abe grabbed him as he started to turn. "The fuck you're not."

"I can't—"

Abe's fingers had the collar of Lee's armor and he gave Lee a violent shake as though to jar the stupid out of him. "Everyone scattered! You have no fucking clue where they are. Best bet is to head for Appomattox. If Sam and Jones are still alive, they'll be heading that way."

Lee swore, knowing Abe was right. As much as he hated to run away without knowing where they were, it'd be flat-out idiotic to run back towards those two helicopters. Sam and Jones were smart. They'd know to head for the settlement if they got out of there in one piece.

Then he remembered something called a radio.

Christ. That blow to his head must've really knocked his senses out for him to forget something like that.

He immediately keyed up. "Sam or Jones. Sam or Jones. Can either of you copy?"

"I already tried," Abe said.

Lee could hear Marie moving Gale and her small crew of survivors away. Abe followed. "Come on, brother. Let's fucking go."

Lee hissed through clenched teeth, then spun and followed the others.

Chapter 14

Jones had thrown himself through the window to get out of the farmhouse. Unfortunately, he'd really committed to that head-first dive. He'd intended to tuck and roll, but only managed to land square on his back.

That had rearranged a few discs.

The second that the shock of the impact dissipated, he'd sworn and started scrambling to his feet. Then he'd heard the Little Bird roaring overhead, and thought better of it. The pilot was blazing away with that minigun of his, splattering anyone that was running. Jones didn't want to be one of them, and decided to make himself very small, hiding between the foundation of the house and a massively-overgrown holly bush.

Then he heard the screech of rockets, said "Aw, fuck!" and barely managed to throw his arms over his head before the whole section of the house he'd just been standing in went up.

The explosions kind of felt like the impact of falling flat on his back, if you could fall flat on your back a half dozen times in a second.

His brain went to whiteout as it was overwhelmed by the pummeling. The explosions melded into a single, apocalyptic roar that became his entire universe for an indeterminate amount of time.

He had no idea how long he'd been out, but when he opened his eyes, the world was spinning in nauseating loops, and he was choking and hacking on the smoke. He couldn't make sense of what he was seeing—all was darkness, except for one blinding light ahead of him.

Oh, shit, he thought. *I'm fucking dying.*

Honestly, he felt a little relieved. This simulation had been bullshit.

But then, if he was dying, why was he smelling the stink of high-explosives? Why was he choking on the smoke? Why was he feeling pain in his back?

He thought the transition out of this plane of existence was supposed to be peaceful and painless. So far, it was definitely not painless, and as for peaceful—well, he could still hear the fucking Killer Egg overhead, and the sound of its minigun spitting.

Oh, shit, he thought. *I'm NOT fucking dying.*

Well. He better do something then. Because as long as you're still in the simulation, you had to keep fighting. Those were the rules.

He tried to move and found himself pinned.

That's when the darkness and the blinding light ahead suddenly made sense.

He was buried in rubble, looking at daylight ahead.

He tested his limbs to find if any weren't fully pinned. Seemed he could move his right leg and his left arm just a bit.

He had a brief memory of his older brother pinning him down and dangling a gob of spittle over his face. Anytime that fucker drank a glass of milk, Jones knew what was coming next. Nothing gave his brother such delight as having a mouthful of milky mucous, so he could issue a thin rope of what looked to child-Jones like alien slime, letting it stretch from his pursed lips until it almost touched Jones's cringing nose, and then sucking it back up into his mouth, cackling.

Oh, the panic he'd felt in those moments. The claustrophobia of the powerless.

So Jones did exactly what he'd done as a pinned-down, tortured child: He began thrashing with everything he had, punching, kicking, contorting, writhing, trying to create some space to work with under the rubble.

The rubble was unforgiving. Nails and jagged ends of wood caught him and jabbed at him. The claustrophobia of it made Jones not care—he just kept going until he got that left arm up over his head, reaching for the daylight.

He watched the sunlight touch the skin of his hand, seeming to make it glow like the sudden hope in his chest. He grabbed the lip of the opening and tried to pull himself toward it, but whatever had him pinned wasn't giving him up that easy. The debris he'd gripped with his left hand felt a little loose—not quite so weighty as the rest. So he shoved it instead, and was rewarded with more daylight as a broken section of farmhouse wall fell away.

He heard voices. Shouting. They were close by.

"Hey!" he screamed, his voice ragged, as he waved that hand in the daylight. "I'm fuckin' stuck! Help me out!"

He wasn't sure if he'd been heard, but then a moment later, he felt the debris covering him shift, as people began pulling sections off. They were calling out to him, but nothing they said made sense to Jones's ringing ears.

The daylight began to expand.

Yes! They were gonna get him out of this hell-hole!

Hands grabbed onto his and pulled. He felt sharp things gouge at his legs, catching on the fabric of his pants and raking painfully over his leg. He didn't care. He just wanted to be free.

Then he was out, splashed in daylight so blinding white that he knew his eyes were still affected by the explosions—still fully dilated after having the sense knocked out of him.

Then someone shouted, "Don't move!"

Jones squinted into the light and saw fuzzy shadows around him. He blinked rapidly, and tried to roll onto his belly so he could get his hands and knees under him.

Then he felt an impact to his ribs and flopped onto his back again.

What the fuck? Some asshole had just *kicked* him?

"Hey! Fucking stop—"

At that point, his vision cleared just enough that he realized he was staring into the muzzle of a rifle. He froze, blinked rapidly, then looked at the wielder of that weapon.

He saw a man in OCP fatigues glaring down at him.

"Don't move!" the man repeated, though there was something very odd about the way he spoke. Or maybe Jones's ears were too busted?

"Alright, okay, chill out!" Jones managed, bringing his hands up and realizing that he hadn't been saved by friendlies. Hadn't been saved at all.

He was being fucking captured.

Then he saw a buttstock flying at his face, and everything went dark.

Sam lay in a section of thick brush, fifteen yards from the front of the farmhouse.

Just before the rockets struck, he'd followed Marie out of the house. And rapidly realized that he couldn't sprint as fluidly as he thought on a calf that had a bullet hole in it. He'd gotten in four or five loping strides before a massive cramp seized his leg—not just the calf, but going all the way up into his thigh as well.

This had happened at a very inopportune moment, when Sam had a full head of steam, trying to get to the woods. Mid-stride, his leg suddenly decided not to bend, and he pitched forward onto his face.

He'd started to rise, but then a blaze of fire from the Little Bird's minigun chopped the weeds overhead, strafing into the forest. He decided to stay in the dirt for a moment.

That moment had become several as the helicopter circled overhead. It wasn't pursuing the fleeing people into the woods, but instead stuck to the clearing around the farmhouse.

Sam became certain that the second he got to his feet, he'd be seen and chewed to shreds.

So he'd waited, trying to control his breathing as his heart slammed. Hissing in pain as the cramp in his leg reached an agonizing peak, and then began to loosen up.

Then he heard another helicopter. He instantly recognized the deep, drumbeat sound of a Blackhawk's rotors. Shit, this was bad.

By then, the Little Bird was no longer firing its minigun—just circling overhead, like a wasp guarding its nest.

Sam was on his stomach, trying to go unnoticed, but he needed to get eyes on the threat. He couldn't wait there forever. He'd have to make a move at some point in time. So, he rolled onto his back and slowly eased himself up to try and see over the weeds.

He could see the belly of the Little Bird, directly over the house.

He could also see a Blackhawk coming into a hover over the brushy field, its side doors open, and a squad of troops in OCP fatigues ready to deploy. The Blackhawk began to lower itself to the ground, not far from the destroyed back-end of the farmhouse.

Sam squirmed around, keeping the Blackhawk in view while he tried to get his feet under him, all while staying concealed.

The Blackhawk touched down, and the troops disgorged, several moving to secure a perimeter, while several others moved into the wrecked farmhouse. Three of them peeled off just before entering the back of the house. Sam couldn't tell what they were focused on, but they began yelling and pointing their rifles at something.

Sam glanced to the Little Bird, but it seemed to be focused on the woodline, not the field, so Sam decided to risk coming up a little bit more. Peering through the brush, he saw the three soldiers around a pile of debris on the side of the house. Two of them were pointing their rifles at the rubble, while the third pulled big chunks of wall out of the way.

With the helicopters' rotors still chopping away at the air, Sam could just hear their shouts, but not what they said.

Then he saw one of them haul something out of the rubble. More shouting and pointing of rifles. Then one of the soldiers stepped in and loosed a mean buttstroke on something. Then the two others bent down and grabbed something.

When they came up, Sam saw the limp body of Jones hanging between the two soldiers as they hauled him for the Blackhawk.

Oh, shit.

Oh, SHIT!

He had a stupid instinct to charge in firing and try to save his friend. He even started to rise, shouldering his M249...only to remember it was just him. And there were five soldiers standing around, looking for something to put holes into.

The three soldiers that had captured Jones thrust him into the Blackhawk and immediately set to stripping, searching, and restraining him. One of them pulled a black sack out of their pocket and slapped it over Jones's head.

This was bad. This was *really fucking bad.*

Then Sam remembered something else.

All their packs, all their supplies—they were still in the farmhouse.

More important than supplies: Their satellite phone was still in there, packed away in Lee's rucksack.

Without the satphone, they had no contact with the outside world. They could not call for extract. They were dead in the water.

And, at that precise moment, there were five soldiers in the farmhouse. He didn't know whether they were just searching for live bodies to put down, or if they were searching for something else, but if they found the satphone, he had no doubt that they'd take it, and then Sam and his whole team would be way up shit creek.

Jones had just been captured.

Marie had hightailed it into the woods.

Sam thought he'd seen Lee and Abe sprint past shortly after he'd fallen.

There was no time to hail them and come up with some sort of plan.

No one was coming to help. It was up to him.

Or, as Lee liked to say: *Do or die time.*

Swearing under his breath as he accepted this, Sam began to crawl through the brush, back towards the farmhouse. Doubts began to swarm his head like gnats. He was one fucking guy with a wounded leg. He was going to try to be stealthy, but he also had to be fast, and no matter which way he cut it in his mind, he was going to end up going toe-to-toe with those bastards inside the house.

Maybe this was dumb. Maybe he shouldn't—

No, he told himself. *Just go. Just do what you gotta do.*

His heart raced as he reached the front of the farmhouse. For a few beats, he lay there, almost clutching the ground. The ground felt safe. He didn't want to let it go.

Focus. He needed to focus on the task.

Get inside. Find the satphone. Get the fuck out. Kill anyone that got in the way.

His M249 was fully loaded with a fresh belt of two hundred rounds. Only hostiles remained in the house. He didn't need to target ID. That simplified things: If anything so much as moved, he just had to put it down. It actually gave him an edge. The soldiers inside might have a bare moment's hesitation as they tried to determine if he was friend or foe. He would have no such hesitation.

It was a small comfort.

He lurched to his feet and scrambled up the front steps as quietly as he could with his wounded leg. The door hung open. No threats were visible.

The Little Bird had retreated from overhead, and the house was blocking some of the Blackhawk's rotor noise, so Sam could hear voices and things being tossed around inside the house.

He immediately moved to the side of the front door, his breath heaving despite his best efforts.

Calm. He needed to be calm.

Be cold. Be pragmatic. Be ruthless.

Slow and smooth, like none of this shit mattered.

He took a few more deep breaths, as though preparing to dive into icy waters, and then he pivoted and plunged through the front door.

The front door opened on a short hall with bedrooms and bathrooms on either side. On the other end of that hall was the kitchen, and then the living room. He could see a soldier's back as he bent over to sift through some rubble.

They were still poking through the wreckage of the exploded living room.

Sam didn't stop—couldn't stop, because he was exposed, and there was no place to hide in the atrium. He aimed himself for one of the bedroom doors, trusting the background racket to hide the thumping of his stiff leg.

The bedroom door was open to his left. That's where they'd been sleeping. Their rucks should be in there.

Eyes fixed on the back of the soldier straight ahead of him, willing the man not to turn around and spot him, Sam slipped into the bedroom door.

And found two soldiers inside, rifling through their rucksacks.

There came the strangest moment where Sam felt like his heart had just stopped completely. Feedback filled his brain, as he looked at the two soldiers, and both of them straightened, turning towards him, their expressions saying they clearly expected one of their teammates. That instantly changed to alarm as they realized they did not recognize the man standing there with a light machine gun leveled on them.

Sam didn't even aim. He just pulled the trigger. The SAW belched out an ear-ringing cavalcade of automatic fire, the muzzle rising as Sam fought to keep it level. The first rounds stitched the ground at one of the soldier's feet, just as the man was trying to bring his rifle up. Then they climbed, eating up his legs and pelvis, shattering the structures that kept him standing.

Sam didn't let up on the trigger, but simply muscled the barrel down and swept it across to the second soldier, cutting him right across the midsection and sending him stumbling backwards.

The first guy hit the ground, but he was not out of the fight. Sam realized this right about the same instant that the guy slumped onto his side and fired. Sam felt the rounds smash into his chest plate, knocking him back.

He hit the wall with a thump, his SAW sending rounds into the ceiling.

He felt a bullet slice through his trapezius muscle, and knew without conscious thought that the guy was trying to track his bullets up into Sam's face. Instinct told him to go low, and he didn't question it—just let his legs out from under him.

His ass hit the ground as bullets pulverized the sheetrock where his head had just been. In the same movement, he rolled onto his side, mirroring the other man's position and directing his unended stream of fire down into the other guy's face, turning it to some bloody, shattered visage that was no longer human.

He heard a roar of effort, and jerked to look towards the second soldier. The man was now sitting against the far wall of the bedroom, his legs splayed, his rifle coming up. Sam saw blood spurting out of a hole in the guy's neck, but he was still fighting, his teeth bared.

Everything in Sam clenched as he realized he was not in a good position to maneuver. Nor was the man across from him. They were too close to each other to miss, so it came down to who could get a round off first.

But Sam had done what he'd been trained to do—everywhere his eyes went, his weapon tracked with them. So when he'd twitched to look at the soldier, he'd instinctively brought the M249 in line with his gaze.

The recoil of the machine gun into his shoulder was the best sensation he'd ever felt in his life. His rounds hit the soldier in the chest, neck, and head, killing him before he got a round off.

Sam didn't wait. Didn't take a breath. Didn't fixate on the bodies he'd created. His cover was blown—the other three would be coming. He scrambled to one knee, ripping the M249 up and pointing it at the wall that adjoined the living room. Sheetrock didn't stop shit—it might as well have been paper.

He squeezed the trigger and kept it depressed as he shot through the bedroom and into the living room, raking the automatic fire along the wall, from left to right, and then all the way over to the wall adjoining the hallway, creating a string of bullet holes at about waist-height.

He didn't stop there. They might've dove to the ground. He swept the machine gun back across the walls, now firing in rapid bursts so he could control the recoil a little better, pummeling the wall at knee height, and then doing it again even lower.

The sharp report of the M249 became a dull thud in his head as his eardrums gave up the ghost. The room was choked with gunsmoke and drywall dust.

Then the last of his ammunition belt went clattering through the M249's feeding mechanism, and the beast fell silent.

Two hundred rounds sure goes awful quick.

He heard the screaming of wounded men, and felt exultant.

Then he heard the pounding of footsteps coming down the hall, and felt panic.

"Fuck!" He thrust himself off the wall, trying to get clear of the bedroom door. There was no way in hell he could reload the M249 in time. Belt-fed weapons were fantastic for fire superiority, but they did not reload as quickly as mag-fed weapons.

He let the sling take his M249, and snatched up his pistol—a Glock 19.

Two pairs of boots stamped to a stop just outside the bedroom door.

Sam moved to his left, getting himself out of the "fatal funnel." At the same time, he fired through the wall to the left of the open bedroom door. He heard a grunt and a shout. A rifle appeared around the doorframe, blind-firing into the room. The rounds went wide, but Sam still flinched against the muzzle-blast, and fired his pistol through the doorjam.

The rifle retreated. Immediately after, a small, round object clattered through the door, skipping across the ground.

Sam leapt forward with a yelp, catching the grenade with the inside of his boot as though passing a soccer ball. He kicked it back through the door.

He barely had time to hunch his shoulders and turn his face away before the grenade went off. The pressure wave buckled the doorframe, and sent a geyser of smoke and shrapnel erupting into the room.

Sam felt the moment of action come upon him like an unstoppable wave, and he flew for the doorway, even as the smoke was still billowing through. He hit the doorway and cut the corner hard, his pistol tucked tight into his chest.

Through the haze of smoke, he saw two soldiers—one with his legs blown off at the hip, atop another that was scrambling to get out from under his comrade.

Sam started to punch out with his pistol, but his feet caught on something. He tripped, falling forward and landing on hands and knees over top of the two soldiers.

He got off a single round. It smacked into the floorboards just to the left of the live soldier's helmeted head. The guy lurched forward with a cry and clamped down on Sam's pistol. Sam fired again, the bullet punching out a chunk of the man's shoulder, but his hands gripped the slide too tight, and prevented the pistol from cycling.

Sam yanked the pistol back, but the guy wasn't letting go. Both of them snarling and thrashing, fighting for control of the weapon, with the dead man's body sandwiched between them.

The soldier shoved the pistol away from him, keeping a grip on it with one hand while the other rocketed up at Sam's face, delivering a palm-heel strike to his nose that turned his vision to sparkling stars. Then the guy's hand latched onto the flesh of Sam's face, clawing at him and trying to plunge a finger into his eye.

Sam was forced to squeeze his eyes shut as fingernails scraped over his eyelids. Blind, he roared and got his support hand up, slamming the forearm into the guy's hand that was still attached to his pistol. He raked backward and felt the pistol come free.

But it still had a dead round in the chamber.

Sam struck out with the pistol, clocking the guy in the forehead with the muzzle.

The fingers clawing at his eyes immediately relented. Sam wrenched his eyelids open just in time to see the guy snatch the pistol in both hands again and rip it off to the side, forcing Sam to sprawl out so he was practically face-to-face with the soldier.

All he saw was blood sheeting down the guy's face, and two, brilliant blue eyes staring back at him with ferocity and terror.

Sam's free hand scrambled about his rig as the guy twisted and writhed, trying to get the pistol out of Sam's grip. But Sam wasn't letting go. His free hand found the hilt of his fixed blade, right next to his mag pouches. He ripped it out and immediately rammed it down, only for the point to hit the guy's armor.

The soldier wasn't letting go of the pistol either, but he tried to use his elbow to swipe at the knife.

Sam slavered out some nonsensical curse, reared the knife back and plunged it into the guy's shoulder. The soldier didn't exactly scream so much as he mewled through his clenched teeth, and Sam felt his grip slacken on the pistol.

Immediately, Sam ripped his gun-hand back again, freeing the pistol.

The soldier twisted, actually trying to bite at Sam's knife hand. Sam ripped the blade out of his shoulder and slashed it across the soldier's face. The well-honed blade sliced into the man's cheek, rattling across his teeth.

In the same instant, Sam reached back with his pistol, got the rear sights hooked on his belt, and racked the dead round out.

The soldier got his hands on Sam's knife, heedless of the razor's edge as it cut into his palms.

Then Sam swept his pistol up and contact-shot him in the temple.

It was over instantly.

Gasping, Sam rolled, clattering his way to his feet. He kept the pistol trained on the two bodies for a second, then raised it towards the living room as he backpedaled through the bedroom door again.

He spun, looking over the two dead bodies in there, and the rucksacks on the ground.

There was Lee's. Sam didn't have time to search for the satphone—he'd just take the whole goddamn pack and figure it out later.

He heard voices from outside, and there was a distinct edge to them, but still, Sam couldn't make sense of anything they said. Didn't matter. He needed to grab the ruck and get out of there.

Hands shaking uncontrollably, Sam shoved the pistol back in his holster, the knife back in its sheath, then snatched up his M249. For an instant, he considered ditching the machine gun and snatching one of the dead soldier's rifles. But then he remembered he was all alone, and fire superiority might end up being his only saving grace.

He did not, however, have time to reload a full belt. Luckily, the M249 was designed to accept standard M4 magazines as well, which was a slightly-quicker reload. Sam shucked the spent ammo pouch from under the weapon, then slammed in one of the two spare rifle mags he'd been carrying for just this eventuality. He racked the charging handle and was ready.

Then he grabbed Lee's rucksack by one shoulder strap and headed for the door.

He took one brief glance down the hall towards the living room, but saw no threats. He exited the bedroom and took off, tearing through the front door and immediately diving into the brush.

He lay there heaving, his ears straining to hear the shouts of alarm that he was oh-so-sure were coming. But after a few seconds, they didn't come. No one had seen him exit the house.

Still prone, he worked his arms through the shoulder straps of the ruck and got it seated on his back. As soon as he did, a sharp stab of pain reminded him of the bullet hole in his right trapezius. But thank God for armor—nothing had penetrated his vitals, despite the fact that Sam knew he'd taken multiple, close-range rifle rounds to the chest.

He'd only been in the house for maybe a minute, from start to finish. But, holy fuck, he was gassed. That fight on the ground had taken a shocking amount of stamina. Now he had a sixty-pound ruck on his back, a twenty-pound machine gun in his arms, and fifty yards of low-crawling ahead of him.

"Fuck my life," he seethed, as he began crawling for the woods.

Every second of the next five minutes of misery, Sam expected to be spotted—if not by the soldiers, then by the Little Bird, which he could still hear chattering away overhead. All he could do was keep pushing forward, and keep praying that he would make it.

Stopping. Breathing raggedly into the dirt. Sweating buckets despite the chill air.

Then continuing on.

Elbows and knees raw from grinding across the ground. Leg wound smarting—trap wound smarting even worse. Lungs like fire.

Just keep moving.

He hit a tangle of briars, and had no choice but to go right through them. The damn things were almost as bad as barbed wire. Thorns raked across his exposed face and hands, snagging on his clothing, slowing his progress.

Just keep moving.

Then he was in the woods.

He didn't stop crawling until he reached a slight swale. Exhausted, he forced himself to go on hands and knees for another twenty yards, then peeked back over his shoulder to discover a decent bit of undergrowth between him and the enemy. Only then did he dare to rise to his feet, though he still kept himself low to the ground, scrambling between points of cover and concealment.

It took nearly twenty minutes to get to a point where he felt safe enough to stand.

He paused before he did that, taking a moment to lean against a tree and catch his breath. Then he figured he'd better confirm he actually got the satphone. He hadn't had time to search the bodies, and now a nightmare scenario came to his mind, as he imagined that one of them had already found the satphone and pocketed it, and all that Sam had just done had been pointless.

He slung the ruck off and plunged inside, alternately swearing and praying under his breath.

His hands hit hard polymers. He drew it out.

Satphone.

He breathed a heavy sigh of relief.

Good. Great. It hadn't all been for nothing.

He stuffed it back in the ruck, then got the pack seated on his shoulders again.

Now all he had to do was find his way through primal-infested territory, and try to link up with his team. Were they still alive? Had the situation at the farmhouse solidified their alliance with the people of Appomattox, or had it only made things worse?

Sam reached for his PTT, but stopped before pressing it.

Jones had been captured. Shit.

These soldiers were obviously professionals. They would've taken the radio from Jones, and if they had half a brain—which Sam was certain they did—they'd be listening.

Sam realized he hadn't heard anyone transmit. Then realized his earpiece had fallen out somewhere along the line. He got it back in his ear and listened for a moment, hoping that the surviving members of his team weren't giving themselves away over compromised comms.

He heard nothing. Which was good in a way, but he hoped whoever was still alive was listening.

He pressed the PTT and spoke in a calm, businesslike voice: "Point Break. Point Break. Point Break." Then he waited about twenty seconds and repeated it.

That was their code for compromised comms. Assuming they'd heard, everyone would switch their radios to a pre-programmed secondary channel. That didn't magically make their comms secure again, as the process to switch channels wasn't difficult to figure out, but it gave them an extra layer of obfuscation. If something urgently needed to be said, they could use that channel, but with coded language.

Asking the rest of his team for directions to Appomattox would be difficult to do using coded language, and it also didn't rise to the level of an emergency.

He knew he needed to head west. Judging by the moss growing on the north side of the trees, Sam oriented himself. Then he swapped out the thirty-round rifle magazine in his SAW for another two-hundred round belt.

Praying he wouldn't have to use it, Sam pointed himself west and got to stepping.

Chapter 15

Lee reflected how odd it was that he could be so relieved to hear Sam's voice over the comms, and still be so worried about Jones.

They were hoofing it through the woods, still following Gale. A few of her people, both hybrid and human, had coalesced around her as they'd made their way, and their party was now fifteen strong, including Lee, Abe, and Marie.

"Should we switch off?" Marie asked about their radios.

Lee shook his head. "Negative. I wanna know if Jones tries to hail us."

Abe made an uncertain noise in the back of his throat. "I think Jones mighta got snatched."

Lee didn't contradict his partner. He'd had the exact same thought process. Their comms were encrypted, and while that didn't make them completely crack-proof, it would take a helluva lot of computing power to decrypt their net—more than he thought would be available to the strike force. Which meant the only way Sam might've known that their comms were compromised was if he'd seen one of their radios fall into enemy hands.

One possibility was that the strike force had recovered the radio that Gale had dumped in the field along with Kat's armor and clothing.

Another possibility was that Sam witnessed Jones getting taken captive.

On the one hand, that was a relief in and of itself: It meant that Jones was alive.

On the other hand, it made Lee mighty fucking pissed.

This strike force had wounded two of his teammates and snatched a third. They were officially cruising for a bruising.

Then there was the issue of Kat. While Lee didn't feel the same depth of emotion as he did for the team that'd been with him through thick and thin for years on end, he did feel personally responsible for her.

What the hell had happened to her? Why had she decided to strip off her clothes? Had she gone native and abandoned them? Or was there some other part to this that he wasn't seeing yet?

A strange whistle echoed through the woods. The entire party rocked to a halt. Lee, Abe, and Marie immediately raised their rifles in a defensive posture, but Lee noticed that none of Gale's people did the same.

Instead, Gale cupped her hands over her mouth and hollered, "It's Gale! We got three strangers coming in with us!"

Shapes melted out of the woods, emerging from positions of concealment about thirty yards ahead. Several armed humans, along with several hybrids.

Christ—how many hybrids were living in Appomattox? There seemed to be as many of them as there were humans.

"Gale!" a man cried out, running forward. He was armed with a shotgun and wearing a bright red jacket.

Lee couldn't see Gale's face, but he could see the way her shoulders slumped with relief as the man trotted up, worry sketched all over his features.

"What the hell happened?" the man demanded, putting a hand on Gale's shoulder. "We heard fucking helicopters and guns and explosions—where's the rest of your people?"

Gale shook her head slowly. "They hit us out by that old farmhouse. I didn't...I didn't realize it was outside the cordon zone."

"Aw, Jesus, Gale!" The guy spotted Lee and his two teammates and stiffened. "Who the fuck are they?"

Gale turned to look at them, her face drawn, and her eyes red. She'd clearly been crying, and Lee couldn't blame her. A lot of her people had been torn up back at the farmhouse. "It's okay. They're not with the military." She fixed her gaze on the man in the red jacket again. "We found a pile of clothing and some tactical armor with a radio on it. Baba tracked the scent back to the farmhouse. That's why we were there. That's where we met these people. There were two others, but they didn't make it out."

Her voice drew down, nearly to a whisper that Lee's still-ringing ears could barely decipher. "Greg, they say they've got a hybrid on their team. They said she was the one wearing the armor and clothes we found. Baba confirmed that the scent came from a hybrid."

The guy in the red jacket—Greg, apparently—pulled his head back as though he'd been slapped. "Wait. We found a hybrid. She was sneaking through the woods towards town."

Right about that instant, Lee didn't give a fuck about hurting anybody's feelings, and he stalked forward, shouldering through Gale's people to come right up to Greg and Gale.

Greg's face got all tight, and he took a step back, half-raising his shotgun as his eyes locked onto Lee. "Hey—don't come up on me like that, man."

Lee ignored him. "You say you found a hybrid? What'd she look like?"

Greg issued a flurry of blinks, eyes flicking from Gale to Lee. "I dunno, man. Uh...she had reddish hair. The fuck else you want me to say?"

"She give you a name?" Lee demanded.

Greg shook his head. "She wouldn't say shit. I had a handful of my people escort her back to town." His face screwed up. "Why're you comin' at me like this? Who the fuck—"

Lee turned to Gale. "I'm guessing that's Kat—our teammate." Then he whirled on Greg again, his one eye flashing with unholy fury. "Did you fuck with her?"

Greg didn't seem to understand. "Did I fuck with her? Whaddaya mean?"

"I mean did you end up fighting with her? Is she hurt?"

"No, she's not hurt. She was fine. Gale, who is this motherfucker?"

Gale intervened. Too tired and grief-stricken to be diplomatic, she put a hand on both of their chests and shoved them away from each other. "Both of you chill the fuck out. Greg, this guy's name is Jax." Then she skewered Lee with a highly-offended look. "And who the fuck do you think you are charging up here and demanding answers of us? If it hadn't been for your people fucking around where you shouldn't be, we wouldn't be in this fucking mess!"

Lee dipped his head and took his foot off the gas. "Apologies. If it's any consolation, we're not having loads of fun either. None of us expected to be in the situation we're in, but here we are." He looked at Greg. "Sorry for comin' in a little hot there. Just worried about my teammate is all."

Greg gave him another long look, then said, "S'alright," and turned to Gale. "We need to get back to town. Judy's freakin' the fuck out. You sure you're comfortable with taking these people in there?"

Gale turned so both she and Greg were now facing Lee and the others. "Well, they're clearly not with the military. The helicopter was trying to kill them too." She looked at Greg, her expression pinching a bit. "They say they were hired by someone to...rescue the scientists."

Greg got very stiff. His eyes darted between Gale and Lee. "We don't know anything about—"

"He already knows," Gale interrupted.

Greg swallowed. "Knows what?"

Gale shook her head. "This is a conversation for them to have with Judy."

"How do you know they're not here to kill Judy?" Greg thrust a hand at Lee, talking about them like they weren't standing right there. "Maybe this is all just a trick to get inside and take her out."

Abe had clearly had enough and stepped forward. "Look. Greg. Gale. I hate to burst your bubble, but the military doesn't need us to infiltrate your compound to kill this Judy lady of yours. Fuckssake, they just sent a Little Bird with a minigun after us. Pretty sure if they wanted to kill Judy, they could do it without a bunch of subterfuge. Gale, you already went over all this shit with Jax when we were back at the farmhouse. Do we gotta go over it again?"

Gale bowed her head, sighing deeply. "He's right, Greg. We don't have time to go over every bit of it right now—I need you to just trust that I did my due diligence. The rest of it's up to

Judy. So let's just keep them under guard and take them into town."

Greg looked aghast. "Keep them under guard? They're armed to the fucking teeth!"

Abe's grip on his rifle got a little tighter. "And we're gonna fuckin' stay that way. Don't know if you've noticed, but there've been a lot of bullets flying around these parts."

"I don't trust them," Greg stated.

Gale leaned into him and spoke in a low voice. "Greg. They fought with the UES."

Greg's face transformed. All at once, his suspicion and hostility turned to something much more akin to hero-worship. "Like...with Lee Harden and shit?"

"We didn't know him personally," Lee said quickly. "But yeah, we fought with the UES."

Greg mulled that over for a moment, a bit of the suspicion coming back to his eyes. "Tell me something only someone from the UES would know."

Lee chuckled in humorless frustration. "How the fuck am I supposed to know what rumors got this far north? Half the shit you think you know probably ain't even true."

"I knew Lee Harden," Marie suddenly declared.

Lee turned and gave her a strong warning look.

Tread carefully, Marie.

Marie acknowledged his look with a tiny nod, then raised her chin at the others. "I worked with him on several occasions, back before it was even called the United Eastern States. Back when it was just the Camp Ryder Hub. Frankly, he was an asshole that put his mission above everything and everyone else." Marie took a step forward. "You probably heard all kinds of white-knight hero bullshit about him. But I bet you never heard that he took one of his own men that'd double-crossed him and burned his face off on a stove. I bet you never heard that a group of people tried to oust him from power. He crushed their coup attempt, and let the people of Camp Ryder hold trials for some of the survivors, so that they could feel like there was still some justice in the world, but really, after every single individual was found guilty and banished from Camp Ryder, he was waiting in the woods to kill them. Left their bodies by the road to get eaten by the primals. He was a cold-hearted sonofabitch. But he was a good fighter." Marie squinted at Gale and Greg, her eyebrows arched. "So yeah, I gotta agree with Jax here. Whatever you think you know about the UES probably doesn't jive with what we remember from being there firsthand."

Lee stared at her, feeling slightly betrayed by what she'd said. He tried to tell himself that she was only trying to prove a point. But he wondered if that's really what she thought of him.

And hell, those things weren't even close to the worst things he'd done.

He directed his gaze to Gale and Greg. Then he shrugged. "It's true. Any other tales from bygone times you want us to relate?"

The two people from Appomattox regarded him for a long moment. Then they exchanged a series of hooded looks.

Finally, Greg seemed to relent. "Alright. We'll take you into town. But I shit you not—you pull anything that I even *slightly* don't like?" He made a gesture towards the hybrids surrounding their party. "No amount of firepower is going to save you."

Lee gave him a longsuffering look. "Should I get a list of things you *slightly* don't like? Or should I just assume you meant for us to be cooperative, but you wanted to say it real scary-like?"

Marie laid a hand on his arm. "Jax is an asshole too, by the way. But he means well."

Greg glared for a moment, then chuffed. "Whatever. Come on."

If Lee had felt it was strange to see all the hybrids surrounding the farmhouse, walking into Appomattox was positively surreal.

They were fucking everywhere.

As they stepped out of the woods and onto the blacktop of an old, neighborhood road, he could see a multitude of people out and about—many of them beginning to rubberneck. As he scanned over all the curious and suspicious faces, he noticed that for every few humans, he spotted a hybrid.

It also became jarringly clear that these hybrids were not segregated in any way. They were standing right alongside humans. Helping with chores. Hell, Lee even saw one of them holding a human toddler on their hip.

What the fuck was going on here?

Lee tried not to gawk, and turned his attention to the general layout of the place, and whether or not it looked like they were doing well, or just getting by. This was an assessment that Lee had done so many times at other settlements, he knew exactly what to look for.

Unlike many other settlements that Lee had been to, Appomattox was not overgrown with trees and brush. On the contrary, it seemed that every patch of dirt—lawns, medians, shoulders of roads—had been converted for crops. It was late fall now, so there wasn't much growing, but Lee saw the remnants of harvested corn stalks, pumpkin vines, now brown and wilted, and huge patches of what he thought had been sunflowers, though all their heads had been removed.

Several areas looked recently-tilled, and Lee could see the green fuzz of newly-sprouted grains coming up to overwinter.

The houses were in generally good repair, and it seemed every structure was occupied. Nearly every place he passed disgorged a multitude of bodies, so that it seemed everyone lived with another family, and every family was a mix of humans and hybrids.

Lee eyed them as he continued to follow Gale and Greg. He was curious if the obviously-extensive interbreeding was open to the point that he might see mixed human-hybrid couples. But most obvious pairs he saw were just the usual—human men and women.

So how the hell did they have so many damn hybrids?

It was a sticky issue that he didn't exactly feel comfortable asking Gale or Greg about. Perhaps when they met this Judy character, he might work the conversation around. Honestly, it was just a matter of curiosity for Lee, and had very little bearing on his mission.

Or did it?

Gale had said that the scientists were there to study *them*. To study their relationship with the three primal colonies, and, presumably, with the hybrids that populated the town as well.

Obviously, Lee was missing some crucial bit of information. Because if that's all the scientists were doing, then why had they been killed?

They crossed a street that looked like a main thoroughfare through the town. Looking north, Lee could see clusters of commercial buildings down the road a bit, though the area they were walking through was still mostly-residential.

"Nice setup you guys got here," Lee commented.

Gale nodded, tiredly. "It's worked out well for us. Better than most, as I hear."

"You guys have much contact with the outside world?"

"Not really. I guess after the UES blew all the bridges along the border of North Carolina and Virginia, we were kind of cutoff. No one was travelling north—not with all the hordes of infected coming south. And everyone further north of us was wiped out."

"Yeah, I gotta ask: How did you guys make it through that? I saw those hordes coming out of the northeastern city centers. There were millions of them."

Gale gave him a small smirk. "Primals."

Lee frowned. "They protected you?"

Gale sighed, then came to a stop in the middle of the street. "Wait here."

Lee found himself a little disgruntled by the hush-hush attitude of his hosts. What kind of dirty secrets were they trying to cover up?

But he supposed he couldn't complain too much. He'd managed to make contact with the people of Appomattox, and so far, aside from a little tension—which was to be expected—things seemed to be proceeding peacefully. That was step one in his plan to figure out what the hell was going on around here.

Gale and Greg left them surrounded by humans with guns, and hybrids with claws and teeth. They made for a cluster of people standing in a nearby driveway. In that cluster, there was a mix of humans and hybrids, which seemed to be the norm for this place. In the center of them, Lee caught a glimpse of a middle-aged woman with blonde hair fading to gray. She was small, but carried herself with authority and appeared to be issuing orders to the others.

Lee guessed that this was Judy.

Gale and Greg stopped at the outskirts of the group, waiting patiently as teams of three or four individuals at a time dispersed to some duty or another. The humans were armed, and every group of humans had at least one hybrid with them. After receiving their orders, they took off at a trot, and seemed to be heading south, towards the edge of town.

Once the entire group was gone, Gale and Greg stepped up to the lady and a brief conversation ensued, with a lot of pointing in Lee's direction. The lady listened, glanced at Lee a few times, asked a couple questions, and then started walking over, flanked by Gale and Greg.

As she drew closer, Lee saw that her face showed the signs of premature aging due to stress. She only looked to be about forty, but it was a gaunt and tired forty. She had cold, blue eyes that fixed on each of them in turn. There was no warmth or trust in that gaze. This was a person who'd been through it enough to know that everyone would fail her eventually.

She was surrounded by her own people, and yet she seemed totally alone.

The woman stopped right in front of Lee, hands stuffed into the pockets of a tan canvas jacket, faded and dirt-encrusted. The rest of her clothes seemed fairly clean though, and, all in all, she didn't seem like a dirty person. Actually, most of the people he'd seen—even the hybrids—seemed clean.

"You must be Jax," she said, her voice husky and rough, like she might've been a heavy smoker back in the day. Her accent sounded more cosmopolitan than country, though still with the slightest bit of southern twang in it.

"I am," Lee said. "You must be Judy."

The only confirmation she gave to this was a slow blink as she shifted her eyes to Marie, and then Abe. "And your friends here?"

Lee gestured to them in turn. "This is Marie, and this is Lincoln," he said, using Abe's pseudonym. Then he paused, wondering if a handshake would be called for, but Judy's hands remained firmly planted in their pockets.

Judy squinted at him. "Gale says you got a hybrid on your team. Kat, right?"

"That's right, ma'am. Greg mentioned she might be here."

Judy gave him a small nod. "Yeah. Come with me."

"One second," Lee interjected.

Midway into turning around, Judy stopped and arched an eyebrow at him.

"We got two other members of our team unaccounted for. One I know is alive, and he should be making his way here. His name's Sam."

Judy considered this for a long moment. "Okay. And what do you want me to do about that?"

"Well..." Lee glanced back the way they'd come. "I'd like for your people to keep an eye out for him and maybe *not* try to kill him when he shows up. He's gonna be kitted out like us, and I don't want them thinking he's with the military."

Judy tilted her head to one side. "Is he dangerous?"

"Not if you don't provoke him."

The ghost of a smile crossed her lips. She looked at Greg. "Grab a few people and spread the word along our picket line that we'll have another guest incoming. Jax, can you describe this Sam for us?"

"Five-eleven. Eighteen years old. Middle-Eastern. And there might be another guy—his name's Jones. Six foot. Blond hair. White. Both of them will have armor and weapons, but they'll be dressed in civilian clothes."

"You got all that, Greg?" Judy asked.

Greg nodded. "Got it."

She jerked her head, and Greg headed out, motioning for a handful of the humans and hybrids around them to follow.

"Anything else?" Judy asked, a bit impatiently.

"No, ma'am," Lee answered.

Judy simply turned and started walking towards the house she'd been standing in the driveway of.

Lee shared a look with Abe and Marie, then fell in step behind Judy.

"Can I ask where Kat is right now?" Lee queried the back of the woman's head.

She didn't turn. Just nodded at the house as they stepped into the driveway. "She's inside. She's fine. We found her some clothes." She gave Lee an odd look. "She always run around in the buff?"

"No, ma'am. Not sure why she thought it was a good idea this time."

"And how long has Kat been a part of your team, Mr. Jax?"

"It's just Jax. And she's been with us for...about forty-eight hours now. Give or take."

A concrete walk branched off from the driveway towards the front door. Judy started down this, but then stopped and turned, her weathered face getting an unpleasant look to it. Like she'd just figured something out, and it apparently didn't reflect well on Lee.

"Ah, I think I see," Judy said in a low tone. "So, you were sent to infiltrate my town, and you thought it'd be a bit easier if you had a hybrid in your crew. Make us think that you're just like us. That about the size of it?"

Lee heaved a sigh and folded his hands on the buttstock of his slung rifle. "You know, I think I see, too. You got a bit of a chip on your shoulder about how your people live their lives, and you think everyone's out to get you."

Lee probably should've been a bit less confrontational there, but he found himself pleased to see a little flare come to Judy's eyes. She was such a cold fish, he was just glad to see *any* emotion break through.

Judy sniffed loudly. "If I have a chip on my shoulder, Jax, it wasn't me that put it there. I have good reasons for seeing the world how I see it."

"I'm sure you do. But you don't know me from Adam. So save your judgment until you have the whole picture."

"Oh, brave words, Mister Army Man. So, I assume from your self-righteous airs that you haven't judged us yet? You're waiting to get the whole picture?"

Lee smiled. "Actually, I am. No judgment from me. If you think a bit of interbreeding is gonna shock me, well, that just goes back to my original point: You don't know me. As for Kat, you have it partially right, ma'am. Yes, we convinced her to help us out on this mission. But not so we could ingratiate ourselves with you."

"Then why?" Judy asked flatly.

"Because we were made aware that there were shit tons of primals in this area, and we thought Kat might help us not get chomped on."

Judy chuffed. "Oh my. You're an honest fellow, aren't you?"

Lee shrugged. "It's not always the best policy. Just usually."

"Good." Judy turned and began walking again. "I don't like being dicked around."

As they took the walkway to the front door, Lee noted that six of Gale's people were still following close behind—four humans with an assortment of firearms, and two rather large hybrid males. They stayed with them as they pushed into the atrium. Judy made no welcoming gestures, outside of leaving the door open behind her as she continued on deeper into the house.

Gale looked over her shoulder and motioned for them to follow.

Lee took a quick note of the house's layout. Upon entering, there was a wall to the left, which adjoined the two-car garage he'd seen on approach. To the right was a dining room. Ahead, a short hall that fed into the center of an open area—judging by the carpeting to the left, and the tiling to the right, he figured it was a living room and kitchen.

Judy reached the end of the hall and made a right into the kitchen.

Lee heard her say, "Your man Jax is here."

He turned into the kitchen, and discovered Kat sitting in a cozy little breakfast nook. Her head snapped to him, and she shot out of the nook to stand, looking guilty as sin. She wore an ancient-looking hoodie that was big enough to hang down to mid-thigh.

"Jax. I..." she began.

He held up a hand to forestall any further excuse-making, and gave her a once over. "How are you? Any new injuries?"

Kat shook her head, looking tense, as though waiting for the other shoe to drop.

Oh, it was coming. But Lee wanted to make sure she was alright before he got into that.

"How are those gunshot wounds from last night?"

"Fine."

"Alright. Good." He dipped his head a bit, looking her earnestly in the eyes. "I'm glad you're okay. You had us worried for a bit."

"I—"

"Now." Lee's voice switched from concerned to pissed-off in an instant. "Why in the fuck did you think it was appropriate to take off your radio? I'm not even gonna get into your clothes—that's your prerogative. But the radio? The armor? That's fucking *equipment*, and you don't leave *equipment* lying around all willy-nilly, and you certainly don't ditch your radio so your team has no fucking clue where you are or if you're even alive."

Lee had more that he would've liked to vent, but Judy's voice broke in from the side.

"Hey, Mister Big Dick."

He swiveled his eye to look at Judy.

She shook her head, gaze withering. "Don't talk to her like that."

Lee regarded her with an expression that said *Oh, you've got a set of balls on you, huh?* "All due respect, Judy—"

She issued a loud, derisive snort. "Every time someone says 'all due respect,' they follow it up with something disrespectful." She leaned towards Lee. "Don't disrespect me in my own home, Jax."

He could see that she was not scared of him whatsoever. He realized it wasn't because she thought she was invincible, or that she didn't think Lee was dangerous. She wasn't scared, because she was too tired to be scared.

That bled over into Lee, reminding him of how exhausted he was as well.

"All due respect," Lee repeated in a measured rhythm. "She's a member of my team, and I'll say whatever I deem appropriate to *my team*. We're not a fucking knitting group. We're a very small tactical team, and everyone has to be squared away, or we all get fucked."

Judy stared back with half-lidded eyes for a second, then nodded, once. "Alright. You do what you need to do, then." She pointed a warning finger at him. "But watch your language in this house."

Lee gave her a humorless smirk. "Will do, ma'am." Then he turned back to Kat and raised an eyebrow. "Well?"

Kat's large, copper eyes held his, unblinking. "You said you wanted me to get close. If I got close, I might be seen. If they saw me with clothes and armor and radio, they would think I was an enemy. If they saw me naked, they would only think I was a primal."

Lee sighed. "Yeah, and how'd that work out for you?"

Kat bobbed her shoulders. "Not good."

"Exactly."

Kat frowned. "I took a risk. It didn't work out." She quirked her head to one side. "This has never happened to you?"

Abe chuckled. "She got you there."

Lee nodded slowly. "Yeah, I guess she does. Alright." He looked to Judy again. "Ma'am, you mind if we take a seat? We're all a bit tired." That was an enormous understatement. None of them had gotten more than a few hours of sleep in the last forty-eight.

Judy's response was to move to the breakfast nook, sit on the detached bench, and wave a hand towards the bench seats that lined the corner of the kitchen. "Come on. We've gotta talk."

Chapter 16

The second Lee sat down at the breakfast nook, a wave of complete exhaustion washed over him. He sighed and grumbled and groaned as he situated his aching leg, and finally let the muscles of his core relax under the constant weight of his combat loadout.

He knew this sensation well. You could keep pushing and pushing, so long as you stayed moving. The second you became static, inertia enveloped you like a wooly mammoth in a tar pit.

He barely knew the people of Appomattox, but scrunched into the nook with Kat on his left and Abe and Marie on his right, Lee felt just safe enough that he thought if he closed his eyes, he'd probably fall asleep immediately.

First, get to the bottom of shit, he told himself. *Then, hopefully, get some sleep.*

He rested his hands on the table, shoulders slumped, and not really caring that he didn't cut the strongest figure at the moment. He looked across the table at Judy.

"You always nicer with strange hybrids than you are with strange people?" he asked.

"People lie," Judy said. "Hybrids don't."

Well, that's great, Lee thought, wondering how much sensitive information Kat had already spilled. "So, what has Kat told you about us?"

Judy gave a facial shrug. "Nothing different than you said yourself. You're not with the military. You were asked to come in and find out what happened to the scientists."

Gale was still with them, hovering over Judy's shoulder. The four humans and two hybrids that had escorted them into the house were hanging back, but still very much present.

Lee glanced them over, resting his gaze on Gale for a moment. "So...what happened to the scientists?"

Judy's thin lips formed a bitter smile. "Thought you already knew what happened to them."

"Well, we found a burn pit with some human bones in it."

Judy gave absolutely no reaction to this. Lee wouldn't have liked to play poker with her.

"Was that them we found in the burn pit?" Lee pressed.

Judy interlaced her fingers on the table and narrowed her eyes at him. "And if I told you that it was—what then?"

"Then I would ask why you decided to kill them."

"Who said I killed anyone?"

Lee rubbed his face. "Yeah. So, I get the impression not a whole lot goes down in Appomattox without your say-so. Am I wrong?"

"No."

"Well, there you have it." He pressed a forefinger into his gritty, burning eye. Released and squinted groggily at her. "Can we cut through the crap-cake, ma'am? I know this has the feel of a homicide investigation, but I ain't a cop, and you're not under arrest. Yes, I was sent to find out what happened to the scientists. But it sure seems like the people that brought us into this want us dead, so my focus has shifted. Now I wanna know the why of it all, so I can figure out how exactly to keep my team alive, and not become public enemies number one-through-six for the IAG."

"I understand that," Judy said. "And I can appreciate it. You seem like a good leader. I also try to be a good leader. Just like you, I want to keep my people alive. So, let me ask you this, Jax: Are our goals mutually exclusive?"

"No," Lee answered, honestly. "Frankly, we need your help right now, Judy."

"Oh? And what do we get in return?"

"Information that could keep your people alive. And six operatives that might be able to lend a hand when it comes to surviving—though in what aspect depends on what we're dealing with here."

Judy's expression hardened. "So you have information that could keep my people alive? And you're going to hold it back?"

"I could ask you the same question," Lee retorted. "Why'd you kill the scientists?"

Judy put her hands on the lip of the table and pressed herself back. She thought about it for a long moment, her inner machinations a mystery beneath her impassive face. Eventually, she turned a quizzical gaze on Kat.

"Is he telling the truth?" Judy asked the hybrid.

Kat seemed a bit surprised to be called upon. Then she frowned and leaned forward. "I *can* lie," she rasped. "I just choose not to. And yes. He is telling the truth."

Judy regarded Lee for another moment, drumming her fingers on the tabletop. Then, abruptly, she slapped them down and stood up. "I'll tell you what, Jax. You and your people look like you could use some shut eye. You have my word you're safe here."

Honestly, nothing had ever sounded better to Lee. But he was also getting a bit tired of the stalling. And while it was nice that Judy had given her word and all, trusting others was not a primary principle of survival.

"Judy," he heaved out. "I'd really like it if we could just handle the business end of things first."

Judy sniffed. "Well, the situation is very complicated, Jax. I have to talk to someone first, before we go exposing all our dirty little secrets to each other."

"Really? You gotta talk to someone? Because my impression was that you were the one running things around here."

"Your impression is correct. But some secrets are not mine to tell."

Lee huffed a disgruntled sigh, then checked his wristwatch. "Alright, Judy. I'm gonna do you a favor right now. I'm gonna give you some information on good faith, because it's germane to how much time you and your people are wasting dancing around with me." He did a quick calculation in his head, then looked up from his watch. "Seventy-nine hours."

Judy looked momentarily stymied. "Seventy-nine hours? Until what?"

"Until a strike force comes in here and turns Appomattox into one more ghost town out of thousands."

Judy's suntanned face got an unhealthy pallor to it. "What?" she practically choked the word out. "How do you know this?"

"Because I was told to have my team clear of this area before that time, or we were gonna get steamrolled with the rest of you."

Judy's immaculate poker face crumbled. In her eyes, Lee saw the terror of a waking nightmare. He stared back at her, unmoved.

Let's see how long they want to stall now.

Judy spun and whispered something to Gale, who rapidly nodded, spun, and marched out.

Judy turned back to them, eyes hardening like cooling lava. "Alright." She gestured towards the living room, where a mighty-comfy-looking sectional sat, in possibly the best condition Lee had seen an item of furniture in six years. It looked to Lee in that moment how an oasis might look to a dehydrated man in the desert. "In the meantime, grab some rest while you can."

Then Judy turned and looked at the four armed humans and the two hybrids. "Trig, keep an eye on these folks, but don't bother them." She gave Lee one last glare. "I want them as fresh as possible."

Lee didn't like that phrasing overmuch.

Judy turned and went out of the house.

Marie leaned into him. "I got some solid sleep back at the farmhouse. I'll stay awake."

"Not tired," Kat said, eyeing their six guards. "I'll stay awake too."

"You ladies are too kind," Lee sighed as he shoved his way out of the breakfast nook and tottered stiffly over to the sectional. Abe followed, and with one glance, Lee could see the blankness of fatigue in his eyes. He'd had even less sleep than Lee.

Lee collapsed onto one portion of the sectional, and Abe took the other.

Very briefly, Lee wondered how dirty he was. He made sure that his boots weren't on the couch, and fell asleep about thirty seconds after closing his eyes.

The two men were both snoring softly within a minute.

Marie stood on the backside of the sectional, between the kitchen and the living room, looking down at Abe and Lee with wry affection. She loved the fuck out of both of them, but God, they required mothering. They'd both push themselves into an early grave if she wasn't around to tell them not to.

Luckily, Marie had long ago learned how to sleep in pretty much any conditions. Abe liked to tease her, saying she was like a parrot—all you had to do was drape a cloth over her and she was out. Which wasn't far from the truth. She had a neck gator that she more often used as a sweatband. Put that over her eyes like a sleep mask, and she could snooze through an artillery barrage.

So she'd actually gotten decent sleep on the C-130, and then grabbed a couple more hours at the farmhouse before everything went to shit.

All in all, for being on an op, she felt pretty chipper.

She turned to Kat. "How are those bandages doing?" she asked, referring to the bandages she'd applied to Kat's wounds.

Kat blinked, then looked slightly sheepish. "I took them off."

Marie wasn't exactly surprised. "Alright. Let's have a look."

So far, Kat had displayed a marked lack of shame concerning nudity in mixed company. But when Marie asked her that, she glanced back at their guards, who were now clustered around the kitchen, all of them watching.

"They're weird about me being naked," Kat observed.

"Hon, that's not weird. That's called 'common decency.'"

Kat's brow furrowed. "Not common for hybrids and primals."

"Yeah, well, we're all living together now. It's a brave new world." Marie looked over at the men in the group of guards, which was all but two of the humans. "You gents mind giving us some privacy?"

One of the men spoke up, seeming like he didn't really know how to handle this situation. "Sorry, ma'am. We're supposed to be watching you."

Marie nodded to the two women. "They can watch us just fine. And you don't need to go anywhere. Just turn around for a minute."

The men in the group exchanged a whole lot of glances and shrugs, and then silently turned to face the wall. The two women—one armed with an AR variant, the other with a crossbow—gripped their weapons a little tighter.

"Alright," Marie said to Kat. "Let's see it."

Kat gave a thoroughly teenagerish roll of her eyes, but complied, lifting the hoodie up. Marie had half expected her to be naked beneath, but she was wearing a pair of threadbare running shorts. Marie leaned in and inspected the wound to her left breast.

She wasn't sure how much movement Kat had done, but she was surprised to see that the wound wasn't seeping. Slightly swollen and red, but no visible, branching veins. Marie took a quick sniff and smelled nothing but normal body odor. Gently pressed the back of her fingers to the flushed swelling. It didn't feel abnormally warm. So far, no infection.

"Looks good. Your back?"

Kat turned and hiked the hoodie up to show the red stripe across her back. Marie found this wound much the same as the other.

"Damn. You heal fast, huh?" Marie said, giving her a pat on the shoulder to let her know she could cover up again. When she had, Marie nodded to the two women keeping an eye on them, and they notified the men they could turn around.

Marie leaned against the back of the couch. "So," she began, hooking her hands in the collar of her armor. "How'd y'all come to have so many hybrids in this settlement? Seems like there's as many of them as there are humans."

The same guy that'd spoken before gave her a cagey look. "I'm not sure how much we're supposed to say at this point."

"Why?" Marie asked, evenly.

The guy blinked. "Be...cause...I don't wanna piss Judy off."

"Fair enough. I'll ask something more general." She looked at the two big, hybrid males. One was clearly Caucasian, while the other looked like he might have some Pacific Islander in him. The white hybrid was glaring suspiciously, while the darker-skinned one just seemed to be hanging out.

She nodded to the darker-skinned one, simply because he appeared less hostile. "What's your name, Hon?"

The hybrid seemed surprised to be called on. He glanced at his friends to see if this was some sort of violation, but no one told him not to answer. When he spoke, it was with the usual growling aspect that Marie had come to expect from hybrids, but his voice was almost comically high for such a large man.

"Cade," he stated.

"Nice to meet you, Cade. I'm Marie. Your parents—do they live here in Appomattox?"

Again, the glance at the others, and again, no one stopped him. "My father."

"And your mother—is she a full-blooded primal, or a hybrid?"

"She is half primal and half human," he said.

Interesting. So he was a quarter-primal hybrid, like Kat. The mutations he displayed were similar to Kat's in that, if you just covered his slightly-protruding snout, you'd think he was human.

"And how old are you, Cade?"

Somewhat childishly, Cade raised a massive hand and spread all five, claw-tipped fingers. "Five."

Even *more* interesting. Cade had been born only a year after the plague hit.

Marie smiled. "Well, that makes you the oldest hybrid I've met so far. Does your mother live in one of the primal colonies? I hear there are three different colonies, all in Appomatox."

Cade opened his mouth to respond, but the woman with the crossbow issued a warning grunt, and he snapped his sizeable jaws shut.

The woman peered at Marie. "Why you wanna know all this shit anyway?"

"Honestly? Just curious. Up until a few months ago, I didn't even know folks like Kat and Cade existed, and there's still a lot I got to learn."

The woman's gaze became surly. "We're not some science experiment for you to poke and prod."

Marie looked at her evenly. "That why y'all killed those scientists?"

Before the woman could respond, the sound of voices and footsteps came from outside the front door.

Marie had a clear view down the hall, and saw the door fly open, banging on its stoppers. Marie shifted her stance and put her hands on her rifle, fingers tingling. Lee and Abe were instantly up, rifles in hand, bleary eyes stretched wide and scanning for threats, though their minds were probably only half conscious.

First through the door came Greg in his red jacket, moving backwards, shotgun gripped in his off hand while the other hovered around as though preparing to catch someone.

Next came a hybrid female, also backing through, and for a moment, Marie thought she was supporting a limp body.

That body—equipped with armor and a slung M249—limped through the entryway, jerking arms out of helpfully-unhelpful hands.

"No, I'm fine!" Sam said, exasperated. "I can walk on my own, for chrissake!"

Marie felt an instant flood of relief to see his face—dirty and haggard as it was, with his hair all mussed, bits of forest detritus clinging to it.

Greg spun around, his eyes worried, which was odd to Marie, because it seemed he was worried for Sam. "He's wounded!" Greg declared to the whole house.

The six guards had come spilling out of the kitchen and now all huddled in a cluster, craning necks to see past each other and down the hall.

Sam spotted Marie and started limping towards her. "It's fine, Marie. I'm fine."

He had a big bloody spot on his shoulder. Red had stained the collar of his armor. But his eyes were clear and sharp, albeit slightly irritated.

"Sam?" Lee called, still standing in the living room, just now lowering his rifle.

"It's him," Marie shot over her shoulder, moving quickly to Sam's side. She did not attempt to support him, since he'd apparently had enough of that from the others. Instead, she immediately stopped him, gently tilted his head to one side, and examined the wound to his shoulder.

"It's just a graze," Sam grumped. "It's already stopped bleeding." He pointed down to his leg. "That one started up again, though."

Marie ushered Sam quickly out of the hall and towards the breakfast nook. She took a moment to look back and give Greg an appreciative nod. "Thank you. He didn't give you any trouble, did he?"

Greg's look of concern switched to exasperation. "After a whole lot of yelling and threats to mow us down with that fucking machine gun...no. We were able to calm him down and talk."

"I was surrounded by hybrids and guys with guns!" Sam defended. "The fuck was I supposed to think?"

Marie reached the breakfast nook and instructed Sam to sit on the bench. Lee and Abe appeared on either side of her.

"I left my medical pack at the farmhouse," Marie said. "Gimme your IFAK."

Easing himself onto the bench with his wounded leg held out stiff, Sam twisted, pulled the IFAK from the side of his plate carrier and shoved it into Marie's arms, then took the tube of his water bladder and sucked noisily on it a few times. He spat it out, frustrated.

"Anyone got any water?" Sam asked. "I'm out."

Lee went down on one knee at his side, offering the tube of his own bladder. "What happened?"

Sam drank greedily from Lee's water for a moment.

Opening the clamshell IFAK, Marie glanced over at the guards. "Any way we can get some more water in here? We're running a bit low."

Cade raised his big paw again. "I will get water." He immediately spun and ran out the door, juking nimbly through the crowd of onlookers hovering around the entryway and front stoop, the door still hanging open.

Sam finished drinking and gasped for air. After a few breaths, he started digging in his dump pouch. "They took Jones. Squad of soldiers came down in a Blackhawk. They grabbed him before I could do anything. I killed four or five of them." He drew his hand out of his dump pouch. In it was their satphone. "I was able to grab it before I had to get out of there."

Lee grabbed the satphone like a priceless object—which it kind of was. "You went back in the house?" he asked, his voice slightly hushed, though filled with a sort of pride.

Rather than answer, Sam leaned forward to look at the entryway. "One of them has your rucksack. Sorry I couldn't grab the others." He chuffed, mirthlessly. "Should've at least grabbed Marie's medical pack."

"You did good, brother," Lee said, rising to his feet, looking at the satphone in his hands. Then he frowned at Marie. "How long was I out?" He checked his wristwatch and answered his own question. "Oh. All of ten fucking minutes. Super."

Marie moved to the bench at Sam's side and began tending to his shoulder wound.

"You gonna make a call?" Abe queried.

Lee flapped his lips. "Shit, man. Jones got nabbed. This is getting way outta control. I don't know how the fuck else we're supposed to get him back." He looked at Abe. "We gotta bring Ron in on this. Figure out what the hell's going on and try to get some help out here."

Abe grimaced. "I don't wanna leave our boy high and dry. But how sure are you that Ron's not in on it?"

Lee shook his head. "I'm not sure. But we don't have a choice at this point. If there's any way he can get word to the strike force and tell 'em not to fuck with Jonesy, then we gotta do it. 'Cause we sure as shit can't go infiltrate an entire battalion to get him back."

Abe heaved a disconsolate breath. "Alright. I'm with you. Let's shake the tree and see what falls out."

Chapter 17

Jones was hooded and bound, kneeling on a dirt floor, and trying not to shiver too hard. He was pretty sure there were two guards watching him—he could occasionally hear them shift their weight, though neither spoke. He was cold because they'd stripped him of everything but his pants.

Boots and socks—gone. Armor and weapons—obviously gone.

Did they have to take his shirt? Fucking assholes.

He couldn't see shit because of the hood over his head. It stank of other men's stale sweat. His hands were behind his back, wrists snugged painfully tight into a pair of plastic zip-cuffs. He'd been kneeling in the dirt for almost an hour now, and his knees were aching and his hamstrings were hinting that they'd like to start cramping sometime in the near future.

"Guys," Jones said, trying to sound friendly. "Look. Are you Army? Because I was Army, too. Eleven-bravo. You guys eleven-bravo? You seem like eleven-bravo. Definitely not some POG ass motherfuckers, amiright?"

For this attempt at rapport, Jones received a kick in the ass.

"Ah!" Jones twisted his head from side to side, as though he might see his attacker. "Christ, man! You put your boot right in my fucking anus!"

"Quiet!" one of them thundered.

Jones hissed between clenched teeth, clamping a cold, numb hand over his ass crack as though to protect it. Damn. It was surprisingly painful to get kicked right in the butthole.

This was all very bad.

Aside from a few, monosyllabic commands, none of these bastards had said a thing to him. He'd taken a brief helicopter ride, then been shuffled into wherever he was, stripped down, and left there.

He had to assume he was at the strike force's outpost. His only comfort was that these guys were fellow American soldiers. And that was a slim comfort considering the fact that they'd tried to kill him twice now. But maybe it was all just mistaken identity. The strike force hadn't been told that a secret team would be infiltrating their area.

This would all get cleared up.

That's what Jones told himself to keep his head on straight.

It's all a misunderstanding, and as soon as you can talk to someone, you'll straighten it all out.

Then maybe they could get the fuck out of here and go back to Oregon. Maybe, in another forty-eight hours, Jones would have another exciting story to tell those sweet young ladies he and Sam had been housing with back in Gearhart.

It was a thin fantasy that he clung to, just to stay calm.

He heard a sharp rustle of fabric. Footsteps approaching.

Again, no one spoke.

What was with these people? Why wasn't anyone talking? Was it some sort of intimidation tactic?

He heard the guards hustle to either side of him. Iron hands seized him under his armpits and hauled him to his feet. They dragged him forward, his feet stumbling to catch up, then shoved him down.

His ass hit cold metal. It felt like a folding chair.

Then one of the guards ripped the hood off his head. They took a bit of his hair with it, and Jones regretted letting it grow out.

He blinked, trying to get his bearings.

He was in a large tent. Sitting in a metal folding chair. Two guards hovering over his shoulders. And a third guy sitting in another folding chair, oddly close to Jones. The guy was hunched forward, elbows on knees, his face only a foot from Jones's.

Jones leaned away, eyeing the guy. The man was smallish, but powerfully built. A big, brown beard, streaked with gray. A black ballcap shaded two pitiless shark eyes. He wore a black soft-shell jacket, black jeans, and black boots. It was a whole motif.

Jones opened his mouth to speak, but in a flash, the guy had a callused, ramrod finger squished against Jones's lips.

"Ssh," he said.

Jones blinked. The guy's finger smelled like cigarette smoke. He sealed his lips and nodded.

The man in black retracted his finger slowly, as though prepared to shove it back into Jones's mouth if he so much as breathed too loudly. The guy leaned back in his seat. Adjusted his shoulders. Clasped his hands in his lap.

"Name."

It was a command, not a question.

Unlike Abe and Lee, who had been declared war criminals and domestic terrorists, Jones never had a need for a fake name. He thought about coming up with one then, but after a few seconds decided that honesty would be best if he was actually going to clear up the misunderstanding.

"Calvin Jones," he answered.

"Rank."

Jones squinted. "Well, see, I technically don't have rank anymore, because I'm not technically in the US military. But I *was* a corporal."

The man's face remained stony, save for just the slightest upward twitch of an eyebrow. "You are not with the military?"

This was the first time any of the soldiers had spoken more than a single word to Jones. Now he realized why.

This guy—his accent…

"I'm sorry." Jones's eyes narrowed. "Are you Russian?"

The man's lips pursed, but he didn't respond.

Jones twisted in his chair, looking at the two soldiers to either side of him. Their uniforms were OCP, but that didn't mean jack shit—lots of countries wore that camouflage pattern.

But their weapons! Their weapons had all been standard US military shit!

"You guys aren't Russians too, are you?" Jones asked, his mind now racing. Maybe the guy in black *was* Russian, but maybe the IAG had brought him into this strike force for some reason.

Rather than answer, the big fellow to Jones's left clocked him good and solid right in the temple. Jones let out a grunt and a slack-mouthed curse as he reeled in his seat, head swarming with flickering lights.

He was dazed for a moment. Then the pain came together to form a sharp, splintered ache on his left cheek bone. As his vision cleared, he began laughing. First, it came out bewildered. And then it became bitter.

"I fuckin' told 'em," Jones railed at no one in particular. "I fuckin' told 'em it was Russians, but no! No one ever fuckin' believes me, but I was right! I *am* right! I'm right all the fuckin'—!"

The guy in black gave an irritable nod, and the next thing Jones knew, the soldier that had punched him sank him into a headlock. The burly soldier's forearm and bicep cinched his throat shut and cut off his diatribe.

Jones gagged, struggled for air, and got just the barest wheeze. It wasn't quite enough to calm his thundering heart. For a second, he thrashed against the sudden assault, but quickly realized he was screwed and decided to be still and save his oxygen.

The guy in black crossed one leg over the other, all casual and languid, his eyes bored as he watched Jones choking.

Fuck. This was so bad.

And if Jones got out of here alive, he swore in that instant that Lee and Abe were gonna hear it from him. Oh, he was going to let them have it.

His vision clouded. He was running out of air already.

Surely they weren't going to kill him like this. What would be the point? They'd captured him. Might as well pump him for information, right? They could've killed him already, but they hadn't.

And yet, the thick arm did not release, and Jones's vision shrunk to a pinpoint, wherein all he could see was the guy in black's merciless, dark eyes peering at him like he was a bug.

Then the guy flittered his fingers, and the arm disappeared from around Jones's throat.

Relief and oxygen flooded him. He gasped, coughed, shook his head and worked his jaw.

The interrogator—because surely, that's what he was—gave Jones a moment to settle. When he stopped heaving and hacking, the guy leaned forward onto his elbows again.

"Let us try this again," he said. Yup. Definitely a Russian—his accent was as thick as Siberian permafrost. "You say you are not with the United States military. And yet you seem to have all of their equipment, despite the fact that you have no uniform. Please. Explain this."

Jones hung on a few choice words.

The interrogator had referred to it as the "United States" military. Everyone knew there was no "United States" anymore. There was only the IAG now. Also, the way he'd said it clearly implied a separation between the "United States military" and whoever these people were.

Was that even possible? Were these foreign soldiers? Was this the start of a fucking invasion?

Jones's mind snapped back to imperatives, and disregarded speculation.

Imperative Number One? He needed to make himself valuable.

If Jones could convince them that he had information they wanted, then they'd keep him alive. The second they felt like he was a waste of their time, he was a dead man.

That didn't mean he had to spill all the beans right at the get-go. And doing so would royally screw his team over—particularly Lee and Abe. If the IAG ever found out that they were still alive, they'd stop at nothing to hunt them down and either capture them to rot in a prison, or, more likely, just kill them outright.

Jones was going to have to lead them on.

Unfortunately, that probably meant he was about to get his shit beat in—if he was lucky. Nightmare scenarios of various banned torture techniques he'd heard of went flying through his mind like a cloud of bats.

The worst one stuck in his mind, instantly making him queasy.

It involved a hammer and a glass thermometer stuck in a very sensitive part of Jones that he held quite dear.

"Alright, okay," Jones gasped, as though the interrogator were approaching him with those implements in hand. Despite the chill in the air, sweat had broken out all over Jones's body, making him even colder. "I'll tell you whatever…" he cracked his voice theatrically and then coughed, making a show of it. "Sorry," he rasped. "Water? Please?"

The interrogator thought about it for a moment, then shrugged and nodded to one of the soldiers.

A moment later, a plastic bottle of water appeared. The soldier unscrewed the cap and put the bottle to Jones's lips. He drank, using every second to let his mind scramble through what exactly he could and could not afford to say.

He was not given as much time as he would've liked. In the midst of gulping down his second mouthful of water, the interrogator lunged forward and slapped the bottle right out of Jones's face, sending it spiraling across the room.

Jones smacked his lips, thinking *Well, that was fucking rude*, but what he said was "Uh, thanks." He cleared his throat. "Much better now."

"Speak," the interrogator demanded.

"Okay. Look. I was telling the truth. I used to be a corporal in the US Army. After the plague hit, obviously there was no US Army anymore, so I just, you know, made my own way in the world."

"Your armor, your weapons, your ammunition, your radio."

Jones blinked, as though he didn't understand what the interrogator was getting at.

The man's eyes narrowed. "If you are not military, where did all your military equipment come from?"

"Oh, that shit. Pff. You know. You wander around the wreckage of society long enough, you find some goodies. Know what I'm sayin'?"

"And your friends?"

Jones managed to look confused. "I don't have any friends."

The interrogator's eyes flashed to the soldier on Jones's left again, and Jones knew what was coming.

Another canned-ham-sized fist rocked his face.

"Ah! Fuck! Jesus, man! Could you stop with that shit?"

The interrogator scooted closer, which was unnecessary, because he was all up in Jones's face already. "We found four rucksacks inside the house where you were captured. One of your friends killed five of my men. I will give you this warning once: Do not say things that I know are untrue, or things will get very bad for you."

"But how am I supposed to know what you know is untrue?"

The soldier punched him again, but this time in the solar plexus.

Jones had seen it coming and managed to tighten his core against the blow, but it still made him feel like he might puke. He groaned and wheezed for a moment.

"Right," he strained out. "You misunderstood me, sir. Those aren't my friends. They're just some people that were hired to do this operation with me. I barely know them."

"So, you were hired. That makes you...what?"

"Uh, I guess...a mercenary or something? Look, I don't ask questions. I mean, who can afford to turn down job offers these days? Shit's crazy around here, if you haven't noticed. Whole country's fallen apart. Gotta take what you can get when it comes. You know what I'm talking about. I mean, if I'd've known *you guys* were gonna be here, then obviously, I woulda turned it down. Hindsight's twenty-twenty, ha ha."

"You say many words that don't mean very much."

Jones nodded. "Yeah, I've been told that before. But I thought you wanted me to talk. So I'm just, you know, talking. Really trying to be cooperative here. I don't want any trouble. I just—"

The interrogator slapped him. Not even a hard slap. Just a cuff across the face to shut him up. Still stung, though.

"I want information, not just words. Make sure your words have information in them. We will continue." The interrogator interlaced his fingers between his knees. "What is your mission here? What were you hired to do?"

I was hired to buttfuck your mother.

Jones was just pissed off enough by the slap that he was tempted to say it out loud, but then he remembered shattered glass up his dickhole and thought better of it.

No chance in hell he was going to admit to the real reason they were here. He needed to make some shit up quick, and he needed to say something that would get them to back off and stop beating him. At least for a while.

He met the interrogator's gaze and sighed heavily, as though he were struggling with whether or not to give up the truth. "There's a girl. Twenty-five years old. Her name's Stacey Peabody. She's the daughter of...well, shit, I'm gonna be honest, I don't know who she's the daughter of, but it's someone that's *real* high up in the IAG. Some fuckin' bigwig that can pull secret shit like this, you know? Anyway. Apparently, she ran off last year and joined this cult over in Appomattox or some shit. I dunno. Point is, whoever this government bigwig is, he caught wind of the fact that y'all are about to kill everyone in Appomattox, and he secretly hired us to go in and extract his daughter before y'all moved on the town."

Jones was actually pretty proud of himself there. He'd just started talking and let the lie tell itself, like those old cartoons where the tracks were being laid out right in front of the speeding train. But hey, it sounded pretty good, didn't it?

Jones was rewarded by having the interrogator lean back in his chair.

Was that a whiff of concern that had just crossed over the grim man's features?

"How much?" the interrogator asked after a moment of silence.

Jones frowned. "How much what?"

"How much are you being paid for this...operation?"

Jones swallowed, and tried to hide it by bobbling his head. "Well, that actually depends." *Just lie. Just make it up as you go.* "I was promised fifty thousand rounds of ammunition in various calibers just for coming out here—but you know how politicians lie, so I'm not holding my breath that the guy who hired us is *actually* gonna come through on that if we don't succeed. I tried to convince him—our go-between, that is—to pay us the ammunition up front, but he wasn't having it..."

The interrogator sucked on his teeth, impatiently.

"Aaaanywho," Jones stumbled on. "If we get her back alive, I get a JLTV guntruck. If we get her back alive *and unharmed*, we get five hundred gallons of fuel to go with it. I mean, that's a pretty sweet deal, don't you think? To extract one chick? Of course, I guess it's not so sweet now that I've been captured by you guys." He let out a nervous chortle. "But it *would've* been sweet. Still could be sweet, if you guys don't, like...hurt me too bad and stuff."

All was silent for a long, uncomfortable moment as the interrogator considered Jones.

Abruptly, he slapped his hands on his knees and stood up, his crotch homoerotically close to Jones's face as he stared blankly down at him. "Mister Jones, you have interesting things to say. I feel it is my duty to make some calls and find out if you are telling me the truth. However, just so you know, I think you are lying. So, while I am gone, I would like you to think about the consequences of lying. My friends here will help you think."

"Goddammit," Jones moaned, as the interrogator strode away, and Jones felt himself lifted from his seat by the two soldiers and thrown roughly to the ground, where they commenced to kicking the shit out of him.

Stas Obolensky of the Spetsgruppa Alfa swept out of the tent, leaving the American to his beating. But, one step out the tent flap, he hesitated, and glanced back. The flap was already falling closed, but he still got a snapshot of the man's body folding around a swiftly-delivered boot to the gut.

Then there was only OD green vinyl, and grunts and groans and fleshy impacts.

Stas reached up, grabbed the bill of his black hat and shuffled it up and down a few times to itch his forehead. Then he turned and stalked away.

This was all very interesting.

Stas was not perturbed in the slightest. He appreciated the chance for some real action. Unfortunately, the last few years had been dark and dreary for him. The reunification of the Russian state had been accomplished through means that most would see as "harsh." Some might even use the word "massacre."

He understood why Spetsgruppa Alfa had been ordered to do the things they'd done. This was no time to handle matters gently. For the first time in a very, very long time, his country was on top, while western powers scrambled to catch up. Russia was poised to be the leader of the post-FURY world, and it would not have been possible if they had not taken decisive—and yes, sometimes cruel—actions.

Because of its unique terrain and culture, Russia had fared better than many other world powers after the plague. Yes, many of their citizens had died or become infected. Yes, some of them had mutated—or "evolved," according to some schools of thought. But the Russian infrastructure and government had not taken the nose dive that so many others had.

While every other country seemed to have been knocked to the mats, Russia had come out with a black eye, but had kept its feet. And then they'd begun to hit back.

Much like everyone else, they'd had to deal with disparate factions, headed up by this warlord or that. Sometimes entire military units had defected and used the plague as an opportunity to establish their own little fiefdoms. But mostly it was civilians who thought to divide their great country up into a multitude of city-states, erroneously believing the Russian government to be dead.

They'd been very wrong.

While western powers wrung their hands about population concerns—oh, we don't want to kill too many people, because there's so few of us left as it is!—the new Russian government had acted swiftly and decisively to quell rebellion and exterminate anyone that couldn't be trusted to have their homeland's best interests at heart.

On the one hand, Stas was proud that his Spetsgruppa Alfa had been instrumental in the pacification of the rebel factions. On the other hand, how proud could you be to wipe out gaggles of hapless civilians? One did not get to be in Spetsgruppa Alfa because they enjoyed easy things.

And that's why Stas found himself excited by this American operative they'd captured.

When Stas had been given this special assignment, it had been moderately interesting to him because it would take place in America—a place he'd never operated in before. But the mission itself seemed to offer no challenge bigger than what he'd faced in the pacification of so many rebel factions.

All they were required to do was keep everyone in the nearby town contained, and, should the order be given, eliminate the entire population and retrieve the research—because, apparently, American troops couldn't be trusted to carry out the unpleasant task of killing a few country rebels for the betterment of their nation.

That was consistent with what he knew of American soldiers. Willing to obey their superiors—so long as it was *convenient* for them, and popular to do so.

How had such a soft people managed to rule the world for so long?

It didn't matter anymore. They had been Rome, and just like that ancient empire, they'd grown fat and weak, and decayed from the inside out.

In any case, Stas had not expected much of a challenge on this mission.

But that had all changed.

This Calvin Jones character could claim all he wanted that he was merely a mercenary, but Stas knew a professional warfighter when he looked one in the eye. This one liked to play the fool, but Stas could see the steel in him. He was some sort of special forces, and while Stas disdained the average American soldier, the special operations community of *any* country deserved respect. And Calvin Jones was most definitely an operative—not merely a soldier of fortune.

Which meant there was at least one team of American operatives on the ground.

That made sense—the small reconnaissance patrol they'd lost the previous night had been made to look as though they'd been killed by mutants, but Stas had been in the command tent when they'd radioed in. They'd seen a group of six moving through the woods, attempting to breach the cordon around the town of Appomattox. Stas had ordered them to set up an ambush. That was the last he'd heard from them.

Which meant those six operatives weren't "mercenaries," as Calvin Jones claimed. Because Stas did not believe for one moment that his highly-trained men had been taken down by something so pedestrian as "mercenaries."

All of this led to Stas being genuinely excited.

He'd never gone toe-to-toe with American special forces before.

And what were they here for? Well, that was easy enough to figure out: They were here to steal the research, because that was how America *always* maintained its superiority—by stealing secrets from others. They were very good at it. And that was just an added level of challenge.

Stas felt re-energized as he entered the command tent.

Inside, a series of folding tables had been erected with a dozen computer stations on them, his specialists working diligently to monitor their area of operations. A white screen was pinned to one wall of the tent, on which was projected a satellite view of Appomattox and its surrounding terrain.

Stas swiped a protein bar from a tray beside their coffee station. He unwrapped it and ate the whole thing in two bites. This was the first time since landing on American soil that he'd actually had an appetite. He crumpled the wrapper and stuffed it into his pants pocket, chewing manically as he stood over a simple desk phone—the same as you might find in any office the world over.

He swallowed. Reached for the phone. Thought better of it, and grabbed a bottle of water instead. Took a long draft to swish the rest of the food particles out of his mouth, then swallowed again and took up the phone.

He punched the number in from memory, then brought the handset up to his ear.

A curt, female voice answered in Russian, and he replied in kind with his credentials.

The woman took a moment to confirm them, then asked him to state his request.

Stas turned and looked at the projection of Appomattox. "The colonel, please. Tell him it is urgent."

Chapter 18

Fifteen hundred miles away, in Aspen, Colorado, Major Ron Paige was in his office, preparing to get himself another cup of coffee.

He needed the extra caffeine—and, God, what he wouldn't do for some Adderall.

Unfortunately, because he was dealing with super-secret squirrel shit, he didn't have any underlings he could delegate the task to, so he himself had to remain in his office, hovering over the satphone, and waiting for Lee to call for his extract.

For a moment, he regretted booting Angela Houston off the case. Normally, she was the single point of contact for Lee and his team when they needed something. And it wasn't that he couldn't trust Angela—hell, they'd trusted her to keep Lee's existence a secret for three years already. And Angela was highly motivated not to screw them over. Her daughter, Abby, had been shot in the spine three years ago during the battle for Greeley, Colorado. The girl was paralyzed from the waist down, and Angela needed their medical assistance to keep her daughter alive and healthy.

So, no, he didn't believe for one second that Angela couldn't be trusted with knowledge of this operation over in Virginia.

But, when ICAO Griffin had issued his orders to Ron, he'd specifically said, "I want you to handle this *personally*."

So, being the dutiful soldier he was, Ron had given Angela a few days off and taken over the satphone-monitoring duties himself.

He considered the satphone lying on his desk. Should he take it with him? Nah. Probably not necessary. He'd only be gone for a second, and it was still very early in the game for Lee to be calling for his extract—which was the only reason he *should* be calling.

Ron headed for the door, thinking about the pretty girl who ran the coffee kiosk, and how she always smiled real nice for him.

Then the phone rang.

Ron stopped, hand on the door of his office, and looked back at his desk, frowning.

Really? Lee and his team had only been on the ground for about twelve hours now. No way in hell they'd actually found the scientists and got them out already.

His frown turned to a full glower as he wondered what kind of illegal shit Lee was going to try to pressure him into doing this time. He stomped back to his desk, swiped up the satphone, and stabbed the talk button.

"Cloud Nine," Ron said, cautiously.

"This is Archangel," Lee's voice gave his codename.

Ron immediately dispensed with subterfuge, lowering his voice so the next office over from his wouldn't hear. "You better have some fucking scientists to extract."

Ron stood listening as Lee began to talk. At first, his brow remained hotly furrowed.

Then it relaxed. Then his eyes widened.

"Shit," Ron said. He listened some more. After another minute, he again proclaimed, "Shit," and leaned heavily on his desk, his head drooping as his shoulders tensed up into a knot.

By the time Lee was done bringing him up to speed, Ron had an accelerated pulse, and his hands were feeling a little clammy.

"Well, what the fuck do you want *me* to do about this?" Ron seethed into the phone.

"So you didn't know about any of this horseshit?" Lee asked, betraying some skepticism.

Ron found this highly offensive. "Jesus, man! What kind of an asshole do you think I am? No, I didn't know about any of this! What the fuck did you do? I told you not to go anywhere near that strike force!"

Lee's voice sounded like he might choke Ron through the airwaves. "We didn't. We took the same track that was prescribed in the mission briefing. They were waiting for us. As for them hitting the farmhouse, these folks in Appomattox say they're being kept inside a cordon zone. Apparently, they got too close to that cordon when they came to the farmhouse, and that's why the strike force hit us there."

"Fucking fuck," Ron spat. "Hang on." He lowered the satphone and stared at the ceiling, feeling his pulse in his neck. Lee's team had been hit twice by elements from the strike force, and now one of his guys had been snatched, and was likely being interrogated.

This was an absolute cluster. If Jones cracked and told the truth, not only would Lee and the rest of the team be in a whole lot of danger, but Griffin's secret would be outed. Ron didn't even want to imagine the hellfire and brimstone that would rain down upon both Griffin and Ron if the higher-ups in the government found out they'd been keeping Lee's team of war criminals as a private little black ops project.

Okay. Problems abounded. That wasn't unusual. Ron's entire life was a string of emergencies that needed to get handled.

He put the satphone to his ear again. "Alright. So. What do you want me to do here, Lee?"

"Well, for starters, I need you to get on the horn with Griffin and get some more information about what the hell is going on around here. Clearly, we were not given the full picture here, and it doesn't sound like you were either. As it stands right now, I can't help feeling like I've been set up."

"Griffin wouldn't do that."

"So you say."

"Motherffff—so, what? You want me to interrogate my own fucking boss? The *Interim Commander of American Operations*?"

"Ron, don't be stupid. You're a smart man, so act like it. You can get additional intel from Griffin without accusing him of anything. But more important than any of that shit—if Griffin doesn't want his entire world shattered in the next seventy-five hours, he needs to figure out how to get Jones out of there."

Ron pressed a breath through clenched teeth.

"Also," Lee continued. "We had to unass the house without our gear."

"You gotta be fuckin' kidding me."

"No, I'm not fucking kidding you, and I don't want any grief about it, Ron! We had a Little Bird with a minigun crawling up our asses, so, yes—we abandoned our shit. I need a resupply."

Ron scoffed in disbelief. "Are you fucking high? Not a chance. I told you that from the get-go. No resupply."

"Yeah, you said a lot of shit from the get-go, but here's the deal: Original plan is toast. Now we adapt. Your only other option is to abandon us in Virginia. And that ain't gonna work out well for you."

"Oh, I'm sorry, are you threatening me?"

"Am I threatening you? Well, gee, Ron, I dunno. You sent us into a giant vat of bullshit with bad intel, two of my team have been wounded, one's been captured, and now you're talking about leaving us in the lurch. So, you tell me, Ron. If you'd been buttfucked by your handlers, how pissed would *you* be? How much *more pissed* would you be if it resulted in the deaths of your very dear friends and teammates? And then ask yourself how much restraint you really expect from a disavowed war criminal and domestic terrorist who has no home, no family, no ties, and technically doesn't exist?"

It might've been tempting to call Lee out for blustering and making idle threats.

Except...Ron had actually witnessed Lee Harden topple an entire government. Acting President Erwin Briggs had wound up with a hole in his head, his forces scattered, his regime utterly destroyed, and the city he'd called home turned into an irradiated wasteland.

So...no. He would not be accusing Lee of idle threats. At the moment, Lee seemed pretty damn pissed, and Ron was a big enough man to admit that it made him very nervous when Lee got pissed.

"Alright, alright. Cool your jets. Let me make a fuckin' phone call before you go all murder hobo on me."

"And the resupply?" Lee demanded.

"Goddammit—why're you twisting my nuts here? You realize how screwed we *all* could be if I send a resupply your way? You think no one from the strike force is gonna notice a fucking C-130 dropping shit in their backyard? Lemme talk to Griffin first and see what kind of exposure we're dealing with here."

"Please tell me you didn't just mention 'exposure' when my team's life is on the line."

"Stop. Just stop, Lee. Stop all your self-righteous bullshit. I know in your heart you're still a ground pounder who don't think much past the muzzle of your own rifle, but for fuckssake, you need to be worried about exposure too. We're not talking about me and Griffin getting busted down a rank. We're not even talking about court marshals—you think anyone in this fucking government gives a shit about due process anymore? I'm talking about complete and total slate-wiping, Lee. That includes your team too. So unless you want the entire IAG coming down on *all* our heads, then shut the fuck up and let me do my job."

Lee was quiet for a moment. Then a sigh rattled through the speaker against Ron's ear. "Alright, Ron. I trust you. Just put some pepper on it, alright? We don't have a lot of time."

"You're right. So how about you stop wasting it and hang up."

The satphone immediately clicked to a dead line.

Ron smacked it down on his desk, his mind racing.

Then he pulled a key ring out of his pocket, unlocked the bottom drawer of his desk, and retrieved an entirely different satphone. He extended the antenna, punched in a number from memory, and placed the call.

Chicago.

The good ol' Windy City.

A desecrated warscape.

And also the location of the First MCR Summit—MCR being the Multinational Coalition for Reconstruction.

It was the strangest thing General Perry Griffin had ever been a part of. They were holding it in one of the conference rooms of the former Loews Chicago O'Hare Hotel, which was now Griffin's FOB in the nine-month-long battle to retake Chicago.

The conference room felt dumpy to him, considering the fact that delegations from all over the world were present—many of them led by that country's current head of state. The conference room had once been grand, to be sure. But what made it feel inappropriate to the occasion of hosting world leaders were the multitude of bullet holes in the walls, the faded remnants of bloodstains on the carpeting, and the stink of death that they hadn't quite been able to fumigate.

The powers that be had tried mightily to strongarm Griffin into letting them hold the summit at the iconic Willis Tower—you know, for the symbolism and all that. Griffin hadn't even been diplomatic about it. He'd told them straight up, "That's the dumbest shit I've ever heard suggested, and a really good way to get some foreign dignitaries killed on American soil."

Technically, the Willis Tower—formerly known as the Sears Tower—was inside the Chicago Green Zone. But only by a margin of two city blocks, on the other side of which was some of their fiercest fighting.

In the years since society fell, Chicago had gone from one of the main epicenters of the plague—thanks to having multiple international airports, as well as one of the densest urban populations in the world—to being a home for hordes of infected. Those fuckers hadn't been able to withstand the harsh Illinois winters, but their mutated cousins, the primals, had managed it.

But after the primals had run out of food, they'd moved on to greener pastures, and left a ghost town behind them. That had all happened in the first two years. Then, in the following four, humanity had begun to creep back in from various points, and, as humans are wont to do, they set up about twenty different factions, all of which seemed to be at war with each other by the time Griffin had come along nine months ago.

The IAG—with assistance from the MCR—had invaded the city from three points: Ground troops coming in from the west; an amphibious invasion from Lake Michigan courtesy of the Canadians and Brits; and an air-assault straight into Chicago O'Hare International airport.

Some of the factions welcomed them. Others fought with them. And several welcomed them at first, in order to receive guns and ammunition, and then fought against them, because that was apparently a mistake that the American government was going to continue to make until the end of time.

Honestly, the whole debacle was a joke to Griffin. They didn't need Chicago. It didn't help their efforts to restabilize the country one iota. It was just a drain on manpower and resources, and, frankly, a distraction from what they *should* have been focusing on, which was expanding their borders out from the interior states to retake the coastlines.

But the newly-elected president—and Griffin used the term "elected" in the loosest possible terms—had insisted. Caught between a hard-nosed president and the pack of military brass that were all too eager to wrest the title of Interim Commander of American Operations away from Griffin, he had caved.

Griffin shouldn't have even been a general. Three years ago, he'd been a captain. Only by pure circumstance had he landed in the position he was in. He did not cling to the position because he loved the power, but because he had a functioning moral compass, unlike all the vultures that were ready to take his position the second he screwed up.

The last thing Griffin's country needed was more sociopathic warlords, who saw the end of the world not as the tragedy it was, but as an opportunity to be a member of the new ruling cabal.

The cabal that now surrounded Griffin in the conference room.

And that...*that* is what made this the strangest thing Griffin had ever been a part of.

Delegations from the UK, France, Germany, Japan, Russia, China, the UAE, and of course, Canada, were all present. Except, this didn't feel like a UN or NATO meeting. This felt like a meeting of mob bosses, and Griffin couldn't escape the feeling that they were all very interested in getting their fingers in the pie of what had once been the United States of America.

Like vampires, Griffin thought, as he looked across the gathered heads-of-state and all of their accompanying staff. *Once you invite them in, they'll never leave, and they'll drain you dry.*

Currently, the German prime minister was going on and on about how well they'd quarantined at the outbreak of the plague. Which kind of felt like a jab at the US, seeing as how America had been one of the hardest-hit countries, and still didn't have their act together.

As a former Project Hometown Coordinator, Griffin found this darkly amusing.

Perhaps if previous administrations hadn't pulled the Big Red Handle every time there was a new strain of the sniffles, the American people would have taken the FURY outbreak a little more seriously. Unfortunately, in an attempt to constantly cover their asses, the government had become The Boy Who

Cried Wolf, and by the time people realized that Fury was a very real wolf at their door, it had been far too late.

The German prime minister stumbled in his bragging as the whole room trembled to the sound of the nearby artillery battery delivering a fire mission—which would probably splash somewhere around the Willis Tower. He recovered quickly and went on, raising his voice to be heard over the guns.

Griffin couldn't help a small smirk.

An aide appeared between Griffin and the president sitting to his left. She leaned in close to the president and whispered something in his ear. Griffin eyed his new Commander-in-Chief.

Fairly young as presidents go, James Morton was fifty-five years old, and a retired Air Force colonel who looked like everyone's fantasy of a strongman president: Six-three, strong jaw, keen eyes, and a full head of iron-gray hair.

Those eyes narrowed as he listened to his aide. Then President Morton slid quietly out of his seat. Griffin made to follow him, but Morton motioned for him to stay and then discretely exited the conference room.

The German prime minister went on, now talking about how his country had so excellently dealt with the primal threat. Just some good, old fashioned, German efficiency, applied to an ongoing eradication campaign. It sounded a bit Wermacht-ish to Griffin, but then again, he couldn't judge. Neither could anyone else at the summit.

Of the countries that were clawing their way back towards being civilized, every single one of them had accomplished it by becoming stratocracies. Of course, no one called it that. They preferred to sanitize it with such terms as "an ongoing state of emergency" and "long-term martial law."

They all claimed that power would be returned to the people once things had been fully stabilized. But they were also the ones that got to define what "fully stabilized" meant, so Griffin would believe it when he saw it.

Again, he couldn't judge them. Griffin himself was now a member of the new American stratocracy. Sure, they were touting President Morton as "democratically elected." But what they weren't saying was that the election had consisted of a paltry five thousand ballots, three thousand of which had come from the military, and there'd been no other name on the ballot.

The German prime minister began to outline some multi-step plan for a joint European reconstruction, with the clear implication that the American government should be taking notes. Griffin tuned him out, his mind drifting towards more immediate concerns, such as how he would pacify the several remaining resistance factions in Chicago without the whole thing turning into a massacre.

He felt a hand rest gently on his shoulder. He twisted to find the president's aide leaning very close to him. A strand of her hair tickled his face, her breath warm against his ear as she whispered, "The president would like to speak with you."

Griffin was all too happy to be free of the summit, even for just a few minutes.

He rose and quietly exited the conference room, following the aide down the adjoining hallway to another nearby conference room. This one had been divided into several small rooms, each acoustically-sealed, so that the members of the summit could have private conversations. Each room was labeled with a sheet of paper bearing the name of the country.

The aide escorted Griffin to the one marked "USA." That had actually been a source of conflict between Griffin and President Morton. Griffin didn't think it was right to call themselves the United States of America, when half of those states were not represented. He'd suggested they label it "Interim American Government," because that's what everyone called it now, but Morton was adamant that he was the president of the USA, and not just the handful of midwestern states they'd managed to stabilize.

Griffin entered to find the president seated at a small, round table with a satphone laying in front of him.

President Morton gestured to the chair across from him. "Have a seat, Perry."

Griffin sat as the aide left the room and closed the door behind her. "What's the problem, Jim?" Because he could tell by the rigid expression on President Morton's face that there was, indeed, a problem.

Morton eyed him for a few beats, then raised his chin. "Tell me about this team you sent to Virginia."

Griffin sat forward, a slight grimace on his lips. "I don't think that would be wise. For your protection, of course," he quickly added. "You need to be very careful about your exposure here."

Morton chuckled mirthlessly. "You remember the story of the Emperor's New Clothes? That's kind of what I feel like right now. You keep telling me I'm covered, but it sure seems like my dick's hanging out."

Griffin nodded to the satphone. "Wanna tell me what the call was about?"

Morton sniffed. Put a hand on the table. Tapped the satphone with an index finger. "Seems like one of your super-secret stealth squad was captured by the boots we already have on the ground."

"Motherfucker," Griffin heaved, smearing a hand over his face.

"Funny, that's exactly what *I* thought."

"Has he talked?"

"Oh, he talked. But don't get your panties in a twist—it was all bullshit. But, Perry, I need to know who these people are."

"A few days ago, you were happy to be kept in the dark. Why do you suddenly want to be in the know?"

Morton's face remained blank as he leaned his elbows onto the table. "Because I need to know if they're worth saving."

Griffin frowned. "I have an exfil plan in place for them."

"They may not get the chance. The strike force is getting worried about *their* exposure in this situation, and they're thinking about moving the schedule up."

"No," Griffin shook his head. "You told them a week. We've still got three days left."

"First of all, don't say 'no' to me—I'm the goddamn CIC. Second of all, we only have as much time as the guys on the ground *decide* we have, and right now, that's not looking like much."

"Yeah, Jim, you *are* the CIC. So tell 'em to stand the fuck down."

Morton grunted. "It's not that simple."

"No, it is that simple," Griffin said, making sure to really emphasize the *no*. "I don't know what private army you've been holding back from me, but they're American soldiers, and therefore, what you say goes."

Morton sighed heavily and broke eye contact. "They're not Americans."

Griffin blinked. "I'm sorry—what?"

Morton looked at him again. "They. Are not. Americans."

Griffin came out of his seat. "Jesus Fucking Christ. Who are they?"

Morton smirked meanly. "I wouldn't want to *expose* you, General Griffin. Now quit acting like a pantywaist and sit down."

Griffin complied, but very slowly.

Morton went on: "And yes, I requested some outside assistance—sue me. We need every soldier we have working on Operation: Freedom's Wind."

Griffin barely controlled a cringe. He fucking hated that name. "The pacification of Chicago—"

Morton winced. "Don't call it 'pacification.' It sounds so...Evil Empire."

Griffin gestured around them. "We're in a sound-proof box. And OFW—" he couldn't bring himself to say the full name "—was *your* idea. I told you we'd be overextending ourselves."

Morton looked put-upon. "Well, I didn't want to have the MCR summit in some Podunk town in Minne-fucking-sota. Come on, Perry. You see the vultures in there. They're circling, waiting for any excuse to come in and take what's ours. If we ever want to be a world power again, we need to look strong and capable, like we have shit under control."

"Oh, yeah. Hearing fucking artillery barrages really sends the message that we have shit under control."

Morton glared and jutted a finger at him. "Hey. I wanted to have the summit at the Willis Tower, not in some gun-blasted hotel right next door to the fucking battery. But here we are, and like every good compromise, neither of us is happy, so how about we stop arguing about shit that's already been done and start talking about what we're going to do *right now*."

Griffin closed his eyes and pinched the bridge of his nose. "Who are they?"

Morton was silent for long enough that Griffin opened his eyes to stare at his president. He found the man's expression to be distressingly like a little boy that's been caught messing with his father's power tools.

"Russians," Morton finally admitted.

Griffin covered his face with both hands. "Oh. My. God." Then he thrust himself back in his seat. "You're serious. You're actually fucking serious."

Morton just sighed and started spinning the satphone on the table.

"Jim. Mister-fucking-President. You invited Russians...Russian *troops*...to conduct a combat operation...on American soil. You couldn't at least have asked the Brits? Or the Canadians? Or literally *anyone else*? You know—a country that we've actually been allies with in the past?"

"It's complicated."

"It only takes one fucking person to say they saw Russian troops wiping out an American town, and it's gonna be all over your precious goddamn newspapers! I told you this newspaper thing was a mistake. I told you to wait until we were actually running a fucking democracy. Journalism does not coexist with a stratocracy."

"There you go with this 'stratocracy' thing again," Morton moaned. "I was democratically elected—hence it's a democracy. And please, Perry, don't insult my intelligence. Nothing goes into those newspapers that I don't approve of, and no one's going to see Russian troops because I made sure they had nothing but standard US military gear—right down to their uniforms and vehicles. Hell, I even gave them a couple of our helos."

Far from mollifying Griffin, this only pissed him off more. Sure, it solved the problem of an eyewitness identifying Russian troops massacring an American town. And apparently freedom of the press wasn't an issue. But just the fact that James Morton had pulled warfighting equipment right from under his nose—especially the helicopters—was both infuriating and highly concerning.

As ICAO, Griffin was *supposed* to know where every bullet was. How the hell had Morton managed to get helicopters without him knowing about it?

"So," Morton said. "I've shown you mine, now show me yours. Who's this team you sent in to nab the researchers?"

No way in hell Griffin was going to tell the truth. "Just some tier one guys I used to work with," he fudged. "Not associated with the IAG. I keep them on a leash, but I'm very intentional about not dealing directly with them. I've got a guy for that."

Morton nodded. "Well, it's good that they're not IAG. That keeps it from getting too complicated. Sounds like you won't be crying yourself to sleep if they buy the farm on this op."

The casual way he said it rubbed Griffin in all the wrong ways. Yes, he kept Lee and his team at arm's length, but that didn't mean he'd willingly toss them into a meatgrinder. Griffin did not think of any of his troops—whether they were IAG or not—as expendable.

He was rescued from saying something extremely disrespectful to the president by a vibration on his hip. He glowered at Morton for another heartbeat, then twisted and snatched the buzzing satphone from where it was secured to his belt.

"Griffin here."

"Cloud Nine," Ron Paige's voice replied. "We got problems."

CHAPTER 19

Lee considered himself a pretty experienced guy, given all the stuff he'd gone through, and it took a lot to surprise him. But he was shocked as hell when a dead man walked into the house.

Lee was sitting on the back of the sectional couch, his team crowded around him while their six guards stood in the kitchen and watched them argue about whether or not Ron Paige and Perry Griffin could be trusted to have their best interests in mind.

That's when the front door swung open, silencing them.

As one, they all turned to look at Judy as she came through the door. Lee could clearly see someone standing behind her. She left the door open, gave Lee a troubled look that he couldn't quite interpret, and then stepped aside.

A young man scooted through the opening, his hands wrestling with each other, his expression wary.

Lee immediately recognized him from his ID photo.

It was the young, bright-eyed scientist, Jeremy Tuttle.

"Ho-ly shit," Abe muttered.

"Language," Judy snapped as she closed the door.

Lee stared at the guy. "You're not dead, Jeremy Tuttle."

Jeremy looked suddenly as shocked as Lee. "Wait. How do you...?" He turned to Judy, lowering his voice. "How's he know my name?"

Judy shrugged as she shooed him towards the kitchen. He didn't look very willing to go. "Ask him."

Jeremy shuffled forward under her urging, frowning deeply at Lee, and then looking at the other members of his team. The guy acted like a dog-shy kid being told to pet a snarling rottweiler.

Lee heaved himself off the couch and extended his hand, which hung for an awkward amount of time before Jeremy relented and gave it a limp-wristed shake. "We were supposed to rescue you and your two friends. We were shown photos of each of you, and given your names." Lee tilted his head to the side. "Do you need rescuing, Jeremy?"

Jeremy shook his head slowly. "No, I..." His gaze bounced around for a moment, found no comfortable place to rest, and wound up fixed on the floor. "I'm fine here. But you should leave."

Lee ignored that. "What about your other two friends? Are they still alive?"

Again, Jeremy shook his head, then quietly muttered at the ground, "They weren't my friends."

"And I take it from your use of the past tense that they're dead?"

Judy's voice blanketed any response from Jeremy. "Alright, this kitchen's getting too crowded." She looked to the guards—specifically the guy that had done most of the talking earlier. "They give you any trouble?"

"No, they were cooperative."

"Good. All of you can leave. Except for Cade. You stay with me, Honey."

Lee eyed the big, swarthy hybrid as the rest of their guards filed out. Interesting that Judy would've gone with him over any of the others. He seemed so placid, his bulk leaning over the kitchen island, propped up by his elbows. He didn't frown at anyone. Wasn't trying to look intimidating—not that he had to try. His eyes were wide and guileless, displaying a sort of childish curiosity.

Except...

Lee had noticed the way Cade's eyes never rested, and never wandered from the five strangers. Occasionally, he would make eye contact with one of them, but mostly it seemed he was looking at their body language—specifically their hands.

Lee suddenly had no doubt in his mind that Judy had picked Cade because he was the most dangerous. What Lee found most unsettling of all, was that he didn't think Cade's innocent expression would change one bit if he got violent.

No warning snarls or menacing looks from this one. He'd just pull their heads off with the same blank focus of a child testing the structural integrity of a Barbie doll.

"Come on," Judy said, as the last of the guards trickled through the front door and closed it behind them. She was angling around Lee, heading for the living room. "Let's sit and talk things out. We got a lot to go over, and I didn't preserve a couch through the end of the world just for looks."

She went to the far end of the sectional where Lee had taken his short nap. Lee saw the way her brow furrowed. She leaned forward and swiped what looked like a bit of leaf debris from her couch, then gave Lee a dirty look and sat.

Her sour expression morphed into a beatific smile as she sighed in contentment. "Not many luxuries left in the world nowadays. But a soft place to land is one of 'em."

Jeremy stuck close to Judy, taking a seat beside her. He looked far less comfortable than her.

Thinking of the big hybrid in the kitchen, Lee made a decision. "Judy, if you don't mind, I think we'd all like to get out of our armor."

Judy frowned. "Why would I mind?"

Lee smiled as he unslung his rifle and began pulling at the Velcro straps of his plate carrier. "Because it's gonna smell like a men's locker room in a minute."

Judy grunted, amused, then waved a hand. "It'll air out. Might as well make yourselves comfortable."

Sam, Abe, and Marie had no qualms in getting out of their armor, nor in removing their rifles. Over the years of meeting potentially-hostile strangers in their own homes, they'd all developed a bit of a sixth sense for when they could afford to let their guard down. By silent consensus, it seemed they all agreed that they didn't need to be on guard anymore.

Lee simply didn't want anyone to accidentally grip their rifle in a way that Cade might interpret wrong.

They flipped their armor inside-out to help them dry, propped them near their feet, and set their rifles close-by. Equipped only with their sidearms now, they each took a position on the couch, Lee choosing to seat himself right next to Jeremy, which caused the young scientist to shrink up and lean subtly away from Lee.

Kat hovered over the back of the couch where Marie, Sam, and Abe sat.

Cade moved into the living room, shockingly quiet and graceful for his size. He lowered himself into a cross-legged position on the floor and continued to watch them.

Lee went into his pants pocket and drew out the three-banded ring they'd recovered from the burn pit. He held it out towards Jeremy. "You recognize this?"

Jeremey stared at it for a moment. Swallowed. Then nodded.

"It belong to one of the other scientists?" Lee pressed.

Jeremy looked at Judy.

Judy seemed to get a little irritated. "Go on, Jeremy. We talked about this."

"You sure we can trust them?" Jeremy hissed.

"No," Judy said. "But I'm sure we don't have a choice at this point. I explained the situation to you. Nothing's changed in the last hour, except we have less time until we get invaded by some government death squad."

Jeremy sighed and hung his head. He avoided eye contact, but when he spoke next, Lee intuited it was directed at him.

"That belonged to Misha."

Lee pulled his head back, frowning. Cast a glance at his team, and received blank expressions and a few bewildered shakes of the head. He looked back to Jeremy. "Misha wasn't one of the scientists we were sent for."

Now Jeremy did make eye contact, perplexed. "There were only three of us."

Lee nodded hesitantly. "Yeah. You, Bruce Ballmer, and Michael Schwartz."

Jeremy blinked like he had something caught in his eye. "I don't know who those people are."

Lee compressed his lips, staring at the ring for a long moment, turning it to see the inscription inside. The inscription in Russian. And wasn't Misha a Russian name?

Had their briefing packet given them false names? But why would they give the right name for Jeremy, and false names for the other two?

"Alright," Lee said, slowly. "What were the names of the two scientists that were with you?"

"Misha Sidorov," Jeremy answered. "And Yevgeni Balakirev." He nodded at the ring. "That belonged to Misha."

"So, both of the others were Russians," Lee said.

Jeremy nodded.

"Seems to be a lot of Russian shit going down around here," Abe observed.

"Jeremy," Lee prodded. "Do you know anything about the military unit that's stationed off to the northwest of Appomattox?"

Jeremy wet his lips, knuckling his glasses back up his nose. "Well. I mean. I know they're there. That's about it."

Lee pocketed the ring again. "So, the intel we received before getting dropped out here gave us completely different names for Misha and Yevgeni. American names. Any reason you can see why they would've lied to us about the nationality of the other two scientists?"

Jeremy squirmed in his seat, then shrugged. "I guess they didn't want you to know they were Russian."

"Well, yeah, that's pretty obvious at this point," Lee said. "But we're talking about scientists here. I don't feel like it's beyond the pale to have a few foreign scientists help with research. I know the IAG is working with other countries. Why would they need to hide that?" Lee held up a hand to forestall Jeremy's response. "What were you guys researching? Because, cards on the table here, we were instructed to rescue three scientists *and their research*. And between you and me, Jeremy, there was a clear implication that the IAG was way more concerned about getting the research back than the scientists."

Jeremy hung his head. It seemed to take him a long time to summon the words.

Judy reached over and patted his knee. "Go ahead. I think it's about time we tell 'em everything."

"I didn't know," Jeremy said, suddenly straightening with shame all in his eyes. "Okay? You have to understand that. Look." He splayed his fingers on his chest. "I'm an evolutionary biologist. And I thought that's what we were here to do—to study a new form of *homo sapiens*. By which I mean both the primals and the hybrids. I thought we were here to research how Appomattox had figured out how to live in peace with them."

Lee sat back on the couch. "Yeah, well, don't feel too bad about being hoodwinked. That was the impression we were given as well—that y'all were just researching the relationship here between humans and primals and hybrids."

Jeremy seemed slightly relieved to be absolved of his ignorance. Getting more comfortable now, he met Lee's gaze and held it. "But that's not what Misha and Yevgeni were here for. I didn't know this at first, though I'll admit, I was curious why two Russian *microbiologists* were in charge of a research mission that had to do with evolutionary biology—I mean, that's *my* wheel house. *I* should've been the one in charge. But I wasn't. I started to realize that this whole thing wasn't even run by the IAG. Misha and Yevgeni, they both spoke fluent English, but it wasn't IAG they were reporting to. When they made the calls to issue their status reports, they were speaking Russian. That's when I started to suspect that we weren't even working for the IAG. At least, not directly. Then Misha and Yevgeni started to take a lot of blood samples from the hybrids. I asked them about it, because it didn't seem very germane to what we were here to research, but they said they were just trying to isolate where the genome split from regular *homo sapiens*. Okay. I could buy that."

Jeremy got a haunted look, and lowered his voice. "But I started snooping around. Started looking into what they were doing with those blood samples." He slumped forward. "They were testing a virus. I mean, I'm not a microbiologist, okay? So, take what I say next with a grain of salt, but...the virus they were working with wasn't anything I'd seen before. I think it was made in a lab." He looked at Lee, and then each member of his team, his eyes filled with earnest conviction. "I think they're trying to design a virus that will specifically attack cells with primal or hybrid genetics, but leave humans unharmed. They're trying to exterminate anyone whose genome was mutated by the plague. The primals, yes. But also everyone like Cade." He looked at the big hybrid, then swiveled his gaze to Kat and nodded. "All of them."

Jones had reached an inevitable conclusion.

The Russians were going to kill him.

Nothing else made any sense. It was clear they were putting a lot of effort into the subterfuge of appearing like IAG forces. They wouldn't go through all that trouble if it wasn't very important that it remain undiscovered that Russian troops were operating on American soil.

Which meant one poor bastard that knew the truth would have to die.

That poor bastard being him.

So, his choices were simple, albeit unattractive.

Option One: Stick it out and see how many hours he could squeeze out of his life. They would likely be filled with some solid beat-downs, and possibly worse. Possibly glass thermometers and all that shit. And really, after the two guards had tooled Jones up pretty solidly, he didn't want a repeat.

And, of course, after they'd taken all their sullen, anti-American rage out on him, they would kill him. The method did not so much concern Jones as the fact that he would be irrefutably dead.

He did not want to be dead. He liked living.

Which was interesting, if you really thought about it. Because for a long time he'd been wondering about the state of the universe, and what it all meant. And when you get into that headspace, you tend to start thinking that it's all pointless, because what other conclusion can you come to? None of it actually makes any sense.

And yet, when you're faced with the alternative of oblivion, all of the sudden it doesn't seem so bad to stick it out a little while longer.

Which led Jones to Option Number Two, which he greatly preferred: Escape.

Yes. A hair-brained plan, to be sure. Because his plan consisted of *hurt them, then get away*. The "hurting them" part wasn't really integral to getting away, but as close as the two guards were hovering, Jones figured it couldn't be avoided.

No, he didn't have some grand scheme for his escape. He was just going to have to wing it. He fully realized that this might all end very badly for him. But however it ended, it couldn't be worse than glass up his pee-hole and an ignoble death at the hands of some foreigners.

Fuck them. If they wanted to kill him, they were gonna have to work for it. No one got to take Calvin-Fuckin'-Jones out of this world without at least breaking a sweat.

That was a satisfactory epitaph, wasn't it?

Here lies Calvin Jones. They had to sweat to kill him.

He had one, minute advantage: They hadn't put his hood back on.

A pessimistic person might not have called it an advantage, but Jones liked to think positively, especially when his life was on the line.

He was still restrained, and currently curled up in an aching fetal position, wherein he swore he could feel his kidneys bleeding into his bladder.

But...no hood.

So he had his eyesight. Hands restrained behind his back, sure. But his legs were free. That was a good thing. Also, the two guards only had their sidearms on their persons. And no armor.

Yeah. Easy-peasy.

Now, for all of Jones's bluster and talk, he actually wasn't that full of himself. Much like many other people in the world, he played a character that had been designed and curated to allow the person inside to live in a world gone mad. Part of the character that Jones played was "The Clown." Why? Because it amused him, and keeping yourself entertained was half the battle of surviving.

But here was the reality: Jones had been active-duty infantry. Then, after the world ended, he'd survived. Then, after surviving, he'd been a part of a Hunter-Killer squad that specifically tracked down and eliminated primals—which was no easy task. Then he'd been an undercover operative inside of Greeley while Lee and his forces surrounded the city and prepared to invade. Then, for a while, he'd been kind of an all-around recon/raider/killer until Greeley had been nuked off the map, and he'd wound up on The Squad of Misfit Operatives with Lee Harden.

Over the last three years, under the tutelage of Lee and Abe, Jones had learned all manner of crazy shit, half of it being on the subject of "how to make people work with you" and the other half being on the subject of "how to kill people that refuse to work with you."

So, yes, Jones was The Clown. He enjoyed being The Clown. It fit his personality, and, really, every team needed a Clown. Teams that didn't have Clowns wound up all emotionally tangled by the violence they had to distribute, whereas teams that had a Clown were always reminded that humanity and all their foibles were really quite laughable. That perspective helped maintain sanity.

But...

Jones was a *Killer Clown*.

He didn't like to pull that out too often because, frankly, it disturbed him. He didn't like how easily killing others came to him these days. It was weird to be able to do it with such practiced precision that it seemed inconsequential.

Jones liked people. He didn't want to kill them.

But sometimes they forced his hand.

"Guys," he said, with a weird, tremulous voice. "Do you speak English?"

Neither responded.

Jones began to subtly twitch. "I'm...I'm an epileptic. I can feel a seizure coming on. Guys—do you understand me?"

It was clear that they didn't, given the smattering of Russian they tossed back and forth at each other.

Then one of them kicked him—not hard, but kind of testing to see what was going on.

Jones decided to stop talking—so he could gather some spit in his mouth, slosh it around between his teeth, and foam it up. He started making little moaning noises, and let his gyrations become a little more obvious.

The tone of the guards became concerned. But, as any ham-fisted soldier would do, they decided to kick him a little more to see if he was fucking around.

Jones endured the handful of half-hearted strikes to his bruised midsection, continuing to moan, and slowly bringing his thrashing up to what he hoped were worrisome levels.

The kicking tapered off. The guards' jabbering took on a more concerned quality.

Jones decided to let it all out and began fully thrashing on the floor, garnering a series of shouted words from the guards which meant nothing to him.

Then he gave them the *piece de resistance*: He began to leak frothy drool out of his mouth.

He writhed his way onto his side, keeping an eye on how the two Russian soldiers responded. One ran for the tent flap, hollering. The other went down on a knee right next to Jones.

He couldn't have asked for better positioning.

In one explosion of movement, Jones wrapped his legs around the guy's neck, pitched him forward onto his face, then rolled until his bound hands touched holstered pistol. He'd locked the guy good and solid into a triangle choke and put everything he had into cinching it tight around his neck.

It worked. The guy's hands went to trying to free himself, instead of protecting his sidearm.

Jones's fingers scrambled at the unfamiliar retention system—but only for a fraction of a second. It was just like the Safariland holsters Jones was familiar with: *Thumb forward, thumb back*.

The weapon came free.

He had the guard pinned good and solid with his triangle choke, so he didn't try to shoot him first. Of course, shooting with your hands tied behind your back was no easy feat, but he hunched over the bucking soldier underneath him and pointed the pistol at the one that'd gone to the tent flap.

The soldier beneath him flailed, realizing the danger of his predicament. He tried to get his hands around Jones's throat, which Jones could do nothing to stop.

Jones let the guy cut off his airway—he could afford to be breathless for a few moments.

Twisting, he fired wildly in the general direction of the tent flap. Even as he did it, he knew how low his chances of success were. But he could see his target's back, and he registered where the fabric of the tent was twitching as his rounds poked holes in it, and he did his best to track them into his target.

He'd fired nearly ten rounds. The pistol was close to running empty. And the fleeing guard was close to slipping out of view.

Jones was shocked as hell when he saw the guy jerk, and then topple, screaming as only a man can scream when they've discovered a new hole in their body.

He was so surprised he almost froze.

He really didn't think that was going to work.

The guy beneath him lurched again, reminding Jones that his one improbable success didn't make him a free man just yet.

He immediately thrust himself backwards, stuck the gun in the crotch of the soldier he was straddling, and fired. The effect was instantaneous. The man's grip released from around his throat and his eyes went wide.

Jones felt a modicum of pity for the poor fucker, then fired again.

He rolled off the guy, and then to his feet.

Both guards were screaming at this point.

Jones let out a slurry of curses as he awkwardly sidestepped and twisted, trying to aim as best he could with a gun that was behind his back, then fired at the soldier on the ground next to him. The bullet struck him in the gut, causing more screaming.

"Goddammit!" Jones shrieked, then redirected his aim and fired again. This one caught the guy in his chest, dead center. Jones was pretty sure that had severed his aorta. He wouldn't last more than a minute.

He immediately whirled and scrambled to the soldier that was writhing near the tent flap, trying to get at a hole in his back which he'd never be able to reach.

This was all very awkward, but Jones half-squatted, pointing his backside at the guy, as though he could fart supersonic lead. He fired again. There was another scream, which was a good thing because it meant he'd hit his target, but it was bad, because Jones hated the sound of people screaming in agony—particularly when he'd caused it.

He tried to pull the trigger again, but the pistol had gone empty.

Jones had no choice but to wheel around and let loose. Just as much as he normally committed himself to being a clown for the betterment of others, he now committed himself to being a cold-hearted killer for the benefit of his life. Sinking into the role, he slavered out a bunch of curses and he set to stomping the guard's face in with his bare feet.

He felt the guy's teeth cut into his heel as he slammed his foot down.

But he also felt the guy's face cave in.

The soldier's screaming turned into strange, guttural moans. Jones figured that meant he was out of the fight, and he wasted no time turning and plunging through the tent flap. The second he did, he thought, *Should've grabbed the other pistol!* But it was too late, and he was consumed with the need to get the fuck out of there.

In that moment of panic and confusion, his awareness of his surroundings was slim—impressionistic. He saw tents. He saw vehicles. He saw trees. He saw the sun.

The sun was setting.

He needed to head east to get back to Appomattox. He wasn't sure if Appomattox was friendly, but he was very sure that the Russians were *un*-friendly, so he turned his back to the westering sun and began sprinting east for all he was worth.

He heard voices behind him, shouting in Russian, as his bare feet slammed through weeds, the pain of sticks and brambles inconsequential to his need to escape.

You're almost free! He told himself, because he needed a little positive affirmation at the moment, and, really, he'd done a pretty good job, hadn't he?

Rifles barked behind him.

"Oh, fuck!" he yelped, deciding to juke left and right, though he wasn't sure if that would help him or plant him firmly in the path of a bullet. He was running entirely on instinct now.

Then a bullet found him.

At first, he didn't realize that's what had happened. One second, he was racing headlong through the forest. The next, he was on the ground, gasping as an incredible, unholy agony wracked his midsection.

Run now, worry later, Jonesy!

As though to spur him, another smattering of bullets raked the trees over his head.

Jones heaved himself to his feet and forced his tingling legs to start moving again. Everything was a hundred times more difficult. But he had no choice but to press on, even as his pace felt nightmare-sluggish.

The next few moments were just blind, senseless flight. The need to get away remained the first priority, but a sickening panic began to descend on him, braiding itself into the cords of pain that tightened around his guts.

Somewhere in there, he realized there was pain in his left arm too.

He glanced down at his midsection and saw no blood, which confused him for several strides. Then he realized what it meant.

The bullet's still in me.

And he had a long way to go until he reached Appomattox.

The fact that they might not welcome him, or that he might get shredded by primals before he even got there, were factors he did not even entertain at the moment.

He was still conscious, and he was still mobile, and that meant running was still his best chance of survival.

CHAPTER 20

GRIFFIN SAT IN THE private meeting room across from President Morton, his face a rigid mask as he listened to Ron Paige tell him the situation. By the time Ron was done, Griffin was hunched forward onto the table, his legs bouncing beneath.

"Is that all?" Griffin asked, laconically.

"Yeah, that's it," Ron answered.

Griffin looked at the president. Morton looked mildly curious about what was happening. To Ron, Griffin said, "Can you give me five minutes and then I'll call you back?"

"Uh, yeah, I guess. Situation's deteriorating, though, so..."

"I'm aware. Five minutes and then I'll have an answer for you on how we're going to proceed." Griffin didn't wait for polite goodbyes—he just hung up.

The president spread his hands. "Hit me."

"Intel on the ground is that the scientists are dead. How important is it to you that this research get recovered?"

Morton rubbed his chin, making a scratchy sound against his five o'clock shadow. "It's important."

Griffin's eyes narrowed. "You never really gave a shit about saving the town, did you?"

Morton huffed. "Jesus, Perry. Of course I give a shit what happens to them. They're an American settlement. I didn't *want* them to get railroaded. But there are bigger things at stake here."

"Such as?"

Morton pursed his lips, but didn't answer.

"Jim," Griffin said with a warning tone. "I need you to tell me what this fucking research was that's so goddamn important we're willing to spend the lives of an entire settlement—and a team of good operators to boot."

"Alright," Morton grunted. "Then tell me who these operators are."

"We don't have time for this shit."

"Then quit wasting it."

"What? You want me to give you their names?" Griffin was incredulous.

Morton nodded, as though it were obvious. "Uh, yeah. That's exactly what I want. And the fact that you're so unwilling to tell me makes me think I'll recognize these names and not be real happy with you for using them."

Griffin glared. "You invited Russian troops onto American soil. You don't really have a leg to stand on."

"Point taken. I guess we both got dirty hands, huh? So, now that we're both on a level playing field—fuckin' spill it."

Griffin stared down at the table as he ran his hands back and forth across the surface. He'd managed to keep Lee and his team a secret for three years now. The only other people that knew that Lee Harden and Abe Darabie had not died in Greeley, Colorado, were Ron Paige and Angela Houston.

What would happen if the president knew?

Griffin had an inkling. And that was the only reason he decided to tell the truth.

"Three of the five names won't mean shit to you," Griffin said. "But the other two..." he sighed, then looked his president in the face. "...are Lee Harden and Abe Darabie."

Morton's face was a fascinating study of human emotion. At first, it remained blank. Then it showed disbelief. Then complete and utter shock.

And then, just as Griffin had predicted, intense interest.

Morton let out a wheezy little chuckle. "Oh, Perry. What have you been up to?"

Griffin sneered. "Things were complicated after Greeley."

Morton scooted to the edge of his chair, leaning in, conspiratorially. "You've had Harden and Darabie in pocket *since Greeley*?"

Griffin nodded.

"What've you been using them for?"

"Probably not what you'd think."

"Oh, but I can't wait for you to enlighten me."

"First off, you gotta understand—they didn't do all the shit they were charged with."

Morton lifted an eyebrow. "So there were no civilian massacres in Greeley? That's odd, because I read the reports from the Brits and Canadians. Were they lying?"

"No," Griffin admitted. "There were civilian massacres. But neither Lee nor Abe were a part of them, nor did they sanction them. They had a guy that was leading a part of their rebel troops that'd become a little...unhinged. He was killed, but we still needed a sacrificial lamb to take the fall. So we said Lee and his team had been caught in the blast. Which, technically, they were. Except they were in Erwin Briggs's underground bunker when the warhead hit. I found them when they came topside again and made a deal with them: I would provide them with supplies and equipment, and they'd stick to the abandoned coastal zones, going from settlement to settlement, trying to stabilize things there in preparation for us to expand our borders."

Griffin took his satphone in both hands, running his fingers over its lightly-stippled shell. "When you came to me needing a team that could get the scientists and the researchers out, while keeping you insulated, they were the ones I called on. That's who's on the ground now."

"Was it one of them that got captured?"

Griffin shook his head. "Just a member of their team."

"Huh." Morton leaned back again, looking thoughtfully into the middle distance.

"They got hit by Russian patrols that are keeping Appomattox cordoned off. They lost their supplies. They're requesting a drop. No intel on the location of the research at this time. Which brings us to my question for you. Care to answer?"

Morton rallied himself with a big intake of breath. "What's the research about?"

Griffin nodded.

Morton flapped his lips. "Shit. Russians were pretty hush-hush about it, so they only gave the bare minimum of details. Apparently, they designed a virus that affects the primals. That was part of their process for restabilizing their country, though, admittedly, between their low population density and the Russian winters, they didn't have near the same problems we've had. The primals over there never formed large colonies—just isolated, nomadic packs." Morton shrugged. "So they never had to deal with the hybridization problem we're seeing here in the States. And…" Morton gave Griffin a pointed look. "The virus is apparently ineffective against hybrids."

The facts swarmed, and then began to coalesce into a logical framework in Griffin's mind. "So the scientists were trying to figure out how to make the virus work against hybrids. That's why they went into Appomattox."

"It's also why this needs to stay quiet," Morton said, sternly. "Look, Perry. We need a leg up against the primals and hybrids or we're gonna be stuck fighting a losing battle against a creature that can outbreed and outcompete us. We are the neanderthals here, and they're the wily upstarts that are going to wreck our shit if we don't figure out how to exterminate them. But I don't need to tell you the kind of shitstorm that's going to come down on us if people learn about this."

No, Morton *didn't* need to tell Griffin. He could intuit it all on his own. Part of the shitstorm would be foreign soldiers inside their country. But the other—and perhaps bigger part—was the fact that the populace would be understandably concerned about the unleashing of an experimental virus, six years after a plague had shattered their whole world.

Honestly, Griffin found the concept wildly disconcerting. Were they really going to fuck around with something like this when they barely had their feet under them from the last pandemic? What happened when the virus mutated and started affecting humans too? You'd think people would be a little more gun-shy about trying something like this. The hubris of it was astounding.

"I'll tell you what," Morton said. "I never bought the party line about Harden and Darabie. Erwin Briggs was a fucking despot that should've never been allowed to take control. Frankly, I've always been a bit of a fan of Harden for taking it to Briggs's ass. After all, someone had to do it, and if he hadn't stepped up, we wouldn't have made as much progress as we have towards reconstruction. So..." Morton planted his palms on the table. "You give that man whatever the hell he needs to find that research and get out of there." He held up a finger. "But *quietly*. The Russians are all too willing to wipe the settlement out and call it a loss—but I want that fucking research."

Griffin frowned. "So you want them to get the research and then *not* tell the Russians that we retrieved it?"

Morton nodded. "The Russians are assed up right now. They're gonna end up swooping in on Appomattox and wiping it out. There's nothing we can do about that without completely ruining our alliance in the MCR. But they don't need to know that we recovered the research."

A satphone buzzed.

It wasn't Griffin's.

Morton picked his satphone up, eyed the display, then answered. "You have the president."

Then he listened.

His face became drawn. Weary.

"Any way I can convince you to hold off on that?" Morton asked whoever was on the other line. He waited, listening again. Then sighed and nodded. "Alright. Do what you gotta do. Just make sure none of this shit blows back on me, or we're going to have some serious problems."

He hung up and placed the satphone face-down on the table.

Morton's gaze was deadly serious. "You better get on the horn, Perry. Whoever it was the Russians captured—he escaped. They're in full panic mode. They're not waiting any longer."

Griffin felt a cold flush on the back of his neck. "They're gonna move on Appomattox?"

Morton stabbed a blunt finger repeatedly into the tabletop. "Get that research, and get your team out of there."

Stas watched with a sneer of disgust as his two men were zipped into black body bags. Stas would be damned if he'd bury them in foreign soil. They both deserved to be put to rest in their own homeland.

They would be added to the four other body bags from the eviscerated recon patrol.

Six casualties already. And the real fight had not even begun.

Was this his fault? He didn't think he had taken the captured operative lightly. Ilya and Lev had been two of his best men. Man to man, he would pit them against any other operative the world over, and be confident in their ability to handle their opponent.

So, how had one man, with his hands restrained behind his back, managed to kill both of them?

Was it a fluke? Had there been deception involved?

Who the hell were these American operatives?

Perhaps he should not have been so excited about the challenge they posed. Perhaps that had been foolish of him.

But if that were the case, then Stas Obolensky was a great fool. The loss of two men who'd been his brothers, who he'd spent years of his life with, having each other's backs in a dozen warzones the world over, both before and after the plague—it nearly crushed him.

Nearly.

But the sadness came with a cold determination. And rather than freezing him, it animated him. Pushed him. Put his mind into overdrive. Woke him up from a certain brand of placidity that he'd developed over years of near-effortless victories.

He hadn't exactly become complacent. But he certainly had not expected this level of resistance from his enemies.

He'd been confident in the beginning, like a boxer testing their opponent for openings and weaknesses. And now that opponent had let fly a solid blow that had sent Stas reeling.

Okay. One did not exit the ring because they'd been rocked. Nor did one turn into an enraged bear and start wildly swinging.

No. You simply took your opponent more seriously. You shook it off, you cleared your head, and you got back to work, now with the knowledge of just how hard your opponent could hit.

This was no exhibition bout.

This was going to be a knock-down, drag-out brawl.

Someone in the Interim American Government had dispatched one, small team of operatives. Clearly, they were a force to be reckoned with, even as small a unit as they were. But Stas had at his disposal two hundred of the best counter-terrorism operatives in the world.

All he needed was a green light from the colonel, and Stas was going to throw everything he had at Appomattox. He would pull no punches. He would hit hard, and fast. He would be merciless. He would leave no survivors.

"Lieutenant Colonel Obolensky!"

The call came from behind him, and Stas spun to see one of his warrant officers hanging out of the command tent. He raised his eyebrows at the man.

"The colonel is holding for you."

Stas's chest felt like a whirlwind of fire and electricity. He stormed across the camp to the command tent and swept inside. He stalked to the desk phone, snatched up the handset, and pressed the button for the waiting call.

"Obolensky," he said, without preamble.

Then he listened. Nodded. Gave a single acknowledgement, and hung up.

His warrant officers waited, eager as greyhounds in the slips.

Stas turned his back on them and looked at the projection of the town of Appomattox.

"Green light," he announced.

Sam had followed everything Jeremy Tuttle said so far. It was just interesting enough to keep him awake.

Well. That and the fact that the mouthful of ibuprofen he'd swallowed wasn't really doing much for the bullet holes in his leg and trap.

But now Jeremy was getting into a bunch of minutiae, and Sam was starting to get that irritable, drowsy sensation, like he was going to slip into a listless doze. Wincing, he shifted on the couch to try to get his shoulder in a more comfortable position.

He was consistently aware of Kat's presence behind him.

He wished she would find some other place to loom.

The voices droned on. The room seemed washed-out of color and details.

What were they going to do about Jonesy? They had to figure out a way to get him back. Sam didn't even want to entertain the notion of just leaving Virginia without him. Didn't want to think about losing his loud-mouthed friend. Who was going to make inappropriate jokes at inappropriate times? Who was going to give them pop-quizzes when they were all too tired to think?

Without Jonesy, this team would be as colorless and ill-defined as the room Sam was in.

His leg throbbed.

Kat was kneeling there. How had she gotten around the couch without him noticing? And what the fuck was she doing? Was she sniffing his leg?

"Hey," he grumbled, but was too tired to move his leg out of her reach. "Leave it alone."

Kat ignored him. Just crouched there, staring at his wound like the smell of blood had lit off something in her brain. That made Sam wildly uncomfortably. God, it was a mistake to work with a hybrid.

Kat raised a hand. Maybe it was the weird, evening light coming through the windows, or maybe it was just his imagination, but her fingers seemed longer than they should've been. The hardened nails seemed more like talons. It looked like the hand of a demon.

Then she began to very gently scratch at the bandages over his leg.

"Cut that out!" Sam snapped, waving a hand ineffectually at her. "Don't fucking touch it!"

Again, Kat ignored him. Those talons of hers started scratching harder, and the wound smarted.

Sam's heart started slamming. What had gotten into her? These fucking animal-people were disturbing as hell. He tried to turn and request help from Marie, but he couldn't seem to tear his gaze off of Kat.

Then she swiveled those copper-colored eyes on him.

"What're you doing?" he moaned.

She opened her mouth and issued a strange buzzing noise.

Sam was suddenly terrified beyond all reason and control. His right hand dipped to his holstered sidearm, and he drew it in one smooth movement. "Get the fuck away from me!" The sights trembled in his shaking hand as he settled them on her face.

Her mouth was still open, still issuing that weird buzzing noise.

Her talon began to sink into his leg.

He cried out in pain and reflexively pulled the trigger.

Except...he *couldn't* pull the trigger. He was trying, but the damn thing wouldn't move, no matter how hard he pressed.

Kat's gaping, tooth-filled mouth began to stretch wider.

Sam kept straining at the unreasonably-heavy trigger, groaning with fear and effort.

Then someone hit him in the side.

"Hey. Sam. Snap out of it."

Marie's voice.

Sam snorted, jerked, and blinked.

It took him a moment to make sense of his reality. The room was back to being full-color. Kat wasn't crouching at his legs, sinking her claws into his wound—she was still hovering over the back of the couch. Also, he did not have his pistol in his hand.

Everyone in the room was staring at him.

Lee was standing now, withdrawn to the other side of the room, but looking over his shoulder, frowning at Sam. He had the satphone to his ear.

Sam turned shakily to Marie, and felt relief drench him. She had her hand on his arm and was gently squeezing him. He must've passed out there for a second or two.

"You alright?" Marie asked in a low voice.

Sam sat up, still shaking, a thin layer of fresh sweat over his entire body. "Yeah. Sorry. Nodded off."

Lee pulled the satphone's mic away from his mouth and snapped a finger at Abe. "Get geared up."

Abe immediately came off the couch and hefted his armor from where it was drying out on the floor.

Lee brought the mic back to his mouth. "Roger that." He looked at his wristwatch. "Timeline?" A pause. "Alright. Got it." Then he hung up and immediately whirled on the others, his face grim. For a moment, he seemed at a loss for words. Then he started moving, tossing the satphone to Marie and snatching up his own armor. "Folks—Judy and Jeremy, too—we are in the middle of a category five shitstorm here. Good news: Jones escaped. Bad news: we're outta time and the strike force has decided to move on Appomattox."

Judy erupted off the couch. "Now? They're moving on us *now*?"

"Now. Soon. In a few hours, or sometime tonight—I don't know. But they ain't waitin'." Lee slung the armor over his head, then paused to take a breath. "Worse news: Jones was right. Those aren't IAG troops in that strike force. This whole thing is a Russian operation."

Now Marie rocketed to her feet too, and Sam decided he might as well get geared up too.

"What?" Marie gasped. "Is this a fucking invasion?"

Lee shook his head. "Oh, no. Way worse than that, Marie. Apparently the IAG is in on it somehow. Ron's either holding back details, or Griffin's holding them back from him, so I don't know who signed off on the Russians being here, but *someone* did, and now the Russians are spooked because Jones escaped, and they've decided to wipe the slate clean."

Sam started to wrestle his still-damp armor up, but Lee made a negative noise and shook his head.

"Nope. Sorry, Sam. You need to stay put."

Sam was aghast. "I can still operate!"

"Yeah, I know you can," Lee soothed, slinging into his rifle. "We're gonna head out straight west and try to find Jones, but I want you and Marie to stay in town, in case Jones makes it back here."

Somewhat peeved by this announcement, both Sam and Marie dropped their armor on the floor and glared.

Lee ignored them and spun on Judy. "You need to think about getting out of here."

Judy recoiled like she'd been slapped. "We're not leaving! This is our home!"

Lee rolled his eye, and Sam felt his frustration—they'd heard this argument time and again. People didn't like to be ousted from their homes. But most of the ones that stayed despite Lee's advice, wound up dead.

"Well, that's your choice, Judy," Lee sighed. "I can't force you to do anything. All I can do is warn you that they're gonna kill everyone here. You do with that what you will." He looked at the scientist. "Jeremy—the hard drive and laptops with the research—do you still have them?"

Jeremy's mouth worked with a few silent syllables before he managed to say, "Uh...yeah. I still have them."

Lee seemed to consider him for a few seconds, making some internal decision that he didn't let the rest of his team in on. Then he nodded. "Alright. We'll deal with that after I get my teammate back."

Jeremy shied away from Lee. "I'm not giving them up so they can—"

"We'll deal with it later," Lee snapped, then looked to Abe and Kat. "Y'all ready?"

Abe was geared up. Kat seemed eager. They both nodded.

"Cade, go with them," Judy ordered.

Lee held up a hand. "No, I don't—"

"My house, my rules," Judy declared.

"Might be your house, but it's my op."

"Cade knows this territory better than Kat. Also, he knows our resident primals. Now, you can take your chances that Kat can dissuade them because she's a female hybrid and most primals will defer to her." Judy gave Lee a significant look. "*Most* primals. But there's some males out there that'll still see her as an outsider. Take Cade, and your chances of getting back in one piece are much better. Trust me on this."

Lee huffed, but relented. "Fine. Cade, you're with us. But Kat's in charge. Kat? You think you can scent Jones out?"

Kat nodded without hesitation. "I know his smell."

Lee turned to Sam and Marie once more. "If I were to hazard a guess, I'd say the strike force will move after dark." He pointed a finger at both of them. "If we're not back with Jones by the time shit starts to pop off, you guys call for extract and head for Point Charlie."

"Got it," Marie said, clearly unhappy.

"What about the supply drop?" Sam asked.

Lee shook his head. "No-go on the drop. Not enough time for it to get here."

Sam's brow furrowed, his eyes snapping between Lee and Judy. "So what're we doing here? We just gonna leave?"

Lee's jaw worked. "Right now, I'm focused on getting Jones. Once we have him in hand, we'll figure out our next steps."

Sam blew out a breath. "Alright. Go get him."

"I'll be in touch," Lee said as he and Abe started to move towards the back door. "We're gonna have to fly this by the seat of our pants, so be ready for anything."

Sam threw up his hands and let them flop. "We always are."

Cade and Kat met at the back door, each giving the other an odd look. Then Cade took the lead and went out, followed closely by Kat, then Lee and Abe.

Then it was just Sam, Marie, Judy, and Jeremy.

Of all of them, Jeremy was clearly the most assed-up.

His hands were back to wringing each other, his feet turning him this way and that, as though he were searching for a way out of the situation. "What do we do? How are we gonna survive this?"

Marie put her hands on her hips. Sam noticed how close her right hand was to her sidearm. "What *you're* going to do is take me to wherever you've got that research stored, so I can confirm that you have it."

Jeremy immediately began shaking his head. "No. I told you. I'm not giving it to you guys."

Marie's hand rotated to rest on the grip of her pistol. "You don't have to give it to me. But I need to put eyes on it."

Jeremy glanced at her still-holstered pistol, then at Judy. "She's threatening me."

Marie barked a nasty-sounding laugh. "Hon, if I was threatening you, it'd be way more explicit. I don't fuck around. But I need to be ready, with the research in sight, depending on how things shake out. You want that shit falling back into the hands of the Russians?"

"It shouldn't be in *anyone's* hands!" Jeremy wailed.

"Then why didn't you just destroy it?" Marie demanded.

That caught him off-guard. "Because...I..." Then he girded himself up. "You know what? You're right. I should destroy it."

He started to move, as though to leave the house.

Marie's left hand shot out and grabbed the front of his shirt, while her right established a full grip on her pistol. "Do that and I'll kill you. There—*that* was a threat."

"Hey!" Judy shouted, moving to intervene, but Sam lurched into place, blocking her. Judy's eyes went wide, not with fear, but with absolute rage. "Who the hell do you think you are?"

Sam was typically a quiet guy, but he knew how to bellow with the best of them, and he broke out his full command voice then: "Everyone calm the fuck down!"

It must've taken them by surprise, because everyone froze—even Marie.

Sam addressed Judy first, lowering his voice back to its usual soft register. "Sorry for cussing. Now, listen to me before things get outta hand. The only thing we know right now is that your people are about to get massacred. Judy, you need to be focusing on that, not Jeremy and his research. That's *our* problem."

"If that research gets in the wrong hands," Judy seethed. "It's gonna be used to exterminate hybrids, and that absolutely *is* my problem. What about Kat? You got a hybrid on your team! You want her to get sick with some mystery virus and die puking blood or whatever the hell it does?"

Sam didn't have an answer for that. He was too conflicted about the whole thing, and didn't want to get into it at the moment. So he deflected. "Let's not jump to any conclusions. This is still a developing situation. Marie's right—we need to put eyes on that research. We might need to destroy it, or we might need to extract it and Jeremy with us. We don't know yet. Point is, it can't stay here, or it's gonna wind up in the hands of the Russians, and I think we can all agree that's definitely the worst-case-scenario."

Judy folded her arms over her chest, still glaring. "So my people are just a write-off to you, huh? You think we're as good as dead."

Sam looked at her earnestly. "I think that, to the people with all the power, you and your people are expendable. And as soon as you can stop looking at this emotionally, you'll realize I'm right. You wanna try to fight and defend your home? We won't stop you. But do you think it's gonna be just troops on the ground that they send in? Because if that was the case, yeah, you might have a chance. But I highly doubt that's what they're gonna do."

Judy chewed on that for a moment. "What do you think they're gonna do?"

"Surround your settlement," Sam answered, matter-of-factly. "Hit it with those helos. Maybe artillery, if they have it. Maybe even an airstrike—I don't know what they have available to them. But if they have the capability, they'll kill most of you from afar, and only then will they move ground forces in to clean up the rest."

Jeremy fidgeted in Marie's grip. "What if we just gave the research to the Russians?"

Marie scowled. "Two seconds ago you couldn't bear the thought of it falling into their hands, and now you wanna give it to them?"

"I'm just trying to figure out a solution where everyone here doesn't die!" he cried.

Sam shook his head at the scientist. "It's not about that anymore, Jeremy. Yeah, they want the research. But more than that, they don't want anyone to know what went down here. Even if you gave them the research, they'd still kill everybody to keep it quiet."

The strength seemed to flow out of Judy. She stumbled backwards until her legs hit the couch and she collapsed into it. Her eyes were haunted, her hands coming up to cover her mouth. "What am I gonna do?" she whispered, as though to herself. "I don't...how can we stop them?"

Sam wasn't sure if he should answer, so he turned to Jeremy again. "Take Marie with you. Let her confirm you have the research, then pack it up and bring it back here. Like I said, maybe it needs to be destroyed. Or maybe we can use it as a bargaining chip. Let's just hold off on any decisions we can't take back. You understand?"

Jeremy gave a shaky nod.

Marie released her hold on his shirt and brushed her fingers across the wrinkles she'd made. "Come on." She looked at Sam. "You good here?"

He gave her a thumbs up.

She moved with Jeremy around the couch and out the front door.

Sam's leg was aching something fierce. He wanted to get off his feet. Judy was still sitting there with her hands covering her mouth, staring off at nothing in particular.

Sam limped back to his original seat, so that they were on opposite ends of the sectional. He slumped into the cushion and immediately felt the pain lessen. He breathed a sigh of relief, got his radio off his pack and put the earpiece in. All was quiet on the radio for now.

"Judy," he said, gently.

Slowly, her eyes drifted to his.

"If there's a way out of this for your people, we'll do everything we can to help make that happen. You don't know us, but this is what we do—we help people survive. This mission we got sent on put us at odds at first, but right now, we're in the same boat."

Her voice was muffled behind her hands. "Y'all are just gonna end up abandoning us."

Sam couldn't deny it, so he shrugged. "We might have to exfil, Judy. But before that happens, we'll do what we can." He leaned forward. "In order for us to help you, you need to be honest with me about how things work around here."

She stared at him, unmoving, for a long time.

Slowly, her hands wilted off her face to lay limp on her lap, and she plopped back, looking wrung out and desperate. "Alright, Sam. Whatever you want to know. You ask. I'll answer."

Chapter 21

Sam considered his train of thought carefully, and tracked it back to where so many thoughts go: the beginning. That might've seemed like a waste of time, but his instincts told him that a more complete understanding of this place might show him a solution that surface-level knowledge wouldn't.

"Let's start with how you've survived for six years right alongside primals. Why are they not aggressive with you? Why haven't they slaughtered everyone in Appomattox for food? And how have you come to have so many hybrids here?"

Judy blinked slowly. "That's four different questions."

Sam gave her a shrewd look. "Something tells me they all have the same answer."

She wheezed out a chuckle without actually smiling. "You're sharp for your age, huh?"

"I pay attention, and I listen to my gut. It's served me well so far."

Judy sniffed and swiped a finger under her nose, her gaze drifting to fix itself on the wall across from her. "My husband, Dirk, got infected. Right here. In this very house." A faint twist of her lips. "But I was never afraid of him. Didn't report him being infected. Didn't run away, or kick him out, like everyone else did. And yeah, he lost his mind, like they all did. Or, at least, a part of it. But not the part that knew me. No, Dirk always remembered me. Remembered that he loved me." Her hands came together and she began toying with a wedding ring Sam hadn't noticed until that moment. "Won't lie—it was weird. Like living with a werewolf or something. Couldn't keep him indoors. Honestly, didn't particularly want to. So he'd run off. But he'd always come back. Didn't really try to interact with me much, but when he needed to sleep, he'd come back here. I'd find him at random odd hours, curled up on the floor like a dog." She chuffed. "Naked as a jaybird."

She finally returned to looking at Sam, some of the emotion falling from her face as she began to tell the facts. "After a few months, I started noticing the changes. The mutations." She gestured briefly to her arms and mouth, then waved it off. "You know what primals look like. And that's what he was becoming. Shoulda figured Dirk wouldn't die because of the plague—he always was stubborn as a mule. No, he did what all the primals ended up doing—took something that turned everyone else into gibbering psychopaths, and made himself stronger. Adapted. Evolved." She sighed. "Anyway. Other infected would come around and...well...you know how the primals were with the infected, right?"

Sam nodded. Before most of the infected died out that first winter, the primals had themselves quite a feast. Treated the regular infected as a primary source of prey. Which, to the scared twelve-year-old boy he'd been, had turned the primals into something of a sympathetic villain in his young mind.

Still terrifying, though.

Judy continued. "Yeah, he'd kill them, and...well, anyway. Other primals started showing up. They formed a pack around Dirk and went wherever he went. They weren't exactly friendly, but they left me be. Actually protected me when the hordes out of the cities came through this region. Kept them from getting too close to Appomattox. And by then, there were lots of primals, and quite a few humans that had figured out that they could survive if they just stuck close to me." She skipped her hand through the air. "And...here we are today."

Sam digested this in silence. At the same time that he'd never seen or heard of anything like Appomattox before, it was not entirely surprising. Not everyone that got infected had turned into raging lunatics. They all seemed to lose a good portion of their ability to reason and speak, but not all of them became hyper-aggressive.

This was the first time he'd heard of an infected retaining some memory of a loved one and actually protecting them, but he could believe it. For a guy who'd spent his formative years in a world of chaos and cruelty, Sam still had a romantic streak a mile wide, and he firmly believed that there were matters of the heart and soul that no plague could ever touch.

"Is Dirk still alive?" he asked.

The corners of Judy's eyes tightened with emotion, but that was all the expression she let show. "I don't know," she admitted. "No one's seen him in about a year. The mutations—they cause horrendous premature aging. And Dirk was no spring chicken to begin with. So maybe he's passed on. Or maybe he's just too old to get out much anymore." She blinked and was emotionless again. "You know, we live alongside those three colonies, but we don't go into their dens, and they don't come into our houses. So, it's not like I can waltz in there and look for him."

Sam noted she'd skipped over the part about how they had so many hybrids here in Appomattox. But he needed to approach that topic gently, and without judgment.

In his experience, the hybridization between humans and primals occurred either through rape or sexual aberrancy, neither of which your average person was keen to talk about.

Sam had known for years that male primals would capture human females for forced breeding, in order to produce the half-primal, half-human matriarchs that ran the colonies. Only recently had he discovered that these matriarchs would also breed with human males, if they got their hands on one that was willing. That breeding resulted in hybrids that were three-quarters human, like Kat and all the other hybrids in Appomattox.

Thinking about that, a memory occurred to him. About three years ago, Sam had known a guy that had been captured by the primals. They'd ended up rescuing him, and after he'd recovered, he'd told them about the female that seemed to be in charge of the primals, and whose mutations did not seem as extreme. That was their first encounter with a matriarch.

According to that soldier, one of those matriarchs had, apparently, made some advances on him. Why this instinct to interbreed existed remained a mystery. Perhaps it was just the instinct to maintain genetic diversity inside the colony.

In any case, Sam remembered the guy talking about the matriarch. He'd never admitted it, but Sam recalled having the notion that the guy had been somewhat...attracted to the matriarch.

Jones had brushed it off in typical Jones fashion: "You remember hentai? Anime porn with tentacles and shit? Yeah, man. Dudes can get turned on by some weird shit."

But then, Sam also remembered when they'd infiltrated the colony that Kat had been born into. That'd been the first time he'd seen a matriarch for himself. There'd actually been three of them in that colony and...

Well. Sam had been focused on the mission of saving a friend. But looking back on that experience, he had to admit—at least to himself, if not anyone else—that there *was* something strangely erotic about them. The easy answer was that, while their faces were decidedly not-human, their bodies were almost idealized female forms.

But in his ponderings, Sam had always felt that there was more to it. Something almost hypnotic, as though the matriarchs exuded some powerful pheromone that blanked out higher thinking. Of course, humans weren't supposed to have pheromones. But then again, humans weren't supposed to have claws or long, predatory canine teeth either.

Just because science couldn't explain a phenomenon, didn't mean it wasn't real.

He rubbed his palms slowly across each other, choosing his words carefully. "It's clear there's a significant level of interbreeding between the humans and primals here. Or at least, more than I've witnessed before." He almost went on, but decided to simply let that observation hang, and see what Judy had to say about it.

She watched him for a time, as though waiting for a full question to be asked. When it became obvious he wasn't going to continue, she let out a long, nasal sigh. Her hands began to move back and forth along the tops of her thighs—a self-soothing gesture that Sam recognized.

"The first hybrid matriarch—the one that still runs the biggest colony of primals…" Hesitation. Guilt. Fear of judgment. "She's my daughter."

Her gaze flicked to Sam's, but he gave no reaction. Honestly, he'd been expecting something like this. Whether or not that daughter had been conceived out of love or terror, he didn't know. And didn't *need* to know. So he simply nodded at her to continue.

Judy seemed relieved that he hadn't displayed disgust or moral outrage. "The other two colonies are led by *her* daughters—my granddaughters—though I have no idea who the fathers were, or whether they were primals or humans. As for the rest of the hybrids around here? Well..." She hunched forward, seeming very small in that moment. "You have to understand the relationship between the humans and the primals here. Not the hybrids—they're kind of caught in the middle. But between all the people that settled here in Appomattox, and the colonies of primals that grew here. We have what you might call..." she made a circular motion with both hands. "...a symbiotic relationship. They keep us protected. We keep them fed."

Sam frowned. "They don't hunt for themselves?"

"Oh, they hunt," she confirmed. "But there's three colonies—probably somewhere in the neighborhood of five hundred primals, all sharing this one territory. They can't get all the food they need from hunting alone. They rely on our crops, just like we rely on their protection." She gave him a hooded look. "And they rely on the genetic diversity we can offer."

She seemed to want to leave it at that. Sam was hesitant to push her, but found himself grossly fascinated.

"Do the matriarchs come to you?" he ventured.

Judy was silent for moment, but then begrudgingly continued. "You ever heard of the mating flight of a queen bee?"

Sam shook his head. "I don't know much about bees."

She stared at her hands. "Once a year, the queen bee leaves the hive and goes flying around, attracting drones from other hives. They don't mate with drones from their own hives or they'd become inbred. She mates with several drones and returns to her own hive to lay genetically-diverse eggs." She flashed a palm at Sam. "I'm not saying that's exactly how it happens with the matriarchs—I'm just using it as an example, because it's similar. You're aware of the gestation period for primals and hybrids?"

"A few months, right?"

Judy nodded. "Between three and four, depending. The matriarchs like to keep breeding. So, for them, it's usually four times a year—pretty much seasonal. The matriarchs don't seem to want to breed with primals or hybrids. They want to breed with regular human males. And we...accommodate them." She looked at Sam sharply. "To keep the peace, you know."

Well, that *was* a bit shocking to Sam, but he managed to keep it from his face and lied, "No judgment from me. I just want to know how things work." He suddenly felt very uncomfortable, and figured he didn't need the dirty details of how they conducted that seasonal grotesquery. But his mind conjured images of all of Appomattox's young men standing in a line by firelight, while the sinuous shapes of the matriarchs emerged from the darkness, hungry.

It probably wasn't so cultish. Was it?

"Alright," he said, working to keep his tone level. "Thanks for being honest. Let's bring it back to how we're going to keep Appomattox alive."

Some part of him that despised the strangeness of it all thought, *Should you even be helping these people survive? Maybe it would be best just to let them get wiped out.*

The primals were already outbreeding humans. And there weren't many humans left on the earth to begin with. If this kind of shit went unchecked, what would the future look like?

It stirred in him an existential fear for the human species. They were already up against the ropes, barely surviving against the threat of growing populations of primals—most of which had no form of truce with their human counterparts, as was seen here in Appomattox.

The primals were a storm surge, threatening to drown all that was left of humanity.

And here was Appomattox, willfully dismantling their levees.

It took a real force of will for Sam to put all of that aside for the moment. Lee had promised to help these people if at all possible, and Sam would honor that, even if he disagreed with it on a soul-deep level.

"How much control can you exert over the primal colonies?" Sam asked.

Judy laughed bitterly. "Control? We have no control over them. We remain alive to this day by playing nice. Call it a policy of appeasement if you like. And yes, I recognize how that might eventually go very bad for us. But put yourself in my shoes, Sam. I'm just trying to keep my people safe."

Sam understood that academically, even if he couldn't quite accept it in his heart. "So, there's no way to get the primals to fight? Or at least direct their aggression at the Russians?"

Judy considered it. "Okay. Here's what you gotta understand: Female hybrids can control the primals—but only to an extent. They can call on them, and they'll answer, and if a female hybrid puts her foot down, *most* primals will back off—though not always, which is why I sent Cade with your friends. He's a big boy, and most of the primal alphas will respect him, even if they don't respect a hybrid female they don't recognize. But it's not like our hybrid females can *control* them. So if you're imagining being able to organize them into some sort of strategic resistance—banish the thought. Ain't gonna happen. Best you can hope for, our hybrids can howl and probably get a pack of primals to respond to a certain location. But once those primals get there, what they actually do is anyone's guess. Maybe they fight the bad guys and tear them apart." Judy shrugged. "Or maybe they get a wild hair up their ass and decide to kill *everyone*, friend and enemy alike. They can be unpredictable when their blood is up."

Sam grimaced. He'd been hoping there would be some way to utilize the three colonies of primals in the defense of Appomattox. But apparently that was a no-go. Or, at the very least, a massive risk.

"Alright, let's switch tacks then," Sam said. "Tell me about the population here. I wanna know how many people with guns you can field, and how many hybrids you have."

Judy rubbed her forehead. "Well, it's not like I take a regular census, but..." A few moments passed while she ran the numbers in her head. "We got maybe fifty adults with firearms that have at least *some* ammunition, though don't expect a lot—no one's found any ammunition in years. Maybe another twenty people with stuff like bows."

"And the hybrids?" Sam prompted.

"About a hundred."

Sam ran the numbers in his head. Hard to say what the strike force would throw at them, or if 170 combatants would be enough to even slow them down. But if that's what it came to, what other choice did they have?

Tracing his fingers slowly along his jaw, the beginnings of a plan started to form in Sam's mind.

"Well," he said. "Gotta work with what you got, right? I think I have an idea."

Chapter 22

Jones was in a world of hurt.

The pain coursing through his insides had become so immense that he'd blacked out several times. A few times, he'd come back to himself, somehow still standing. But mostly he woke up with his face in the dirt and leaves.

Every time he awoke, it got harder and harder to force himself to move again. Not to mention, it was no easy task to get to your feet with your hands bound behind your back. His only saving grace—if you could call it that—was the fact that, when he remembered his situation, a burst of panic would hit him like a runaway semi, and he'd writhe and contort his way back to his feet.

No matter how hard he tried—and oh, how he tried—he couldn't budge the damn zip-cuffs that bound his wrists. These weren't the chintzy zip-ties that he'd seen some people use as restraints. These were hardened polymers, with thick straps, designed not to let the wearer free until they were cut loose by a sturdy pair of shears.

He'd tried to staunch the flow of blood from the hole in his back by pulling his restrained wrists tight against it. But eventually, his shoulders wore out from the strain, and began to cramp, adding one more layer of misery.

He lost all sense of time. It was growing dark, so he knew it couldn't have been *that* long, but the lost segments made it feel like ages had past, so it seemed his entire world had become an endless slog of agony and endurance.

In his more cogent moments—which were becoming fewer and farther between—he realized that he was a dead man walking. That bullet had gone in just above his kidneys, and it was still in there.

He felt the blood oozing from the wound, soaking his back all the way down his pants, nearly to his left knee. And that was just the blood that had come out. Chances were, there was just as much blood, if not more, sloshing around inside his abdominal cavity.

The fear of that sickened him. Or perhaps he was already going septic.

Several times he'd stopped, his ragged breath rattling in his throat, his mouth beyond dry now, his thirst ravenous, even as he knew that if he drank the bucket of water he fantasized about, he'd probably puke it all up. In those moments, he was so tired, and in so much pain, he thought about giving up.

He was doing that right now.

Hazy. Everything was hazy. He couldn't tell if the twilight woods were just that shadowy, or if his vision was failing him. It seemed he could only see whatever was directly in front of him. His peripheral had melted into a slurry of darkness. He felt ice cold, but burning with fever at the same time.

He put his back against a tree, using the pressure of it to keep his wrists against his wound, for all the good it would do.

It was a miracle he'd gotten this far.

But he didn't even know how far that was. He'd stopped running a while back. All he could do was stumble forward on legs that felt like they belonged to someone else. If he fell down again, he didn't think he'd have the strength to rise.

He'd done his best. Which wasn't all that bad, but for fuckssake, he was shot in the back and bleeding internally. There'd be no shame in giving up, right? Wouldn't it be better to lay down and try to get comfortable for his last moments on this earth, rather than continuing to push through the torture and still wind up dead in the forest?

Might be nice to just lay down and stare up at the sky, while there was still light to see it.

He'd always known he was going to die a bad death. Dying of old age? He'd let that idea go right around the time the world had gone to shit. No, he was a fighter, and there was only one eventual end point for people that spent their lives fighting. No one's luck lasted forever.

No shame in acknowledging the inevitable.

Except...there was.

To him at least. No one would know it—but *he* would know it. He would know, in his last moments, that he could've put a little more into it.

"Don't be a pussy," Jones wheezed into the chill air.

That was all the breath he had to spare on lambasting himself, but he continued in his mind, much more forcefully.

If you act like it's a big deal, you'll trick yourself into making it a big deal. And this? This is some piddly shit. It's just one fucking bullet wound, you giant, blubbery bitch. That's fuckin' nothing.

You know how you know when you're dead?

When you die.

Until that happens, you're just giving up like a coward.

Come on, Jones, he wrangled himself, blinking furiously to get the stars out of his eyes as he looked around the forest ahead of him. *Just get to that tree, right there. Get there, and you can have another quick rest. That's not so hard. It's barely ten yards.*

So he heaved himself off the tree. Tottered a bit, and the spike of fear at the idea of collapsing put a bit more strength in his legs. Just enough to stagger forward. A few steps. A few more. And then to the tree.

Boom. Easy. See how easy that was, Jones? You can do that again.

Yeah, Other Jones, I sure fuckin' can.

Alright, well, stop dawdling and do it then.

So he picked another tree, and stumbled over to it.

Pfff—so fuckin' easy.

That's right, Other Jones. Easy as pie.

Don't puss out on me now, Jones!

Okay, Other Jones. I'll do it again.

Damn right you'll do it again.

Except that, as he stood, gearing up to shuffle forward another ten paces, he heard a quiet hoot.

The breath caught in his chest, burning as he strained to listen. His eyes darted off to the right. The sound had come from somewhere over there in the deepening gloom. Had it been what he thought it was? Or was he just—

Another hoot, far off to his left.

"You gotta be kidding me," Jones gasped out.

Two more calls—one from behind, and one from ahead.

He'd known there were primals in these woods. He'd just kind of hoped that, with a bullet rolling around in his guts, maybe the universe would say, *Hey, maybe that poor Jonesy guy has had enough abuse for one day—maybe we stop fucking with him for now.*

But no. This simulation called reality was clearly run by a cruel DM that delighted in fucking with its victims until they could be fucked no more.

The question was...

Curl up in a ball and hope for the best?
Or run and hope for the best?

They had him surrounded. He could barely stagger between the trees, let alone outrun a pack of primals that was slowly closing the noose on him. His hands were bound behind his back. He couldn't even fight them.

Exhaustion and hopelessness made curling up in a ball sound unreasonably attractive.

But then he saw himself.

Well, no—not himself, because he was a battered, bloody mess.

He saw Other Jones, clear as day, standing right in front of him like a drill sergeant inspecting a fat slob of a recruit. Other Jones was...glorious. He wore an OCP uniform that looked like it'd been tailored to fit his frame, which was noticeably more muscular than Regular Jones. His arms were crossed over his chest, the sleeves of his uniform rolled up to expose gnarled muscle.

Other Jones did not yell, or scream, or berate him.

Other Jones simply sneered, disappointed.

"Fuck you, Other Jones," Jones said as he heaved himself off the tree. He remembered a motivational poster he'd seen once, showing a line of perfectly sharpened pencils, except for one, which had been worn down to a nub. He recalled the caption that went along with the image, and he spat it at Other Jones with significant venom: "Easy to look sharp when you haven't done any work!"

Other Jones's eyes flared. "The fuck did you just say to me, you mouth-breathing little shitstain?"

"You heard me, dickwallet," Jones growled as he staggered past.

Except he didn't pass Other Jones. Other Jones started keeping pace with him. "Speaking of shitstains—I can smell your guts leaking out your back." Other Jones sniffed the air theatrically. "So can every primal in a mile radius. You wanna die today, son?"

Jones got his feet moving a little faster. "Not today, Satan."

Other Jones was running alongside him now, face thrust in close, voice menacing. "Then you're gonna have to keep up with a real man. How fast can a six foot stack of shit run, huh? Let's see, motherfucker."

Jones was running. God, did it hurt. It hurt everything there was to hurt. But he couldn't stop. Not with Other Jones pushing him on.

The hooting turned to sharp barks. Between the stamp of his own feet through the leaves and brush, Jones could just hear the movement of the primals closing in on him.

"They're gonna eat your fucking liver!" Other Jones gnashed out.

"Joke's on them," Jones croaked between gasping breaths. "Pretty sure mine's shot to pieces."

He may not have actually said any of this aloud. It might've all been in his head. Because the very next moment, Other Jones wasn't there, and what had replaced him was a churning mass of dark, sinewy limbs, hurtling through the trees at him.

Jones knew he couldn't outrun it. Knew he couldn't fight it.

Knew he couldn't give up either.

So he did the one thing he could think of to do, which used every last bit of his already-exhausted energy. He skidded to a stop, faced the onrushing primal, and delivered one, final, defiant kick—a front kick with all the force he could muster, as though he were trying to breach a heavy door.

His foot connected with the primal's chest, just as it was in midleap.

But it had a lot of mass, moving with a lot of momentum. Jones's kick did little more than stop its progress, while it put Jones on his back.

By the time Jones lifted his dazed head off the ground, the primal had already recovered from its momentary shock. It was a male with an abnormal amount of body hair, giving it a gorilla-like appearance. Jones watched its muscles tense as it prepared to leap.

Jones couldn't even raise his hands to ward off the coming attack.

So he roared at it. For the fact that he was damn near dead, it came out loud enough to make the primal recoil its head just slightly. They were not accustomed to their prey bellowing at them like that. Screaming? Yes. But not *roaring*.

It was a good effort. But it only bought Jones the time of a flinch response, and then the primal leapt.

Kill me quick, you fucker, Jones thought, as he shut his eyes against the incoming violence of his death.

He felt its weight crush down on him.

Felt something scuff across his face, and heard a crack like a starter pistol going off.

That had been the crack of his skull breaking, he was pretty sure.

And yet, mercifully, he felt no pain.

The weight came off his chest. There was a snarl and the sound of thrashing leaves as multiple bodies tore around Jones. Then a raspy, dangerous bark, that sure sounded like the primal version of *fuck around and find out*.

Jones's eyes snapped open.

He found himself staring up two strong legs, muscle striations standing out, even in the low light. Those legs were planted right over Jones, and above them was a hunched form, a wild mane of auburn hair, feral eyes darting around, snout-like nostrils flaring, and bared teeth that would have been more at home in the mouth of a mandrill.

Horrific. And yet, in that moment, Kat was the most beautiful thing Jones had ever seen.

She swiveled, glaring, claw-tipped fingers curled and ready to maul anyone or anything that dared test her.

Jones twisted his head to look around him, and saw no less then five primals circling, but keeping their distance. Jones was no expert on the facial expressions of primals, but despite their mutations, they were, at their core, human faces. So he could hazard a guess that these primals were feeling a bit pissed at having their dinner taken away.

But Kat was not alone. While Kat had planted herself over Jones's body, there was another hybrid—a big, Māori-warrior-looking motherfucker with arms as thick as Jones's legs—standing at his feet. He was also baring his prodigious canine teeth and growling so deeply Jones swore he could feel it rumbling in his chest.

Jones remembered to breathe. Stale air gusted out of his lungs, and he sucked in more, his gaze snapping around to the primals, which had retreated to a greater distance, and now mostly sat on their haunches, looking peeved. They were doing something odd that Jones had never seen before. All of them were baring their teeth, but their heads were turned away from Kat and the other hybrid. It struck Jones as both a gesture of submission and a warning of their own.

Alright, you can have him, the posture seemed to say. *But don't start anything.*

Kat had stopped her raspy barking, and the other hybrid had stopped growling.

"Kat," Jones husked. "Are you saving me?"

He felt hopeful, but his innate fear of Kat had not entirely gone away, and for a moment, he felt like it was possible that she just wanted to savage Jones herself. Perhaps because he'd offended her with aloofness.

He swore to himself that, if she didn't bite his throat out in the next few seconds, he was going to be a helluva lot nicer to her.

Kat glanced down at him. "You're injured. Can you stand?"

That sounded like she wanted to help him rather than eat him, and Jones's fear was immediately washed away in a tide of the strangest, most earnest affection Jones had ever felt for another individual.

Being saved from certain doom can have that effect.

"Yeah, I can stand." He immediately tried to roll to his hands and knees, but the pain was suddenly too much for him. He had nothing left in his tank. "Ah, fuck!" he groaned, curling up on himself. "Maybe not."

"Cade," Kat said, seeming to address the other hybrid. "Watch my back."

Then she bent over Jones, rolling him onto his belly. There was a moment of stillness as Kat seemed to inspect his bindings. Then he felt her face press against his wrists, her nose cool from the chill evening air. He felt her sharp canines slip between his flesh and the plastic cuffs, snipping them as easily as a pair of heavy shears.

Jones was reminded of what long canine teeth were for: Scissoring through spines.

For the first time, Jones was incredibly happy to have Kat on his side.

The tension came out of his shoulders in a gust of relief. Jones wanted to push himself up, but his arms were numb, and simply flopped.

Kat seized him by his right arm and lifted him to his feet as though he were no bigger than a toddler. She draped the arm over her shoulders and hugged his midsection tight to hers. She was shorter than he was, but she bore his weight effortlessly.

They backed away from the pack of primals, then turned and began moving quickly through the forest.

Feeling safe for the first time since the farmhouse, all the fight withered out of Jones, and darkness encroached.

"Hey, Kat?" he burbled.

"Yeah?"

"I'm sorry."

"What for?"

"Sorry for being mean to you," he said, realizing how childish he sounded, even as a knot of emotion formed in his throat, born from relief and the utter exhaustion of being near-to-death. "But I'm also sorry…that you're gonna hafta carry my ass…"

The last words came out in a breathy whisper, and Jones passed into the darkness.

Lee and Abe crouched in the dim forest as the sounds of snarling and barking subsided.

Lee had to force himself to keep scanning. All he wanted to do was look in the direction that Kat and Cade had run off in. All he wanted to hear was Jones's voice, cracking some stupid joke.

This was the problem with letting himself get so close to his team: Whenever they got themselves into trouble, Lee's guts knotted and his nerves frayed.

The two hybrids had caught Jones's scent on the wind and gone sprinting forward, faster than Lee and Abe could keep up with. Kat had already warned them that she smelled primals close-by, so when she snapped at them to stay put, Lee had listened.

They'd been out of sight for a few minutes now. Then came all the snarling and barking. And now there was silence.

Lee stood up from his kneeling position, still scanning, but continuously glancing ahead for any sign of the hybrids or Jones.

"What're you doing, Lee?" Abe asked in a low, warning tone.

"Well, I'm thinking about running in there."

"Mm."

"You're *not* thinking of running in there?"

"No, I'm thinking about it," Abe admitted. "Just haven't decided if it's smart."

"Smart would've been to never come out here in the first place," Lee grumbled, then started moving. "Come on."

Abe's support hand shot out and smacked Lee in the shoulder. "Hold up. Be quiet."

Lee halted. He knew Abe's hearing was better than his. After so many years of gunfire and explosions, neither of them would score high marks on a hearing test, but Abe typically picked up on noises quicker than Lee.

Abe motioned for Lee to get down, and they both sank low again. "Motion ahead," Abe whispered, so low Lee barely understood him.

Then he heard it for himself: Footsteps approaching at a good clip.

It sounded like walking, rather than the rhythmic gallop of a primal on all fours.

"It's them," Abe said, but Lee had already spotted the three figures—Kat and Cade, with a limp Jones hanging between them.

"Ah, shit!" Lee exploded from his position and took the last hundred yards between them at a dead sprint. He churned to a stop, then reversed direction to run alongside Kat. Even with Jones hanging over one shoulder, she was still keeping a pace that Lee felt was a solid eight-minute mile. "Is he alive?"

"Yes," Kat grunted. "Still alive."

"Was he shot?"

"Not sure. Probably. Hole in his back."

Abe appeared at Lee's side. "Stop for a sec—lemme check his pulse!"

Kat glared at Abe. "I already said he's alive."

Abe juked in front of her, putting a hand to her chest and forcing her to stop. "Did I ask for your fucking opinion? Do what I tell you to do." Without preamble, he unlimbered Jones's arm from around her shoulder and pinched his wrist, checking for the radial pulse.

Cade misunderstood and started to let Jones down.

"No, hold him up," Abe snapped. He held Jones's radial pulse for a moment, then jammed his fingers into the very top of his thigh, where it connected to his hip.

Lee understood. It was a quick and dirty method of getting a rough blood pressure reading. In order to feel a radial pulse, the body had to be kicking about 70-80 systolic. For the femoral pulse, where Abe was feeling now, it had to be about 60-70.

Abe switched to checking Jones's carotid pulse, which was not a good sign. If all you could feel was the carotid pulse, that meant the blood pressure had dropped into dangerous territory. And, obviously, if Abe didn't feel a carotid pulse, that meant Jones was dead, or close enough as made no difference.

"Got a carotid pulse," Abe announced, pulling his hand back. "But that's it. He's lost a lot of blood."

"Stuff the hole while we move," Lee ordered. "Kat, let's keep moving."

She slung Jones's arm over her shoulder again, and she and Cade took off once more. Abe hustled behind, wrangling hemostatic gauze out of his IFAK while Lee touched off his comms. Their channel might be compromised, but Lee judged this to be enough of an emergency.

"Team Mom, you copy?" He transmitted, using Jones's old nickname for her, rather than her real name. "Need Team Mom to answer up."

She came back. "Here. You find him?"

"We got him. GSW, lower left back. *Not* conscious. BP's around fifty-to-sixty. I need you to beg, borrow, or steal whatever the fuck you need for a blood transfusion. We're twenty minutes out."

Twenty minutes was a long time to be at such a low BP, and Lee could only assume it was continuing to drop. They were racing against whatever internal bleeding Jones had, and the prognosis was not good.

The only positive thing Jones had going for him at that moment, was that God must've wanted him to survive, because he gave Jones AB-positive blood type—the "universal receiver." Any of them could give their blood to Jones, with a low likelihood of a negative reaction.

And Lee intended to give his man every drop he could spare.

CHAPTER 23

Lee sat on a table, slowly draining.

Jones lay face down on the floor under Lee's feet, still unconscious.

Marie was on her knees, hunched over Jones's back. She snipped the excess from one final suture, then sat back on her heels, wiping a wrist across her brow. In the glow of a solar lantern and four small flashlights, her face looked drawn and exhausted.

They were *all* exhausted.

Except maybe for Kat.

She was holding one of the flashlights. The other three were held by Abe, Sam, and Lee, the beams directed at the hole in Jones's back at a variety of angles so that Marie had enough illumination to operate. Their flashlight beams jiggled slightly in hands that trembled with nerves and fatigue. But Kat's beam was steady.

Marie waved a nitrile-gloved hand at them, the fingers coated in blood. "Kill the lights. Save the batteries."

They all clicked off, leaving them in the scant glow of the dying solar lantern.

They had been lucky. Appomattox had a little family practice medical center. It was right on the border of the primals' half of town, but Judy had assured them that the primals knew their boundaries. They were all crammed into one of the smallish patient rooms now. The medical center didn't have many supplies left, but Marie had at least been able to gather the very basics of what she needed to seal off Jones's bleeding, and jury-rig a direct transfusion.

Judy had been there with them as well, but she'd left to prepare her people for the assault they all knew was coming any time now. It was just Lee and his team now.

"Will he live?" Kat asked.

None of the others would have asked, because they already knew what answer Marie would give—it was the only answer she *could* give.

"No way to know, Hon," Marie said, both her voice and her face blank. She was pushing her emotions down, as they all were. None of them could afford to let their mindsets slip. Not until they got extracted to safety.

Marie looked up at Lee. "I stopped the bleeding, but he still needs surgery I can't perform. All I can do is try to keep him alive until we get back to Fort Campbell. They have an OR setup there."

Lee nodded. They'd beaten the clock on Jones's dropping blood pressure, only to be racing against septic shock. The bullet had skipped off of one of Jones's lower ribs, shattering it in the process, then tumbled through his intestines. Marie had done the best she could, cleaning the piss and shit out of Jones's body cavity, but sepsis was just a matter of time.

On the positive side of things, Marie had been able to remove the bullet, and the bleed had been from just a few severed veins, which she'd sutured off.

"As soon as his BP's up enough," Lee said, looking to the others. "We need to get him out of here. Not only does he not have any time to waste, but the assault on this settlement is imminent. I don't wanna get pinned down here. My guess is that they're already moving their ground troops in to secure the cordon, and we need to get out before they close the circle. Our evac's on standby at the Kentucky outpost. They'll be at Point Charlie ninety minutes after I place the call for extract."

While Lee spoke, Marie was checking Jones's blood pressure.

"I'm guessing he'll be at a stable BP in maybe twenty minutes," she said. Then she looked sternly at Lee. "But it can't all come out of you."

"I know that." He nodded to Abe.

"I'm next," Abe confirmed. "Just tell me when."

"How you feeling?" Marie asked Lee.

"Fine."

She rolled her eyes. "Of course you are. Couple more minutes, then I'm switching to Abe."

"In the meantime," Lee said. "Anybody got any bright ideas on how to help these people make it through the night alive?"

Marie squinted. "Is that what we're doing here? Because I think we should just take Jones and get out. I convinced Jeremy to exfil with us. We need to get him and the research out of here before the Russians get their hands on either."

"Great," Lee said, curtly. "But, if nothing else, we can at least provide Judy with a better plan than she's currently working with. As of right now, she's planning to sit and hold and take potshots at the Russians. We all know how that's going to turn out."

Sam fidgeted, drawing Lee's attention. He was staring back at Lee from under his eyebrows, arms crossed over his chest.

"Something to say, Sam?" Lee asked.

Sam sniffed. Raised his chin. "Yeah, as a matter of fact, I do." His gaze flicked to Kat. "Kat, you mind giving us some privacy?"

Lee held a hand up. "She's a part of the team. She needs to know what the rest of us know."

Sam huffed, but nodded. "Alright. Fine. Kat, this might offend the fuck out of you, but I'm gonna say it anyway." He looked at Lee again. "I talked to Judy while y'all were gone. She told me all about this place, and frankly, I don't see why we need to stick our neck out for them. This isn't some poor settlement that's being bullied by a warlord or the cartel. They're breeding like fucking rabbits. Lee, there's already over a hundred hybrids living here. And she says these matriarchs like to breed *every season*. They're popping out fifteen to twenty hybrids a year."

Again, Sam looked at Kat. "I get that you're a person. And I'll always be grateful to you for saving Jones." Back to Lee. "But none of that matters in the long run. What matters is that human beings are going extinct. They can say we're rebuilding all they want, but what does that look like twenty years down the road, when there's ten times as many primals and hybrids as there are humans? Extinction. That's what it fucking looks like. And yeah, maybe Appomattox is just a drop in the bucket, but no single raindrop thinks they're to blame for causing the flood. I know it feels fucked up to just let people die, but, big picture? Maybe it's the right thing to do."

Lee let out a protracted hiss, and glanced at Kat, feeling a prickle of discomfort skitter down his spine.

Kat was glaring at Sam, and Lee saw the way her fingers tensed and curled.

He started to say something, but she cut him off.

"What has a hybrid ever done to you?" she asked, her voice flat.

"Really, Kat? You don't remember what happened when we met?" Sam was entirely unintimidated, which surprised Lee. He would've been a bit more cautious if he were the one spitting offensive shit at a hybrid.

Lee's hand drifted to his pistol.

Kat noticed his movement and snarled—but not as though she was going to pounce. It felt more like withering derision to Lee. "You think I'm going to turn on you?"

Lee held her gaze, unflinching. "Tempers are high. I wouldn't put it past anyone to start swinging. It's just that your swing is likely to take someone's head off. If I could control you physically, I'd just do that, but we both know I can't, so..." He rested his hand on his pistol.

Kat nodded, slowly. "Fear. You all stink like fear." She pointed a dog-like claw at Lee, then switched it to Sam. "The only reason you're scared of hybrids is because you can't control them. And just like a scared animal, you hate what you fear. So who's more dangerous? The hybrids that just want to live? Or the monkeys with guns that are scared of them?"

She dropped the hand to her side and chuffed. "I remember what happened when we met," she said to Sam. "I held you down by your throat. But did I rip it out? No. I never actually hurt you. You've never been hurt by a hybrid."

"Yet," Sam amended, bitterly.

"But how many times have you been hurt by another human being?" Kat demanded. "And yet, you don't fear other humans. Because you understand them. Us? You're too scared to even try to understand us. So instead, you decide we all need to die. It's bullshit," she spat. "Hybrids haven't done anything wrong. The only reason you're afraid of us, is because we *look* like the things you *should* be afraid of. I'm getting tired of scared little humans that can't think through their fear. Because if you could think, you would realize that we hybrids? We might be the only thing that can protect you from extinction."

Silence.

Lee glanced between Kat and Sam. The hybrid was all seething challenge. Sam was all disgruntled resentment. But he could see in the young man's eyes the same realization as was in all of them at that moment.

They *hadn't* thought of it like that. And what Kat said might very well be true.

Lee thought back across every scar that was on each of their bodies from their years of fighting. However many wounds they'd suffered at the hands of primals, they'd suffered twice as many at the hands of other men. Of all the friends and loved ones that they'd lost, the vast majority had been killed by other human beings.

Hybrids were not responsible for any of the scars on their bodies, nor any of their dead friends and family. In fact, at this point, hybrids had now been responsible for saving their asses on multiple occasions.

Maybe they *were* the only chance humanity had.

Still sitting on the floor between Kat and Sam, Marie reached out and patted Kat's foot. "Your speech has really improved in the last few months."

"Thanks," Kat said, distractedly.

Sam threw up his hands in begrudging surrender. "Alright. Fuck it. I got an idea that Appomattox might be able to pull off."

Lee retracted his hand from his pistol, now feeling moderately guilty for having distrusted Kat. But, in his defense, this was all very unfamiliar to him. He was just now starting to understand that hybrids could control their violent instincts better than he'd given them credit for. And he wouldn't let himself feel foolish for being cautious around an unknown quantity.

He looked at Sam and nodded. "Go ahead with it, then."

Sam took a deep breath. "From what I can determine from talking to Judy, they have pretty much zero control over the primal colonies, so there's no way to use them against the Russians in a way that doesn't also put Judy's people in danger. However, she does have about fifty people with firearms, and a hundred hybrids. Now, best I can tell, the Russians want to contain Appomattox, so, like you said, Lee, I think they're going to try to encircle the settlement with ground forces. I don't know what kind of indirect fire they can bring to bear, but even if they don't have arty, we know they got those two birds. So I'm thinking they'll at least roll in with those to soften the target before they have their ground troops move in." He raised a questioning eyebrow to Lee.

Lee motioned for him to continue. "I'm with you. That's certainly how I'd do it if I was going to exterminate a town."

Sam continued. "I think Judy should pull everyone out of Appomattox—not far, just into the woods where it'll be harder to target them. Then she takes her fifty guns and her hundred hybrids, and she punches through the cordon at a single point. Chances are, the Russian strike force will have to commit most of their ground troops to the cordon if they actually want to fully encircle Appomattox. They'll be anticipating scared civilians hunkering down, not a counter-assault, so I'm guessing the outpost will be lightly defended. Judy's assault team hits the Russian outpost, eliminates the indirect fire if they have it, and disrupts command and control of the operation. How'm I doing so far?"

Marie had risen at that point, motioning Abe to switch out with Lee.

"Good," Lee said, as Marie slid the catheter out of his vein and Lee relinquished his seat on the table to Abe. "What about the rest of the ground troops on the cordon?"

"Well," Sam said, scratching at the back of his neck. "The way I see it, either the ground troops are going to try and retake their outpost, in which case the extermination op is disrupted, or they're going to push on and move into town, in which case they won't find anything but three colonies of primals."

"Depends," Abe put in, as Marie tapped his vein. "On what the Russians are more likely to target first—the people, or the primals. I'm assuming they have the same information that we have, so they'll know the locations of the primal colonies. They might try to eliminate those colonies first."

"Or," Lee said. "They might focus on the humans that know their secrets. In any case, we don't know, so there's no point in speculating. And, chances are, even if they do target the colony locations first, there will still be primals that survive, and they'll be mighty pissed."

"All the more reason to pull the people out of town," Sam agreed.

Abruptly, Kat spoke up. "Just use the hybrids."

All eyes turned to her.

"Just use the hybrids for what?" Lee asked.

She looked at him. "For breaking through the line and attacking the base. Don't use the people with guns. One hundred hybrids will do it better. Have the people with guns stay with the rest of the humans."

Lee arched his eyebrows. He hadn't expected hybrids to have good control over their violent instincts, and he certainly hadn't expected them to be able to think strategically. This would be interesting. "I'm listening."

Kat pressed on. "The hybrids make a hole in the line. Then, while they're attacking the base, the people with guns can get the rest of the humans through the hole. Then the bad guys will be stuck between them, and the primals in the town. That's when the hybrids can call on the primals. If the bad guys move into the town, they'll get killed. If they try to take their base back, they'll get killed."

Lee, Abe, Sam, and Marie all exchanged a cautiously-optimistic look.

"Makes sense," Sam admitted, somewhat painfully.

Kat nodded. "I will go with the other hybrids and help."

"No," Lee said. "Y'all need to focus on getting Jones and the scientist and his research to Point Charlie."

"Y'all?" Sam said, voice suspicious. He glared at Lee. "Why'd you say 'y'all'? You not gonna be with us?"

Lee heaved a sigh. "It's a good plan, Sam. But I trust Judy's ability to execute it about as far as I can spit. She might be good at running civilians, but it's gonna be darkness and chaos out there once things go down. She's gonna need help."

Abe swiveled to look at Lee. "If you're staying, then I'm staying."

Lee held up a hand. "No, I'm not—"

"Don't fucking argue with me," Abe said, dismissively.

"I need you to help evac Jones."

"No, you don't. Marie, Sam, and Kat can manage that just fine. I'm sure we can convince Cade to help. They'll get Jones and the scientist out to the extract point."

"And how are *you* guys gonna get out?" Sam asked, with mounting concern.

Abe waved him off. "We'll call for a second extract once we handle shit here. Most important thing is getting Jones to a surgeon, and Jeremy and his research away from the Russians. Helping Appomattox survive is...personal."

"Personal?" Sam demanded. "How's it personal? You've known them for twelve hours."

Abe glowered at Sam. "I give zero fucks about Appomattox or Judy or their weird-ass breeding program. It's personal, because fuck the Russians, and fuck whoever thought they could just wipe out a town and not be called to account for it. Also, if someone thinks they're going to unleash some experimental super-virus on my country, after I just spent six goddamn years spilling blood, sweat, and tears to piece it back together? Well, they can just fuck right off."

"Yeah," Lee concurred.

"Yeah," Abe nodded.

"What he said," Lee concluded.

Sam stood there, gaze sliding between the two men. "Okay. Alright." He pointed at them each in turn. "Is this another one of y'all's crusades? Like with *Nuevas Fronteras*? Or Briggs?"

"Hey," Abe growled. "Not our fault other motherfuckers are always starting shit with us. What are we supposed to do? Bend over and let them have their way with us?"

Sam rolled his eyes. "Aren't you two always telling me—" and here, Sam put on a dumb voice. "—'You gotta pick your battles, Sam'?"

"Whoa." Lee threw up a stop-sign hand. "First off, we don't sound like that. We're very wise in the ways of war, and you're welcome for all that we've taught you. Second, you *do* have to pick your battles. It just so happens that we're picking this one."

"Why?" Sam asked, in earnest. "Why not live to fight another day? There's so many other settlements that need our help, and you're gonna spend your life on *this one*?"

Lee made a face. "Jesus, Sam. Don't pronounce us dead before the fighting's even started."

"Anything could happen out there."

"Anything can happen at any time."

"You're not going against some band of yokels or outlaws. Those are professional soldiers, with a whole lotta firepower. It's an unnecessary risk."

"An unnecessary risk?" Lee echoed, quietly. "Sam, you remember the day we met?"

Sam seemed to clam up a bit. He got straight and stiff, crossing his arms over his chest. "Hard to forget, Lee."

Lee patted the air. "Yeah, I took an unnecessary risk to save a twelve-year-old boy, but that's actually not what I was getting at. Just before our paths crossed, I'd been burying a friend and his family. They were neighbors of mine. He was a cop. We'd sit around and drink beers, and he would tell me his woes. You know what he hated about police departments and how cops were trained?"

Sam shook his head.

"Officer safety. That's what he hated. He hated how people whose entire job it was to put their lives between civilians and a threat, would basically be fucking cowards because of 'officer safety.' A school would get shot up, and the officers that got there first would stand around and wait for backup while kids were getting killed, because, in their minds, it was *too risky* to go in without help. They were trained to worry about *officer safety* and were told not to take *unnecessary risks*. My friend was a big part of changing his department's policy on that. The new policy that he worked so hard for? If people are getting hurt, you get your ass in there and take it to the threat."

Lee spread his hands. "We signed up for this job, Sam. By doing that, every one of us has agreed to put others' lives ahead of our own. We don't train to *stay safe*. We train so that we can take it to the threat and win."

Sam groaned and shuffled his feet. "Well, shit. You got me all ashamed, and now I wanna stay and fight with y'all."

Lee shook his head. "Sorry, brother. You got bullet holes in you. You did your part—you went back into that farmhouse and got our satphone back. We would've been screwed without that. Besides, I want you watching Marie's back. She needs another good rifle with her."

Reminded of Marie, Lee turned his attention on her as she checked Jones's blood pressure again. "You've been shockingly quiet this whole time. Nothing to add?"

She glanced up at him, then snorted. "Lee, after all these years I've learned when you and Abe have made up your minds about something. I have objections—I actually agree with Sam—but I know y'all ain't gonna listen. I've made my peace with it." She ripped the blood pressure cuff from Jones's arm. "He's at a stable BP. It's time to move."

Chapter 24

By 1900 hours, Sam and Marie were out of the city of Appomattox, heading southwest for Point Charlie.

After hearing the plan, Judy had not wanted to commit Cade to helping them get Jones to the extraction point. She'd wanted every hybrid she had available to help breach the cordon. Instead, she'd committed two stout guys that would've otherwise been doing nothing but hunkering down in the woods. They carried the improvised litter that'd been constructed for Jones's unconscious form. They, along with Jeremy Tuttle and his precious research, stayed between Marie and Sam, while Kat took point in their column.

Off they went, into the darkness.

By 1930 hours, Judy had the entire population of the town crowded into an intersection, where she assigned roles and delegated tasks. There were over five hundred people living in Appomattox, including the hybrids. Those few with firearms and enough ammunition to make themselves useful were assigned to Gale, who appeared to be Judy's second in command. Judy herself would be staying back with the unarmed civilians. She'd begrudgingly admitted she wasn't much of a fighter, had never used firearms, and would be better used keeping the contingent of non-combatants calm and orderly.

There were fifty-two individuals with firearms, including Gale. They had a mix of weaponry that ranged from nearly-useless .22 pistols, all the way to one guy who had a SCAR Heavy, and a healthy stockpile of .308 rounds.

Then there were the ninety-six hybrids that were old enough to comprehend the strategy and execute violence. They ranged in age from a few two-year-olds that looked and thought like teenagers, to a dozen "elders" that were all of five years old, though they looked and acted like adults.

Abe took control of the fifty-two armed humans, and Lee took the ninety-six hybrids. Though their comms might be compromised, they hoped to be able to coordinate the two elements over their secondary channel with a series of code words.

By 2000 hours, everyone in Appomattox knew what they were supposed to be doing, and dispersed from the intersection.

Lee knelt in the middle of the hybrids. They were positioned near the westernmost edge of the town, in an elementary school's track field. The night was clear and cold, with a half-moon rising above the trees. For the hybrids, with their mutated, night-adapted eyes, it was almost as good as daylight.

Lee was lucky. Because Sam had rescued his rucksack, he was the only member of the team that still had their NODs. That was why he'd elected to go with the hybrids. He had his monocular flipped up on his helmet for now, as the moon was sufficient illumination to organize the hybrids.

For just a moment, as he knelt there, surrounded by the hulking, shadowy figures of ninety-six hybrids, he allowed himself to feel the utter strangeness of the moment.

Was he comfortable with this assignment?

Absolutely fucking not. It weirded him out to his core. It was one thing to have Kat embedded with his team of humans. It was an entirely different thing to be the lone human in charge of a company-sized element of hybrids.

It felt…precarious. As though at any moment, they could turn on him, or run off and decide to do their own thing. Or they might all just get slaughtered.

Who knew?

Certainly not Lee, as he'd never been good at predicting the future.

He pushed all that other stuff out of his mind and focused on what he could control: Clear and concise communication of a simple plan that *should* be easy to execute.

Out of all of them, Lee only recognized Cade, so that's who he spoke to first. "Cade, come in here with me," he said, motioning for the hybrid to join him.

The big guy lumbered through the crowd, a head taller than most of the others. He stood, looming over Lee, until Lee waved for him to take a knee and he complied.

"Do the other hybrids listen to you?" Lee asked.

Cade gave a small shrug and said, "I'm big."

Lee had to crack a smile at that. It made sense. For most of human history, strength, size, and fighting prowess made you the chief. It was instinctual. Why would it be any different for the hybrids?

"Good," Lee said. "I want you to pick seven of your friends who you think the others will listen to and follow, and have them step in here with us."

Cade nodded, as though picking teams were a normal occurrence. He rose to his feet and quickly selected seven others, rattling off a string of names as though he'd already had them in mind. They stepped into the center with Cade and Lee.

"Alright." Lee panned his gaze over them. "This is how it's going to work. Cade stays with me. I'll tell Cade what to do, and he's in charge of everyone else. That's called chain of command. You seven that he just picked? You're the team leaders—or alphas, if you prefer. You're each going to select a team of eleven others." He stopped, then squinted at Cade. "Everyone can count, right?"

There came a chorus of murmured affirmatives. No one seemed offended by the question. That was something Lee actually liked about the hybrids—it seemed to take a lot to hurt their pride, so pussy-footing around feelings and sensitivities was typically unnecessary.

"Great. Cade and the other alphas will each choose eleven teammates. Do that now, and everyone stand with your team."

Again, unlike with humans, where there would be social alliances and hurt feelings to navigate, Cade and his seven team leaders just went about selecting who they wanted. Within two minutes, the ninety-six hybrids had divvied themselves up into eight groups of twelve.

Lee continued. "Look around at your team. Make sure you know who they are. Get their scent, or whatever else you need to do. This is your pack. You stay with your pack, no matter what. You work with your pack to approach and eliminate the enemy." He thought better of his phraseology. "By which I mean you're going to hunt them down like prey and kill them as quickly as possible."

That seemed to strike a chord with them, and there were a whole lot of bobbing heads and eager growls.

That kind of creeped him out, but he told himself it was a good thing. It was what he needed of them.

It was what they needed to do if they wanted to survive the night.

Lee tapped his own ear. "Listen up for Cade's voice. If he tells you to do something or go somewhere, you immediately move *with your pack* and do what he says." Lee stood up and pointed west. "We're going to be heading in that direction. Our job is to make a hole in the enemy line. It needs to be a big hole—big enough that all your human friends can get through it. I don't know where the enemy will be, so keep your noses in the wind and your eyes open for any movement. Be careful. The enemy is not going to be easy to kill. They are professional soldiers. They have big guns, and lots of ammo. They also have night vision—" Lee jiggled the NOD on his helmet. "—just like these. That means they're going to be able to see in the dark just as good as you can. Maybe even better. They might also be able to see your body heat, so don't rely on leaves and thin brush to hide you. Use the terrain to your advantage. Move on all fours, and try to stick to low ground and thick trees. Be very careful when crossing open ground, like a field or a roadway. Chances are, that's where the enemy will be hiding, trying to catch you out in the open."

Lee bit his lip, wondering if he'd covered all his bases. He also didn't want to overwhelm them. He didn't know how much new information they could retain. But then again, was hunting really new for any of them?

"Does everyone understand?" he asked.

He heard a few "yesses" and a lot of grunts.

"Is anyone unclear on anything?"

No one appeared to be unclear, or have any questions.

Lee took a deep breath, then lowered his monocular NOD over his eye. "Alright, then. Let's go hunting."

There were pros and cons to Lee being with the hybrids, just as there were pros and cons to Abe being with the armed humans.

At that particular moment, Abe was noticing a lot of cons.

First and foremost, the firearm safety on display—or lack thereof—was sphincter-puckering. He started off trying to correct it person by person, but then realized that would take too much time. Instead, he stepped back from the group and used his command voice—he really didn't want to be a dick, but they needed the information nailed into their skulls, en masse.

"Form up around me," Abe called, making a circular motion in front of him. "Everyone needs to be able to see me and hear me."

The fifty-two fighters—a term Abe felt was a bit generous—shuffled into position around him.

"Listen to my words, and do what I say," Abe said. And then, because they were civilians, he decided to give them the why of it: "Because if you don't, most of you are gonna die from friendly fire."

There was a lot of worried glances at that.

"Fingers." Abe held up his rifle and demonstrated, turning in full circle so everyone could see. "Off the trigger and outside the trigger guard. I shit you not, you *will* end up flinching when the bullets start flying, and that flinch will cause you to crank off a round into yourself, or one of your buddies. Best case scenario, you fire it into the dirt, waste a bullet, and give your position away. Again—fingers off the trigger, and outside the trigger guard until you are aiming at something you want to kill.

"Muzzles—that's where the bullet comes out. Do not point them at your friends. This is called *muzzle discipline*. I want you to imagine there's an infinitely-long lightsaber coming out of the end of your muzzle, and you have to move your weapon in a way that doesn't chop up your friends.

"Target identification. It's going to be dark in those woods. You won't be able to see shit. Hopefully, our hybrids will punch a big enough hole that we won't come into contact with the enemy. But if we do, you need to make sure you're shooting at the enemy and not your friends."

"How are we supposed to see what we're shooting at if it's dark?" Someone called out.

That was another con: Too many questions. Everyone had a hundred worries, some of them reasonable, some of them less so, but they all seemed to think that Abe should be able to soothe every single one of their anxieties, as though combat was going to be mentally comfortable.

"You won't," Abe answered. "And that's why we're going to form two lines to either side of the civilians we're guarding. Each line will be facing *away* from the civilians, and each line *will* maintain its integrity—by which I mean, I don't want to see anyone running out ahead of anyone else. If you take fire from one direction, everyone on the line finds the nearest piece of cover and fires back. Should we take contact, it is going to be chaotic and confusing. Luckily, I'm here, and I will do your thinking for you. All you need to remember is four simple things..."

Abe raised four fingers in the air and dropped them one by one. "First: Face away from the civilians. Second: Point your weapon towards the threat and shoot until there's no more threat. Third: Don't muzzle-sweep your buddies. Fourth: Keep your finger off the trigger until you're ready to shoot. We can all remember four simple rules, right? Easy-peasy."

There was a general murmur that sounded more affirmative than negative.

"Where's Gale?" Abe asked, craning his neck to try and find her in the moonlight.

"Here," she said, raising her hand and stepping forward. She was armed with some piece of shit, chromed-up knock-off of a Beretta 92—currently holstered.

As she came to face Abe, he lowered his voice to a more conversational tone. "You and I are going to be at the front. You're in charge, so I need you to stick to my ass like glue and don't go running off anywhere. I tell you what to do, you just turn around and repeat it to your people. It won't be anything complicated. If we take contact, I'll basically be telling you where I want your people to shoot. All you gotta do is make sure they're doing what they're supposed to be doing." He pointed to the group of fighters. "Now, divide them up into two, equal lines."

Gale got to work splitting the group in two, and Abe turned to find Judy. She was standing at the head of a column of four hundred terrified civilians. She didn't look much more comfortable than they did. Behind them, Abe could just make out the houses on the west end of town.

He strode up to her. "Judy, no matter what happens, you and your people don't stop moving. I need you to be ultra-clear on that point."

Judy nodded stiffly. "Don't stop moving. Got it."

Abe bobbed his head at the crowd. "We don't want anyone getting split up or left behind, so you need to get everyone to hold hands. You move as one body. If shit kicks off, get low and keep moving. If you see this—" Abe flashed his weaponlight. "—that's me. That's your lighthouse. If you're ever unsure of what direction you're supposed to be going, look for that light. I'll be staying at the front of the column, guiding you west." He lowered his voice. "However you need to explain this next part to your people is up to you, but...there's no stopping for casualties. Someone in your column goes down? Leave 'em."

Judy balked.

Abe raised a hand. "It sounds harsh, I know. But chances are, if we take contact, some of your people are going to get hit. If we let that stop us, *more* people are going to get hit. You're gonna have to think about what is best for the many, which might require the sacrifice of a few. You with me?"

Judy swallowed, looking pained. But she nodded. "Yeah. I'm just—"

And that was when the sky shook with a thunderous sonic boom.

Before people could even cry out in alarm, half the neighborhood behind them erupted in fire and smoke.

Then everyone was screaming and losing their goddamn minds.

There's command voice—which is what Abe had been using—and then there's battlefield voice. And Abe had a helluva battlefield voice.

As the shockwaves of multiple explosions rocked the crowd of people, Abe bellowed at the top of his lungs: "Everyone calm the fuck down and start moving! Civilians—link hands!" He was already running towards the fighters. "Gale! Get your lines into position! Move! Move! Move!"

Like a single, churning beast, the people of Appomattox began to move. At first, it was a confusing jumble, but then, by some miracle, they managed to form themselves up into a semblance of what Abe had wanted.

He sprinted for the front, keying his comms as he did. "That was an airstrike! They got fast-movers!"

The distant booms rumbled through the ground beneath Sam's feet. He immediately spun in the direction of the noise, but couldn't see anything through the trees. That had been multiple explosions, and he was just beginning to question whether it was artillery or airstrike when Abe's transmission answered his question.

He shot back around, and started picking up the pace, moving from a stiff march to a hobbling jog. He was in the rear of their column. Jeremy and the two guys hauling Jones's stretcher had come to a full stop, necks craning.

"Don't stop!" Sam snapped at them as he passed. "Keep moving!"

Marie was at the front, with Kat kicked out ahead about fifteen yards—just a barely-visible shadow in the gloom. Marie was walking backwards, letting the stretcher-bearers catch up after their pause. Sam fell into step with her.

"We need to hoof it," he said. "If they're hitting Appomattox, they might already have the cordon set up."

"We might already be past it," Marie said. The words were hopeful, but her tone sounded like she didn't believe they were that lucky.

They weren't.

A sharp hiss came from in front of them.

They stopped, both peering into the trees, looking for Kat's form. She was kneeling, twisted around and facing them. Her hand peddled through the air, calling them up to her.

She must've smelled something.

Sam and Marie hustled up to Kat, flinching as another series of explosions came from the town five miles north of them. Reflexively, Sam looked back, even though he knew he'd have no visual.

"Fuckin'-A. How many airstrikes are they gonna send?" he whipped around to meet Marie's gaze. "And who the fuck authorized them to be in our airspace?"

Marie shook her head, waved his comments off, and directed her attention to Kat.

Sam followed suit.

Kat turned and pointed westward. "Wind is coming from that direction."

There was a slight breeze tickling the trees, moving from west to east.

"I smell them," Kat went on in a whisper. "Several. I think they're moving this way."

Sam and Marie made eye contact again.

"If they're moving, they haven't closed the loop," Sam observed.

Marie nodded. "That's what I was thinking. We can make it through if we push."

Sam slapped her on the shoulder. "Go. I'll make sure the others keep up."

Marie rose from her crouch and told Kat to kick out again on their right flank, between the column and the approaching hostiles.

Sam lurched up to the stretcher-bearers and Jeremy. The guys carrying Jones—Trevor in the front, Mike in the back—looked like they'd been doing hard labor all their lives, and weren't even breathing through their mouths. Jeremy, on the other hand, already looked gassed. Despite the fact that all they'd done was walk, and all he had was a backpack with a laptop and a hard drive in it. The whole package couldn't have weighed more than ten pounds.

But what did Sam expect from a scientist?

"Russians are close, but they haven't closed the loop. If we don't wanna get gunned down, we need to hustle up." Trevor and Mike immediately double-timed it. Jeremy looked like he might wilt.

Sam grabbed at his backpack. "Lemme have that."

Jeremy batted his hands and twisted away. "I'm fine! You're wounded!"

"No," Sam said, grabbing the shoulder strap and forcing it off of Jeremy. "I'm fine, and you're soft and out of shape. Save your breath for running." He slung the little pack onto his shoulders and used his M249 to shove Jeremy into motion.

"Hey, I work out!" Jeremy protested.

Not enough, Sam thought, but just said, "Shut up and move."

Chapter 25

Lee heard the sonic boom and instantly knew what it was.

Seconds later, the ground shook.

Lee swore under his breath, but didn't stop moving. That quiet rage that had been simmering in his gut since things in Virginia had gone bad, now began to flare up, sending tendrils of heat through his chest and up into his brain.

A fucking airstrike. Someone had authorized an airstrike.

Some asshole in the IAG had decided to get in bed with the Russians, because they wanted a quick fix to the primal problem, and apparently thought it'd be a great idea to let the Russians unleash an experimental virus on them. And now, either they'd allowed Russian fast-movers into American airspace, or, more likely, they'd ordered the mission themselves, and those were IAG flyers dropping guided munitions on them.

He wasn't mad at the pilots or their flight command. Those poor bastards probably didn't even know what they were doing. In all likelihood, they'd been kept in the dark just as much as Lee had been.

Abe's voice came through Lee's earpiece: "That was an airstrike! They got fast-movers!"

"What was that?" Cade hissed from beside Lee.

"Airplanes with bombs," Lee said. Then glanced at Cade, gauging his comprehension.

There was none. "What's that?"

Lee shook his head. "It's bad for us. They're destroying your town."

"Motherfuckers," Cade growled.

Cade might not know about planes and bombs, but at least he had a solid vocabulary.

Up ahead, Lee could see the trees open up into a field. Just the kind of place where the Russian troops would be waiting for any escapees from Appomattox to reveal themselves. That thought just spiked his anger even more.

The Russians were anticipating scared families, fleeing the destruction.

And what would they do when those families crossed into the field?

Mow them down.

Lee held up a hand and came to a stop.

Cade followed suit and the two of them sank down to the ground, shoulder to shoulder.

"Possible danger area ahead," Lee whispered.

Cade rolled slightly so he was on his side, then issued a few soft hoots that sounded indistinguishable from an owl to Lee's ears.

He glanced sidelong at the hybrid. "What's that mean?"

Cade rolled back onto his belly. "Caution. Danger. Be careful."

Well. You learn something new every day.

"Right," Lee breathed. "Everyone else needs to stay low. You and me are going to crawl forward, real nice and quiet and low, and see if we can spot any bad guys on the other side of that field. Got it?"

"Got it."

They began to snake their way across the forest floor towards the edge of the woods. The field beyond was brushy and choked with weeds, and the edges of the woods were crowded with undergrowth. Their heat signatures would likely be hidden. But so would the heat signatures of the Russians—if there were any.

A cold breeze kissed Lee's face when they were about ten yards from the woodline.

Cade's hand took hold of Lee's arm. He didn't say anything, but when Lee turned his head, he found Cade scenting the wind. The hybrid's shoulders tensed and he got an unmistakably predatory look on his face that did strange things to Lee's insides.

"Bad guys," Cade husked. "Many bad guys."

Lee felt his heart give a few hard pulses as the nearness of enemies tingled through him. Once things went down, he'd be in the flow of combat. But always—no matter how many times he experienced it—the lead up to the fight was always shot through with jittery dread.

Lee continued crawling forward, angling for the thickest tree in his vicinity.

Abe transmitted a coded phrase, sounding out of breath and a bit piqued: "Whiskey neat. Whiskey neat."

That meant he'd gotten the people to a position of relative safety, and was waiting for Lee to breach the line and give a location.

Lee clicked his PTT twice in silent acknowledgement.

A distant drumbeat reached Lee's ears as he came to the base of the tree. It rapidly grew louder, and became the sound of multiple rotors. The high, snare-drum sound of the Little Bird, along with the low kickdrum of the Blackhawk.

Lee went still, praying that the helos wouldn't be scanning the woods with infrared. He keyed up, knowing the background ruckus would prevent the enemy from hearing his voice. "Copy whiskey-neat. Gin-and-tonic inbound," he said, using their code for the enemy helicopters.

Then he laid there as the rotor noise grew to a crescendo, and then began to fade. No rotorwash lashed the trees. They hadn't flown directly over Lee's element. But if they spotted Abe and the civilians, they'd certainly park over them and shred them to bits.

There was nothing Lee could do about that. He had to focus on his task.

Keeping himself very small and tight against the tree, Lee eased onto his knees, then his feet. Moving at the measured pace of a chameleon, he leaned his right eye out just until it cleared the edge of the tree.

The enemies' heat signatures were obvious. They'd taken no pains to hide from thermal imaging. They weren't even using cover all that much. Just a lot of guys with guns, crouching or kneeling next to trees, waiting for unsuspecting victims.

They were clustered in what looked like ten-man squads. Two squads on either end of the field. Lee and his hybrids were facing the empty space directly between them. There was about a hundred and fifty yards between Lee's position and enemy squads.

He took a mental snapshot of their locations, then very slowly lowered himself back to the ground. He lay there for a moment, just breathing and thinking. This was a good location to breach the cordon. Tempting to try and sneak right up the middle, but it would only take one of their heat signatures to get spotted through the weeds, and then they'd be pinned down by overlapping fields of fire, with no cover.

Lee leaned onto his left side, looking at Cade. He pointed with a knife hand, far to the right. "Ten bad guys over there." He switched to the far left. "Ten bad guys over there." He pointed straight up the middle. "Nobody right across from us. Here's what we're gonna do."

Cade listened carefully as Lee walked him through the plan, stopping multiple times to make sure that this point or that was fully understood. Again, the hybrid didn't take offense, though he did cock his head and give Lee a curious look the final time he asked.

"Fighting and killing," Cade said, slowly, as though Lee were the dim-witted one. "Might be hard to understand for regular humans. But for us? It makes sense."

Lee cracked a nervous grin. "Yeah, you and me both, buddy." Then he patted the hybrid on the shoulder. "Go."

Cade slithered back across the forest floor to disseminate the plan to the rest of his hybrids.

In the distance, another airstrike cracked and rumbled. God, they were really trying to pound that town to dust. If the people of Appomattox even survived the night, they wouldn't have much to go back to.

After only a minute, he heard rustling behind him. He took a peek over his shoulder. Through the thermal-overlaid NOD, he could see the white-hot forms of the hybrids moving stealthily on all fours. Two packs split off in one direction, and two packs split off in the other.

One, solitary heat signature went straight back, disappearing into the brush after a hundred yards. That one would connect with Abe's element and guide them in to the breach point.

This would all be a lot easier with GPS coordinates and some synced up tech, but they had to work with what they had, and go old-school with it.

Lee keyed up. "Got a runner coming to you. Standby for rum-and-coke."

Rum-and-coke being the actual point at which the cordon would be breached and the civilians could get through.

"Copy direct," Abe intoned.

Once again, Lee worked his way slowly up to a standing position behind the tree and readied his rifle. The second shit went down, he was going hot. First priority was clearing the breach point, but he was also cognizant of the need to conserve ammo. Otherwise he'd be taking the Russian outpost with a knife.

Assuming he got that far. But when you were about to throw yourself into a gunfight, the worst thing you could do was think about all the ways you could die. Better to think about all the ways you could kill.

As General Patton so famously said, the point of war isn't to die for your country, but to make the other poor bastard die for his.

Hua, and all that moto bullshit.

Time seemed to trickle by.

Another thunderous airstrike.

Had they hit the primal colonies? Or were they only concerned with killing the people that could talk?

Was it the same planes dropping payloads? And how many were there? Or was it multiple sorties? He hadn't heard any other sonic booms, but maybe they'd come from a different direction.

Lee really wanted to know if those were Russian jets, or IAG. But either way, someone had some shit to answer for. Every bomb that went off got Lee hotter and hotter, until the men across from him weren't even soldiers anymore—they were just obstacles. The Russian outpost? A speedbump.

The ultimate destination? Find whoever the hell was responsible for this abortion of justice.

And when Lee did, they better have a good goddamn reason, or Lee was going to handle them like he had Briggs.

Was he developing a problem with authority?

When it happened, it came from the left side of the field.

First, a yell. Then multiple men screaming. Then a whole lot of suppressed gunfire.

Lee didn't move. Just breathed, everything in him wanting to surge forward, to start finding targets to put down—obstacles to remove from his path. But he forced himself to be patient.

Snarls. Barks.

Someone let out a blood-curdling shriek.

Then there came shouting and gunfire from the right.

That's when Lee moved—when he knew both squads had their attention diverted.

He swung his rifle up and braced it on the side of the tree, still breathing steadily out as he looked for targets. The area to the left was a mess of heat signatures. But despite the confusion, it wasn't hard to identify what was human and what was hybrid.

The soldiers were on their feet, trying to group themselves into fireteams, rifles spitting plumes of hot gasses. The hybrids were all around them, bounding off of trees, erupting out of brush, running on all fours to tackle men from behind, and skittering out of the path of any soldier that faced them.

The left flank seemed to have things well under control. Lee snapped his rifle to the right. He immediately spotted four, human figures—two standing, and two trying to bring a crew-served weapon to bear.

Lee thumbed his IR laser on and the second it touched the machine gunner, he fired. The man writhed, still alive, but clearly hit. There was no hesitation on Lee's part—he transitioned to the second gunner, already trying to take his wounded friend's place, and put three rounds into him. His body slumped over the machine gun.

The two soldiers on their feet were scanning wildly for who was shooting at them, their own IR lasers piercing the night air in brilliant beams. But Lee had toggled his off between targets. They couldn't see him. He pointed his rifle in the general direction of the soldier that was closest to facing Lee, then hit his IR laser again.

The beam went over the soldier's head.

The enemy soldier saw it, and immediately pivoted, firing wildly at the source of Lee's aiming laser, but his shots were too fast and panicked. Lee heard them smack the trees around him, but remain unmoved. All he did was dip the muzzle just a fraction of an inch. His laser touched the man's chest, and Lee squeezed off five quick rounds, stitching him right up center mass and into his face, spilling him backwards.

By then, the fourth guy had Lee's number.

A bullet thwacked against the other side of the tree, and Lee doused his IR laser and dropped. The second he hit the ground, he rolled, then skittered on all fours—far clumsier than the hybrids did—like a low bear crawl.

The rounds chased him, spitting up dirt in his face.

Fucker still had him in his sights.

Lee put his belly to the ground, and gritted his teeth, thrusting with his legs and low-crawling as fast as he could manage. Something skimmed off of his hamstring. The pain was sharp and immediate, but Lee could tell it had only split his skin.

Bad gunshot wounds took longer to feel. If your brain could register the pain instantly, then it wasn't that bad.

He lurched into place behind a rotted-out tree stump, which wasn't much, but it was better than nothing. The bastard was still locked onto Lee. Just over Lee's head, the top of the stump shattered into a cloud of punky sawdust. He heard the round go whining off into the distance.

Lee swore, then twisted to get his eye on Cade and the remaining four packs of hybrids, all of them so flat against the ground that their numbers seemed far less than they were. "Cade!" he barked. "Get ready to move!"

One last bullet hit the stump. Lee felt the shock of it through the wood.

There was a lot of screaming coming from over there. Still a lot of shooting.

Had the guy that'd been locked onto Lee been taken down? Or was he patiently waiting for Lee to peek out?

Can't hide under the blankets.

Lee lurched out from behind the stump and ran for the nearest large tree. No bullet impacts chased him. No rounds whined through the air. And by the time he slung himself into cover behind the tree, he registered that there were no more screams. The woods had fallen silent.

Lee took a look, rifle up and ready.

The locations where the squads had been were still alive with heat signatures, but they were all low to the ground, prowling about. He saw a lot of still-warm bodies laying around, unmoving. Too many. There were dead hybrids mixed in with the enemy.

How many hybrids had been killed?

How many had been wounded?

He was about to find out. "Cade! Go! Move!" Lee rapidly swung his arm through the air, and Cade and the other four packs of hybrids exploded off the ground and went sprinting into the field, right through the middle.

Lee waited for the last of them to pass, then fell in behind. Even at his fastest sprint, he was still being left in the dust. God, those things were fast!

He transmitted as he ran. "Rum-and-coke, rum-and-coke, how copy?"

Abe's response was immediate. "Solid copy. Enroute."

CHAPTER 26

IT WAS CLEAR FROM the Americans' use of coded language that they knew their comms were compromised. But that was no matter to Stas. He was watching their movements with a pair of reconnaissance drones that circled the area.

The feeds from those two drones were projected onto the screen in the command tent. On that screen, the image was mottled charcoal terrain, with the small, gray-white shapes of thermal signatures swarming around like frenzied insects.

Stas was not a man prone to emotional outbursts. Or...emoting of any kind, really.

So when his subordinates saw the corners of his eyes tighten as he muttered a curse under his breath, they knew he was pissed in the extreme.

One segment of the Americans had just managed to break through the cordon. The drone that currently had them in sight had arrived too late to give those two squads warning. But not too late for Stas to watch twenty of his men get ripped apart by animals.

Except...these must've been the human-mutant hybrids, because they were moving with too much coordination. It appeared they'd divided themselves up into squads of their own, and had just performed something of a pincer movement on his men.

He didn't need to ask if there were any survivors—he could see there were not.

Clenching his teeth and sucking in a big breath through his nose, as though preparing to plunge into icy waters, Stas forced his attention away from the breach in his lines. That one drone was working at high altitude, and so had a wide view of the area. In addition to the hostile element that had just savaged two of his squads, there was another, much larger element, about a kilometer west of the town.

This larger element seemed to be trying to organize itself into some sort of tactical column, though what they intended to do with that remained a mystery to Stas.

The second drone was much farther to the south, tracking a third element that had come out of Appomattox. This element was much smaller. Only six individuals. And one of them was being carried on a stretcher. They appeared to be trying to escape.

That concerned Stas a great deal.

Was that the American special forces team? Were they just running away? That would be disappointing, but Stas didn't think it was true. He had a hunch that this six-man element was in possession of the research Stas had been assigned to recover. And they were trying escape with it.

Stealing Russian secrets, as the Americans were prone to doing.

Stas pointed to that side of the screen and glanced over his shoulder at the warrant officer that was manning that particular drone. "Who do we have closest to that enemy unit?"

The warrant officer glanced at Stas, then back to his screen with a frown.

On the projection, the drone's feed zoomed out.

Roughly five hundred meters west of that escaping element, there were several squads of Stas's men, trying to complete the encirclement of Appomattox.

The warrant officer rattled off the designations of those nearby fire teams.

"Send two teams to intercept and eliminate that enemy unit," Stas commanded. "Have them search the bodies when they're done. Recover any electronic devices."

Then Stas turned to his air controller. "Do we have any more airstrikes available?"

On the projection, the town had been reduced to a smear of white-hot rubble and billowing smoke. But that's not what he wanted another airstrike for. There was no one left in Appomattox—unless you counted the mutants, but Stas didn't care about them.

They wouldn't be telling anyone what had happened.

His air controller shook his head. "No, sir. The aircraft have delivered all their munitions and are heading back to their base. Would you like me to contact the colonel and see if he can arrange for the Americans to send another sortie?"

Stas considered it, but shook his head. That would take too long. "Negative. Divert the helicopters. There's nothing in the town worth killing anymore." He pointed to the main body of hostiles, just west of Appomattox. "Have them engage that larger element."

Finally, he turned his attention back to the breach in his lines.

His stomach sickened at the thought of what had been done to his men. Frankly, he was sickened by the whole town of Appomattox. Simply the concept of human beings defiling themselves with mutants—God, what was wrong with these people?

But then to add to that, using their mutated offspring as attack dogs?

Everyone in this God-forsaken settlement deserved to die.

He frowned deeply as he watched the enemy mill about the breach in his lines. Judging by how they moved on all fours, he concluded that they were hybrids.

Except they weren't *all* hybrids, were they?

There was one heat signature that wasn't moving as fast as the others. It looked like it was running on its feet, like a normal man.

Stas immediately stalked around the table where the drone operators were positioned. He hunched over the appropriate monitor, leaning in to scrutinize the image. Then he jabbed a finger at the single heat signature of a man amongst mutants.

"Zoom in to that individual," he ordered.

The drone operator complied.

The imaging tech in these drones was top notch, and with just a few clicks, the drone zoomed in so that it seemed to be hovering directly over that man's head, tracking with him as he ran.

All the details that had been invisible when zoomed out, now became crisp and clear.

Stas saw the outline of body armor, a rucksack, a rifle, and a helmet.

That was no random gunman from Appomattox.

That was an operative.

Stas swore and leaned back, his mind racing.

If one of the American operatives was there, then the little six-man element fleeing to the southwest wasn't them. Or, at least, not *entirely* them. Which meant that the special forces team that'd been disrupting his operation was *not* running.

They were trying to organize the deranged people of Appomattox and their twisted spawn, into fighting back. And given the direction they were heading, it wasn't hard for Stas to figure out their plan.

They were going to try to take the fight to him.

Stas straightened. His fingers tingled coldly with some mix of apprehension and excitement.

"Abort the cordon," Stas snapped, and pointed to the zoomed-in view of the solitary American operative amongst the mutant hybrids. "I want all available teams to converge on that motherfucker, right there."

Lee had lost eight hybrids while taking those two squads down. Honestly, he was pleased that the body count hadn't been higher, but he kept that to himself.

The surviving hybrids, for their part, did not emote like normal humans. It would've been difficult to discern expressions or tears through his NOD anyway, but he heard no wailing or sobbing for their dead friends.

Rather, they seethed with rage.

For a moment, things felt very tenuous. Lee had seen trained soldiers lose their shit and make bad decisions when their buddies went down. How much worse would these hybrids react?

But, once again, he was surprised at the level of control they displayed.

It was clear from their hunched postures and heaving chests, and the way their voices scraped with raw fury, that these hybrids wanted blood. But as he moved quickly through them, checking for wounds and getting a casualty count, the hybrids simply told him what he needed to know, and then waited for further orders.

There were several wounded amongst them, and some of those wounds were bad.

Much like Kat, those with flesh wounds shrugged it off like it was nothing. But there were a few that likely wouldn't make it. One had been shot in the chest and was developing tension pneumothorax. Another had four holes in their gut. A third's femur had been shattered by a bullet, and they had an arterial bleed.

Lee hesitated for only a moment before using his own IFAK to do what he could for them. He just had to hope he wouldn't need those medical supplies in the near future. But what else was he supposed to do? Tell them, "Sorry, I don't want to waste my shit on you, because my life is more important"?

Such a thing was as impossible for Lee as it was for him to grow wings and fly away on the breeze.

As he went along from hybrid to hybrid, he looted a few of the dead men's bodies of ammunition. Magazine pouches refreshed, and IFAK depleted, Lee hustled to Cade as the rest of the hybrids formed up.

The second he got the big hybrid's attention, he pointed to the right and leftmost edges of the field they'd just crossed. "I want a pack on either side of this field. The bad guys might try to come in and retake this ground. We *cannot* let that happen until the rest of your people get through this breach, you understand?"

Cade nodded, twisted, barked out the name of two pack leaders, and told them where to go. Then he turned back to Lee. "What are the rest of us doing?"

Lee pointed himself west, towards the Russian outpost. "The rest of you are coming with me."

It's one thing to notice a noise where before there'd been none. It's another thing entirely to notice that a noise you've been hearing for quite some time is getting louder.

The helicopters circling Appomattox had been a dull background hum in Abe's ears as he pushed the citizens of that town through the woods. They'd settled from their initial panic when the airstrikes had hit, and managed to order themselves: unarmed people in the center column, flanked on either side by lines of people with guns.

All in all, Abe was thinking they weren't doing half bad for a group of civilians that didn't know their ass from a hole in the ground.

He was at the head of the formation, following the runner that Lee had sent to guide them to the breach in the cordon. They had to be getting close.

Then something in his subconscious sent a little whisper of anxiety through him.

He stopped, all of his senses immediately perking up.

"Hey!" he whisper-shouted at the hybrid ahead of him. "Hold up!"

The hybrid halted and twisted to look at him.

Abe held up a hand to call for a stop as he glanced back at the column. Moonlight glinted off of nervous faces. The sound of hundreds of clumsy feet scuffing through fallen leaves and stepping on every dry twig ebbed as they all accordioned to a stop.

As soon as everyone was still, he realized what it was.

The helicopters were getting closer.

That whisper of anxiety turned into blaring alarm klaxons in his head.

He stared at the people for a moment, his brain screaming options at him, none of which were a sure thing.

Run? No, movement would just make them more visible. Maybe those birds were simply heading back to the outpost for a refuel. But then, that didn't make any sense. They hadn't been in the air long enough to be low on fuel.

So maybe they were looking for these people. It was impossible to pinpoint the direction of the noise, and the helos were flying blacked out—there was no way to see if they were going to go right over their heads, or pass wide of them.

The trees were winter-bare, offering them little-to-no concealment from the thermal imaging scopes both of those birds would be using. So there was no point in telling the people to hide, either.

This felt a lot like when you're walking along and a wasp comes buzzing right up to your face. Flailing around only increases your likelihood of getting stung. Better to simply freeze and hope it loses interest in you.

The people began to realize what Abe had already figured out.

"The helicopters are coming!" several people cried out, in various wording.

Also no point in telling them to shut up—not like that would save them either.

They just had to freeze and hope the two helicopters passed them by.

The Blackhawk was one thing—it only had door gunners. Sure, they could still do a lot of damage with dual M240's, but Abe was far more worried about that fucking Little Bird.

There was a reason they called them "Killer Eggs."

The sound was mounting into thunder and hurricanes.

Abe's heart started slamming.

"What do we do?" someone cried out.

"Just shut up and hold still!" Abe snapped. No, the shutting-up part wasn't a strategy. That was just for him.

They shut up. Mostly. And anyone that was still moaning and crying was quickly drowned out in the rotor noise.

Abe got the distinct feeling that the birds weren't going to pass them by.

Then he heard that terrible buzz-saw noise.

He screamed, "Scatter! Scatter! Scatter!" even as he watched the back of the column erupt in chewed up flesh, the blood painted in monochromatic tones in the moonlight. In an instant, that line of death raked through the people, charging right at Abe.

"Scatter, motherfuckers!" Abe bellowed, and started to run.

He felt the impact of the bullets through the ground as he ran. Trees writhed in the rotor wash, saplings splintering under the onslaught of copper-jacketed lead.

There is something terrifying beyond measure to be faced with a threat you can't even strike back at. Abe knew fear. It had been a constant, unwanted companion for years on end. But at least in all those other times, he'd had something to shoot back at.

All he could do now was run, and hope.

"They're coming for us," Kat hissed.

Sam's heart started squirming up his throat. "How do you know that?"

Sam and Marie were huddled on either side of Kat, while she peered out into the dark woods and scented the air. Then she turned a look on him. Hard to say by moonlight alone, but he was pretty sure it was a withering glare.

"Because they're heading right at us," she said.

"You can tell that by the smell?"

Kat huffed and briefly hung her head, her patience with ignorant humans clearly exhausted. "No," she growled at him. "I can tell because I can hear them."

"Shit," Sam husked. "How are they tracking us?"

"I don't know," Marie said. "But we need to move. Even if it's just one squad, that's more than we can handle right now."

"How many are in a squad?" Kat asked.

It seemed to be a question born of random curiosity, and Sam almost dismissed it, but then decided he might want to trust his point man a little more.

"Depends. Five to ten guys, usually. Why?"

Kat nodded in the direction where, apparently, they were coming from. "It's more than that. At least twenty. Hard to tell."

"Yeah, we definitely don't wanna fuck with that," Marie said, already rising.

Sam followed suit. "Think we can outrun them?"

Marie simultaneously shook her head and shrugged. "What other option do we have?"

Sam hissed through his teeth. "I can't beat them on a wounded leg."

Marie didn't respond.

Kat spoke up. "The guys carrying Jones can't beat them either."

Sam didn't want to admit it, but she was right. "Even if we do stay ahead of them, what happens if they track us to Point Charlie?"

Marie let out a quiet string of curses. "Kat, can you tell how close they are?"

"Three or four hundred paces."

Sam looked at Marie in a way that was unmistakable to anyone who's ever been crushed between the rock and the hard place. "I can't move fast enough. But I have a SAW. I can slow them down. You guys get to the extract."

"Bullshit," Marie spat, barely letting him get the whole thought out.

"Yeah, it is. But that's the only way Jones gets on the helo."

"No, I can—"

"You can't stay and help me—those guys can't get Jones to Point Charlie on their own. You're the one with the DAGR. You're gonna have to lead them there. Also, we don't have fucking time for arguing about who's doing what. Those fuckers are breathing down our necks, and the extract's going to be here in ten fucking minutes." He gave Marie a shove. "Go. Get your ass moving. Do it for Jonesy."

Marie stuttered back a few steps. "What about you?"

Sam scoffed. "Shit, girl. I'm hard as a muhfucka." He slung out of the backpack he'd taken from Jeremy, and pushed it into Marie's arms. "That's got the laptop and hard drive in it. Now go."

Marie was clearly unconvinced about leaving Sam behind—as he'd known she would be.

She began rapidly shaking her head. "This feels wrong," she blurted out. "This feels like a terrible fucking idea. I don't like it."

Sam decided to use the same trick he'd seen Lee use time and time again: Acknowledge the danger, then invite the detractor to provide an alternate plan.

"Yeah, I don't like it either," Sam said. "But do you have a better idea for making sure that Jonesy gets out of here?"

He gave her two or three seconds to stare blankly before he shook his head.

"Marie," Sam said, feigning a confidence he didn't feel. "If there was another way, don't you think I'd rather do that? Of course I would. But we're out of options, and out of time. Now get the fuck out of here before it's too late and we *all* get blasted."

Marie swore viciously, her teeth bared for a flash. Then she whirled on the hybrid who had just now risen to her feet. "Kat, you stay and help Sam. I'll get Jonesy out of here."

Without waiting for a response, Marie ran back towards the others.

Kat watched her go, seeming confused. Then realization struck her. She looked at Sam. "Okay. Guess I'm helping you."

Marie got Trevor and Mike on the stretcher again, and they started hustling off with Jones's body. Then she prodded an exhausted Jeremy after them. She turned to look at Sam and Kat one more time, then ran to the front of the column.

They disappeared quickly into the darkness.

And Sam was alone with a hybrid.

Great. Just the position he wanted to be in.

"Get down," Sam commanded, lowering himself to the ground as well. Kat settled herself down beside him.

Sam readied his M249, popping the bipod and settling in behind it. He was surprisingly calm. He thought that was just the fatigue though. That was one good thing about being tired and in pain: You worried less.

"Keep me updated on their movements," Sam whispered.

"They're closer," Kat said, and he couldn't tell if she was being sarcastic.

"Distance?"

"Listen."

So he listened. And he heard them.

It wasn't loud, but it was unmistakable now: The slight swish of careful, stealthy movement through the forest.

He guessed they were closing within a hundred yards of him.

God, he wished he had his NODs. He could only assume *they* did.

But his goal was not to kill them—although he'd take any kills he could get as icing on the cake. No, his goal was to slow them down long enough for his wounded friend and the all-important research to get evacuated.

"You remember what you did that first night when we got ambushed?" Sam breathed, barely even a whisper.

"Yes," Kat said, equally quiet.

"Do that again. I fire—you move. Cause chaos. Then fall back with me."

"Okay."

Inside the command tent of the Russian outpost, Stas was focused on the horde of hybrids led by one American operative, as they closed within a kilometer of him.

"Lieutenant colonel," one of the warrant officers barked from behind him.

He glanced over his shoulder, saw which one it was, and then looked at the corresponding screen on the projection. It was the one focused on the fleeing team of six. "What's the problem?"

"That team just split," the warrant officer told him, right about the same time that Stas saw it for himself. "Four continued on, but two have remained behind. Should I divert the squads towards the four?"

Stas considered it for a moment, scrutinizing the projection. He could see the four heat signatures, still moving on a southwesterly tack. The stretcher with the wounded individual was with that group. Behind them, two heat signatures were hunkering down in the path of his three pursuing fire teams, which were closing within a hundred meters.

They were about to take contact.

Stas pursed his lips in hard thought. His priority was recovering the research, and he strongly believed it was possessed by *someone* in this fleeing group. But was it with the two that had remained behind, or with the four that had gone on?

He suspected what they were trying to do: Two people staying behind to ambush his men and slow them down, so that the wounded man—and presumably, the research—could get away.

But...he didn't know that for certain.

And he didn't particularly want to split his three teams up. Together, they could easily eliminate the two that had remained behind, and catch up to the four.

"Negative," Stas decided. "Keep the teams together. Have them eliminate the two, and then go after the remaining four."

The warrant officer acknowledged the command and disseminated it to the three teams of Spetsgruppa Alfa operatives on the ground.

Stas suspected the American operatives had called for an extraction, which would almost certainly come in the form of a helicopter. If worst came to worst, and his teams couldn't catch up to the fleeing four, Stas had a small surface-to-air battery that he could use to blow their extraction helicopter out of the sky—preferably with them in it.

That was a dangerous game. Clearly, someone in the IAG was working to counter someone else in the IAG, or these American operatives wouldn't have been dispatched in the first place. If Stas blew up an IAG helicopter in its own airspace, it might create an international incident between America and Russia.

But America was not the force to be reckoned with that it had once been, and Stas was willing to risk pissing them off to keep that research from falling into their hands.

He believed his superiors in the Kremlin would agree.

Chapter 27

Sam couldn't see shit.

But Kat could.

The last thing Sam had ever thought he'd be doing was working as a two-man team with a hybrid. He didn't like it one bit, but his preferences were immaterial at the moment. So he'd humbled up, and whispered to Kat to direct his fire the second she got sight of the enemy.

One moment, they were laying prone, shoulder to shoulder, listening to the rustle of the approaching soldiers.

The next moment, Kat went stiff. She grabbed the muzzle of his M249 and shifted his aim a few inches.

"Shoot!" Kat hissed.

Sam didn't hesitate.

He let his first string of fire belch out into the woods, holding the trigger down as he swept his muzzle back and forth, spraying the woods ahead of him—and hopefully striking close enough to the enemy that it made them hunker down.

The second his SAW started chattering, Kat leapt to her feet and took off at a sprint. He didn't know where she went. It was up to her not to run into his lane of fire.

He let his weapon eat for fifty rounds of continuous, cyclic fire, then began to send quick, three-to-five round bursts downrange.

In the silence between his bursts, he realized they were firing back at him. Bullets whined by his head and smacked the ground around him. Dirt from the impacts erupted into his face, blinding one eye, but that didn't really matter, since he couldn't even see what he was shooting at anyway.

Their aim was clearly more accurate than his. He was just spraying and praying, but they had NODs and IR aiming lasers.

He needed to keep firing. He needed to keep giving it back to them until—

Men started screaming.

Kat had just made contact with the enemy.

Sam leapt to his feet—or at least, he'd intended to. His wounded leg apparently thought that the minutes of laying prone meant it was time to sleep, because it buckled under him the instant he put weight on it.

"Shit!" He hit the ground on one knee, still in the process of trying to turn himself around to sprint away and establish a new base of fire.

He struggled to both feet again, rounds pocking the trees around him.

The round that hit him square in the back knocked his breath out and sent him stumbling forward. His wounded leg couldn't keep up, and he sprawled, face first, gasping for air.

He knew his plates had stopped the round, but—God! That had felt like being kicked in the spine by a horse.

Gotta move! he screamed at himself. *Get your ass up!*

Wheezing, he crawled forward until he had some semblance of cover behind a tree. Forcing himself upright again, this time he didn't put too much trust in his wounded leg. He took off at a limping run, while the sounds of men being savaged ripped through the night air behind him.

Then they went silent.

He ran for another handful of strides before it registered that Kat was no longer on the attack. Then he spun, did something like a baseball slide, landed prone on the ground again, and immediately began firing. Hopefully, he was pointing in the right direction.

The return fire was more sporadic this time, but no less accurate.

A round hit his helmet, jarring his brain into fuzzy gray like he'd just taken a punch to the face. Sam reeled, his respirations skyrocketing with sudden panic as he wondered if his skull had been pierced.

He didn't know how long it took for things to clarify. And clarity was a generous term, because all was darkness and the chatter of suppressed weapons, and the multitude of impacts around him. But he was still firing, so that was a good thing, right? He probably wasn't dying, right?

He desperately wanted to touch his head to see if there was blood or brain matter leaking, but some supremely logical part of him knew that would be a pointless waste of time. He was conscious, and that's all that mattered. If he was leaking brains, there wasn't shit he could do about it anyway.

His hearing had been badly dimmed by the blow to his head—not gone completely, but everything was muted. He kept listening for the sounds of men screaming that would tell him Kat was on the attack, but all he could hear was the gunfire.

Should I move?

You should move.

He fired two more bursts, then scrambled to his feet.

He didn't even have a chance to spin around—the second he was upright, two more rounds hit him. One in his chest plate, which caused something in his sternum to crack like a dry twig, while in the same instant, he felt his left elbow explode.

For a moment, there was only numb horror as he staggered in a circle, only knowing that he didn't want to get hit again—he needed to fall back and find cover.

His legs started moving, animated more by instinct than by conscious thought.

I'm up. He sees me. I'm down.

Sam just let his legs go out from under him—didn't even have the wherewithal to point himself in the right direction. He collapsed into the leaves, and for a moment, just smelled dirt and mold, and every survival instinct in him screamed to burrow down and hide.

He tried to move to face the enemy again, but stupidly planted his left elbow on the ground, and what had been an approaching tidal wave of pain crashed over him.

He couldn't even scream. His brain switched off, and all that came out was a gag.

How long he existed in that nightmarish liminal space between consciousness and never-ending blackness, he did not know. When he became aware of himself again, there was only pain. He'd collapsed onto his machine gun, his face against the hot shroud. It seared his skin and he jerked his head up with a gasp.

There was too much agony to pin point any particular injury.

Higher-order thinking had fled. He did not remember Jones, or Marie, or the extraction. All that remained was what had been drilled into him time and again. All he knew was that he was in the middle of a fighting retreat, and had to continue on until he couldn't.

The thought flitted through his head like a dragonfly—*Should I TQ my arm?* But then he remembered he needed to be pointing his weapon at the enemy and firing it. So he did that instead.

He fired, and fired. Tried to remember to keep shifting his aim. Tried to point it generally towards where he thought the return fire was coming from, but everything was too confusing. There was no right action for anything. Just a bunch of guesses, based on a wonky stream of data from his overwhelmed senses.

You're doing okay, he tried to soothe himself. *You're doing good. Shake it off.*

Every burp of gunfire sent the stock recoiling into his shoulder. He'd never been bothered by the recoil of this weapon before—it was a *light* machine gun, after all. But every burst lit off fireworks in his ruined elbow.

How long had he been shooting from this position?

He should probably move again.

A bullet smacked his right ass-cheek. The pain didn't even register. There was only so much of it the human mind could process, and Sam was already topped out. But he knew it was a bullet. And something about it made him certain it had come from his right, and that there were invisible enemies over there trying to flank him.

He rolled onto his left side. Almost fainted as his arm was pinned beneath him. Everything was a dull roar, like being caught under a pounding waterfall, helpless and thrashing. He just managed to keep his wits and angle the SAW off to his right, then pulled the trigger.

It chattered out a dozen rounds, and went empty.

By some miracle, he must've actually hit someone, because he heard a grunt—surprisingly close—and then yelping.

He needed to reload, but more than that, he needed to move.

It was hard to do. His left arm wasn't cooperating anymore, and just hung there at his side, screeching for attention but being absolutely useless. He had to pull his knees up under him, then get to his feet. Surprisingly, the hole in his ass cheek didn't feel all that bad. More achy—like an extremely sore muscle.

He hefted the M249 in one hand and staggered away from the enemy. That was all he could do. Fall back. Shoot at them. Fall back again. And on and on.

He was going as fast as he could, but it felt slow and dreamy. The pain wasn't exactly fading, but it was becoming...abstract? More feverish and queasy than agonizing. Almost like he wasn't fully in his body anymore. And that worried him. He'd never experienced that before.

Was he dying?

He *couldn't* die. He still had work to do.

Another round hit his back plate. This time it was just a bass-hit that seemed to reverberate through his skeletal structure, but he was too far away to care. It was immediately followed by another bullet that must've *just* cleared the top of his back plate, because it went through him, high on his left shoulder blade.

He just so happened to be running through a patch of moonlight, and he marveled with sickened fascination as he watched a cloud of his own blood puff into the air before him. Saw a little tatter of fabric, so clearly that it might've been a figment of his imagination.

He said, "Ow. Fuck." As though he'd stubbed his toe.

He was still running, but he could feel himself losing his balance, pitching forward.

That was okay. This was as good a place as any to turn and fire again.

Oh, yeah, he needed to reload.

Shit. He should've been doing that while he was running.

Come on, Sam. Think. Use your fuckin' head, man.

He twisted as he fell, so that he would land on his right side and save himself some pain. He clattered to the forest floor. Realized he should have some cover while he attempted to reload—it would take him longer with only one arm, and he didn't want to be out in the open where he could get shot.

Get shot *more*, anyway.

Just breathe. Remember the basics. Think.

He saw the dark outline of a tree to his right and squirmed towards it, using his legs to push himself along on his side, dragging the M249 with him. He got behind the tree. Mostly.

Time to reload.

His right hand—the only one that was working—shook uncontrollably. His fingers felt numb, like he was wearing thick gloves. It made it hard to get the cover up on the machine gun. He scraped clumsy fingers across the chamber to clear it of any errant brass or ammo links. Then he reached for another ammo belt...only to realize his pouches were empty.

Fine. Whatever. He still had a spare rifle mag. Thirty rounds was better than nothing. Besides, it'd be a quicker reload. And he really needed to get moving. Time was wasting.

Wait. Had he just fallen asleep?

He had a rifle mag in his hand, and was, apparently, just staring at it.

For how long?

Didn't matter. He was awake now. There was still some life in him. He fumbled the magazine into the M249's canted well. Slapped the cover closed. Racked the charging handle.

Which way was he facing again?

Which way was the enemy?

He felt bullets impact the opposite side of the trunk he was leaning against.

Right. Somewhere over there.

He hefted the M249 across his lap and blind-fired in the direction of *somewhere over there.* Hazily, he noted how quiet his machine gun sounded now. That distracted him, and before he knew it, the magazine was empty.

Well, damn. He should've made that last longer.

Time to move again?

Yeah. He really should. But man, this tree felt good. It felt safe. And he was suddenly so tired, that even just getting to his feet sounded hard—let alone sprinting another handful of yards.

Who was he kidding? There'd be no more sprinting for him.

Sam shook his head groggily. "Go," he husked at himself. "Just go."

So he did. He struggled onto hands and knees. Tried very hard to keep as much of himself behind cover as possible, but he was losing proprioception in the fog of pain and looming unconsciousness.

He was just trying to get to his feet when something blasted through his pelvis.

All structural support from the hips down left him.

He collapsed onto his side.

For a moment—he didn't know how long—he lay on his side, staring through the moonlit woods, and trying to breathe.

Even that was difficult now. Things were rattling and wheezing. He couldn't seem to catch his breath.

You should reload your weapon, Sam.

Were those shapes he was seeing?

Figures, flitting from tree to tree in the moonlight. They weren't far away.

Rounds impacted all around him, spraying dirt in his face. He just blinked when that happened—barely even a wince.

Get another rifle mag.

He let go of the grip of his weapon. Drew his arm across his body. Grabbed the rifle mag. And held it. And forgot what he was supposed to do with it.

There was so much screaming. So much darkness. So much pain.

And yet, he marveled: *I'm not even scared. I thought I would be scared, but I'm not.*

Reload your weapon.

So he did.

Kat flew through them without thinking. She moved on instinct alone. Each passing instant was a flow, a stream of action and reaction—a dance, one might say, except she seemed to be the only willing partner.

She felt where the enemy was going to be before they even began to move. She felt danger, like a voice in her head telling her when to duck, when to juke, and when to turn around. Except a voice would have been too slow. Words were clumsy. This happened in blinks.

That all sounds superhuman. But she wasn't.

She was a hybrid—somehow both more than human, and more than primal, and yet less than both. Still made of flesh. Still governed by physics.

She could not avoid *all* the danger.

She could not kill thirty heavily-armed and armored men by hand.

But she certainly tried.

Launching herself out of the darkness, she took a soldier in his blindside, ripping the night vision from his head, which turned into ripping his helmet off his head, which was still strapped to his chin, which turned into snapping his neck.

She rode his body to the ground. Hit the dirt with him atop her.

No active, articulable, tactical thought. But an amalgamation of subconscious data, from which her instincts provided her with instantaneous solutions that she did not question. She did not really *see* the men to her right, and she did not really *hear* their popping rifles, because she'd been focused on the victim she'd just taken. But her brain had taken in the information whether she knew it or not.

She rolled, still clinging to the man atop her, putting his armored body between her and danger. It'd worked before, maybe it'd work again.

The rounds hit him. Punched through him in places. Burrowed sudden holes into Kat. Through her thigh. Through her upper arm.

Those were not the first bullet wounds she'd taken.

She was already coated in blood.

She did not think about that, because wild things do not succumb to thoughts like, *I've been badly wounded, I can't go on.* They simply keep going until they can't.

Kat exploded out from behind the man and took off running on all fours, cutting a sharp diagonal away from them, because she knew without knowing that it would be harder for them to hit her if she was moving across their vision, but she also wanted to be moving away from them.

Into the trees. Into the darkness that the moon and her night-adapted eyes had turned into broad daylight. Bullets chased her. Pain wracked her with each muscle contraction and jarring footfall. But her brain blocked that out for her—it knew that now was kill or be killed, and pain would only hamper her self-preservation. Hamper her need to kill.

Distance. Cover. Concealment.

A momentary, logical thought broke through to her: She couldn't hear Sam's machine gun anymore.

That was concerning. His volleys of fire had been keeping the soldiers distracted while Kat maneuvered to attack them again. Without that suppressive fire, their focus would be on her, making it harder to surprise them.

She'd killed ten of them so far. The man whose neck she'd just broken had been the eleventh. A few had fallen to Sam's blind hails of machine gun fire. But they had not fallen into a panic. These men were not prey, as hard as she'd worked to make them so. They were just as much predators as she was. They did not run about in confusion. They stuck with their teammates, stayed organized, and didn't give into fear.

She respected them for that. But she was fully capable of respecting a person while she ripped their guts out.

Sam.

What happened to Sam?

Bullets smacked the trees around her as she ran. They buzzed by her ears.

A slight depression in the earth ahead—a spillway of sorts, though currently dry. She went low, sliding into it on her side, dirt and leaves sticking to her bloody leg. She thrashed and came up on hands and feet, belly low to the ground.

Her left arm immediately gave out, causing her to faceplant.

Shit.

Aware of it only because it had refused to work, the pain in her arm raised its voice. But it was dim, and she quickly smothered it. The pain was informative, though. It told her that the bones of her arm remained intact. The shredded muscle fibers were simply weak due to the trauma. So they just needed to be pushed harder.

Correcting herself and putting more energy into her wounded arm, she began to skitter along the spillway like a spider. The enemy bullets did not track her. They'd lost sight of her.

Kat had a supreme sense of herself and the space she occupied. Not once in the fight had she gotten turned around. She knew precisely where Sam was, and where her enemies were.

The enemy was to her right, and a bit behind her.

Sam was ahead, and to the left.

She rapidly drew abreast of his position. The smells of gunsmoke and blood were dominant, but she could pick out the unique flavor of Sam in all that. His sweat had the sour tang of a creature close to death.

For the first time since the fight had started, Kat felt something like...fear.

Not fear of death. Something worse than that.

Fear of failure. Of betraying the trust that this team had put in her.

Why should that matter to her?

She didn't ponder it for more than a fraction of a second.

It mattered. Sam's life mattered, because it mattered to his team, and for some reason, they mattered to her.

She did not need to peek up over the lip of the spillway to get a fix on the enemies' positions. She was able to picture where they were by the sounds they made—the clattering of rifles being reloaded, the swish and stamp of feet, the voices speaking in a language she did not recognize.

They were fifty paces behind her.

Sam would be about five paces to her left.

The trees here were thicker—growing close to the spillway where water would feed their roots.

She would need to move fast and low, but she was confident she could do it without being spotted.

She slithered out of the spillway and immediately spotted Sam, slumped against a tree.

She crawled up to him. His helmeted head leaned forward, chin on his chest plate. Drool and blood seeped from between his open lips. His breathing was ragged and labored.

She scrambled up and grabbed him by his chest plate.

"Sam!" she hissed.

His eyes were closed. He didn't respond.

She shook him, but that had no effect beyond forcing a breathy groan out of him, which splattered blood and spit in her face.

Straddling him for a moment, her knee squelched in wetness. She glanced down and saw that his pants were soaked in blood from the waist to the knee, and had turned the ground under him into mud.

That was a lot of blood.

That was bad. He wouldn't last. He couldn't stay out here. He needed help, and he needed it fast.

Kat took a few hard breaths of her own and let her body tell her what was wrong with it. She did this only to figure out the best way to carry Sam.

The gunshot wounds to her arm and thigh were bleeding, but neither was gushing. She'd also taken two grazes—one to her side that might've cracked a rib, and one to the hip bone. She didn't think she'd bleed out, but with a cracked rib and a busted hip, could she make it to the extraction point while carrying Sam?

It was the first time in her life where she'd ever been forced to doubt the capabilities of her body. If it had just been her, she'd be confident she could get to the extract in time.

But with Sam on her back, she wasn't so sure.

She knew she could follow the scent of Jones and Marie to the extract point, but she didn't know how far away it was.

But she had to try, didn't she?

The enemy was getting closer, though they were approaching cautiously.

Kat's hands scrambled over Sam's body. She unslung the heavy machine gun from his chest and heaved him up. It was harder than she thought it would be—not because Sam was heavier than she'd thought, but that she was weaker than she'd hoped.

Still, she managed to hoist him up and over both shoulders while she was in a kneeling position, then stood up.

The pain was immense. Particularly in her shattered rib.

She ignored it.

Lick wounds later. Right now, run.

So she ran.

Chapter 28

Abe hated everything about this moment in his life.

He'd never felt so useless, so cowardly, so vulnerable.

He lay on his back, staring up at blackness, and he seethed. The big, fallen tree trunk he had squirmed underneath was so close to his face that he could smell his own breath wafting back, mixed with the scent of the bark. It'd been a split-second decision, as a strafing run from the Little Bird had cut a path of destruction just behind him. He'd seen the upturned root system in the moonlight—seen the thickness of the trunk, and what seemed like a narrow space between it and the ground.

He'd flattened himself and scooted sideways, digging through years of accumulated leaves to get himself under the trunk. It was just big enough to hide him.

Hide him.

He was hiding, while others were dying.

Logically, he knew there was no shame in this decision. There was absolutely nothing he could do to save the people of Appomattox. The helicopters circling overhead had them dead to rights. Equipped with thermal targeting, no one was getting away. Abe could not protect them, nor could he fight for them. Any attempt to do so would be pointless, and would result in his death, as well as theirs.

Logically, he knew all of this.

But logic was a cold comfort when faced with the screams of dying civilians.

The rotors beat the air and whipped the treetops into a frenzy. The buzzsaw sound of the minigun ripping through life and limb. The shriek of rockets, followed by earth-shaking explosions as they detonated in rapid succession, turning whole swaths of forest into burning embers and charred, torn flesh.

It could not last forever. He knew that as well. He'd already heard both rocket pods fire off their payloads. The minigun was loaded with four thousand 7.62mm rounds, and every three-to-four second strafing run used hundreds.

All Abe could do was lay there, and wait for the storm of lead to be over. Who would survive? He didn't know. Not many. Any attempt to render aide to the wounded would also be mostly-useless. What could he accomplish with his IFAK? Maybe keep one or two people alive for another ten minutes, only to die anyway because they had no place to evacuate to?

No. The people of Appomattox were gone. He struck them from his mind, and with them, the shame of having to hide while they were slaughtered. They should've hidden as well. They should've used their fucking heads. But they didn't, so now they were dead, and he was alive.

Let the helicopters do their work. They couldn't go on forever. Eventually, they would have no more ordnance to pour out, and then they'd have to fly away. And when that happened, Abe would move.

In the meantime, he processed his shame. He smelted it down, and applied cold pragmatism to it, and through some process of mental alchemy, turned it into wrath. Not hot and heady and mindless. But cold, and cruel, and determined.

Oh, those bastards didn't know who they were fucking with.

Let them get their licks in. Let them think they'd won. They didn't know about Abe Darabie. They didn't know what he was capable of. And when he got like this—when assholes pushed him to the brink—he was capable of quite a lot.

Abe had never claimed to be a good person. He had too much hate in his heart to ever be good. He did his best to keep that under wraps, so he could function amongst other human beings and not be seen as a complete psychopath.

But it was always an option. A switch that could be flipped, if he wanted or needed it.

So he thought of all those foreign troops. He thought of their faces—men who were sons, and brothers, and husbands, and fathers. Every one of them had someone who loved them, and wished for them to be safe and return home in one piece.

But that was just too goddamn bad.

If they'd wanted that bright future, they shouldn't have come here.

Abe was going to murder them. Not kill—murder. Because there would be no white flags, no begging for mercy, no hands-up-don't-shoot. They should've thought of that before they did what they were doing. Abe would give them no quarter. He would execute every God-forsaken one of them, in a line, like an extermination.

Then he'd eat their rations with a hearty appetite, and sleep like a fucking champ.

His body was rigid as he thought all of this. Hands gripping his weapon in bloodless knuckles.

One final strafing run, somewhere out there in the woods. He waited, continuing to listen. Rotors. The chatter of the Blackhawk's door gunners. But they fell silent after a moment as well. And then it was just the sound of their blades beating the air. Now fading. Retreating.

It left the woods in a state of gruesome shock.

People's voices lilted to him through the night. Whining. Moaning. Weeping.

So very few of them now.

Growling like a rabid dog, Abe clawed his way out from under the fallen tree and immediately keyed his comms. "Jax, this is Lincoln, how copy?" he ground out as he pointed himself west.

Lee's response came back, breathless as though he'd been running, and quiet, as though he might be close to the enemy's encampment. "Solid copy. Go ahead."

"Plan is White-Russian." He used their code word for complete disaster. They'd both agreed it was not only appropriate due to who they were dealing with, but that they both found the creamy cocktail abhorrent. "Recommend Bloody Mary, immediately." Then he started running with a full head of steam and violence. "I'm coming to you."

Lee felt sick.

He'd heard the helicopters in the background—not only their rotors, but their guns blazing. He'd just...he'd hoped it hadn't been that bad. He'd hoped the civilians from Appomattox had been able to find cover and save themselves, or...something.

He'd hoped. And now it crashed down, and took his stomach with it, plunging his guts into his boots.

"Copy," Lee breathed into his mic. "Bloody Mary it is."

For just a moment, he kept the PTT depressed, and considered telling whoever was listening in on their channel that this was their last chance to abort their mission and save their lives.

But then he thought, *Nah, fuck 'em*, and released the PTT.

Lee and his four remaining packs of hybrids were maybe five hundred yards from the outpost. He could just make out the moonlight glimmering off of manmade structures—tents, vehicles, etcetera. He turned to the hybrid kneeling in the woods beside him.

"Cade," he said in a low voice. "Call in the primals."

The big hybrid looked at him, his face unreadable in the gray-wash of Lee's NOD. But Lee thought there was hesitation there.

They were not supposed to call in the primals until all of the civilians were with them, and the Russian ground troops were between them and Appomattox. That was the only way to make sure that the enraged primals wouldn't turn on the civilians in their bloodlust.

Lee shook his head. "Cade. I'm sorry, Bud. Those enemy helicopters..." Lee grimaced. "You gotta call in the primals. Do it now."

Lee didn't know how many survivors there might be, if any, so he hadn't told Cade that his friends and family were most likely dead. But the hybrid seemed to understand what was meant in the absence of those words.

His shoulders hunched, and his head dipped. He let out a quiet, mournful sound. Then it turned into a growl that made Lee's skin crawl.

Cade tilted his head to the sky and howled.

And all through the woods, the other hybrids took up the call, until the air seemed to tremble with it.

Lee did not know many of the sounds and calls that hybrids and primals used to communicate between themselves. But he knew that one. He'd heard it many times before. And he knew what it meant.

Dinner is served.

Stas Obolensky heard the eerie howl, and his head snapped towards the flap of the command tent. Not like a wolf's howl. This was…something different. Something uniquely mutant.

One voice turned into ten. Ten turned into twenty. Twenty turned into forty.

Stas's skin prickled and contracted around itself. Then he gnashed his teeth and pushed the fear out of himself. Fuck these animals. And fuck the idiot humans who were trying to use them against Stas.

His eyes whipped back to the projection. His drones were doing their work: They'd let him see every bit of the enemy's movements, so that nothing caught him by surprise. He knew that forty-some-odd number of hybrids were in the woods not far from his outpost. Even now, he could see them spreading out to encircle.

He could also see the killing ground where nearly every civilian in Appomattox had been massacred. There were a few little heat signatures, still running around here and there. Once the helicopters re-armed, they could get back out there and hunt the survivors down. Same for his ground troops, though, at the moment, he needed to pull them back here.

As he'd requested, they were hustling. They'd been a few kilometers away, but the teams under Stas's command were nearly Olympic-level athletes, and already four teams were coming down on the hybrids outside from the northeast, and two more were coming up from the southeast.

They'd make contact in a few minutes.

Problem was, Stas wasn't sure he *had* a few minutes. He only had a single team of ten pulling security here. Currently, he had them spread around the perimeter of their encampment. Against local militias and firearms, that was tactically-sound. Against a horde of forty hybrids, being spread out only made them weaker.

Stas clapped a hand in the air, piercing the veil of fear that had gripped his staff at the sound of all those howls close by. "It's good!" he bellowed, turning in a slow circle. "Let the abominations come to us! Pull the security in and have them surround the command tent!"

One of his technicians immediately transmitted the order directly to the security team.

"Sir," another piped up. "We have an unknown aircraft on approach, several kilometers southwest of us."

Ah, the extraction helicopter, on its way to pick up the six operatives that'd fled with the research. Stas immediately whirled on the drone that had been keeping track of them. Stas had been a little distracted by the goings on elsewhere, but he focused now on the three teams he'd sent to intercept those operatives.

Then he frowned deeply.

Where before he'd had thirty men, he now only saw fifteen.

The warrant officer handling those teams had reported that they were "taking casualties." But the bastard hadn't said they'd been cut down to half strength.

He whirled on that officer, who spotted his commander's incensed gaze and immediately looked guilty.

"What happened?" Stas demanded. "They only had two hostiles to take down! Why are half of them dead?"

The warrant officer stuttered, blinking rapidly. "I believe...sir...I believe one of them was a hybrid, sir. It was fast. And the one with the machine gun—"

Stas whirled back to the projection. The fifteen remaining members of those three teams were currently running headlong through the woods, in pursuit of one, rather large heat signature that didn't look like a person at all until Stas focused on it, narrowing his eyes.

No, not a large heat signature. It was one individual, carrying another.

And somehow *still* staying ahead of his men.

The warrant officer preemptively answered Stas's question: "The machine gunner was wounded. The hybrid went and picked him up, and now it's running to catch up with the others."

Stas grimaced.

"Sir, the incoming aircraft?" the other warrant officer prompted him. "Would you like us to take it down?"

"Negative," Stas immediately snapped. He couldn't afford to just go shooting what was most likely an IAG helicopter out of the sky. He would if it was necessary to keep the research from falling into American hands, but there was still a chance his men might overtake the fleeing operatives before they reached their extract point. "Target it, but do not fire until I tell you to."

Before he'd even finished speaking, another warrant officer piped up, concern evident in his voice. "Sir! Appomattox!"

Stas instinctively whirled on the man that had spoken, but he was standing up and pointing at the projection screen, and Stas immediately redirected his attention there.

He didn't need an explanation for what he was seeing.

Stas was well-aware of the nature of Appomattox—how it was divided down the middle, with the northern section belonging to three colonies of mutants, while the southern section belonged to the humans and the hybrids. He had not been concerned with the mutants, because mutants could not talk, and therefore could not tell anyone that Russian soldiers had exterminated an American settlement.

His airstrikes had been focused on the southern section, which was now only shattered ruins.

But in the northern section, Stas could see the three, large structures that'd been marked with red danger icons, denoting the location of the mutant nests.

Bodies were streaming out of those three structures. Hundreds of them. They moved rapidly on all fours, en masse.

And they were all heading west.

Straight towards Stas's teams, and his outpost.

For the first time that evening, Stas was legitimately concerned. For his men. For his operation. And for his own life.

There had to be between four and five hundred mutants, bearing down on his men, as they, in turn, bore down on the hybrids encircling his outpost.

Then the howl he'd just heard made sense to him, all in one crash of undeniable, and terrifying logic.

The hybrids had called their mutant friends in to help. Stas hadn't even been aware that such a thing was possible. They didn't have mutant colonies in Russia—just packs of them. And for all his experience in fighting the mutants, Stas had no experience with the hybrids, and had never even considered the fact that they might be able to call upon the mutants.

His first, clear thought was, *We can't survive against that many.*

But then he stuffed that down. They were Spetsgruppa Alfa. They'd fought against longer odds than this and come out on top. And Stas would be damned to hell if he let some mutants and their freakish offspring win against his battle-hardened teams.

If he failed, he'd never be able to show his face in Russia again, so he might as well commit himself to the fight.

Stas jabbed a finger at the projection. "Notify our teams they have mutants coming in behind them. Have them divert and engage. We'll handle the hybrids on our perimeter."

Then Stas spun and stalked to one end of the command tent, shouting as he did, "And tell those helicopters not to come back here! This location is compromised!"

He reached the far end of the command tent, where a rack of AK-74s was stowed. He snatched one up. "Everyone grab a rifle! We hold this position no matter what!"

Marie's legs and lungs were burning. This was made all the worse by the fact that she was dragging and pushing a grown-ass man to force him to keep up.

She tried not to resent the fuck out of Jeremy Tuttle for being such a weak piece of shit, but that's really hard to do when the enemy is right on your ass, and said weak piece of shit was increasing your chances of getting shot full of holes.

They were *so close* to Point Charlie.

"Come on, Jeremy!" Marie gasped as she moved from pushing him along to pulling him by his arm like an unwilling child.

Jeremy didn't even have the breath to respond. He'd wasted what spare oxygen he had by repeatedly claiming "I can't go on!" a few minutes earlier.

And then, abruptly, they burst out of the dark woods and into a moonlit clearing.

Point Charlie. And they only had a minute or so to spare before the extraction helo reached them.

The second Marie came to a stop and let go of Jeremy, he collapsed into a wheezing heap of useless flesh. For their part, Trevor and Mike had kept up, though they were clearly exhausted from hauling Jones's body through the woods for so many miles.

Heaving for breath and blinking sweat out of her eyes, Marie snatched the IR signaling device from her chest rig and activated it. Of course, the pursuing squads of Russian soldiers would be able to see the infrared signal as well, but there was nothing to be done for it. Point Charlie was not, as the name suggested, a single geographical point, but rather a general area encompassing a several hundred-meter radius. Marie didn't have time for the bird to go squirrelling off five hundred meters away from them. She needed it to land *right-fucking-here*.

She hurled the device into the field. To the naked eye, it would be invisible. But through a pair of NODs it would be a bright, strobing light.

Trevor and Mike put the stretcher bearing Jones down, then both of them doubled over, coughing and gagging from the effort of their exertion.

Marie jogged on stiff, fiery legs back towards Jones, keying her radio as she did. "Marie to Sam. Marie to Sam. You copy?"

She reached the stretcher and dropped to an exhausted knee, shoving her finger against Jones's carotid artery. He still had a pulse. It was rapid, and weak, but he was still alive. That was a huge relief. But it was immediately overshadowed by the silence on the radio.

She transmitted again. "Marie to Sam. I need your location. How copy?"

Nothing.

In the distance, she began to hear approaching rotors.

Mixed feelings slammed into her. God, she'd never wanted to hear an extract helicopter as desperately as she did right at that moment. They were so close to getting out of here, and hope was blooming in her chest that they might actually make it.

But in the same instant—*where the fuck is Sam, and why is he not responding?*

Nightmare scenarios clouded her brain like a thick, toxic fog.

What if he hadn't made it out? One guy with a machine gun and a hybrid against multiple squads of hostile soldiers—that was no one's idea of a sure thing. But it was only supposed to be a delaying action! He was just supposed to fire and retreat and slow them down a bit.

So why the hell wasn't he responding?

"Marie to Sam!" she practically shouted in her radio, knowing the Russians could likely hear her transmission, and not giving a shit.

The helicopter rotors went from a distant buzz to an all-too-present drumbeat.

Where moments before, that had filled her with relief and hope, now it filled her with an urgency that bordered on panic.

Goddammit, Sam! Answer your fucking radio!

She transmitted again, and again, got no response.

The rotor-noise became too loud to even hear her own voice, let alone a response on the radio. Wind buffeted through the field, sending dirt and bits of grass flying in a whirlwind. Marie squinted against it, and saw the dark bulk of the Blackhawk descending out of the night sky.

Marie scrambled over to Jeremy, who was now curled up in a ball with his back to the helicopter, shielding his face from the rotor-wash. She took him by the shoulders and shook him hard, screaming, "Get the fuck up! Get up! Now!"

Dazedly, he swirled upright and let her drag him towards the helicopter.

Behind her, Trevor and Mike hefted Jones's stretcher and followed.

The helicopter's crew chief was hanging out the open side door, waving them on. Marie noticed they had both doors open, and a machine gunner was in each, scanning with dual-tube NODs over their eyes. She was happy about that. At least they'd come prepared.

She hustled Jeremy through the buffeting wind and up to the side door, shoving him forward into the crew chief's waiting hands. He seized the scientist and half-helped, half-threw him inside the Blackhawk. Regardless, Jeremy seemed all too happy to get off the ground.

Marie was next in. She posted up beside the door gunner. He didn't seem to mind or give her much notice. Her eyes tracked through the dark woods as Trevor and Mike brought the stretcher bearing Jones on board.

The second they got Jones situated, they started backing away.

"Trevor! Mike!" Marie shouted. "What're you doing? Get on!"

Trevor simply shook his head, yelling back at her, though his words were washed out. Something about needing to get back to Appomattox.

"You go back out there, you're gonna get shot!" she insisted.

But they wouldn't listen. They'd already turned their backs and were heading away.

The crew chief must've noticed her conflicted expression and intuited that she was considering running back out for them. He put a hand on her chest plate and shook his head. "Leave 'em!"

Marie swore, then leaned in close to the door gunner. "We got hostiles on our ass, but we're still waiting on two friendlies!"

The crew chief slapped an in-flight headset against her arm so she could talk to them without screaming. He waited until she had them over her ears, and his voice immediately came through: "You say you're waiting on two more?"

"Affirmative!" she raised two fingers, just to be clear. "Two more, but there's also hostiles in these woods. Your gunner needs to confirm with me before he lights anything up. You got an extra set of NODs?"

He shook his head. "Negative! And we can't wait!"

Instinctively—and perhaps because she was exhausted and had limited control of her emotions—Marie's grip tightened on her rifle. "The fuck you can't! We're not leaving without them!"

"You can take it up with your superiors when we get back. Our orders are to pick up whoever was here and get out."

Marie couldn't help herself. She was instantly enraged. "I'll tell you what—if I feel this bird lift off, then I shoot you in the face. How's that?"

The crew chief recoiled, shocked. "Christ, lady! We got orders!"

"Fuck your orders! We're waiting on two more!"

He raised his hands. "Alright. Fuck. It's your head. But if command asks, I'm telling them you held me at gunpoint."

"Yeah, knock yourself out, chief," she snapped, then pointed her rifle towards the woods and hit the weaponlight. The beam illuminated the swath of forest directly across from them.

The door gunner jerked his head at the sudden white light, but his helmet was wired into the helicopter's comms, and he must've heard what'd been said, because he didn't protest.

What he did say was, "Multiple contacts coming through the woods!"

Marie tensed, seeing flashes of movement through the trees. "Hold fire!"

A shape burst from the woodline.

No, two shapes—one being carried on the other's shoulders.

Marie's stomach bound itself in knots as she recognized Kat, with Sam slung over her shoulder, running at a full sprint despite the added weight.

Oh, God, why is Sam being carried? Why does he look so limp?

She immediately felt sick to her stomach—a visceral reaction she hadn't felt about a combat casualty in a very long time.

"Those're friendlies!" Marie barked to the gunner. "Don't shoot them! Everyone else behind them needs to die!"

As though to make her point, incoming fire pinged off the helicopter's sides.

The door gunner immediately adjusted his aim and opened up with the M240. Tracers lanced out into the woods as the machine gun thundered over Kat and Sam.

Marie slung her rifle and she and the crew chief moved to the lip of the deck, both of them going down to a knee and extending their hands. The *ping-ping-ping* of incoming rounds faltered as the door gunner laid down an unrelenting volley of suppressive fire. Kat reached the Blackhawk and heaved Sam's limp body into the hands of Marie and the crew chief. They dragged him on board, Kat immediately vaulting in after them.

The second her feet were on the deck, the crew chief yelled over the comms at the pilots, "Dust off! Get us the fuck out of here!"

The bird immediately lifted skyward.

Marie forgot about Russian troops, and uncooperative crew chiefs. She became entirely focused on Sam. He was covered in blood. His eyes were closed. He did not respond when she shouted his name repeatedly, or smacked him in the face. She thrust fingers into his neck and couldn't even tell if what she felt was a weak pulse, or the vibrations of the helicopter.

Crouched over Sam, directly across from Marie, Kat was shouting something inaudible. She glanced up, her eyes momentarily fixed on Kat's mouth. Lip-reading wasn't so easy when the mouth was so different than a human's. But Marie thought she was repeating "I'm sorry" over and over.

As the Blackhawk gained altitude and spun around, Marie's mind could only think of what she had to do to get Sam's heart beating again.

Stop the bleeding. Restart the heart.
Stop the bleeding. Restart the heart.

Everything else faded to a background roar as Marie ripped Sam's armor off his chest and got to work.

Chapter 29

Everyone in Stas's command tent was armed now. They stood at their stations instead of sitting, AK-74s slung to their chests.

Stas stood in the center of the tent, his rifle shouldered, his eyes flicking this way and that. To the projection. To his men. To the tent flap that led outside.

The hybrids on their perimeter had stopped howling. All was quiet outside.

All was quiet inside as well—an unnerving, tense silence.

That was broken by one of the warrant officers: "Sir—enemy operatives got away! They're on the helicopter now, and it's lifting off! We have a positive lock on them, and are ready to fire."

Stas grimaced. Dammit, he'd really been hoping his teams on the ground would be able to run them down before they got to their extraction point. He knew that if he blew that helicopter out of the sky, there would be repercussions.

But he'd known this was a possibility, and he'd already made his decision.

"Take them down," he growled, turning back towards the projection. The drones showed him a wave of mutant heat signatures barreling through the woods towards his men, now closing within a few hundred meters of them.

"Firing," the warrant officer said.

And right as the word was spoken, the air inside the command tent was suddenly filled with the *zzzzip-CRACK* of supersonic projectiles.

For a microsecond, Stas was confused by the way the walls of the tent twitched and jerked like a living thing as holes were punched through it. There came the repeated *thwap* of bullets hitting flesh, along with the *snap* and *crunch* of equipment being perforated in showers of sparks and gouts of smoke.

On instinct, Stas dropped. He hit the dirt floor on his belly, already sighting along his rifle, his finger dropping to the trigger as rounds continued to pummel the interior of his command tent.

Outside, the security team returned fire amid shouts of alarm and cries of wounded.

Growling, Stas whipped his head around to the station where the warrant officer had been about to fire the surface-to-air missile that would blow that helicopter out of the sky and deny the Americans possession of the research.

The warrant officer lay on his side beneath the folding table that served as his desk. His eyes were locked on Stas's, his hands gripping his own throat. Blood squirted between his fingers, his mouth gaping as he choked and coughed out red.

There was nothing Stas could do for that man now. But even if everyone in Spetsgruppa Alfa was killed, Stas was going to launch that missile, and complete his primary objective.

He began to crawl towards the computer terminal.

Lee and Abe hosed the command tent on automatic. It almost felt like a dueling-rifles drill—Lee slamming out an entire mag, and the second his bolt locked back, Abe began to empty his own magazine, while Lee reloaded.

Back and forth they went from their position of concealment on the outpost's perimeter. The command tent hadn't been hard to spot—it was the one with all the men standing sentry outside. Those men were now falling, wailing, screaming, writhing.

Not all of them, though. Several were moving to positions of cover and returning fire.

Except Lee and Abe had selected their firing position very carefully. A big, tri-forked tree, with another tree that had fallen right against its trunk, giving them a nature-made fortification that provided not only concealment from their enemy's thermal-enhanced NODs, but cover from their return fire as well.

To the right and left of Lee and Abe's position, the hybrids began moving in.

"Third mag!" Lee shouted as he slammed it in and dropped his bolt.

The sentries outside of the command tent had scattered, but they knew where Lee and Abe were now, and their return fire was increasing in accuracy. Through his night vision monocular, Lee could see the beams of their IR lasers lancing through the night air and crawling over the trees he was covering behind.

He activated his own laser, flicked his select fire to semi-auto, and started picking his shots.

One soldier leaned out, rifle spitting—but his aim was high, and the rounds impacted over Lee's head. The second the glowing pinpoint of Lee's laser touched the man's head, Lee squeezed off a round that splashed the man through the face, snapping his helmeted head back and slumping him to the ground.

"Third mag!" Abe called, and he also began to pick his shots, though he did not have the benefit of night vision.

Muzzle flashes from unsuppressed rifles flickered. A round buzzed by Lee's head, worryingly close. He lurched fully behind the tree trunk, then kept moving, transitioning his rifle from his right shoulder to his left as he leaned out the other side of the tree, and immediately sent five rounds back at one of the muzzle flashes.

Some of them went wide, but others struck the shooter, causing the soldier to jerk and fall back from his kneeling position onto his ass.

Lee fired again, and this time saw the puff of organic materials flying off the man, the hot blood a smoky gray through his NODs. The target went down on his back, thrashing, and Lee sent a few more rounds into his exposed pelvis for good measure.

Lee had no peripheral vision—not only was he reduced to one eye, but the one eye he *did* have was covered by his NOD. He whipped his head to the right and left to spot the progress of the hybrids, and felt his heart surge as he saw them in amongst the various structures of the Russian outpost. They were no longer creeping—they were running full-tilt.

"Moving!" Lee shouted, wrangling his feet under him.

"Move!" Abe called back.

Lee took off, vaulting over the fallen tree. Rounds snapped the air around him, and he searched desperately for their source, but didn't let his speed falter. He headed for a generator box that'd been quietly humming in the silence before they'd launched their attack.

He slid, feet-first into cover behind the generator. It was just big enough to hide him if he stayed scrunched and small. Bullet impacts pinged off the generator's metal housing. But Lee was not there to return fire. He slung his rifle, plucked one of two fragmentation grenades from his rig and clutched it in both hands, whipping his gaze back to Abe.

Abe was doing work. Popping out on one side of a tree, firing, then ducking back, switching positions, popping out and firing again. He was focused. Workmanlike. Like they were on a flat range, just drilling holes in paper targets.

The rounds harrying Lee's position behind the generator tapered off.

Lee turned his head and chose a new location to sprint to—this one the engine-block of a military truck of an unfamiliar make. On the other side of it, a Russian soldier was firing this way and that, his rounds punching through one hybrid, then another, with expert precision. These were no half-assed ground-pounders. Lee could tell by the fluidity with which the man transitioned between his targets that he was a true professional.

But even true professionals can get overwhelmed.

As the second hybrid faceplanted under a hail of gunfire, a third launched itself into an inhuman leap. It vaulted over the top of the truck's cab, and then came down, feet slamming into the soldier's head and driving him to the ground.

Lee couldn't see the man now, but he could hear his wild screams as he was pulled apart.

"Cover, cover, cover!" Lee shouted in Abe's direction as he pulled the pin on the grenade.

The second he registered Abe's rifle spitting out a rapid fusillade, Lee thrust the grenade into the generator's inner workings, let the spoon fly off, then immediately scrambled for the engine block of the truck.

He slid into place on his knees, covering behind the knobby front tire.

A round cracked through the tire, and Lee felt it smack his boot as the tire deflated with an explosive hiss. He glanced down, but didn't feel pain, and saw no hole in his boot. The round had lost too much kinetic energy as it'd passed through the tire, and had simply bounced off the hard leather.

Lee's brain judged the line between the hole in the tire and the location of his boot, and in an instant, calculated its trajectory and source.

He dropped onto his left side, his rifle shouldered, aiming between the two front tires.

He clocked the shape of a helmeted head and a rifle—close to the ground—prone—weapon pointed at him.

In the same instant that he spotted his opponent, the grenade went off.

Lee had been expecting the concussion.

His opponent had not.

The guy flinched and his attention diverted towards the blast.

Lee feathered the trigger as fast as he could feel it reset. He knew he'd hit the guy, but the reaction was subtle. Already prone, the shape just went slack and still.

Abe's voice, roaring through the chaos of gunfire and snarling and screaming: "Moving to you!"

There is a subconscious sense you develop after being in many a gunfight. You don't have to actively think about it, but your brain knows where you've looked and where you haven't. Those unknown areas nag at your brain until they are addressed.

Lee had taken cover and responded to the guy that was trying to kill him, but everything to his left was a big, dangerous unknown. The urgency to look and identify threats crested to a fever-pitch. Abe wanted to move to Lee's location, but Lee couldn't give him the go-ahead until...

He was a microsecond too late.

As he twisted his body to address the unknown left something struck his dome, and he went out like a light.

"Moving to you!" Abe bellowed.

Lee was twenty yards ahead of him, and slightly to the right, in an "urban prone" position behind the front tire of a truck, firing at some enemy Abe couldn't see.

Then Abe saw it happen: Lee arched his back and simultaneously rolled onto his belly, sweeping his rifle around to clear his left. As he did, a puff of spall erupted from Lee's helmet and his body went limp, one leg kicking spasmodically.

Abe rarely felt horror when immersed in the hectic confusion of combat. Horror was something he experienced after the fact, when the smoke cleared and the bodies stopped weeping and twitching.

But watching Lee's leg spasm—that did it.

That looked like death throes.

Abe had just been about to repeat his call to his partner. Those words caught in his suddenly-constricted throat, and all that came out of him was a pained grunt, as though the wind had been knocked out of him.

Before Abe even had a chance to think about the tactical consequences of his actions, he was up and sprinting. His belly was hot and tight and it forced air out of his throat that came with noises not dissimilar to the hybrids: A low, snarling, growl of effort.

Lee was down. And he was exposed.

Abe couldn't see the shooter—there was a tent in his way.

Tactically-speaking, he should've come at this problem another way. A way that gave him an advantage, gave him angles, gave him time to spot the shooter before the shooter spotted him.

But all he knew in that moment was that he needed to get his body between Lee and the threat.

A second bullet struck Lee's back armor, shredding the plate carrier into Cordura confetti.

Abe cleared the tent that had been blocking his view.

His rifle was already up, the select fire clicked to full-auto.

He spotted the figure of a soldier approaching at a steady, measured jog, his rifle trained on Lee.

The second Abe cleared the corner, he went low, sliding on one knee to put his body in front of Lee, as he simultaneously depressed the trigger.

The approaching soldier stopped and pivoted. His rifle swung towards Abe, the muzzle strobing a rapid volley.

The rounds were wild and reactive, and they went wide of Abe.

That was great. But Abe's rounds weren't on target either. He was a fantastic shooter, but accuracy on full-auto while in the midst of sliding through the dirt only happened in glitzy action movies.

It did cause the enemy soldier to flinch, though.

Abe's slide terminated in a bang as he collided with the side of the truck. He registered the wild climb of his rifle's reticle, and released the trigger just long enough to steady himself and bring it back on target.

He didn't get the chance to shoot the guy.

A muscular shape came flying out of nowhere and tackled the shooter high around his shoulders. In an instant, both the soldier and the hybrid disappeared behind the back of the truck. There was a clatter of gunfire, and for a brief moment, Abe was certain that the hybrid had been shot dead. He prepared to launch himself to his feet again, already thinking about how he was going to clear the backend of the truck and pump bullets into the fucker.

Then the gunfire stopped, and there was only gurgling and snarling.

A second later, a helmeted head went rolling out from behind the truck, trailing a length of tattered, bloody trachea.

What kind of strength did it take to rip a man's head clean off his shoulders?

Right on the tail end of that thought, something snarled, right behind Abe.

He lurched around, letting out a little whoop of surprise, already indignant that a hybrid would be snarling over his shoulder like that. Did it mistake him for an enemy? Or had they all gone wild once they got some blood on their tongues?

But there was no hybrid behind him.

The snarl was coming from Lee—except it wasn't a snarl. It was the tongue-swallowing snore of someone who's had their lights knocked out.

"Lee!" Abe gasped, immediately ripping his gaze away from his friend and checking his environment for hostiles. All he saw was a lot of hybrids sprinting here and there. The gunfire was sporadic, and clearly not directed at Abe's position.

Holding his rifle one-handed, Abe reached down and started lightly smacking the side of Lee's face. "Lee! Come on, man! Wake the fuck up!"

After checking his blindsides once more, he clicked on his weaponlight to provide him some illumination, and shuffled around so he was more at Lee's side, and had a better view of his injuries.

Lee's eye was still rolled back in his head, eyelid slightly open to show the bloodshot white. His mouth gaped, issuing that nasty gargling noise, his body still twitching, almost like a dog dreaming of chasing a rabbit.

Lee'd been knocked out for ten to fifteen seconds. While Abe was glad he wasn't outright dead, being unconscious for that long due to an impact to the head was not good. The longer Lee stayed unconscious, the more likely it was he'd slip into a coma.

Abe quickly inspected Lee as best he could for signs of a neck break or skull fracture. He found no bruising around the neck, jawline, or eyes. So he hazarded the old *head-tilt and chin-lift* to clear Lee's airway, and the gargling immediately turned into heavy, arrhythmic breathing.

"Come on, Buddy," Abe seethed as he unbuckled Lee's helmet and very carefully pulled it from his head, hoping to God he wouldn't find a mess of pulped brains on the inside. But it was clean. There was no hole in the Kevlar. Turning it over, Abe spotted a big, teardrop-shaped divot in the Kevlar.

The bullet hadn't penetrated—only glanced off at a shallow angle.

That was fantastic news—but Lee would still have a helluva concussion and probably some heavy-duty whiplash.

When Abe looked back down again, Lee's eye was open, but unfocused.

Abe immediately shook him by his shoulders. "Lee! Lee, you gotta get up! There's still a fight!"

Lee's one eye swam around, struggling to fix itself on Abe's face. He seemed confused.

"Give the…" Lee burbled.

"What's that, Buddy? Talk to me."

"Give the liver to Deuce," Lee said, frowning, completely earnest. "I fuckin' hate that shit."

"I know, man," Abe said, as he grabbed Lee by the arm and started to hoist him upright. "Liver's pretty gross, isn't it?"

Chapter 30

Stas squirmed under the folding table on which sat the terminal that he desperately needed to reach. He lay there as the fusillade of incoming bullets continued to pepper his command tent.

Another one of his men went down, screeching as they clutched a belly wound.

A warrant officer fired wildly through the tent at unseen targets.

Stas gritted his teeth, taking sharp, bracing breaths. He would just have to brave the storm of lead. He could not let the enemy extract helicopter get out of range. They'd already targeted it, and all Stas had to do was reach up and click the right button to send a missile right up their ass. If he took a round while doing that—well, that was just the price you paid to serve your country.

Right as he decided it was worth the risk of injury or death, the volley of projectiles pouring into the command tent abruptly ceased.

Stas wasted no time thanking the heavens or thinking too much about this stroke of good luck. He grabbed the side of the table with one hand and hauled himself upright.

He was, however, not the one that worked these damned computer systems. What met his eyes as he crouched at the terminal and stared at its monitor, was a confusing jumble of black boxes, outlined in green, with lines of code and data that made no sense to him.

He'd been expecting an easy prompt, like, *Fire missiles? Yes or No.*

He swore, eyes raking back and forth across the monitor, trying to find something that he recognized. The screen showed four different open windows, but none of them seemed to have priority over the others in how they were arranged.

Screams from outside.

Stas knew that sound. He'd fought mutants before. This was the sound of men being attacked, not with bullets, but with teeth and claws and brute, inhuman strength.

He refocused himself.

That lasted for perhaps a single second before something exploded outside, and all the lights in the command tent went out.

The projection screen went dark.

The computer monitor remained on, though it dimmed as the laptop switched to battery power.

Someone had blown up their fucking generator.

Would that affect the missile systems? The guidance systems?

Nothing on the screen gave him a warning or an error. Most of their sensitive equipment had battery backups. The missile system had its own power source.

Then he saw it: One of the windows was labeled with an alphanumeric that Stas recognized as the name of their ground-to-air missile defense system.

Savage glee coursed through him as he focused on that window.

There it was—that's what he'd been looking for: A prompt inside that window, requesting a command code.

The command code was simple. It just wanted to know how many missiles Stas wanted to send at the helicopter.

A minute ago, Stas would have simply sent a single missile.

But what was the point of saving them now?

He decided to send all six. He typed in the command. And then received a second prompt to execute.

His fingers were moving to the correct keys when the tent flap burst open and five shapes launched themselves into the command tent. There was no hesitation on Stas's part—he knew in an instant that they were not friendly, nor were they human.

He roared as he snapped his rifle up at the nearest threat, pulling the trigger as he did and stitching the hybrid from groin to neck with a volley of seven rounds. The hybrid—a female, he thought—went limp in mid-leap and crashed into the folding chair directly in front of Stas, sending it careening into him.

He tried to flinch away, but wasn't quite fast enough, and caught the folding chair across his face. He grunted, blinked, immediately righted himself, and got back into his rifle's sights, swinging the muzzle towards the next closest threat.

This one had leapt onto the folding table Stas was still crouching at. The table legs gave out with a snap of stressed metal, and the table collapsed, pinning one of Stas's ankles. He barely noticed it as his reticle fell on the hybrid's nose and he squeezed off a burst that shattered its head into bloody porridge.

Right about the instant that the second hybrid collapsed in a heap, almost right on top of the first, Stas registered that more hybrids were coming in through the tent flap, leaping on his officers and technicians as their rifles barked in final protest. Throats were ripped out. Rifles were yanked out of hands. Arms were pulled out of socket. Men were falling, tackled by hybrids who bit and slashed and tore.

Stas ripped his ankle out from under the table, leaving a bit of skin behind as he did, but the pain didn't even register with him.

It'd been one thing to risk a bullet for his homeland, in order to protect their secret research.

It was another thing entirely to get pulled apart.

This was not a conscious thought in Stas's mind. He didn't make this decision with logic. It was made for him by years of survival instinct. Years of fighting the mutants. And perhaps, in some way, a part of him had always known it was all futile, and that at some point, the cost he would be asked to pay would not be worth it.

He was halfway through crawling under a wall of the tent when he realized he was abandoning his post to save his life.

He kept going.

For nearly a full minute, Lee existed in some mish-mash of realities past, present, and imagined. He was aware that this was due to the blow he'd taken to the head, but was powerless to stop it. Some things that were real seemed imagined. Some things that were imagined seemed real.

There is a theory that human consciousness exists in all moments of its life. That past, present, and future are merely our way of organizing the cavalcade of information that we process. A defense mechanism, of sorts, to keep your mind from being overwhelmed by the sheer enormity of existence.

Lee was a child. And a young man. And a middle-aged one. And an old one.

He played football under the famed Friday night lights. He ran through cool, dew-soaked grass in his bare feet, catching fireflies. Then he ran through sweltering summer forest, and things were chasing him, and his lungs were raw.

The explosion of an IED rocked his Humvee. The strength went out of him as he held a dying woman on the muddy banks of a lake. He cried because he'd crashed his bicycle into a mailbox and broken his arm. He seethed frothy spit through clenched teeth as he knew his eye would never be saved, and yet he pressed on to finish the fight.

The dying woman he'd held, now held him as his lung collapsed and life left him.

He slammed a kid's face into a locker for pushing him too much at school.

He ran on a beach.

On a beach, where the waves washed memories away and all that there ever was became timeless and infinite, only ever existing in the present, with no past and no future. And yet in the liminal space between land and sea that we call beach, his feet would run.

And they were the feet of a child. And they were the feet of a man. Running to escape. Running to think. Running just to see how far he could go. Those feet changed, but they belonged to the same person, across time.

Then it was night, and there was howling and gnashing teeth and gunfire and Abe was pulling him along, saying, "Stay on my ass, Lee!" and Lee said, "Okay." He saw the shapes of things he knew should have been a threat, and yet something told him not to shoot them—that they were on his side.

What did sides matter? In the long run, everyone dies. Governments rise, and governments fall. Vacuums are created, and then they are filled.

Meet the new boss. Same as the old boss.

Societies grow, and then they wither away, and all that ever remains is...

A beach. A beach with land behind it, filled with governments and men, and beyond the beach, just the endless, unthinking sea, and all you can do is run in the narrow space provided between those two unstoppable forces that you will never have any hope of conquering.

Pop-pop-pop!

Abe sent three rounds into a man that Lee thought looked like an American soldier. Something in him wanted to cry out and tell Abe not to shoot him, but he also trusted his friend, knew he wouldn't fire on someone unless he had a damn good reason.

Shit. What the hell was happening?

He'd blown the generator, and then he'd run—

He'd run on a beach, just as fast and as far as his legs could carry him—

No, he'd run to cover behind a truck. Kind of like how he and Abe were taking cover behind another truck right now.

Wait.

Was this the same memory? Had Abe been there with him? Was this the past or the present? And did it even matter?

An Army doctor smiled at Lee, bright white teeth in ebony skin. The doctor explained to him the weird-ass test he'd just taken that'd required Lee to be asleep while they mucked around with his brainwaves. They were looking for something called "mental flex"—the ability to keep going, even when things made no sense, and reality seemed surreal.

Apparently, Lee had it in spades.

He gripped his rifle and pulled it tight into his shoulder. His head ached. His brain wasn't quite working. He had only the dimmest sense of who was friend and who was foe, but he trusted himself to figure it out in the moment.

"Hey!" Abe was at the back of the truck, about to cut the corner. But he looked back over his shoulder at Lee, concern in his dark eyes. "You with me?"

"Yuh," Lee grunted.

Abe slipped around the corner.

Lee wobbled through a carport, skinny arms straining at the plastic grocery sacks, trying to navigate them up the steps into the house, carrying far too many. He failed in his mission. He dropped the eggs. His mother was mad. His father was reserved.

"You don't gotta carry all the groceries by yourself," his father said.

Around the backend of the truck. Something buzzed by Lee's face. Abe's rifle was spitting. Lee saw a man in a familiar uniform skirting sideways, firing at them both. Lee didn't consciously aim, just pulled the trigger several times until the guy went down in a tumble of limbs.

Abe was running now. Lee realized it belatedly, the distance between him and his friend stretching. He spurred himself on. They were heading for a big tent that looked half torn to shreds. There was a lot of screaming and thrashing going on inside. Abe steered wide of the open tent flap, pieing off the interior before deciding whether or not to plunge in.

Lee pivoted left to cover Abe's exposed side. It was just so...rote.

He'd done this so many goddamn times. A fight here. A war there. All of them the same. All of them bleeding together. Congealing into one big ball of excitement and misery. Except the excitement seemed distant now. From the perspective of his entire life, it all seemed pointless.

How would it end?

Sometimes in victory. Sometimes in defeat. But no matter what, always and inevitably, it ended in death. That was the war that no one could win. No one got out of life alive.

Then he saw someone squirming out from under the side of the tent. The man was wearing all black. He had a beard. He carried a rifle—an AK variant. Lee wasn't sure whether this was someone to help or hurt. The man wasn't shooting—he was fleeing. And he wasn't wearing the same uniform as the other guys.

The man twisted as he came to his hands and knees, looking about. He saw Lee. He didn't raise his rifle. Instead, he simply spun around and ran, disappearing around the edge of the tent, heading for the woods.

Where moments before Lee had been struck with apathy at the pointlessness of it all, now something exploded in his mind. That man, running from him, was like a squirrel running from a dog.

He just needed to chase it and fuck it up.

This was not a conscious thought in Lee's mind. He didn't make this decision with logic. It was made for him by years of fighting instinct. And perhaps, in some way, a part of him knew it was all futile, and that no matter how many of his enemies he killed, more would rise up behind them.

But he went after the guy anyway.

Abe spotted a soldier inside the tent, pumping rounds into a hybrid until they collapsed at his feet. That man's brief moment of victory came to an abrupt stop when Abe put two rounds through the side of his head.

He'd pied off a good bit of the interior through the sagging tent flap now. He was on the right side of the flap, and was pretty confident that the hybrids had taken over inside. Even so, he slapped the side of the tent and hollered, "It's Abe! Coming in!"

Then he glanced to his left, and then behind him.

No Lee.

Lee was supposed to be right on his ass.

Where the fuck had he gone? The guy's brain was still coming online after a hard reboot—had he gone and wandered off somewhere? Or worse—had he collapsed? Had there been bleeding on the brain? Swelling?

Shit!

Abe flashed his weaponlight, hoping against hope to illuminate Lee crouching in some shadow. But there was nothing but dead bodies—hybrids and Russian soldiers alike. No Lee.

"Goddammit, Lee!" Abe made a split-second decision to sweep the command tent before he went looking for his buddy. He plunged through the opening and found...utter annihilation. Flipped-over tables. Toppled chairs. Tangled wires. Smashed computers. Bullet holes everywhere.

Bodies.

Six hybrids stood in the room, chests heaving and feral eyes darting to Abe as he swept in. Their faces and hands were coated in blood. One of them had something in its mouth that Abe couldn't identify. The second Abe looked at him, he spat it out, like he'd been caught. Another had his foot on the head of a still-squirming man in an OCP uniform.

Unlike his friend, this one seemed to wait until Abe looked at him before he thrust his heel down, rupturing the man's skull.

There were human and hybrid bodies strewn about the room. Abe did a quick once-over, but it seemed the six hybrids in the middle of the Russian command tent had things under control. And, frankly, Abe didn't want to be alone with them at the moment.

He slipped out, keying his comms as he went, and forgoing codenames: "Abe to Lee, Abe to Lee, where you at?"

Lee did not hear Abe hail him on the radio. Somewhere along the line, his earpiece had come out. It didn't matter. He wouldn't have responded anyway.

He didn't know why. His thinking was still a bit…loose.

He felt as though he were being carried by a will not his own. Like he was just a dog, and that some power beyond himself was his handler, and it had told him to *Get the bad man!* And then he was off, in pursuit of the fleeing figure, without any real thought as to why, or what the consequences might be.

In truth, Lee was just being himself.

Reduced? Perhaps. Because rational, strategic caution had left him.

But perhaps more as well. Because he was unfettered by all that he'd learned, and simply acted on what he knew in his heart.

What he knew was this: He had to catch the bad man and fuck him up.

Just that simple.

And more than just *had to*—more than a simple sense of duty—he *wanted to*. Was *driven* to. Could no more deny that force that animated him to action than he could deny the force of gravity.

He plunged headlong through the woods.

He had lost his NOD when Abe had ripped his helmet off his head. But there was just enough moonlight for him to catch glimpses of the shape, about twenty yards ahead of him, crashing through the brush, desperate to get away.

But this man was unwounded. He was mostly-fresh. And his legs appeared to not have nagging old bullet wounds to make them stiff and unwieldy.

In short, he was pulling ahead of Lee, the distance growing from twenty yards to twenty-five in short order.

Lee was going to lose this footrace.

That was okay.

The second he realized it, he slewed to a stop in the leaves, shouldering his rifle in the same instant. He registered the red dot. Super-imposed it on the shadowy figure ahead. Tracked it as it disappeared behind a thick stand of trees.

The second it reemerged on the other side, he squeezed the trigger.

The rifle bucked.

The fleeing man flailed and toppled.

Lee didn't know where he'd hit him. He fired again at the downed form. And then again. Didn't know if either of those shots landed either. Maybe not, because, as Lee fired the third round, the man rolled onto his back, his rifle between his knees.

Lee juked for the cover of a tree as the muzzle flashed. He heard the zip of the passing rounds, then the deep, woody smack as they impacted the tree. The enemy rounds just kept coming, the guy firing with reckless abandon.

Lee dropped to both knees, settling back on his heels. He took a deep breath as he calmly transitioned his rifle to his left shoulder.

He felt no fear. Perhaps fear was one of the senses that had been knocked out of him.

A good attack dog didn't operate out of fear.

You ever seen a war dog attack with its tail between its legs? No, an eighty-five-pound dog will take on an armed man twice its size, and it will wag its tail the whole time. To the dog, it's not work. It's not scary.

To the dog, it is fun.

Physiologically, both the dog and the man that it is attacking are experiencing adrenaline, increased heartrate, increased respiration, and tunnel vision.

But do you know what the difference is?

The dog *wants* to be there.

The instant the incoming fire ceased, Lee bent sideways. The muzzle of his rifle cleared the cover of the tree. The red dot touched the man—the bad man—the prey—the victim. And Lee fired.

He heard a yowl that sounded like nothing so much as an offended cat.

Lee ducked back into cover, transitioned his rifle to his right shoulder, and stood up as the man's response came in the form of three bullets that struck the side of the tree and the dirt beyond where Lee had just been. As those rounds were still coming, he leaned out the opposite side of the tree, and did the same thing: muzzle clear of cover, reticle on target, squeeze the trigger.

This time the man flopped backwards, and the noise he made was just a breathy groan.

Lee ducked back behind the tree, and calmly waited for a response.

None came.

He exited cover, rifle up, optic in line with his eye, and fired again. He began to walk towards the dark shape on the forest floor, twenty-five yards away. He wasn't entirely sure if the bad man was still alive, but the body seemed to move, so Lee fired again.

Walking. Red dot on target.

It started to move again. So he fired again.

He was cognizant now of the sound of his impacts. There's only one thing that sounds like a bullet hitting flesh. It's easier to hear when your rifle is suppressed. It reminded Lee of the sound of a kicker punting the football for a return. It threw him back under those Friday night lights.

He fired again.

Striding forward. Realities overlaid with each other. Past, present, and imagination.

He was declared a non-viable asset for leaving his bunker early.

He fired.

A kid shoved him into a locker and said, "What are you gonna do about it, faggot?"

He fired.

Julia was in his arms, gasping out her dying breaths.

He fired.

That damned betta fish, swimming all alone in the glass bowl on Deanna's desk. Bred to fight, and yet trapped in a glass cage.

He fired.

He was in some foreign country, so very far from home, and his commanding officer was telling him that his parents had both died in a car accident and he was being flown back to the States for their funeral. Four day's leave to mourn, and then he was expected back, to keep fighting, to keep operating.

He fired.

He was in an underground bunker as a madman named Erwin Briggs, who'd set himself up as the new President of the United States, rambled on about how all of this had been a plan to destabilize the thing called "Western democracy," because democracy was a sham, and might made right, and once the idiot population had been dealt with, strongmen would arise to lead the world into a better, brighter future.

He did *not* fire.

He stood over the man on the ground.

The man was still alive. He'd been shot ten times. But he wasn't giving up. He lay on his back, wheezing, his breath rattling, every inhale terrible and wet, every exhale splattering blood out of his mouth. But his eyes were wide. They were furious. They wanted to fight, but his body had betrayed him.

Lee gazed down at the man, mesmerized.

He wasn't prey. He wasn't a victim.

He was just another war dog, obeying his master's commands.

It was obvious that the man wanted to raise his rifle and shoot Lee. But he just didn't have the strength anymore.

And it all came crashing down on Lee. His mind buzzed with Jones's words. About how this reality was just a simulation. And the consciousness that kept things running was like a Dungeon Master in a role-playing game.

A game. That's all this was, according to Jones. A game that required each individual to sacrifice, and to pit themselves against other individuals.

And sometimes there was defeat, and sometimes there was victory, but in the end, didn't they all lose? Weren't they all being controlled?

Lee saw the collar around this man's neck. Not a dog-collar. A slave collar. And on it was written the words *Duty* and *Honor* and *Sacrifice*. And it was an iron collar, unbreakable, and forged by men who did not know what duty, or honor, or sacrifice actually meant.

Lee dropped to a knee beside the man. He yanked the rifle out of his hands. The man's finger must've been on the trigger, because as Lee did it, the rifle went off, sending a round harmlessly into the woods.

Lee didn't realize he was crying until he saw the man's face blur, as though melting.

The man struggled against Lee for a moment, but his breaths were getting shallower and wetter, and every exhale was a cough that issued more and more blood. It was not hard for Lee to control his hands. To grab both of the man's wrists in one grip and press them back into his chest. And then the man was still. No longer fighting. He gazed up at Lee with stricken eyes, seeing his end coming, and Lee knew how that felt, because he'd seen his own.

The firm grip he had on the man's wrist slowly relaxed, and Lee took the man's hand in his. Instead of recoiling and fighting against Lee, the man's fingers wrapped around Lee's. Not aggressively, but like a man seeking something to hold onto. Something to keep him from drowning.

"Hey," Lee croaked, his throat tight as tears continued to stream out of him, unbidden. "What's your name, brother?"

The man blinked, his eyes stark and blue in the moonlight. He must've understood English, because he whispered, "Stas."

It'd been a mistake to ask him his name. Or maybe it wasn't. Lee's brain did not allow all the cold logic. That'd been stripped away, and he was now only himself, and not what he'd been trained, and molded, and contorted into being.

Just a man. A human being. Someone who wanted what was best, and was willing to give everything he had to make that happen. A man whose instincts to help others had been used against him, time and time again.

All he wanted to do was help. All he wanted was a better world. All he wanted was to right the wrongs, and for people to have peace.

And yet, no matter how he tried to accomplish this, there always seemed to be some asshole pulling the strings, trying to use men like him, and men like Stas, to reach their own perverted dreams of absolute power.

This whole world—this whole reality—was a fighting pit.

A dog fighting ring.

And here was one fighting dog, kneeling at the side of another, neither really knowing why they'd come to be in this place. But here they were.

Lee gripped the man's hands with his left, while his right gently stroked the man's head. There was no shame here. There was no competition. That was over and decided. They'd fought their fight. They'd done as their handlers demanded. Now it was just the winner, and the unfortunate loser, in a pit where either could've come out on top.

It just so happened that, today, it was Lee.

He bent over, sobbing without any embarrassment, and put his forehead to Stas's.

"It's all fucking bullshit," Lee whispered.

CHAPTER 31

IN THE WOODS, MEN were slaughtered.

They formed up, and through their thermal-enhanced NODs, they saw the mutants coming at them, just as they'd seen a dozen times—in Voronezh, and Saratov, and Tolyatti. Except they'd never seen so many, working as one.

The men were professionals, though. They moved with practiced precision, without even having to communicate to each other, because they'd been working as a brotherhood for so long, that they rarely needed to verbalize. They were calm and practical. They were expert marksman.

None of it mattered.

The wave of mutants crashed into them. No matter how fast they fired, how smoothly they transitioned from target to target, or how fast they performed their emergency reloads, it just was never enough to stem the tide.

The mutants were in a frenzy, and they maneuvered and fought with a sort of teamwork all their own. But mostly it was because they could be shot a half dozen times without going down, and they were inhumanly fast, and inhumanly strong.

That's really what carried the day.

Not technology. Not training. Not tactics.

Just plain old brute force—being faster, stronger, and meaner than your opponent.

The operatives of Spetsgruppa Alfa comported themselves well. Very few of them fell into a panic. Even fewer still retreated, because, even as death bore down on them, the vast majority would not be so dishonorable as to place their life above their brothers. So they stood side by side, and they fought on.

They watched best friends and brothers die. They watched them get torn apart, and heard their dying screams. They felt everything a normal person might in that instance—the grief, the shock, the spinning, disorienting quality of life when it becomes so unhinged and seems to be flying apart into pieces. The only difference between them and a normal person was that they stayed focused, and kept working, even as their world crumbled around them.

They just weren't a match for this new species that was dominating the planet.

The only moral victory that could be claimed was from the fact that, if anyone had gone in and tallied up the dead that littered that forest floor after the fighting was over, they'd find more mutant bodies than they would Russian soldiers.

The last man died, running.

He was not running away from death.

Rather, he was simply running to give himself time to use the last round in his pistol to go out on his own terms, instead of being eaten alive.

Perhaps, in some small way, that was a moral victory in and of itself.

Abe could just barely make out the distant ripple of suppressed gunfire, but he could hear the screaming of the Russian soldiers well enough.

The primals had closed with them. And it didn't sound like the soldiers were holding very well.

That should've felt like a victory to Abe, but he just felt kind of ill.

Part of that was his worry for Lee, as Abe continued to work his way along the perimeter of the outpost, trying to see where Lee had gotten to. He picked up a hybrid as he went—the big Samoan-looking one, named Cade.

"All dead," Cade announced in a low growl.

For a moment, Abe thought he meant the soldiers currently being torn apart by primals, but then he realized Cade was speaking about the outpost.

"It's clear?" Abe asked, casting a glance over his shoulder at the collection of tents, vehicles, and various other warfighting supplies.

"Clear," Cade confirmed.

That tracked—Abe hadn't seen another live human in the last minute or so. The encampment had become eerily quiet. No more screams. No more snarls. No more gunfire. The shadowy figures of hybrids stalked through the gloom in silence, searching for more prey, and not finding any.

Abe pointed into the woods. "I lost track of L—uh—Jax. Can you scent him out?"

Cade didn't even hesitate. He pivoted slightly and pointed. "He's over there. With someone else."

Abe didn't know what the hell that meant. Rather than relieve him, it only deepened his anxiety. "Lead me to him," he ordered.

Cade immediately took off at a loping stride, Abe keeping pace with him, his weaponlight scouring the dark woods as they moved through it.

It didn't take them long to find Lee. He was only about two hundred yards into the woods. When Abe's weaponlight first hit him, Abe thought he must've been wounded: Lee was on his knees, hunched over, unmoving.

As Abe got closer, he saw that there was another figure there—the "someone else" that Cade had mentioned. Whoever it was lay on their back, as Lee hovered over them.

"Hey, buddy, you with me?" Abe called as he and Cade raced up.

Lee's head came up. Then his body straightened.

Coming up behind Lee, Abe could see that the stranger on the ground was dressed all in black, and clearly dead from a multitude of gunshot wounds. An AK-variant rifle lay in the leaves near the dead man. Lee's own rifle was slung to his side.

Abe crouched down and put his hands on Lee's shoulders, cautiously. "Hey, man, you alright?"

Lee turned and regarded him. His eye looked red-rimmed, as though he'd been crying, which made Abe incredibly uneasy for reasons he couldn't quite pin down. Lee stared back at Abe, his features blank for a long moment.

Then he blinked, as though suddenly coming awake, or perhaps remembering who he was.

He cleared his throat. "Yeah. I'm alright."

"You're not injured?" Abe asked as he looked Lee over.

"Nah," Lee said, casually, then stood up.

"We need to go," Cade rasped from behind them. "The primals—they're coming."

Lee and Abe didn't argue. Abe kept a hand on him until he was confident his friend was steady enough to walk on his own. He still seemed a bit dazed. They began making their way back towards the outpost, Cade urging them to a run, clearly worried about how close the primals were getting.

"Who was that?" Abe heaved as they ran.

"Don't know," Lee answered, tonelessly.

A moment later, they emerged from the forest, back into the clearing where the outpost sat.

Abe was surprised as hell to hear human voices—not the throaty, awkward rasps of hybrids. When they cleared a line of tents, Abe spotted a cluster of bewildered humans, and immediately recognized a few of the people from Appomattox that he'd lost in the woods.

Judy was among them.

Abe raced to her side with Lee in tow. The woman was filthy from head to foot. Her graying hair stood out in wild tangles, with leaves and bits of bark woven into the strands. Her eyes seemed hollow and haunted, a ghost of the strong settlement leader he'd met only hours before.

There were six others with her, and Abe spotted a few more being hustled out of the woods, escorted by a contingent of hybrids. As it turned out, some of the hybrids that Lee had instructed to stay behind and hold the breach had decided to head back to where all the civilians had been massacred by the helicopters, sniff out survivors, and pull them to safety before the primals could overtake them.

Abe wondered what had happened to those two helicopters, because they'd never shown up to the outpost. They must've either been warned away, or they'd seen the outpost getting overrun and decided to fly off to points unknown.

That was an idle curiosity.

As he made eye contact with Judy, Abe fully expected her to launch into recriminations about how he'd abandoned them when they needed him the most. But that was just his latent guilt talking. He'd shoved it down below the level of his recognizance, and replaced it with ferocity, but it still sat like a stone in his guts, souring everything.

Instead of weeping and shouting and screaming at him, Judy wilted into him, seeming almost relieved, which took Abe off-guard. Then her eyes sharpened, and he braced himself.

"Did you get those bastards?" she asked. "Did you kill 'em?"

Abe swallowed, momentarily surprised. Then he nodded. "Yeah. We got 'em." He spun for Cade, intending to tell the hybrid to send more of his packs back to retrieve as many survivors as they could find, but the big guy was already on it.

Hybrids sprinted off into the woods, even as more emerged, shepherding civilians along with them.

"They're getting close," Cade said, after scenting the air. He turned to Abe and Lee, looking concerned. "You should get the people out of the open."

Abe understood. At that particular moment, the truce between the people of Appomattox and the primal colonies had become a fragile thing in the midst of the chaos. Stirred up, the primals would not have as much control over their instincts as usual. If they came across this encampment out in the woods, and saw the humans crowded there, they would only perceive prey, which would make it that much harder for the hybrids to convince them to back off.

Abe began hustling the surviving humans towards the command tent, which he thought would be big enough to hold them all. What was waiting for them inside would not be pleasant to see, but really, given everything that'd happened that night, well...they'd just have to get over it.

Lee assisted, but while Abe barked orders and did his best to give the civilians a sense that they had things under control, Lee simply murmured soft encouragements to them. He still sounded like he was caught in a dream-state. The round to the helmet had really scrambled his brain. But he was, at least, still doing work.

Abe couldn't ask for more than that.

He just hoped his old friend would come back. He *had* to come back.

Abe had seen many a friend with a TBI become a different person entirely. As though the neural connections in their brains that made them who they were and gave them their unique personality had been broken, and when they were rebuilt, the pattern was different, giving birth to a stranger.

That, more than anything else, made Abe incredibly uneasy.

For the next ten minutes, Abe, Lee, and Cade worked quickly to pull batches of survivors out of the woods and put them inside the command tent. Their scent would be all over the place, but there was nothing they could do about that. They would just have to hope and trust in their hybrid friends.

Hybrid friends.

That struck Abe as wildly surreal.

The world just kept changing around him. Kept evolving into something he didn't understand. Abe kept hoping that at some point, things would stabilize, and the constant tide of change would slow, so that he could get his feet under him.

But that was not how this new world was going to work. The plague of six years prior had put the world into a blender, rearranging it, just as surely as those men with TBIs had their personalities rearranged. This new world would always be a stranger to Abe, and he to it.

It would never stop changing.

All Abe could hope to do was stay alive, and try to keep up.

In the end, the hybrids rescued thirty-seven survivors, all of which were packed into the command tent, out of sight. None of the elderly civilians had made it, Abe noted, as he scanned the haggard, frightened faces. But some of the children had. Several of them were hybrid children—too young to have contributed to the fight. But many were human children.

That would give the people of Appomattox some hope, Abe thought. The children would give them a reason to be strong, a reason not to give up.

Abe and Lee stood outside, rifles in hand, flanking the opening to the command tent. They'd already given the people inside multiple warnings to stay quiet, and now the only sound that came from inside were wet sniffles and heavy breathing.

Cade ran up to them, flanked by two other hybrids that Abe didn't recognize.

"They're here," Cade growled with a note of urgency. "Get inside." His eyes fixed on Abe, then Lee, his expression stern. "Do not shoot at them. That will only make things worse."

Abe nodded, and he and Lee retreated just inside the tent flap, while the two hybrids that had accompanied Cade took up positions outside.

Abe stayed very close to the opening, so he could peer out into the moonlit night.

Cade loped off on all fours, and was quickly joined by dozens of his brothers and sisters, all heading for the eastern edge of the encampment. Abe tried to keep an eye on them, but they disappeared behind the outpost's temporary structures, and then everything was very still, and breathlessly silent.

The interior of the command tent was pitch dark. Abe had doused his weaponlight.

He turned his head towards where he thought Lee was, then reached out with his support hand. Felt his friend's plate carrier. Crawled his fingers up to rest on the back of his sweat-slick and dirt-encrusted neck.

"How you doin', old boy?" Abe whispered to the darkness.

The darkness let out a quiet chuff, then whispered back: "Lucky to be alive. Hope to stay that way."

Abe practically melted with relief. That sounded like the Lee he knew. "Me too, brother. Me too."

Then the night came alive with noise.

Once, when Lee had been a kid, living out in rural North Carolina, he'd stood with his old man on their back porch. It'd been night. Clear skies. So dark and removed from city lights, that he could see the celestial band of distant stars for which their galaxy had been named: The Milky Way.

Crickets and frogs sang in the cool night air. The porch was dark—his father hadn't turned the lights on before stepping outside to stare into the darkness, as was his proclivity of an evening. Not because he was filled with dark thoughts, but because he loved the feeling of remoteness, and the stars overhead, and the sounds of all the nocturnal wildlife.

Then, that childhood version of Lee, standing by his father's side, had heard something out there in the night. Something that made his skin crawl, and he stepped closer to his father.

It was a long, eerie howl. Mournful. Piercing. Primordial.

It was the sound of something so far removed from civilization, that, for a moment, Lee did not feel like such a thing as civilization actually existed, or *could* exist. It was as though all the cities and towns and stoplights and cars had all just up and vanished in an instant, and Lee and his father had been suddenly transported back to a time when man did not rule the earth, and cowered around firelight, and feared the dark, and all the monsters it contained.

"What was that?" Lee had hissed, clutching at his father's arm.

His father's voice was quietly amused at his son's concern. "Coyotes," he said.

"Are they dangerous?"

His father made a noncommittal noise. The howl had tapered off by then, and there was only the crickets and frogs again. He never did say whether they were dangerous or not.

What he did say was this: "Howl back."

"What?"

"Go ahead. Howl back. But do it like you mean it. Do it like you're the scariest thing out here."

Lee was entirely unsure about this request, but he took a big breath, lifted his head to the sky, and howled. It was a little hesitant at first, but about midway through, Lee felt something come over him. Some latent instinct that had no room for fear.

He was just a boy. But in that moment, as he expelled the last of his breath, he did so with force, and conviction, channeling some deeper part of himself that, while it had no claws and teeth, was nevertheless the most dangerous thing that had ever walked the earth.

For just a tiny moment after the last of the breath emptied out of his lungs, there was only silence, and Lee, in a flash of boyhood hubris, thought that he had frightened those ancient creatures away with his ferocity.

But then they answered.

Not one, but dozens. All of the sudden, the woods around that little house in the middle of the North Carolina countryside, was filled with the keening of beasts that Lee had not even known were there. Some of those howls were very close—maybe only a hundred yards away from the porch—and Lee was abruptly terrified, as though he had inadvertently issued a challenge that he could not back up, and that those tawny, wolf-like creatures would slink out of the dark woods and come to see how dangerous this boy-human could actually be.

He had only ever seen a coyote once. A solitary figure, caught in a flash of headlights as his family drove down a dark country road. Because of this, he had imagined that there were very few coyotes.

Now, he realized that they were all around him, living unseen in the forests that he would play in during the day, oblivious that he was climbing trees and building forts and plinking beer cans with his BB gun, all while predators lurked in silence, smelling his scent, hearing his clumsy footfalls, and perhaps even watching him with their cold, golden eyes.

The idea of this terrified Lee, and he began to wonder if he should ever go out into those woods again.

But then his father chuckled, lighthearted and awestruck by the chorus of woodland predators now filling the night with their voices, as though defiant of the spread of man and all his endless concrete sprawl.

Then his father howled back.

Lee joined him.

Their human voices melded with the cries of unseen and secretive predators. The coyotes did not falter, unbothered by these brash interlopers to their night song.

In that moment, Lee felt both powerful, and insignificant.

The spiral arm of their galaxy arcing overhead—just one of billions. And in it, a single, tiny orb where life had taken hold, and evolved, and continued to evolve, on and on forever. A world in which the only constant was change, and Lee's life, and the life of every human being, and even the life of their entire species, was just a tiny aberration in an infinite timeline of struggle and survival and adaptation.

Perhaps it was hubris to join their voices with those old creatures of claw and tooth. For what had either of those humans done to earn their place in this savage existence?

Or perhaps it was something else. Perhaps it was neither pride, nor challenge, nor passing amusement between father and son who both would soon be dead.

Perhaps it was something deeper than that.

An acknowledgement of the fragility of the order that they had established over the world. A realization that all would be dust in time, and all those concrete seas and rivers would be swallowed up eventually, and that human beings would only be a memory—a blip in the fossil record of a world that continued to change.

But also a statement that, until that day came, they would fight for their survival, as every creature did, until they fell to inevitable extinction.

Maybe the coyotes understood that.

Maybe that was the only reason they allowed Lee to sing with them that night.

Outside the command tent, the air was filled with hooting and yapping and howling. They did not sound like coyotes, or wolves, or even dogs. They did not sound like humans, either. They did not sound like any creature but what they were—something new. Something original that'd been spawned on this little blue marble, spinning its way through one of billions of galaxies.

The primals chorused, and the hybrids responded. It was not a song, like that night with the coyotes. It was more like an argument. Heated, but at the same time, with a certain amount of deference. Neither side really wanted to fuck with the other.

Even though this moment was very different, it still reminded Lee of that night years in the past. Not because of its similarities, but because of a stark contrast that became all too obvious to Lee.

Back in that childhood night, he'd howled *with* the coyotes, and they had allowed the human to join them.

Now, the humans sat in tense silence, aware that they were no longer the kings and queens of this planet. They'd been deposed. And for the last six years, Lee had been watching their old kingdom crumble to dust, and get washed away in the tide of unstoppable change.

Humanity at large might not realize it, but Lee did. He knew what he was.

He was the last of the old guard. Not even warring to hold their ground anymore, but instead fighting simply to slow the inevitable advance of their extinction. A tactical withdrawal, it was called, in the strategy books. Sometimes referred to as a fighting retreat. Or, as the Marines would put it: Attacking in the other direction.

But it all amounted to the same thing: The war was lost, and now all that remained for people like Lee was to buy time, and postpone their unavoidable end.

Even in the midst of that existential realization, Lee was not hopeless. Because humanity *did* have one last chance to carve out a place for themselves in this ever-changing world. They just couldn't do it alone.

They needed the hybrids.

Many might disagree. But Lee had been paying attention, and what was occurring right at that moment, in that abandoned corner of the Virginian countryside, was just a microcosm of the larger conflict at play across the globe.

Humanity could try to go it alone, and become extinct.

Or they could figure out how to work with the hybrids, and perhaps live on.

In the darkness of the command tent, no one saw it, but a wistful smile had taken over Lee's mouth. Morbidly amused, as only someone whose perspective has just been violently rearranged can be, Lee whispered the words of an old song.

Misunderstanding Lee's quiet susurrations, Abe hissed, "What's that? What're you saying?"

Lee leaned into the man that had been a friend, and then an enemy, and then a partner that had stuck with him through thick and thin, and told him the words that'd been rolling through his brain. Words from an old Bob Dylan song, that now rang with the weight of prophecy:

Come gather 'round people
Wherever you roam
And admit that the waters
Around you have grown
And accept it that soon
You'll be drenched to the bone
If your time to you is worth savin'
And you better start swimmin'
Or you'll sink like a stone
For the times they are a-changin'

Chapter 32

Lee and Abe walked back to where the assault had begun, and where Lee had dropped his rucksack.

It was clear that a primal had become interested in it: It was unzipped, with some of its content hanging out, or strewn around.

After a protracted session of hollering wordlessly back and forth with the hybrids, the primals had retreated, taking the bodies of the fallen with them.

Those colonies would eat well for several days.

Abe grumbled as he stepped up to Lee's disheveled pack: "You fuckin' assholes."

Lee and Abe both had their weaponlights on, and began searching the immediate area for any items that'd been tossed around. Pairs of socks. Spare battery packs for their radios. Extra magazines. A few MREs—though in that case, both Lee and Abe left the rations where they lay, as they'd been chewed through and partially eaten.

Lee gathered his things, feeling a growing unease until he found the thing that really mattered.

He let out a gust of breath as he picked it up. "Found it."

"Thank God," Abe said. "Still in one piece?"

Lee inspected the satphone. "Yeah. Looks fine."

They quickly stuffed what they could find back into the ruck. Lee shouldered it, and they headed out of the woods. Cade had assured them that the woods would be clear of primals—at least around the outpost—but neither Lee nor Abe wanted to hang out any longer than necessary.

Walking back into the encampment, a few flashlights and lanterns bobbed through the midnight darkness, as the remaining survivors of Appomattox worked with an almost spiteful thoroughness to loot everything they possibly could. Weapons, ammo, food, water, medical supplies—it all went into the two trucks.

"Think we should tell 'em to be careful what they take with them?" Abe asked out of the side of his mouth.

"What do you mean?"

Abe shrugged. "I dunno. How's this shit gonna play out? Is any of this Russian equipment gonna be evidence against them? Maybe it'd be best to just get rid of it all."

Lee peered around, uncertain. "Yeah, I guess I don't know either." He lifted the satphone. "We can find out. But honestly, I think they've earned it."

Abe went quiet as Lee extended the satphone's antenna and dialed.

It barely got through the first ring before Major Ron Paige answered, sounding keyed-up and twitchy. "Cloud Nine."

"Archangel," Lee gave the rote response.

A pent-up breath crackled through the speaker. "Fuck. Alright. You at Fort Campbell?"

"Uh, well…" Lee glanced at Abe. "About that."

Ron groaned. "Christ. Where are you?"

"I'm still in Virginia. Currently standing at Point Delta, if you take my meaning."

There was a long silence. "You're with the Russians? Are you under duress?"

"No duress. I'm in the Russian camp." Lee cringed a bit. "But...they're...gone."

Ron's voice was full of sickened dread. "What did you do?"

"Well, how about you send me an extract chopper, and I'll give you a full debrief when I'm back. It's just me and Abe. The rest of the team took the first chopper out. We stayed behind...to help."

The next ten seconds was just Ron cursing. It was muted, as though he'd pulled the mic away from his mouth to have his tantrum.

Lee half-smiled, half-grimaced at Abe.

Abe lifted an eyebrow. "He's freaking out, isn't he?"

Lee held up thumb and forefinger, the tips almost touching. "Little bit."

Ron came back. "You have no idea what a shitstorm you've created. Oh my God, Lee. Do you *ever* think before you do this shit? Do you realize you've created an international incident?"

"Slow your roll there, Major Paige," Lee groused. "As I recall, some bigwig in the IAG invited Russian soldiers to experiment on American civilians. So, no, I didn't *create* an international incident. That shit was created while I was still in Oregon, happy and ignorant. *Y'all* pulled *me* into an already existing shitstorm. In fact, I seem to remember you threatening to blacklist me if I didn't come. Just remember, none of this was my idea, alright?"

Ron just growled.

"And besides," Lee continued. "This shit's all under the table, isn't it? So, while the Russians might be a little pissed at whoever it is in the IAG that gave the go-ahead for this fuckery, it's not like either of them can be too vocal about it. Am I wrong?"

"Things are very tense right now!" Ron cried. "Diplomacy is hanging by a fucking thread!"

"Okay, well, lesson learned, huh? I don't do diplomacy, so maybe next time take that into consideration before you force me to help some dickweed in the government cover up their shady business." Lee huffed. "Can I get a fucking extract or not, Ron?"

Another long silence, which was terminated by Ron making a noise somewhere between lifting a heavy object and being strangled to death. "Yes. Alright. Fine. Extract will be inbound in a few. But when you get back to Fort Campbell, don't say a fucking word to anyone. Don't go anywhere. Don't do anything. I'm on the next flight out to you. We'll deal with this in-person."

"Sounds great," Lee quipped. "I look forward to seeing your sunny face."

"Fuck you, Lee."

"Bye now."

Lee hung up.

"Well," Abe said after a moment. "That sounded…nice."

Lee pocketed the satphone, sighing heavily. "I think I got us in trouble."

"Yeah?" Abe clapped a hand on Lee's back. "Well, they can eat a dick."

In the Loews Chicago O'Hare Hotel, General Perry Griffin lay spread-eagle on the king-sized bed in his suite.

In the silence of the room, it seemed he could hear every noise from the city outside.

Helicopters buzzed in the distance, supporting night operations against the rebels. Muted gunshots popped like an endless fireworks show. Occasionally, a bigger boom, as some piece of ordnance was detonated.

Despite all of this, Griffin was just beginning to slip into a restless doze when someone knocked on his door.

He groaned. "What?"

"General, it's me," a female voice called through the door of the suite's master bedroom.

That would be his aide.

Griffin hoisted himself onto his elbows and looked down. He was wearing only a pair of silkies—his preferred sleepwear for years, and it hadn't changed after he'd been promoted. He still slept like the ground-pounder he was.

Briefly, he considered not giving a fuck. The silkies were small, but they were basically PT shorts. But then he thought about professionalism, and keeping up appearances, and all that.

"Hang on," he grumbled, swinging himself out of bed and snatching up his OCP pants.

"General, it's urgent."

"Yeah, okay," he said, stuffing his legs hurriedly into the pants, buttoning them, then grabbing his undershirt and wrestling it on. "Come in."

The door immediately opened. His aide was in uniform, hair pinned back neatly as though she hadn't slept at all. Maybe she hadn't. The woman's work-ethic bordered on manic.

She was holding a satphone.

She crossed the room to Griffin and held it out to him, her eyes giving him a significant, hard stare. "It's Major Paige, general."

Griffin snatched the satphone from her hand and put it to his ear. "Griffin here. Talk to me."

Then he listened.

And as he listened, his face went dark.

After about a full minute of silence, Griffin said, "I want you there in person. Be on the next flight out to meet them. And keep this quiet."

Major Paige indicated that he was leaving Aspen, Colorado in ten minutes—just as soon as the transport plane finished fueling. He also indicated that he understood the sensitivity of the situation.

But really, he had no fucking idea.

Griffin hung up and handed the satphone back to his aide. "Wake the president," he said, grabbing his uniform shirt from where it hung on the back of a chair. "I'll be in his suite in ten minutes."

"How's your noggin?" Abe asked, as he and Lee stood at the back of one of the Russian military trucks, currently packed with all manner of appropriated goods.

"Oh, you know how it is," Lee answered. He'd already taken a handful of ibuprofen from his personal stash. It barely took the edge off the migraine-like headache. The whiplash had torqued something in his neck as well, making it difficult to turn his head fully to the right.

"How many concussions is that for you now?"

Lee made a dismissive *pssh* noise. "Who knows."

He was being all laissez-faire about it, but that was just an act, and they both knew it. TBIs were serious, and they'd both taken some hard knocks to the cranium over the years. It was best not to think too much about what it would do them in the long run. Mood swings. Confusion. Palsy.

The glorious life of a warrior.

Old soldiers never die, General MacArthur had once said. *They just fade away.*

Fucking horseshit.

Soldiers got blown up, stabbed, and perforated. They drowned in their own blood. They went into septic shock. They bled out. Sometimes, if the Universe was merciful, they just got their brain punched out and went quick. And if you somehow managed to survive all of that and become an *old* soldier, well then you lived in a shell of your former self, the pilot of a body too broken to ever fully heal. And yes, those old soldiers died too, as everyone would die. They didn't miraculously dematerialize. They died shitting the bed, stroking out, gasping nonsense. And that was if they didn't just suck-start their own weapon to be done with it all.

If you ever hear someone talking about *glory* or *honor*, run the fuck away.

Over the years, Lee had wondered many times why he didn't just stop.

But he never wondered it for long. Dark nights could lead to bad thoughts, but no matter the mental contortions, the conclusion was always the same.

You are what you are.

Lee and Abe? They weren't...normal. When God pieced them together, he put a fire in their bones that never went out.

A blessing? A curse? Hard to say. All Lee knew was that he was incapable of turning away. If ever his own sense of self-preservation tried to assert dominance over him, the fire blazed and burned it to ash.

Turning away from a fight to save yourself was what normal people did.

Plunging into the thick of it every goddamned time? That's what fools like Lee and Abe did. Not because they wanted to, so much as they knew they couldn't live with themselves if they didn't.

Standing there, shaky and exhausted, it sure seemed like a curse.

But then, looking out and seeing a little girl clinging to her father, both of whom would've been dead if it hadn't been for that fire in his bones, Lee saw it as a blessing.

Everyone sought meaning in a meaningless life. No matter how hard things got, if you could extract some sense of meaning from it, then you could keep yourself going.

This handful of survivors from Appomattox?

That was all the meaning Lee could ask for.

Judy walked up to them. She looked dead on her feet, but less from exhaustion, and more from the emotional toll. She was accompanied only by Cade. Lee hadn't seen Gale or Greg. He didn't think they'd made it. But that was going to be a common grief for the people of Appomattox over the next few days.

Of those that had survived, Lee doubted that any of them had made it through without losing a loved one or a friend. That little settlement had been a family. And now most of them were dead.

But some had made it. And that's what Lee chose to focus on. That was the only part of this that he could consider a success.

Judy and Cade stopped in front of them. Lee and Abe both waited for her to say something, because she'd come over as though she had a purpose. But she just stood there, staring blankly into the back of the truck.

Lee shifted his weight to give his bum leg a rest. "Judy?" he prompted, gently.

She inhaled sharply, as though he'd surprised her. She blinked, her eyes narrowing into focus as they landed on his. Her mouth hung open for a moment. "It doesn't feel like we won."

Lee sighed through his nose, nodding slowly.

"I mean," she stumbled on. "We beat them. But..." her eyes took on a pleading cast.

Lee reached out and took her hand. She was stiff at first, not sure what he was doing, but when she realized he was just making human contact, she relaxed. "Judy, I'm gonna tell you a secret that not many people know."

She swallowed. "Yeah?"

He leaned in, gently squeezing her hand. "It never does. No one wins in a fight. Everyone walks away hurt. But...you're walking away. And the fuckers that did this? They're not." He shrugged. "That's what a fight is."

He let go of her hand and it just kind of flopped back to her side.

"What do we do now?" she breathed. "We don't have a home anymore. They blew everything up. We can't rebuild. We can't—"

"Look," Lee interrupted, pointing over Judy's shoulder and causing her to turn. "You see that little girl?"

Judy stared at the child, straddling her father's hip, clinging to his chest. "Yes."

"What's her name?"

The breath of a smile came to Judy's lips. "Morgan."

"Just focus on Morgan," Lee said. "She's one of the survivors. She's one of your people. You wanna know what you're going to do, Judy? You're going to pack up your shit, and you're going to get the hell out of here, and you're going to find a place where Morgan can be safe and live her life. She's your purpose now. And if you ever wonder about the meaning of it, I want you to find Morgan and look at her, and remind yourself. She's your meaning. She's the only meaning you're gonna get. And you know what? That's enough. That's *gotta be* enough."

Judy's chest hitched. Her hand came up to cover her mouth as she stared at the girl, tears coming to her eyes. Then she huffed out a few shaky breaths, thumbed the tears out of her eyes, and cleared her throat.

When she turned back to look at Lee, he recognized at least a sliver of the hardness he'd seen in the woman before.

She sniffed loudly, glancing between Lee and Abe. "And what about you guys? What are you going to do?"

Abe blew a raspberry, then let out a long, protracted, "Shiiii-it."

Lee forced a smile. "To be honest, Judy, I don't know. There's a whole shitstorm brewing about what went down here, and we're right in the middle of it. But don't worry about us. Being in the middle of shitstorms is kind of our thing. We'll figure it out."

CHAPTER 33

BY THE TIME LEE and Abe landed at Campbell Air Force Base, the sky had turned gray with dawn.

Lee's exhaustion had been so complete that he'd fallen asleep on the Blackhawk. That was a first for him. He woke up only twice, both times with a sense of confusion and a spike of anxiety. The first time was when they landed at the Kentucky outpost to refuel. The second time was when they landed at Campbell.

Lee did not recall any dreams, and yet, immediately upon waking, his only thought was this: *God, please let Jones be okay*.

He did not wheel and deal with the higher power. Such things felt like folly. What could he offer that would be worth Jones's life? He had nothing. So he just begged.

Begged the entire time as the Blackhawk descended to the tarmac.

Two figures waited at the edge of the landing pad.

Kat was wearing what looked like a borrowed jumpsuit a size too large for her. Despite the cold, she had the top tied around her waist, and Lee could see bandages on both arms, and around her stomach. She also seemed to be favoring one leg.

Marie still wore the filthy civilian clothes she'd been in. No armor. No weapons. Her arms were crossed over her chest. It was a defensive posture that Lee immediately didn't like the look of.

As the Blackhawk touched down and the crew chief opened the doors, Lee exchanged a look with Abe, and saw all of his worries reflected in the other man's eyes.

They slid out of the helicopter and walked stiffly under the whirling rotors.

As they drew closer to the two women, Marie's face came into focus.

Lee's heart felt like it stopped dead in his chest.

In her expression was no joy of comrades reunited. No snarky smile for him, nor a warm look for Abe. None of the things Lee had expected.

Instead, her face was drawn and stricken. Her eyes were swollen and red.

God, I'm fucking begging you...

He stopped in front of Marie, every muscle in his sore and fatigued body pulling tight. "What happened?" he asked, his voice thick. "Did Jonesy make it?"

Marie blinked rapidly. Maybe it was the rotor wash still buffeting them. Maybe it'd blown a bit of grit in her eye.

He wanted that to be true.

He knew it wasn't.

Marie's face tensed, and she reached out and hooked her fingers into the collar of Lee's armor. It was a motion that one might expect to come with a rough shove or a pull, but she simply hung on him.

"Marie," Lee said in a more demanding tone, unable to bear it.

"Jones is alive," Marie said, a jagged smile quirking one side of her mouth, and then immediately falling away. "He just got out of surgery. He's stable. Surgeon says he's optimistic about his recovery."

Lee's knees almost buckled. But they didn't. They stayed tense.

Because her expression was still haunted.

Marie sucked in a big breath. Her eyes went wide, as though falling into some sort of trance, and when she spoke, it was mechanical and dazed. "It's Sam. He...uh..."

She wasn't even looking at Lee, he realized.

She was staring over his shoulder at nothing in particular.

A moment before, his heart had stopped. Now it began to beat so hard and irregular, Lee thought something might actually be wrong with it.

"He didn't make it," Marie said.

No. That's not what she'd said. Lee had misheard her.

"What?" he croaked.

He felt Abe's heavy hand on his shoulder. It squeezed, painfully. Dimly, he heard Abe's breathy voice, as though from a great distance: "Ah, Jesus, Marie. Fucking hell."

"What?" Lee almost shouted at Marie.

Her eyes snapped to his, and she looked very small, and very scared, and very overwhelmed. "He's gone, Lee. Sam's gone."

Lee's mind seemed to shear in two.

Half of him understood the words, and what they meant. The other half seemed unable to comprehend it. And there was an argument between those two halves, which took place in the span of just a few breathless seconds.

Sam is dead. You knew this could happen one day. Today was that day.

No, that's ridiculous. Sam can't be dead.

She just told you he was.

That's impossible.
It is not only possible, it was inevitable.
I don't want this. This isn't real. I refuse to acknowledge it.
Good luck with that.

Still reeling, Lee turned a frown on Abe, as though hoping the other man would offer some clarity on the situation. And he did, in a way. Just not in the way Lee wanted.

Abe detached himself from Lee and faced away, both hands over his face, head tilted back. He made some noises. None of them made sense to Lee.

"I'm sorry," Marie suddenly cried, pulling at his armor, and causing Lee to stumble slightly. He looked back at her, expression unchanged—still frowning, as though confused. But with each passing second, the confusion was leaving, and cold, stark reality was taking hold. "I tried—I tried everything I could!" Marie was crying so hard that snot was running down her lip, and her spittle was forming froth around the edges of her mouth. "I tried, but I didn't have my fucking medical kit, and it wasn't a medevac chopper, and he'd been—oh, my God, Lee!—he'd been shot so many fucking times! I just...I just..."

Lee's split mind knitted itself back together. Reality fell, as heartless as stone. He didn't bother denying the facts anymore. But neither could he accept them. To accept them felt like pulling a knife into his own guts, and he shied away from that pain.

So he disassociated. Life was just a game, after all—just like Jonesy had said. And they were just players. None of this actually mattered.

Maybe that was true, and maybe it wasn't. But it kept him standing.

Left him numb and robotic, but that was better than the alternative.

He reached up and took Marie's hand from his collar, then pulled her into a hug. She sobbed into his dirty armor.

"It's alright," he said, trying to affect compassion, though he could feel nothing but the willfully-ignored horror of a man walking through hell with blinders on. "You did the best you could, Marie. It's not your fault."

Lee held her for a moment as she cried. But with no human emotions that he was willing to let himself feel, he was just rigid and awkward, and he knew it. He gently pushed her away, turning as he did to look at Abe.

The man had fallen into a squat, both hands pulling at his beard while he stared, wide-eyed, at the ground in front of him.

"Abe," Lee said, still in the strange, automatic voice. Playing a character. Playing a guy who had no stock in their grief. As though none of it could touch him.

That was all a lie. But it was a lie that worked. For now.

Abe's eyes listed over to his.

Lee beckoned him with a hand.

He rose and stepped over, and Lee kind of passed Marie to him, then took a step back.

What was he doing? Where was he going?

Did it matter? Did anything matter?

No, he just needed to be somewhere else. This spot of tarmac right here, where Marie had delivered the news that could not be unheard—it'd become the ninth ring of hell. He just needed to get away. Needed to be alone.

Lee continued to step backwards, like a person who hopes to flee without being noticed.

He was noticed. Abe and Marie both watched him.

He hiked a thumb over his shoulder. "Just...I, uh...I'm just gonna take a walk."

Then he turned and started walking, with no clear idea of where he was going.

Just...away.

Anywhere but there.

Kat watched him walk away.

He moved in a straight line, head up, as though fixed upon something in the distance. She wasn't sure where he was going, or how long he would be gone.

She glanced back at Marie and Abe.

They stood facing each other. Close, but not embracing. Abe gently kneaded the woman's shoulders. Both their heads were bowed, but while Marie was staring at her feet, Abe was looking at her.

He muttered soft things to her. A lot of them were questions, to which Marie would offer a short nod or shake of the head.

This was all so very odd for Kat.

She felt bad about Sam. But at the same time...she hadn't really known him. How much grief should she feel for someone she'd only known for such a short time? Was she being a heartless primal bitch right now? Or was this normal?

What *was* normal?

Kat had no idea. She understood, academically, that the world had been very different before she'd been born. But to Kat, this was all she'd ever known.

Violence and death.

What had *not* been normal was the life she'd led at the monastery. To her, anyway. Bran and Shay seemed to love it. Seemed to think that's what life should be like—waking up, working all day, and spending quiet evenings together.

There was nothing wrong with that, Kat supposed. But she...itched.

This? The fighting and the dying? That felt more normal to her.

And yet, she was not standing there happily, oblivious to the emotions of others. She did not feel the same grief for Sam that they did. But she was *not* a heartless primal bitch. She felt pity for those people, because she could imagine what it would be like if she lost someone that she cared very dearly for.

The only person in the world that fit that bill was Bran. So she imagined losing him, and when she did that, she understood what these people were feeling.

Was it her fault? Could she have gotten to Sam sooner? Could she have run faster? Should she have tried to use some of the stuff in the medical pouch on his side to save him? She didn't know how to use any of those things, but maybe she could've figured it out.

But then the bad guys would have caught up with them.

Kat frowned, feeling frustrated at her failure, and sad because the others were sad, and shameful because she could not rid herself of the feeling that she could have done more, if only she had a smarter human-brain to figure her way through problems.

But more than anything, she felt worried. And that confused her. Took her a moment to parse through her feelings and thoughts, and realize why.

Oddly enough, she would have never figured out the source of her feeling if she *did* have that human-brain, because humans were inherently deceptive creatures, and they lied to themselves as often as they lied to each other. Hybrids, on the other hand, were always brutally honest.

She was worried because she feared rejection.

She feared rejection because being on this mission had given her a sense of meaning and purpose she'd never before felt in her entire life. For the first time, she felt as though she were a part of something bigger than herself. And more than that, she felt *useful*.

Everywhere else, she was just a liability.

Cover your face, so the humans don't get too scared of you. Don't give into your violent instincts, because you have to act like a human. Sit down. Hold still. Be nice. Don't fight.

Don't...be...you.

But here, with this team?

With these people, she was an *asset*.

She didn't want to lose that, but she felt like it was slipping away. Because surely they saw her faults just as clearly as she saw them. Surely they had wondered the same things she'd wondered—could she have done more? Could she have run faster? Could she have been smarter?

Could she have saved Sam's life?

Clenching her teeth, Kat looked up at Lee again. He was a few hundred strides away now. He'd crossed to the far side of the airfield, just a dark figure in the pre-dawn light. He stood at the very edge of the black paving, hands on his hips, staring out at the grassy field between airstrips.

Then, moving slow, as though he were in great pain, he lowered himself to the ground. Sat with his legs splayed out in front of him, his shoulders hunched. His movements still sluggish, he unslung his rifle and lay it on the ground at his side. Then he unstrapped his armor, sloughing it off like a skin that's grown too small for the creature within.

Kat began walking towards him, her gait stiff and awkward on her wounded leg.

Abe's voice came from behind her: "Kat."

She stopped and looked over her shoulder at him.

Abe and Marie stood, intimately close with each other, looking wrung out.

Abe shook his head. "Maybe you should leave him be."

She considered that.

Yeah, maybe she should. Maybe that would be the human thing to do.

But she wasn't a human. And here, with these people—particularly Lee, who'd been the first to warm up to her and treat her like an asset instead of a liability—she didn't need to act like something she wasn't.

She gave Abe a respectful nod, but then turned and continued on.

She half expected him to shout after her and make his suggestion a command.

He didn't.

She limped the width of the airstrip, as the nearby helicopter got quieter and quieter as its rotors slowed. The engine was now off, and the spinning blades simply whooshed through the air behind her.

She stopped, just a stride shy of Lee's hunched back.

He didn't seem to register her presence.

She realized she wanted to see his face. Wanted to see if she could determine how much rage, how much resentment, how much accusation there would be in it when he saw her standing there.

Her heart was pounding, which was very strange indeed.

She stepped softly to his side, her eyes fixed on him the whole way, until she saw his face in profile.

There wasn't much there to see.

If you hadn't known he'd just received the news he had, you'd think he was just some tired soldier, resting his feet, and staring off into the east to watch the coming dawn.

She was on his right—the side that still had an eye—and he caught her in his peripheral.

He turned and looked up at her.

Her guts clenched, fearing recriminations.

But there were none.

He looked her up and down without judgment. Or any perceivable emotion, really. Then he went back to staring out at the eastern horizon.

"Kat," he said, acknowledging her.

She lowered herself to sit beside him, restraining a hiss of pain as her wounds throbbed. Moving sucked, but once she was seated, it wasn't so bad.

Marie had tried to get her into the surgery, but the doctors on base refused to treat her.

That was okay. Marie had done a good job. Maybe these wounds would've been more serious if she was a regular human. But she wasn't, so as soon as Marie had her bandaged and stitched, she'd been up and about.

At least she had that going for her.

Silence stretched. It didn't seem to bother Lee, but it made her nervous.

What should she say?

What *could* she say?

Her hands found each other in her lap, the claw-tipped fingers wrestling.

"I'm sorry," she eventually rasped.

He didn't visibly react. But after a moment, he spoke in a somewhat toneless voice: "What for?"

It all burst out of her—the long list of judgments she'd rendered upon herself. "I didn't save Sam. I should have gone to him sooner. I should have used the medical stuff. I should have run faster to get him to the helicopter. I should have killed the bad guys before they could hurt him."

Lee's chest inflated as he drew in a long breath. Then he sighed the word out: "Yeah."

Kat felt hot and prickly all over. This was it. She was done. Lee had just agreed that she'd been a failure...

But then he hung his head and kept talking. "I should have never put a gun in a twelve-year-old kid's hand. I should have never encouraged him to fight. I should have never let him be a part of this team. I should have gone with him, and not stayed to help Appomattox."

Silence.

Kat didn't know how to respond. She didn't know how to interpret what Lee had just said.

Eventually, he turned to look at her with his one eye. "Kat, you know how many people I've lost along the way?"

Kat shook her head.

Lee looked momentarily stymied, then chuffed. "Shit." He looked down. "I can't even remember them all. I mean, I could if I tried. Their faces, their memories—they're all right there. But I don't *want* to think about them. I don't want to keep a list. It's too long, and it only ever gets longer. And what happens if I let those ghosts haunt me? Will they teach me something I didn't already know? Will they show me some...mistake I could correct?"

He sighed again, and, with a breathy groan, drew his feet into a cross-legged position. Then he posted his elbows on his knees, and leaned his chin on his clasped hands. When he spoke again, his voice had just a touch of creakiness in it.

"I don't know, Kat. Mostly, I keep all those ghosts at bay by focusing on the here and now, and what I can control. But every once in a while, they'll get to me. I'll think about them. I'll think about what I could've done differently. But that is..." he made a soft, strangled noise. "A pointless endeavor. All those ghosts have ever taught me is that this life is a gamble. You take risks—you *have* to take risks. Sometimes they work out, and sometimes they don't. I mean, what're you gonna do? *Not* take risks? Well, if that's the case, just find a quiet hole to while away your life. But even that doesn't solve the problem, because if you hide from the risks, they just grow bigger, and they will eventually find you. They always do. Eventually, we all gotta roll those dice, Kat. Sometimes it works out. Sometimes we come up short. And that's all there is to it."

He turned to look at her. "Don't get me wrong—if you fucked up, you gotta face that shit. But sometimes bad shit just happens. We look for someone to blame—either someone else, or, more often, ourselves. But that's bullshit. That doesn't do you any favors. And you, Kat?" He surprised her by reaching out and placing a hand on her knee. "You didn't fuck up. You did what you could in the moment. You took risks that didn't work out. But that's better than not taking any risks at all."

Kat's shoulders drew up. "If I was smarter, I would know how to use the medical kit."

Lee shook his head. "You can't know what you haven't been trained on. Ignorance is not the same as unintelligence."

For some odd reason, Kat found her respiration increasing. Despite the cold morning, sweat was breaking out along her hairline and lower back. She fidgeted uncontrollably, but no matter how hard she fought it, she could not keep the words inside.

"I don't want to go," she blurted. "I want to stay. I want to learn. I want to know how to fight better. I want to know how to fix people. I want to know how to..." she stared out, wide-eyed at the seemingly-endless horizon, and all the land that lay in turmoil beyond it. "Fix all of this!"

Lee withdrew his hand from her knee, frowning. "Why, Kat? Why do you want...*this*? It never gets any easier, no matter how much you learn and train."

Kat had to look away. Staring into that man's eye seemed to have some strange effect on her. It muddled her thoughts and made her oddly panicky, overwhelmed with the need to prove herself and her worth.

But he wasn't asking her about her worth, or what she could bring to the table.

He was asking her why she wanted to be at the table in the first place.

Why did she? Why did she want this, instead of the "normal" life at the monastery, with Bran and Shay and the boys?

She thought long and hard about her answer.

She selected her words like one might piece a puzzle together, to see what image it contained.

"I am not normal," she finally said—equal parts statement, and dawning realization. "I can't ever be normal. I am not good at being normal. But I am good at fighting. And there are so many people that need someone to fight for them. I want to fight for them. And when I think about *not* fighting for them, when I think about just going back to the monastery and trying to be normal, I...It's like..." She bared her teeth at the glowing horizon. "It feels like I'm burning inside."

She thought about what she'd just said.

She inspected it for truth. And for a hybrid, that was not difficult.

This was truth.

When she turned to see how her words had landed, she found Lee staring at her with a small, sad smile on his lips.

"Well," he said, getting slowly to his feet with a grunt of painful effort. Then he locked eyes with her, and in him was truth as well, and there were no lies. "I guess you're one of us."

Chapter 34

Corporal Hampstead really had no idea what the hell was going on.

He stood inside the holding cell with the...prisoner?

Hostage?

VIP?

Well, he wasn't quite sure why the guy needed to be under armed guard—for his protection, or for the security of Campbell Air Force Base. Frankly, it all seemed a bit much to Hampstead. If ever there was an unassuming dude that you just *knew* was not dangerous, it was the guy sitting at the table.

Smallish. Bookish. Nervous-looking.

A nerd, basically.

A nerd with a little backpack that he kept protectively between his feet.

Yes, Hampstead had searched the pack, and no, it didn't contain anything dangerous. Just a laptop and what looked like a plug-in hard drive.

He hadn't been told what the significance of those items was, or if they even mattered at all.

He hadn't been told anything.

He'd woken up in order to be on post by 0500, only for his sergeant to tell him he'd been volunteered for a special duty—thanks, Sarge, you sonofabitch—and to report to the base commander. That was strange. The base commander was a colonel. Colonels did not speak directly to such lowly beings as corporals. That was what the chain of command was for.

Corporal Hampstead was young, but not so young that he hadn't seen some shit. He'd done a single combat tour before the world up and ended. And then his whole life had become a combat tour, for six years straight.

So, despite the fact that he was only twenty-five years old, Hampstead was jaded enough that he did not even allow himself to imagine that this super-secret assignment would be anything glamorous or action-packed. If it was, they wouldn't have given it to a dumbfuck, enlisted grunt like him.

But *something* sure as shit had happened. Perhaps not glamorous, but definitely action-packed, judging by how the Blackhawk had come in hot, and immediately disgorged two dudes that looked like they'd been shot all to hell. There'd been others on the helo, but Hampstead, being the disciplined young soldier that he was, focused on what he was there for.

In the words of the colonel: "Blackhawk's coming in from a hot-zone. There's gonna be a civilian on board, white male with glasses, wearing a backpack. I need you to secure that individual and keep him under guard until I *personally* relieve you."

"Yes, sir," Hampstead had dutifully replied.

The colonel had squinted at him for a moment.

Hampstead was still standing at attention, because this cock hadn't told him "at ease" for some reason.

"Can you keep your mouth shut, son?" the colonel asked.

"Yes, sir," Hampstead said.

Was this guy kidding? Hampstead was a corporal in the IAG. Keeping his mouth shut was a prerequisite for duty.

"Good. Do that. Dismissed."

So, Hampstead had spotted the only guy on the helo that matched that description, fetched him with a simple, "Come with me, sir," and the guy had followed without much fuss.

For the last few hours, they'd been sitting in silence. The mysterious prisoner/high-value target/VIP had tried to start conversations a few times, but Hampstead assumed that keeping his mouth shut included small talk, so he'd shut the nerd down with stony silence.

Didn't make hours of staring at each other any less awkward, though.

So when there was a knock at the holding cell's door, Corporal Hampstead immediately felt relief. Fucking *finally* the colonel had shown up to take possession of this guy, or send him to some black site, or whatever the hell they were going to do with him.

Didn't matter to Hampstead—that was above his pay grade.

But when Hampstead opened the door, it was not the colonel.

Actually, it wasn't anyone that he recognized.

As previously stated, Hampstead had seen some shit in his day. He knew the difference between harmless sheeple, wolves in sheep's clothing, sheep trying to act like wolves, and everything in between.

One look at the motherfucker standing in the doorway, and Corporal Hampstead knew the type of person he was looking at.

Back on his single combat deployment, Hampstead had heard a different terminology, apparently coined by some dinosaur enthusiasts: They referred to non-combat units as "plant eaters," as opposed to the mean sons of bitches whose main job was the execution of violence. Those, they called "meat eaters."

Hampstead had always thought that was a bit much for his tastes—just a tad too overblown, and really trying to lean into the cool-factor, like all the idiots who idolized Roman legionnaires, Spartans, or Vikings.

'Til Valhalla? God, that had always made Hampstead roll his eyes.

However, standing there and looking at the man that had just knocked on his door, Hampstead's brain only knew one way to categorize this guy.

This was a meat eater.

Tall and rangy, the guy bore no obvious military attire, unless you counted the holstered pistol on his hip. Aside from that, he wore civilian clothes, which had clearly just been through some things—was that blood on his pant legs?—and his shirt had an obvious sweat-stain in the shape of an armored vest.

But the eye. That told Hampstead what uniforms and insignia and gear could not. And it wasn't just because there was only one, but because that eye…

Jesus, how to describe it?

It wasn't like the guy was putting on a mean face, or that his single eye was glaring, or even trying for the thousand-yard stare. It wasn't anything about the eye's shape or color or the emotions of the face around it.

You ever yelled into a cave or cavern with no clear concept of how big it was until your voice echoed back to you?

Kind of like that.

"Can I help you, sir?" Hampstead asked, evenly.

The guy tilted his head a bit, looking past Hampstead, to the squirrelly dude sitting hunched at the table. "Jeremy. You still got the devices with you?"

Hampstead didn't look—he had no intention of turning his back on this guy—but he heard the squirrelly guy fidget in his seat and say, "Yeah."

The stranger's eye slid back to Hampstead. Glanced down at the rank insignia on his chest. "Corporal. I need to take possession of that backpack."

There was the sound of a skidding chair.

Now concerned that his prisoner/hostage/VIP might be making a run for it, Hampstead backed up a pace, so he could see his ward, and also keep the stranger in his peripheral.

The nerd—apparently his name was Jeremy—was out of his seat, clutching the backpack.

"No," Jeremy gasped, looking and sounding like a kid that doesn't want to share his favorite toy. "I can't just give you this shit!"

Hampstead raised a hand to Jeremy, giving him a stern look. "Sir, I need you to sit down."

"But—" Jeremy protested.

"Sir." Hampstead used his command voice. "Sit. Down."

Jeremy balked. Then dropped into his chair again, still hugging his backpack.

Hampstead turned to eye the stranger. "Now, sir, I have no idea who you are. I can't release that backpack to you without proper authorization from Colonel Wright."

"Colonel Wright, huh?" the stranger mumbled. "Never heard of him. Look, corporal, I think we both know that Colonel Wright has no fucking clue what's going on right now. You were probably just told to nab this guy and hold onto him until you got further orders, right?"

Hampstead swallowed, not wanting to confirm that the stranger was right.

The stranger nodded anyway. "Yeah, that's because this shit's way over his head. Now, I have orders to retrieve the items in that backpack for *immediate* investigation, as they pose a security risk to the IAG."

Hampstead shifted his weight, now put in a tough spot. His orders from the colonel didn't say shit about the items inside the backpack. He'd just been told to secure Jeremy and wait for further orders from the colonel.

There was the specific wording of an order, and then there was the *spirit* of that order.

But was it really a lowly, shit-eating corporal's job to go about interpreting his orders?

The stranger perceived his reticence and sighed. "How about this, then?" The stranger stepped into the room. "I'm gonna go get that backpack. You don't have to do a thing."

Hampstead's grip tightened on his rifle. "Hang on a minute, sir. I'm gonna need to see your identification."

The stranger hesitated. Then smiled. But it wasn't very warm. "Yeah, that's not gonna happen, corporal. But if you get in any hot water over this, just tell them Jax took the backpack."

Then the stranger started forward again.

With a sudden burst of testicular fortitude, Hampstead shot forward and seized the man's arm. "Sir! I need you to…"

The stranger froze, head swiveling to stare at the hand gripping his arm. Hampstead trailed off, feeling somehow like he'd just put his head in the tiger's mouth.

The stranger was like stone. The only thing that moved was his one eye, which lifted to meet Hampstead's.

He spoke softly. "You really wanna go down this road, corporal?"

Corporal Hampstead rapidly came to the conclusion that he did not.

Interpreting orders was above his pay grade.

Opening his goddamn mouth was above his pay grade.

You know what else was above his pay grade?

Dying over a fucking backpack.

If the stranger tried to take Jeremy with him, Corporal Hampstead would do his duty, because his orders were to secure the *person*. But the backpack? That was beyond his purview. And if that cocksucker, Colonel Wright, wanted the backpack, then he should've issued clearer orders.

Hampstead withdrew his hand. "Whatever, man. Take it and get the fuck out of here."

Private Calloway was pretty sure he was gonna get cancer from this shit.

He stood, a few paces back from the burn barrel as the flames leapt higher, consuming the armload of flattened, cardboard boxes he'd just shoved in. MRE boxes. Boxes that had contained frozen meats of highly dubious quality—probably another thing that was gonna give him cancer—and various bits of plastic and Styrofoam trash—which most *definitely* was gonna give him cancer.

This was the third time in as many weeks that Private Calloway had been assigned trash-burning duty. Hand to God, he had a tickle in his throat that wouldn't go away, and he was developing a cough that sounded like he was a life-long smoker.

He stood there, leaning against a shovel with a fire-blackened head, squinting distastefully against the acrid smoke pouring out of the burn barrel.

The real bitch of it was that his sergeant had it out for him. He'd be out here burning goddamn boxes all day, and the next time his sergeant saw him, he'd wrinkle his nose, tell Calloway his uniform stank like smoke and that this was unacceptable—despite the fact that Calloway only had one fucking uniform and laundry day was once a week. At which point his sergeant would punish Calloway by assigning him more trash-burning duty.

That was fucked up.

His sergeant was literally trying to give him cancer.

The IAG military had recruited young Calloway out of Milwaukee the year prior. They'd given him all sorts of promises about how he was going to help rebuild America. Calloway had thought that meant he'd be out in the hot zones, either on the east or west coast, or maybe down by the southern border, saving lives and doing hero shit.

So far, Private Calloway had done janitorial work, cleared brush along Fort Campbell's perimeter, sprayed weed killer in every goddamn crack on the tarmac, dug latrine ditches, and burned trash. The last time he'd touched a loaded weapon of any sort was when he'd fired a grand total of a hundred rounds through an M4 during basic training.

So far, Private Calloway was pretty disillusioned with the IAG military, and had long ago run out of fucks to give.

Being in that headspace, Calloway had zero reaction to the four figures that approached his burn barrel.

Two dudes, and two chicks. All of them in civilian clothes.

One of the chicks had a bandanna over her face, which was odd, but then Calloway figured, hell, *he* wanted a bandanna to cover *his* face. Maybe she just didn't want to breathe all this goddamn cancer.

One of the guys—a tall, mean-looking motherfucker with one eye—was carrying a backpack in one hand.

Very dimly, Calloway wondered if he should challenge them for base identification. But shit—that wasn't his job. If they wanted him to worry about base security, they should give him a fucking rifle, instead of a shovel.

Besides, security around here was pretty tight. Calloway was certain that, if they were here, then they were allowed to be here.

So, Calloway just leaned on his shovel and nodded to the newcomers as they approached the fire. "Mornin'," he offered up, boredly.

The woman that didn't have a bandanna covering her face—she looked a bit older—gave him a careworn smile and returned his nod. "Morning. How are you today, private?"

Calloway coughed, perhaps a bit dramatically. "Just burnin' fuckin' trash."

The woman stopped, about the same distance from the fire as Calloway—any closer and the heat would singe your eyebrows. Not to mention the smoke would singe your lungs.

She gave him a desultory thumbs up and said, "Good deal."

The tall man with the one eye stepped forward and gave the backpack an underhanded toss, landing it neatly in the burn barrel to a plume of sparks, smoke, and feathery, cardboard ash.

Calloway considered whether he even wanted to say anything at all, then sighed and raised an eyebrow at the tall man. "What's in the backpack?"

The tall man looked at him. "Why?"

Calloway hadn't been expecting a return question. It kind of stumped him for a moment. Why was he asking again? "Uh…just gotta make sure it's trash. This is a trash-burning barrel. So, like, you can't dispose of…uh…ordnance or whatnot."

The tall man nodded. "Huh. Okay."

Momentarily smothered by the new addition, the flames began to lick up again as they consumed the backpack and whatever it contained. Calloway hoped these idiots hadn't just tossed live rounds or some shit in there. He couldn't really imagine why they would do something like that, but people were dumb.

He huffed and shifted his weight. "So?"

The tall man looked at him blankly. "So, what?"

Calloway nodded at the burn barrel. "Is it trash?"

"Oh," the tall man said. Then he nodded, returning his gaze to the toxic flames. "Yeah, it's trash."

Satisfied that he'd done his duty, Calloway shrugged. "Okay. Cool."

Then he bent, took up another armload of flattened cardboard, and shoved it into the flames. Took up his shovel and jabbed at the boxes until they were all stuffed down into the barrel. He did this with his eyes squinted nearly shut, and his breath held.

Then he hurried back to his original position, blinking tears out of his eyes and heaving for slightly-fresher air.

The four strangers were already walking away.

CHAPTER 35

They waited for the C-130 to finish taxiing.

Lee, Abe, Marie, and Kat stood just inside a hangar, a few hundred yards down the airfield. There were two guards watching them, but they kept their distance and didn't give them any grief. Everyone had been very hands-off with them. Lee assumed that the soldiers and airmen stationed at the base had very correctly surmised that this group of strangers was clearly the nexus of a whole lot of shit they didn't want to step in.

"How pissed do you think he's going to be?" Marie asked in a low voice.

Leaning against the rolling hangar door, Abe shrugged. "Somewhere between enraged and having a full-on stroke."

Marie turned and regarded Lee. "You could always just lie."

Lee raised an eyebrow. "Yeah? Like what? I already told him we'd secured the laptop and hard drive."

"Tell him we lost them in the woods while the Russians were chasing us."

Lee wrinkled his nose. "Nah. I want them to know I fucked them over."

That caused Abe to turn around and look at him. Then Abe and Marie exchanged a loaded glance.

"Lee," Marie said in a careful sort of way. "Are you picking a fight with the government again?"

Defensively, Lee pulled his head back. "I'm not picking a fight. I just want whoever's idea this whole bumblefuck was to know that I disagree with them in the strongest possible terms."

Marie winced, as though deeply pained by something. "You're picking a fight with the government again," she sighed.

Lee glowered. "I'm not."

"Okay," Marie said, turning away from him.

"Whatever you say, Chief," Abe grunted.

Standing at Lee's side, Kat gave him a curious look. Then nodded, resolutely. "I'm with you," she said. "Fuck 'em."

Well, that tracked. The research *was* focused on exterminating her kind.

"Thanks," he acknowledged her, glad that at least one person saw it his way.

Abe and Marie would come around. Jones too, whenever he woke up.

Lee held no illusions that he'd successfully put a stop to the eradication of hybrids. The primals? He could give a fuck about those animals. But the hybrids? No, they didn't deserve the same fate. If he'd learned one thing in Appomattox, it was that hybrids were humanity's only chance to adapt to this world.

But clearly powerful people that controlled the world's resurrected governments and their militaries did not see it the same way. In Lee's experience, people in power were incredibly short-sighted. Their entire lives revolved around whatever they had to do to maintain their positions of power, no matter how much it might hamstring the world at large.

They would continue their efforts. Lee knew that. All he had done was buy some time. And what he would do with that time remained to be seen.

It kind of depended on what Major Ronald Paige had to say to them.

One thing Lee *was* sure about?

The Deal was done. He and his team would be blacklisted.

It was all so bitterly ironic to him. The only reason he'd taken this mission to begin with was because they'd threatened to blacklist him and his team if he didn't. So he'd agreed, fought the good fight as best he could, lost a very dear friend and teammate, and put another one in a coma, only to get blacklisted anyway.

He should've just told them to fuck off.

What did being blacklisted mean to him? He'd spent years as a "nonviable asset," which basically meant the same thing. He was accustomed to being a *persona non grata*.

He'd gone along with this mission because having the tacit support of the IAG in the form of supply drops had allowed him to help people in ways he never could have otherwise. He hated to lose it. He hated to think of how many settlements were still out there, barely surviving on the fringes, that would not get the help they needed because some asshat in the IAG couldn't see the forest through the trees.

But that didn't mean Lee had to stop helping people.

Hell, he'd built the United Eastern States without the help of the government. He and his team were capable and resourceful. They wouldn't stop doing what they were meant to do—what Lee firmly believed he'd been placed on this earth to accomplish: Helping people survive.

Out on the tarmac, the C-130 had stopped. An old Humvee rolled up to the side of the plane, and as soon as the ramp lowered, a figure hopped out and immediately went to the Humvee. Even at a distance, Lee recognized Ron. He was alone, and moving with urgency.

Lee girded himself up for the coming tirade, and simply hoped that it wouldn't go so far south that the remnants of his team had to fight their way out of Fort Campbell in order to avoid getting arrested for treason.

The Humvee spun around and raced across the tarmac towards the hangar.

Lee and his team retreated from the open door, moving into the shadows within.

A minute later, the Humvee roared through the opening and braked rather dramatically in the middle of the empty hangar.

It'd barely rocked back before Ron opened his door and scrambled out, looking all kinds of tweaked up. The guy had bags under his eyes and a wild, desperate look about him, like he hadn't slept in days.

He might not have. For all Ron's bluster and combative words, Lee knew the truth.

The guy was a good officer, and he legitimately cared about the people under him, which extended to Lee and his crew.

He marched right up to Lee, giving Marie and Abe a quick nod of acknowledgement. To Kat, who had removed her bandanna now that they were in private, he gave a hooded look.

"How's Jones?" were the first words Ron said.

"His surgery was successful," Lee replied, evenly. "He's still out, but they're confident he'll recover."

Ron seemed relieved by that, and nodded slowly. Then his eyes glanced around, and Lee knew he was realizing that they were one teammate short.

Lee's heart clenched, and his throat thickened, knowing what was coming.

"Where's Sam?" Ron asked. But he said it in a dread-filled way, as though he already suspected the answer.

The grief swelled up in Lee, and threatened to bury him like an unstoppable wave.

But then Lee pushed it down, and floated atop that cresting wave, and came out the other side with a mind as blank and smooth as a frozen lake. "He was killed, attempting to slow down the Russians so we could get Jones and Jeremy Tuttle evacuated."

Ron's expression registered no shock. No horror. His gaze simply fixed on Lee, as though bracing himself and wondering if Lee was going to turn violent.

Lee just stared back.

Ron's shoulders slumped, and his head bowed. "Christ. Lee. Guys. I'm…"

Lee held up a hand. "It's not on you, Ron. You didn't come up with this shitshow. You didn't allow Russians to do some shady fucking op on American soil. You just did what Griffin told you to do."

Ron swallowed. "Griffin didn't know the full extent of it either. Not until shit went bad and he got the full story from the…" Ron cut himself off, snapping his mouth shut.

Lee's eye narrowed.

The…what?

How many different titles in the IAG would start with the article "the"?

Perhaps *the president*?

Lee filed that one away, but didn't push the issue. Instead, he made a general, *over there* gesture and said, "Jeremy Tuttle's being held under guard. He's alive and unharmed."

Ron drew himself up again. Took a breath. "And the research?"

Lee felt Abe and Marie's eyes on him.

Was he really going to do this?

Yeah. Fuck it. He was.

"I burned it," Lee stated.

For a moment, Ron just stared at him, wide-eyed. Then he glanced at Abe and Marie, as though to see if this was some sick joke. They gave him no reaction. He returned his eyes to Lee, now blinking rapidly.

"I'm sorry," Ron's voice almost hitched. "You said—"

"I burned it. Yeah. That's what I said."

Both of Ron's hands went to his mouth.

"Took the laptop and the hard drive and put 'em in a burn barrel," Lee said, casually. "They're toast."

Ron's hands clawed their way across his scalp, disheveling his hair. "What the fuck'd you do that for?"

Lee let just a tiny bit of his own rage show in his face. "Why the fuck didn't we get a full briefing on this mission? Information was withheld, Ron. Information that would have *really* been useful in keeping my team alive and uninjured. But the fucktards you work for didn't think it was *important* that we know those details, and so I decided it wasn't *important* for them to have the goddamn research. And if whoever's pulling the strings on this shit—were you about to say 'the president'? Because I'm pretty sure you were about to say 'the president'—has a fucking problem with that, then you can have that moron come talk to me face-to-face, at which point I will Lee Harvey Oswald his ass into the next dimension."

Ron looked about to tear his hair out. "Did you just threaten to assassinate the President of the United States?"

"I dunno. Was he the one that set this shit up?"

Ron's face turned into a snarl and he spun to face the Humvee. "Get the fuck outta here!" he yelled at the driver.

The driver looked all too happy to get gone. He spun a U-turn, which the size of the hangar accommodated, and sped out.

Ron wasn't done. He pointed to the guards. "You two! Get lost!"

One of them stepped forward. "Sir, we were given orders by the colonel to—"

"I'll fuck your colonel in the ass!" Ron bellowed. "Out! Now! You say another goddamn word and I'll..." Ron trailed off, because the two guards were already moving out of the hangar.

Discipline and chain of command were still a bit wonky in the IAG, Lee noted.

Ron turned back to Lee, one hand on his hip, the other with the thumb and forefinger slowly sliding down either side of his mouth. "You tryna start another war?" he demanded. "Huh? Is that what this is, Lee? You just can't abide anyone being in charge but you, so you're just gonna fight them all until...what? You become Julius Fucking Caesar and run the show as god-emperor-general? What's your end goal here? Or have you thought that far ahead?"

"Yeah, I've thought about it," Lee said. "And no, Ron, I'm not trying to start another fucking war, so calm your tits. You wanna know where my head's at on this shit? Fine. If you'll listen, I'll tell you."

Ron huffed and shuffled. Then made a *get on with it* motion. "I'm listening."

"First off, I didn't threaten to assassinate anyone. If you'll recall my specific choice of words, I said 'if they have a problem with it,' meaning that if they're so assed up by what I've done to their precious Russian research that they decide to come after me about it, then, yeah, I'll lay 'em out. But I'm not lookin' for a fight."

Ron scoffed and rolled his eyes, but didn't say anything.

Lee continued. "And as far as the research goes, let's take a minute and unpack this. First off, fucking Russians. That's a big nope right out the gate. Second, their grand plan for getting rid of the primals is to release a genetically-engineered virus? Really? Come on, Ron. I cannot be the only one that sees how epically fucked that idea is. Even if we hadn't just got through six years of absolute societal devastation due to a pandemic, it'd *still* be a stupid idea. Now? After all the shit we been through? It is beyond the pale, brother, and I can't believe for one goddamn second that you're not smart enough to see that."

Lee took a breath.

Ron arched his brows. "You done?"

"No, I'm not," Lee snapped back. "That's just point one and two. Here's point three: The hybrids? We're gonna exterminate the hybrids right along with the primals? Hey man, fuck the primals. Let's get rid of them. But this girl?" He pointed to Kat. "She saved my team multiple times out there. Also, the only reason me and Abe are standing here, and all the foreign soldiers—who shouldn't have been here in the first place—are dead, is because all the hybrids in Appomattox worked together to help. Because they're not fucking animals, Ron."

Ron managed to look a tad sheepish as he glanced between Kat and Lee. "I didn't know they were tryna wipe out the hybrids, alright?"

"It doesn't matter what you did or didn't know, Ron. You wanted to know why I made the decision that I made. Now you've been educated. Now you can see I'm not just some wingnut that's determined to buck whoever's in power. But if the people in power keep turning out to be idiots and madmen, then, well…fuck, man. Whaddaya want me to do?"

Ron crossed his arms over his chest. Stared balefully at Lee for a long stretch of silence. "So are you done *now*?"

Lee waved him off. "Yeah, I'm fuckin' done."

"Alright." Ron breathed in deep through his nose. "Give me a goddamn second to think."

Then he turned and paced away.

Abe let out a long, sad sigh, once Ron was about twenty yards away. "Well," he said in a low tone. "Guess that means The Deal's over."

"Yeah, I'd say that's a safe bet," Marie said.

"What's that mean?" Kat asked.

Lee gave her a minimal shrug. "It means we've been naughty and the government doesn't want to play with us anymore."

Ron stood with his back to them, head inclined towards the hangar's ceiling. He remained in that pose for nearly a full minute. Then he must have come to some conclusion, because he righted himself, spun, and stalked back.

He parked himself front and center to them. Instead of just talking to Lee, this time he spoke to all of them, making eye contact with each—even Kat. "You said your piece, now let me say mine. You gotta realize at this point that you're all fucked. Which is to say, there's no way in hell I can cover for you, and when the truth comes out—and I will be compelled to tell them the truth—heads are going to roll."

He paused for a long moment, and the ire seemed to bleed out of him. It was replaced with genuine concern. "Lee, I know we've had a bit of a rocky relationship in the past. And maybe I'm just getting soft, or maybe I just feel bad about Sam. But for whatever reason, I don't want your heads to roll. Isn't that fucking weird?" He let out a strange titter. "I know. I've been up for forty hours straight. Shit's a bit tangled upstairs. But here's what I'm going to do."

He pivoted and pointed to the C-130. "That bird's got cargo bound for Florida. We have a base down in the Tampa area—actually, more like an embassy. And when I say embassy, think the old US embassy in Lebanon—the locals have their own thing going, and they don't particularly want to get into bed with the IAG, but we're there, pushing our agenda anyway. The base opened up a public hospital—goodwill, hearts and minds sort of shit, you know? The loadmaster on that C-130 owes me a no-questions-asked favor. I can get you guys on it. Jones too. He'll need that hospital if he's gonna fully recover. But you gotta go, and you gotta go now, because it's wheels-up in fifteen. After that, you're on your own. It's the best I can do for you."

Lee blinked, taken aback by the offer. He had not expected this. And, oddly enough, he felt a sudden welling of affection for the guy, despite the fact that they'd been at each other's throats almost constantly for years.

He was putting his neck on the line for them. He didn't have to do it. He was just doing it because he knew it was the right thing.

There was just one small problem.

"Thank you for that," Lee said, earnestly. "But how are we going to get on base down there? We come walking off a C-130 with no identification or credentials or official orders, we're just gonna get arrested."

Ron shook his head. "Coty Brennen."

Lee's eye widened with surprise. "Like, *Captain* Coty Brennen, the Coordinator?"

Again, Ron shook his head. "He's not a captain or a Coordinator anymore. He got out last year. Now he's a civilian—basically our ambassador to Florida. And as ambassador, he's got broad powers over what happens on that base. I can get word to him that you're coming. He'll cover for you. Find a place for you to lay low while this shit blows over." Ron stepped into Lee and put a hand on his shoulder. "But, seriously, Lee. You need to go *now*. Go get Jones, and get him on that plane."

Lee blinked a few times, then nodded. Because what else was he going to do? This was the only way out for them.

Ron released him and started backpedaling, angling for the C-130—presumably to pull that favor with the loadmaster.

"Ron," Lee called.

The man stopped, clearly impatient.

Lee hustled after him. "I know you're already going out on a limb for me, and, truly, I appreciate it. We all do. But I need a favor."

Predictably, Ron balked. He made a few choked noises. Then he wilted. "Fuck. Goddammit. What is it?"

Lee cringed. "Actually, it's two things."

"Oh, boy, you're tryna give me an aneurism, aren't you?"

Lee waited.

Ron pedaled a hand rapidly in the air. "Well?"

"First thing: Please—take care of Angela and Abby for me, okay? They weren't a part of my shit. They've done their job. Don't take it out on them."

Ron's face became solemn. "I'll do everything I can for them. What's the second thing?"

"You remember where you found me in Oregon?"

"Yeah."

"I need you to drop a package there."

Epilogue 1

Jones had a strange life for a while. But then, he guessed his whole life had been strange.

All he really knew was that he wanted a fucking cold beer, really bad.

His mind took him to all kinds of places—mountaintops, cityscapes, plains. But everywhere he went, he was parched, his mouth aching for cool liquid, but more specifically, a frosty, pulled-straight-out-of-the-ice, Miller High Life. He preferred bottles over cans, but he'd take either.

Also, wherever he went, Sam was there. And that was odd.

He wasn't supposed to be there. Jones wasn't sure why, he just knew it, and seeing Sam follow him around to all those places he went, filled him with a deep unease. A sense of foreboding.

But he was also happy that Sam was there, because it'd be great to drink a beer with him.

His dreams in all those places were centered around him and Sam trying to find this beer. They looked everywhere, but there was none to be found, and Jones was only growing thirstier and thirstier.

At one point, he realized something: "Holy shit, dude! Have you ever even *had* a beer before?"

Sam said that he hadn't. He'd only been twelve years old when the world died. Was only eighteen now—not that anyone would give a fuck about legal drinking ages at this point.

"Oh, man, you're gonna love it. It's cold, and delicious, and it makes you feel better about life."

They were in a city. But no one had any beer—Miller High Life or otherwise. Everywhere he went, it seemed they were fresh out, or didn't sell alcohol, or something along those lines. Always an excuse. Jones was getting frustrated.

Then he was on some cold, snow-capped peak, and he was scrabbling through the ice, and he came up with a bottle of Coors Light, and the mountains were oh-so-blue. It wasn't Miller High Life, but it would do, and he was so, so thirsty.

In triumph, he held it up and turned around. "Sam! Look! When the mountains are blue, it's as cold as…the…"

All around him was just wilderness.

Sam was nowhere to be found.

"Sam?" Jones called into the vast, empty space surrounding him. "Sam? You wanna get in on this beer? We can go halvesies! It'll change your life!"

But Sam was gone.

Wary and perplexed, Jones was nonetheless still parched to the point of desperation, so he twisted off the bottle cap and immediately guzzled the longneck.

Except it wasn't cold, and it wasn't refreshing, and Jones wasn't even sure it was beer.

It was hot, and dry, and it tasted like gunsmoke.

Jones was not at all cogent when he woke up, but he knew he was afraid, and he knew he was thirsty.

He didn't know where he was, or how he'd got there.

He was in a big tube. That's what it looked like. And it was loud as fuck. Buzzing and humming. Like a…a…

Ah, fuck it, he didn't know, and didn't really care. He needed beer. No, water.

There were people. It took a moment for him to recognize them. It was Marie, and Abe, and Lee, and…who was she again? And shit, what was wrong with her face? Damn. She looked scary as hell.

They were all sitting in a row, shoulder to shoulder on little seats. The monster-looking girl was closest to him.

Jones tried to crane his neck to see around the others, because surely Sam was on the other side, but he just didn't have the strength to lift his head.

"Sam?" he called out, but no one could hear him. He couldn't even hear himself. This place was way too loud.

He found himself terrified for Sam. Or about him. He wasn't sure. All he knew was that the fear he'd felt in the dream—that terrible sense of foreboding when he'd turned and Sam wasn't there with him—it had carried through into the real world.

Marie, Abe, and Lee were all out cold. Marie's chin was on her chest. Abe was slumped forward, hands interlaced over his chest, looking oddly peaceful. And then there was Lee, whose head was tilted back, mouth hanging open, and Jones knew that if it wasn't so damn loud in this place, he'd hear Lee's wall-vibrating snores.

But the monster-girl was awake.

Just sitting there, staring straight ahead, as though in deep contemplation.

Jones followed her gaze, but all that was across from her were giant cubes of plastic-wrapped...whatevers. Supplies, he guessed. Cargo netting covered everything. Because this was a cargo hold. And the noise was propellers, and the tube was the round fuselage of a plane.

A C-130, then? They were in a C-130, or some similar prop-plane?

But why? And where were they going?

And where was Sam?

God, I'm so fucking thirsty.

Jones raised a weak hand, and realized he was not in a seat like the others. He was in a bed. A hospital bed.

Monster-girl must've seen the movement out of her peripheral, and snapped her attention to him. She was fast and intense. Like a cat.

Cat.

Kat, with a K.

That was her name. He remembered now.

"Kat!" he tried to call to her, but couldn't even hear himself. So he kind of jiggled his hand in the air, half a beckoning gesture and half a drinking motion.

Here was something interesting: Kat's eyes grew wide when they hit his, and they...sparkled? Or something? Like she was excited to see him. She was, in fact, almost smiling as she hurriedly tore out of her jump seat.

Kat. The quarter-primal, three-quarters-human hybrid girl.

Pretty eyes. Terrifying mouth. Way stronger than she looked.

She hustled over to his bedside, swaying a bit to the rocking motion of the plane as it rumbled through turbulence.

Then she really did smile, and her teeth were too long, particularly her canines, and that was frightening…or at least, it should've been. But the relief and happiness in her eyes was genuine, and that made the smile beautiful, and not scary at all for Jones.

"Jonesy!" she yelled, and he just barely heard it.

He smiled weakly back at her and managed a nod. He realized he wouldn't be able to yell loud enough to be heard. So he raised his unsteady hand a little more and beckoned her closer. His motions lacked the nuance of fine motor skills—his arm just looked like it was spasming, rather than gesticulating.

A frown of confusion crossed Kat's brow, but then she must've realized what he wanted and leaned forward, putting her ear close to his mouth.

"Water," he said, as loud as he was able.

Kat immediately understood, and dipped out of sight, fetching something that must've been stored under or near his bedside. She came up with a silvery packet with a straw stuck in it that reminded Jones of those Capri Sun pouches he'd loved as a kid, except they never did turn him into a molten-metal sky-surfer guy, and this pouch just said WATER in big blocky letters.

He was desperate for it.

She put the straw in his mouth for him and he sucked greedily.

It relieved his ravenous thirst. But that was only half of what ailed him.

After he'd taken as much water as he could, he motioned for her to lean in again, and she did.

"Where's Sam?" he yelled to the best of his ability.

There was a time, a short, maybe two-second period, where all Jones could see was Kat's hair, and the top of her head, and in that moment, he lived in a wonderful world of ignorance. A place where he could believe that everything would be okay, and that Sam was just somewhere else, and that he would see his friend again soon.

That was a nice place to live, those two seconds.

He wished he could've stayed there forever.

But then Kat straightened, and he saw her face, and the expression on it.

And he knew.

She didn't even have to tell him.

Maybe he'd known it in his dream. Maybe that's why Sam had disappeared from his mind. Maybe that's why he'd woken up with the dead-sick certainty that bad news was just around the corner, on an intercept course with poor, frail, Jones. Like a Mazda Miata in the path of a freight train, it shattered him to bits, and just kept on going.

Kat grabbed Jones's hand in both of hers, and squeezed. It was almost painful, but Jones knew it was meant to comfort him, and in a way it did. At least it distracted him. Made him feel pity for the girl who just wanted to connect with others, but didn't quite know how. She was doing her best. And Jones appreciated the effort. Would've wrapped her in a hug if he could've moved his arms a bit more.

He squeezed her hands back, as he found his vision blurring. Felt the drops trickle down his temples.

Kat did not cry. But she looked torn up.

"I'm sorry," she said. Jones didn't actually hear her, because she'd said it too low, but he read her lips easy enough.

Jones just shook his head and managed a careworn smile, and hoped that was enough for her to know that he didn't blame her. He didn't know the circumstances of Sam's death, and right at that particular moment, he didn't *want* to know. Just the fact that Sam was truly gone was heavy enough.

But he knew one thing: He trusted Kat, and didn't think for one moment that she'd been responsible for Sam's death. In fact, he suspected that, when he had the stomach for the full story, he'd learn that Sam died in spite of Kat's best efforts.

In spite of all their best efforts, sometimes death came.

In the insane game called life, you never knew what the Dungeon Master was going to throw at you next. You did your best to use what skills and strategy you had, but in the end, it all came down to a dice roll.

Death came for everyone eventually.

It just seemed to come for people like them a little more often. Tempting to call it unfair. A child loses and says the game is unfair, because they don't understand the rules. But a wise man accepts what fate and chaos doles out because they know the rules are fair, whether they understand them or not.

That didn't make it hurt any less, though.

Jones closed his eyes, then grabbed the hem of the sheet that lay over his body, and pulled it up over his head. There was plenty more cold, harsh reality in store for him. But he would face that later. Right now, he needed to deal with this blow.

But as he lay under that sheet with his eyes clenched against the world, he found that his tears were no longer coming, and the grief was souring into something else. Something he'd never really felt before.

He'd always been able to shrug off tragedy and keep on trucking.

But not this time.

This time, one thought began to dominate his mind.

They're going to pay for this.

Epilogue 2

General Griffin sat, staring at President Morton.

President Morton sat, staring back, as though waiting for more, though Griffin had nothing else to tell him.

They were in the president's suite, in that Chicago hotel, on the final day of the MCR summit. Not the presidential suite, mind you—that honor had been given to the representative of the Russian Federation, though Griffin wasn't sure if Morton had done that to ingratiate himself with the Russians, or to give them the impression that the IAG was doing better than it was.

It was a quiet morning. No active operations happening in the war-torn city of Chicago. An occasional helicopter rumbled by on patrol, but there was no distant gunfire, nor the thunder of artillery strikes or airstrikes.

"So, let me get this straight," Morton said, leaning forward to steeple his fingers in front of his face, his eyes tilting upward, as though reviewing the facts from an invisible projection. "You've had Lee Harden and a team of fellow outlaws and terrorists and war criminals in your back pocket ever since the battle for Greeley. Then you send them on a mission to retrieve the scientists and the Russian research on how to infect both primals and hybrids with a designer virus, except, both the Russian scientists were murdered, and the only survivor was the American scientist, and they rescue him, and he has the research, but then Lee

Harden up and decides to burn it in a trash barrel, rather than turn it over to us."

Morton's gaze came back down to Griffin. "Would you say that's an accurate summary of this past week's events?"

Griffin simply nodded. "Yeah. That's pretty much it."

"Interesting," Morton said. "And how do you think I should handle a rogue operative?"

Griffin opened his mouth, then hesitated. Gave the president an earnest look. "Are you asking Perry Griffin, or the Interim Commander of American Operations?"

Morton smiled. "Is there a difference?"

Griffin nodded. "Yeah. As ICAO, I would tell you to eliminate people that refuse to fall in line, because leaving them to run amok sets a bad precedent."

"Hm." Morton tapped his lower lip with a finger. "And what would Perry Griffin say?"

"He'd tell you to leave Lee Harden alone," Griffin stated flatly.

"Really?" Morton seemed more curious than disbelieving.

"Lee is a special case. I don't like picking and choosing who I apply the rules to, but in this specific instance, I think you're better off leaving him be. He claims he's not going to start another civil war, but let's be honest with ourselves, Mr. President—the name 'Lee Harden' still carries weight with the people. If anything, the mythology around him has only grown, and continues to grow. He's become a folk hero. And my concern is that, if we piss him off enough, he's going to do to you what he did to Erwin Briggs, except this time he'll be coming back from the dead. Do I really need to spell it out for you what happens when folk heroes come back from the dead? You won't be able to stop the groundswell that will move against you."

Morton frowned. "You saying a black-ops team can't just put him toes-up?"

Griffin sighed and shrugged. "You'da asked me that question three years ago, I'd've told you to take him out because he's just a man. Now? Now I worry. He has a knack for surviving things. And if you don't take him out with your first shot, you better be ready for a fucking brawl."

Morton looked pained and scoffed. "I think you're buying into his mythology a bit much there, Perry."

"Well, you've never met the man. I have. You're smart, Jim. You know it's wise to lean on the opinions of those who know more than you. In this specific instance? I know more than you."

Morton grumbled, looking sullen for a moment as he heaved himself out of his chair and turned to look out the window at the Chicago skyline. "I think you're not reading me right. I don't want to kill Lee Harden. But I also don't want him fucking my shit up." He turned and held up fingers, a hair's breadth apart. "We're *this fucking close* to having an actual, viable country again. We're spreading the good news through the papers I'm having distributed, and people are starting to believe that we can come back from this, that we can be the United States of America again. We cannot—*cannot*—let the country become divided again."

Griffin nodded. "I agree. And that's why I think you should leave him alone."

"You think he'll keep his word, then?" Morton asked. "You think he'll actually let this shit go, and not decide he wants revenge?"

Griffin shrugged. "I think that it's very hard to know the mind of another man, but the chances of Lee pulling some shit you really don't want to deal with is a lot higher if you try to go after him."

"So you're sticking with your recommendation to leave him alone?"

"I am."

Morton let out a theatrical sigh, and slumped, hands posted on the table. He stayed there, head hanging, for a long moment. Then he righted himself. "Like I told you before, Perry—I have great respect for Lee Harden. I hate that his team got tooled up. I wish this op had gone off without a hitch, and, to be honest, it *would* have, if he'd just done what you asked him to do, and didn't run off and try to save the poor fucks from Appomattox from the big, bad Russians." Morton was quiet and thoughtful for a moment. "I won't lie, that actually makes me like him more. He's clearly a good man, with a conscience, who just wants to help people. That's all well and good. Possibly a bit short sighted, but I can see he just wants to do the right thing...*BUT*..."

Morton tapped the table, which turned into a slap, which turned into a pounding rhythm. "But-but-*BUT*...he is a fucking maniac and a liability to the stabilization of this nation. So I see the conundrum you're in, Perry. I feel like I'm in the same boat myself. You like the guy, and you respect him, but pragmatically speaking, he is an unknown quantity out there—" he flittered his fingers through the air "—floating around, doing his own goddamn thing, when all we really need is for everyone to stop being think-for-yourselfers and fall the fuck in line so we can put this country back together."

Griffin took a bracing inhale. "It is quite the dilemma."

"I don't like dilemmas."

"Well, you're the president now, so get used to it."

"No." Morton wagged a finger at him. "As president, I don't need to *get used to dilemmas*. I need to solve them. I need to make wise decisions that are best for this country."

Griffin found himself holding his breath.

"So," Morton said, straightening. "Here is my decision. Here is how we're going to handle the Lee Harden issue." He gave Griffin a stern look. "We'll leave him alone. I am going to turn a blind eye on Lee Harden. I'm going to put him out of my mind, and continue on, as though I'd never learned that he was still alive."

This came as a shock to Griffin, but at once, he saw that there was another shoe dropping.

Morton's expression turned rigidly serious. "But he needs to stay quiet and keep his fucking head down. If he makes a nuisance of himself any more than he already has, people who I need to trust and support me are going to want me to take action. My *only* priority right now is getting this country back on top, and if Lee Harden puts himself at odds with that, my hands will be forced. I don't want a war with Lee Harden. And if he's smart—which I think he is—he won't want a war with me either."

Morton stood up straight and tall and spread his hands. "You just let him know the terms of this truce, and make sure he's ultra-clear that I don't want to hear his name come up again. Can you do that?"

Griffin rose from his chair. Gave his president a respectful nod. "I'll make sure it happens."

Epilogue 3

On a crisp and clear November morning in Oregon, the people of Gearhart heard the rumble of rotors, shaking the walls of their cabins.

None of them knew what the hell was happening, so naturally, they were all a bit frightened.

Bethany was already awake, as most of the people were, preparing for another day. Her heart thudding in her chest, she snatched the old shotgun from her bedside and charged outside, uncertain what the noise was, but immediately thinking about Badger and his retinue of assholes.

Was this some sort of trick of theirs? Were they finally coming to try to raid Gearhart? They'd been kept at bay for some time by the presence of Lee and his team, but last week he'd showed up to try to press his luck once more, and there was no group of special operatives to talk him down.

So Bethany and a handful of others had gone down to do their best to ward him off.

They'd succeeded, but not before Bethany had noticed the look in Badger's eyes. It was the look of a predator, spotting weak prey. He'd seen that Lee wasn't there to protect Gearhart anymore, and in his eyes, Bethany could tell he was already planning how to take advantage of their vulnerability.

Bethany had been on edge ever since, just waiting for those assholes from down the mountain to finally come charging into their settlement, guns blazing.

So, naturally, that's what she was thinking as she ran out of her cabin, even though it defied logic that Badger and his ilk would have any sort of aircraft, which was clearly the source of the noise.

When Bethany got outside, she spotted two things in the sky.

One was an aircraft—she recognized it as an Osprey, the very same aircraft that had arrived in Gearhart and caused Lee and his team to leave on some mission to points unknown.

The Osprey was already retreating into the distance, curving slowly towards the northeast.

The second thing Bethany saw in the sky was a big, green box with three parachutes attached to it, drifting towards the ground.

Bethany and practically everyone else in the settlement went running, curious, cautious, and perhaps a bit hopeful.

They found the box lying in the middle of a field they'd recently clear-cut and were working to get the stumps out of the ground so they could extend their cropland.

The others seemed wary of the box, but that's because they didn't know Lee like Bethany knew him. Hell, they all still thought his name was Jax. But he'd confided in her. Told her his real name, and what he really did out there in this American wasteland. He'd told her about the supply drops that he used to help rescue settlements from bandits and madmen and warlords.

Knowing this, Bethany jogged out ahead of the others.

The box was big—actually, it was three boxes, lashed together, each the size of a coffin. They were olive-drab, made of hardened polymers, and had metal buckles holding the tops on. All three boxes sat on a wooden pallet, and were bound by cargo netting.

Bethany pulled the old buck knife from her belt and set to sawing the cargo straps off. That took her a few minutes, by which time the others had caught up to her, full of questions, as though she had all the answers.

When she opened a lid on one of the boxes, the first thing she noticed was a sheet of paper with a handwritten note. This is what it said:

To the people of Gearhart, thank you for the hospitality. Sorry to leave you in the lurch, but shit got weird, as it tends to do. Unfortunately, we can't return to Oregon at this time, but please accept this gift as our thanks for being a safe harbor, and an apology that we had to leave you with that asshole, Badger, still at the foot of your mountain. Hopefully the contents of these boxes will help with that.

P.S. To Bethany, thanks for working my kinks out. I hope our paths cross again, sometime in the future.

Best,

Jax & Crew

Underneath that note, nestled into foam packing, were...

Bethany frowned. And then she smiled.

What was it that Lee always said?

Oh yeah.

Happiness is a belt-fed weapon.

A NOTE FROM D.J. MOLLES

Thank you for reading *Coyote Song*!

I'd like to ask a favor: Would you mind taking a few minutes to review it?

Reviews help others find my work. Without them, my books would be caught in the depths of the interwebs never to be seen. With millions of books online, a higher rated book becomes more visible, and then readers just like you can enjoy this story as well!

So, would you take a minute to share your thoughts?

I'd greatly appreciate it.

-D.J. Molles

To post your Amazon review, please visit:

https://mybook.to/coyote-song

About the Author

D.J. Molles became a New York Times and USA today bestselling author while working full time as a police officer. He's since traded his badge for a keyboard to produce over 20 titles. When he's not writing, he's taking steps to make his North Carolina property self-sustainable, and training to be at least half as hard to kill as Lee Harden. Molles also enjoys playing his guitar and drums, drawing, cooking, and cruising on his Onewheel.

Most nights you can find him sitting on the couch surrounded by his family and three rescue dogs—which he prefers to call "All American Couch Hounds" but are also commonly referred to as "Pillow Pibbles."

Want to be in the know for all things D.J. Molles?
Sign up for the newsletter.
There's a giveaway every month!

djmolles.com/newsletter

ALSO BY D.J. MOLLES

The Remaining Universe Books:
The Remaining Series
Lee Harden Series
The Valley
Sanctuary
Abe
Coyote Song

———

Standalone Books:
The Book of Dog: A Satire
The Santas
Wolves

———

Ashes of Eormun (Grimdark Fantasy):
A Harvest of Ash and Blood
The Orphan and the Queen
The Breath That Breaks the Stone
and more at djmolles.com!

Printed in Great Britain
by Amazon